"HOW OLD ARE YOU, MISS MAYFIELD?"

"That's no business of yours—"

Hunter reached out and wound his huge hand around the ribbon at Felicity's neckline and pulled her closer, till his breath heated her hairline and her brow. He was blended spice and damp fog; his face was dark planes and brusque angles.

"How old?" he demanded.

"Twenty!" she whispered, and then flinched as the word brushed back against her mouth. "I'm twenty."

He drew her closer still, until his teeth blinded her in the firelight. "Then you have committed a felony, Miss Mayfield. Those railway shares aren't yours to sell until you are twenty-five."

"This can't be true—"

"Oh, it's true, my dear little thief. And now you will marry me, or I'll see that you spend the next five years in debtor's prison."

"EVER HIS BRIDE is great entertainment!"
Stella Cameron, author of *Guilty Pleasures*

Other AVON ROMANCES

DESTINY'S WARRIOR by Kit Dee
HIGHLAND WOLF by Lois Greiman
THE MACKENZIES: CLEVE by Ana Leigh
SCARLET LADY by Marlene Suson
TOUGH TALK AND TENDER KISSES by Deborah Camp
WILD IRISH SKIES by Nancy Richards-Akers
A WOMAN'S HEART by Rosalyn West

Coming Soon

DECEIVE ME NOT by Eve Byron
GRAY HAWK'S LADY by Karen Kay

And Don't Miss These
ROMANTIC TREASURES
from Avon Books

FLY WITH THE EAGLE by Kathleen Harrington
HIS FORBIDDEN TOUCH by Shelly Thacker
LYON'S GIFT by Tanya Anne Crosby

EVER HIS BRIDE

LINDA NEEDHAM

AVON BOOKS ◆ NEW YORK

This is a work of fiction. Names, characters, places and incidents either are the product of the author's imagination or are used fictitiously. Any resemblance to actual events, locales, organizations, or persons, living or dead, is entirely coincidental and beyond the intent of either the author or the publisher.

AVON BOOKS
A division of
The Hearst Corporation
1350 Avenue of the Americas
New York, New York 10019

Copyright © 1997 by Linda Needham
Inside cover author photo by Expressly Portraits
Published by arrangement with the author
Visit our website at http://AvonBooks.com
Library of Congress Catalog Card Number: 96-95495
ISBN: 0-380-78756-3

First Avon Books Printing: July 1997

AVON TRADEMARK REG. U.S. PAT. OFF. AND IN OTHER COUNTRIES, MARCA REGISTRADA, HECHO EN U.S.A.

Printed in the U.S.A.

WCD   10 9 8 7 6 5 4 3 2 1

Chapter 1

Kent County, England
1849

"**R**un, Culley! Run hard!"

Felicity Mayfield had a half-crown on the long-shanked village lad, money she should have kept in her purse. But she'd finally succumbed to the thrill of the Robin Hood Race, to the swirl of festive banners, and to all the shouting and cheering.

As the lad rounded the final curve of the intricate turf maze, he teetered for a paralyzing moment on the brink of falling off the narrow, ground-level course into the sandy trench.

"Hang on, Culley!" Felicity shouted, jumping up and down like everyone else in the crowd, staying her next breath as he stumbled forward. But Culley righted himself and broke through the flower garland with a whoop of triumph.

"He won! Bravo, Culley!" Felicity didn't even know the lad, but at the moment she was his greatest champion.

Mrs. Duffle clapped Felicity on the back. "You're a right lucky young woman!"

"I'm most grateful for the tip. He's every bit as fast

1

as you said he was." Felicity was as winded from all
her shouting as young Culley was from his sprinting.
"I've never made a wager on a race before—and I
won!"

Mrs. Duffle beamed as if the Robin Hood Race, the
turf maze, and the rowdy festival were all her own
doing. "Happens every year here in Beacon Chase.
You'll come back and spend May Day with us next
year, won't you dear?"

"Absolutely! And I'll send all my loyal readers, Mrs.
Duffle. You may count on it."

"Ah, that's very good to hear, Miss Mayfield. And
now I insist you come have lunch with me at the
Knotted Mazel—as my guest, of course. You'll find my
pigeon pie's the very best in the county."

Felicity was hungry beyond decency; her stomach
rattled, primed by the spellbinding smell of meat
pasties rising from the warren of food stalls.

"I'd love to join you, Mrs. Duffle. Thank you." She
collected her winnings from a man in a bright yellow
hat, then hefted her portmanteau and followed Mrs.
Duffle through the crowded street, to the cottage inn
tucked against a woodland at the edge of the village.

"Oh, you've a lovely setting, Mrs. Duffle." Felicity
approved immediately of the riotous flower garden
and the ornately woven ridge of the thatched roof. If
the food and lodging proved as charming as the
spacious, sunlit dining room, Felicity would give it an
excellent review in her travel gazette. A perfect spot to
recommend to her readers for a holiday in the Kent
countryside.

Mrs. Duffle's tray of good silver clattered as she set it
down on the table. "The very same tea served at
Windsor, Miss Mayfield. True China tea, not that
secondhand compost served across the street at the
Skipping Toad. None but the best for my guests at the
Mazel."

"It's truly delicious!" Felicity spoke overloud, hoping to mask the indelicate growl of her stomach as the

tea collided with the emptiness there. Breakfast had been a withered apple from last season, plundered from a tree on the way from the tiny railway station. Not a meal she would recommend to her readers.

Mrs. Duffle spread a mouthwatering luncheon for her, and then talked in an unbroken stream about her grown children, her late husband, and her unconventional sister who had married a man half her own age. She was a charming little woman, Felicity's favorite kind of innkeeper, and one of the reasons she liked her job so well.

The front door opened just as Felicity bit into a steaming, jam-filled scone. The glare of noonday darkened the details of the two figures who stood together in the portal.

"Sheriff Hinchcliffe!" Mrs. Duffle clapped her hands together and laughed. "That was quite a race your Culley won!"

The man's chest strained with pride at the buttons of his waistcoat. "Yup. Proud of the boy," he said, sauntering into the room, rubbing his palms together.

"Ooo, I know that look, Sheriff." Mrs. Duffle drew a steaming plate beneath the man's nose. "You come for a helping of my pigeon pie."

The gangly man beside him hissed something into his ear. Hinchcliffe straightened and pushed the plate aside. "Actually, Mrs. Duffle," the sheriff said. "I've come for that pigeon over there." He pointed toward Felicity.

Felicity blinked and glanced over her shoulder. There was no one behind her. The man was pointing right at her! For no reason at all, that last bite of scone turned to lead as it hit her stomach. She stood up, wincing at the scrape of her chair across the stone floor.

"You came here for me?" Her mouth had gone dry as dust. Felicity was a stranger to Beacon Chase, had only arrived that morning to make her notes on the May Day celebration. Few people knew she was here, and even fewer cared. Perhaps the sheriff needed only to ask a few questions.

But Hinchcliffe stopped a scant yard from her table and fixed her with a cold, professional stare.

"Are you sure this is the right girl, Cobson?" he asked from the corner of his mouth, still watching Felicity with a deep-browed suspicion.

Cobson joined him, cocking his head at her as though sizing up a two-headed goat on display at the faire. "A young woman, seven-and-a-half stone. Five feet three'ish tall, wheat-blond hair, green eyes. Yessir. Just as the bailiff said."

"Just as *what* bailiff said?" As dumbfounded as she had ever been in her life, Felicity tried to make herself seem taller, and a bit bigger around. "Who are you, sir?"

The sheriff plunged his thumbs into the fob pockets of his waistcoat and squinted at her. "Tell me, girl, is your name Felicity Mayfield?"

Mrs. Duffle sucked in a long, awe-filled breath. "That it is, Sheriff! That's the name she gave me when she came in here with her notepad and all her fancy words about listing the Knotted Mazel in some kind of travel gazette. What wicked thing has she done?"

"I've done nothing wicked, Mrs. Duffle." Felicity felt very alone at the moment, and wished suddenly that she had a warm place to run home to. "If these gentlemen will tell me their business—"

"I have here an arrest warrant for a Felicity Mayfield." Cobson held up a sealed document.

"An arrest warrant? For me?" Felicity fought the ridiculous urge to dodge her way between the tables and out the door. "What have I done?"

"Cobson, here, is an officer of the Queen's Bench, and is authorized to take you to London—"

"To London?" Felicity tried to bluster away her quickening fear, but her heart was racing, her pulse pounding in her ears. "On what charge?"

Cobson snapped open the document and displayed

it for her. "On the charge of criminal debt, Miss Mayfield."

"Debt?" Felicity laughed at the notion, and a huge weight lifted from her shoulders, though Cobson's scowl only deepened. "You have the wrong person. I owe nothing to anyone!"

Hinchcliffe snickered and poked Cobson with his elbow. "I'll bet you've heard that tune sung a few times, eh?"

Cobson snorted. "And all the verses. If I had a penny for every time, I sure's hell wouldn't be doin' this job! You're comin' along with me, Miss Mayfield." He reached for her, but Felicity stepped backward into Mrs. Duffle.

"I will not go anywhere with you, Mr. Cobson!" Felicity had heard quite enough. She gathered her anger into a hard knot of indignation to help shore up her wobbling knees. "This charge is entirely false. How do I know you're not going to kidnap me and force me to do your will?"

Cobson shrugged. "I guess you don't."

The scone in Felicity's stomach began to burn. "Sheriff Hinchcliffe, how can you let this man do this?"

"I know you're innocent, miss," the sheriff said, shaking his head in conspicuously false sympathy. "And I know this is a great mistake. But a warrant is a warrant."

"Let me see that!" Felicity tore the warrant out of Cobson's hands. The page was official-looking; the script was overfrilled, but it said quite clearly, "Felicity Mayfield to be arrested for criminal debt owing to Mister Hunter Claybourne, London."

Felicity looked up at Cobson, more confused than ever. "*The* Hunter Claybourne?"

"I doubt there's more than one, Miss Mayfield."

Felicity doubted it, too. Just as strongly as she doubted that the sinfully wealthy Hunter Claybourne could possibly have any connection to her at all.

"Come along, Miss Mayfield," Cobson said, clamping his efficient fingers around her elbow, and starting toward the door. "The train to London's due any minute, and you've an engagement at the Queen's Bench Prison."

Felicity overran Cobson with her questions all the way to London, but arrived at London Bridge Station no wiser for her efforts, and completely unnerved. He led her from the platform into the rain-soaked, poorly lit street.

"This is a huge mistake, Mr. Cobson," Felicity insisted for the hundredth time since leaving Beacon Chase. "I don't know Hunter Claybourne. He doesn't know me."

"Master Claybourne is an important man. He don't make mistakes, Miss Mayfield."

"But *you* have! I suppose you round up all his debtors?"

"Been doin' it for seven years now." Cobson reeled an overlong kerchief from his coat pocket, and swabbed at his nose. "All I know is: those that do come his way don't remain debtors for long. He always gets his pound of flesh . . . and then some."

Felicity fastened her thin shawl around her shoulders, her stomach reeling as if she'd dined on live eels. Hunter Claybourne? Railroads, shipping, foreign trade; no man was better known or more feared in the financial affairs of the nation. What the devil did he want with her?

Cobson loaded her portmanteau into a crowded hackney cab and they wheeled away into the drizzling night, only to be deposited in front of a clapboard house not a mile from the station.

"Inside, Miss Mayfield." Cobson took her elbow and started toward the house.

The windows and the front door of the sagging building were barred. The rain had lessened to a fine spray, giving the dirty clapboard a greasy look. It looked like a house of evil intentions.

"What kind of place is this, Mr. Cobson? I'm not taking another step unless you tell me!"

"Then let me welcome you to Cobson's Rest, Miss Mayfield. The missus and I run a respectable sponging house."

"A sponging house!" The prelude to debtor's prison, designed to intimidate and insult as the debtor tried to arrange for repayment. This was a mistake, and even if it weren't, she had no money to spare. Her thousand pounds were tucked away in the Bank of England, intended only for the most dire emergency, a safeguard against starvation and utter homelessness. But what if no one believed her?

"You'll stay here with us until your trial. Unless, of course, you can raise money enough to pay off your debt."

"I tell you, I am no one's debtor!"

"Aren't you now?" Cobson chuckled low in his throat and pointed to the end of the block. "That building way down there's the Queen's Bench Prison. Unless you can come up with the sum you owes to Master Claybourne, you'll be living there for a very long time."

The eels churned again. Felicity had spent most of her life in the countryside, following her father from one railway engineering project to the next. She didn't know London very well, but she'd heard tales of the Queen's Bench, had read the horrible accounts of the Marshalsea and Fleet before they were closed.

"I owe Claybourne nothing. I don't even know him. This is a wasted effort, Mr. Cobson. And when this folly is done, I'll want my fare back to the Knotted Mazel."

But Cobson was a never-shirking force, a transportable jail. Felicity had no choice at all but to do as he bid. Come tomorrow he'd be sorry! So would Claybourne.

She would weather this storm as she had weathered others.

Felicity allowed Cobson to lead her to the sagging stoop, where his three-part tap with the brass knocker was answered seconds later by a more intricate pattern. The latch rattled, then the door opened to the hovering light of a candle flame.

"Ooo! She's a little thing, Cobby." The soupy voice spilled from a fleshy female face that seemed to hover just behind the circle of light.

"May be. But she eats like one of Wellington's officers."

Felicity bristled. "A crust of bread and a carrot is hardly—"

"Bring 'er in, Cobby, a'fore she blows away in the wind."

Cobson's ever-present fingers pulled Felicity into the house. The air inside Cobson's Rest was as dark and close as its shadows: woodsmoke and rancid food and mildewed upholstery all sealed up together by windows long ago swollen shut in the damp.

"He's *here*, Cobby." Mrs. Cobson's whisper was clouded by the reek of day-old onions.

"Claybourne?" Cobson looked agitated for the first time all day. "Now? But it's near midnight."

"He come here just after dark," Mrs. Cobson hissed. "Brought the cold in with him, he did. I had to light the fire."

"He doesn't usually come himself. What does he want?"

Mrs. Cobson's gaze led right to Felicity. "He wants *her*, I think."

Felicity could only stare back at the woman, unwilling to imagine the confrontation to come. She knew Claybourne by reputation alone, and that was enough to keep her feet rooted to the sagging floor.

But Felicity was forcibly edged into a dreary parlor just off the cramped foyer. A low fire glowed red in the grate, the only light in the room, making monsters of sideboard and sofa. Wind rattled against the clapboard siding.

"A good eve to you, Master Claybourne," Cobson said, sliding his cap off his head. "I brought you your debtor. Like I said I would."

An enormous darkness moved across the hearth, cooling Felicity's face, reaching beyond the fragile windows to sap the light from the stars.

"Leave us, Cobson." The voice advanced like a midnight fog overtaking a lighthouse.

Felicity stepped backward, fearing that the sound had substance and might crush her. Shadows hid the man's face, hinting at sharp ridges and strong planes.

"As you wish it," Mrs. Cobson trilled as she bustled into the room and lit the lamp on the sideboard. "Shall I bring you a brandy, Master—"

"Take your wife and leave us, Cobson."

Like a pair of crabs dodging the tide, the Cobsons ducked out of the parlor and slammed the door.

Felicity had been to the Zoological Gardens in Regent's Park; had seen the lions pacing the length of their cages. She felt that same restless power seething in the dark form in front of her. Yet Claybourne stood motionless, leaving his flickering shadow to stalk the walls and the ceiling.

"I know you only by your name, Mr. Claybourne," Felicity said in the void left by his unwieldy silence. "And couldn't possibly owe you so much as a ha'penny. You have arrested the wrong woman."

"And you have stolen from the wrong man, Miss Mayfield."

"Stolen?" Felicity laughed then, still vastly nervous but relieved at the nonsense. "I've never stolen anything from anybody."

Claybourne's greatcoat fluttered, then folded around him as he stepped away from the hearth. The simple act gave the room back its glowering light, but none of its warmth. His profile sharpened as he bent to retrieve a sheaf of papers from a side table. She wished she could see more of him, the slant of his mouth, or the depth of his eyes—something beyond the shadows.

He turned then, looked up at her from his paper. But his eyes only drew her into a deeper darkness.

"Your uncle is Foley Mayfield."

"My uncle?" Felicity swallowed back a lump of foreboding and sidled over to a spindly chair. She gripped the rails of its laddered back, prepared to wield it should Claybourne choose to overtake her. "What does my uncle have to do with this?"

"Where is he now?" he asked evenly.

"My uncle is two days out of London, sailing for San Francisco and the gold fields." Felicity chided herself for confessing the information. Her dear Uncle Foley would be helpless against such a powerfully coercive man. "Why do you want to know about—"

"You gave Foley Mayfield the legal authority to sell the shares held by you as the sole owner of the Drayhill-Starlington Railway."

So that was it! The great financier had come sniffing out an easy profit. "Mr. Claybourne, is this about the shares my father left to me when he died?"

"Your uncle was acting under your instruction in the matter?" Claybourne stepped away from the side table and moved toward her.

Felicity quickly countered his approach, feeling every bit the trapped rabbit. She left the chair and caught her foot on the sideboard, causing the prisms dangling from the lamp to chatter.

"Did you give your uncle permission to sell your shares?" he repeated.

"Yes, he had my permission. I signed a promissory note indicating that I owned the shares and the railway." Felicity backed toward the hearth. Claybourne was mad. And he knew entirely too much about her and her family. "The papers are quite legal, Mr. Claybourne, drawn up by Francis Biddle, a solicitor of good repute. The shares were very valuable, but they've already been sold—"

"Yes, I know."

"Then why—"

"Your uncle sold the shares to *me*, Miss Mayfield. I paid him thirty thousand pounds for the privilege."

The hearth light seemed to intensify and Claybourne's shadow threw itself against the water-stained ceiling. The enormous shoulders she had thought hunched were actually broad and carelessly hooded by a half-cape. His hair was dark and unfashionably long, and he was watching her.

"Ah! So, now the shares belong to you, Mr. Claybourne. I don't see what—"

"No, Miss Mayfield. The shares still belong to *you*." He started toward her, motion without perceptive movement.

"Don't be absurd, Mr. Claybourne. You gave the money to my uncle: a great stack of it—piled into a satchel." Felicity backed away from his towering height until the fire became too warm at her back and she had to stop. "I saw the bank notes with my own eyes, just before he bought the store of goods he plans to sell in San Francisco. I saw the money."

"I'm sure you did." And now he was the whole of her sight, bearing a lime-laced heat all his own, despite the fog-born chill that had hidden itself among the folds of his cloak. "How old are you, Miss Mayfield?"

"That's no business of yours—"

But the horrible man reached out and wound his huge hand around the ribbon at her neckline and pulled her closer, till his breath heated her hairline and her brow. He was blended spice and damp fog; his face was dark planes and brusque angles.

"How old?" he demanded.

"Twenty!" she whispered, and then flinched as the word brushed back against her mouth. "I'm twenty."

He drew her closer still, until his teeth blinded her in the firelight. "Then you have committed a felony, Miss Mayfield. Those shares aren't yours to sell until you are twenty-five."

Now she knew the color of his eyes, as she knew the color of cold malice. Her heart beat madly beneath the heel of his hand, thumping out her fear, confessing her shame.

"This can't be true—"

"Oh, it's true, my dear little thief. And now you will marry me, or I'll see that you spend the next five years in debtor's prison."

Chapter 2

❦

"Marry you?" Felicity wanted to cower from those glacial eyes, fearing the weighty chill that made them dull and dark. But she forced a bravado she didn't feel. "Marry a misbegotten heathen like you? I will not!"

Claybourne straightened as if she'd slapped him—which she would have done, if she thought that a mountain could be moved.

"Will you not, Miss Mayfield?" His touch frosted as he drew his finger along the ridge of her jaw. "This maiden's blush of yours will soon pale to chalk inside the damp walls of the Queen's Bench. Dare you risk it?"

"You haven't got the facts right, Mr. Claybourne. The shares and the railway were mine to sell whenever I wanted. Now, let go of me."

He looked down at his fist, still balled beneath her chin, and crushing her silk ribbons. His gaze faltered as it returned to her face, lingering too long on her mouth before finding its way to her eyes. Firelight imbedded gold in the faint stubble that bristled his jawline. Yes, he looked quite mad.

He released her roughly and Felicity scooted away to the safety of the ladder-back chair, her heart and her stomach doing some kind of spiraling dance together.

"You perform outraged innocence with rare precision, my dear. As precisely as your uncle performed his thick-headed simplicity. Well done." Claybourne slammed his palms together twice in mock applause.

"I *am* outraged, Mr. Claybourne!"

"So am I, Miss Mayfield. No one steals from me. No one."

"Sir, you are a lunatic!" Felicity clutched at the crinkled ribbon at her throat, remembering the heat of his hand, the silk of his breath. "My father left those shares to me as my inheritance. They were mine to spend or to invest as I pleased."

"Do you read, Miss Mayfield?" Claybourne's hand was steady as he held out a sheaf of papers toward her.

"Of course I do!" Felicity reached across the distance and snatched the document.

"Then you can see for yourself: the Bank of England has legal hold of your shares, in trust, until you reach the age of twenty-five. Or until—"

"Yes, I can read it myself, Mr. Claybourne. Until I reach . . ." Felicity hurried along in the paragraph, sure that she would find the error in his interpretation. Her father wouldn't have done this to her! And then she saw it, the terrible phrase laid down like a whispered curse from the grave.

"Until I reach the age of twenty-five, or until I've . . . been married for the period of one year." Her knees came unstrung as the life seemed to drain from her, leaving her wanting air and hope.

Felicity let her gaze rise to meet Claybourne's. He looked like an ill-bred bear who'd wandered into the Cobsons' parlor, his savagery disguised as patience as he waited to snag a tasty morsel from the tea tray. His head was cocked, his shoulders bent forward, his hands clasped behind him—prepared, she was sure, to strangle her.

But the pompous man was right. According to the

document, she had no right to the shares for another five years. She was too far from the hearth for the heat that sizzled the tips of her ears to be anything but shame.

"I knew nothing of this, sir. Truly." An uncomfortable memory of her uncle's vacillating gaze as she signed the power of attorney suddenly clarified. Uncle Foley had deceived her!

Claybourne shrugged and sighed. "Whether you knew of it or not is immaterial to me. You and your family have committed a fraud against me. I want my money returned to me immediately."

"Thirty thousand pounds!" Felicity covered her mouth and laughed at the absurdity. She had a thousand pounds to her name, money left over from the sale of the shares. The rest she had invested in her uncle's venture. "Mr. Claybourne, I haven't got that kind of money. I have barely enough to last me the week."

"Then I will take your shares."

Now the man was being stupid, and she fixed her most scathing gaze on him. "Sir, you know very well that I cannot give you either at the moment. But rest assured that my uncle will return from the gold fields within a year. He expects to quadruple my investment, with the picks and shovels and other indispensable goods he plans to sell to the miners. Allow me that short time to repay you, Mr. Claybourne, and I will double your money . . ."

But Claybourne had gone deadly calm.

"Your uncle is an ass."

"How dare you! Uncle Foley is a kind and gentle man who helped my father when times were lean—"

"He's a witless felon, who will be stripped of his money—my money—long before he arrives in San Francisco with his wares. He'll be lucky if he isn't murdered in his sleep."

"Murdered?"

His gaze was the sort of terror that beckoned. She couldn't look away.

"Thirty thousand pounds, Miss Mayfield. Do you know what a man will do for that kind of money? Do you know how low he will sink to attain it?"

"*I* don't, Mr. Claybourne, but I'm quite certain that *you* do!"

The air grew still. Felicity knew better than to breathe or to move as he approached her. Obsidian—that was the color. His eyes shone like obsidian, sharp and brittle, offering nothing but blackness. The mocking edge to his humorless smile was in truth a small scar on the upper ridge near the corner. Though why she was looking just there, at the fine fullness of his mouth, when she ought to be preparing for his imminent assault, was a matter she'd have to sort out later.

"Repeat such words, my dear little felon, and those five years in prison will turn to fifty."

"Better five hundred years of prison squalor than a marriage to you!" Felicity hurried to the far side of the room to rid herself of the dizzying sensation of looking up at him. "Sir, before we continue this discussion, I beg your indulgence to speak with my solicitor."

"The honorable Mr. Biddle? I think not, Miss Mayfield. Your choice is five years in debtor's prison, or one year married to me. Take it or leave it."

"Married to you? To a foul-tempered monster who would pluck the pennies from his own dead mother's eyelids? I'll leave it, Mr. Claybourne." To make her point, and to keep her knees from knocking together, Felicity sat down.

Claybourne's brow deepened; his eyes darkened and threatened as he stared down at her. She thought for a moment that he might backhand her. But he muttered a curse, then turned from her and threw open both parlor doors.

The Cobsons stood frozen in place as if their eavesdropping had been caught in wax by Madame Tussaud herself. Claybourne peered down at them, nearly as tall as the door itself.

"Evening, sir!" Mrs. Cobson scooted backward and pasted herself against the wall. "We come to ask if you need anything!"

Claybourne ignored the woman and bent his displeasure on her husband. "Lock her up, Cobson."

Cobson brightened. "My wife, sir?"

"Mine," Claybourne said.

"I'm not your wife, Claybourne," Felicity said, feeling recklessly brave as she followed him into the foyer. "Nor will I ever be."

He ignored her and turned to Cobson. "The expense of relocating Miss Mayfield, should she escape, will fall upon your head, Cobson. I'll send word as to what to do with her."

"Do with me?" Felicity caught Claybourne's arm to turn him, but might as well have been trying to turn the Houses of Parliament for all she could move him. "I'm not a potted palm, Mr. Claybourne."

Claybourne shifted his glare to Felicity and she battled the urge to cower. "No, Miss Mayfield. You are a thief."

Then he stalked out of the vestibule and became a part of the damp London night.

"He can't do this to me!" Felicity said, trying to shake loose the inconceivable notion of having to tack his name onto her own. Felicity Mayfield Claybourne. The very thought made her face heat.

"Lock us down tight, Theda," Cobson said, frowning at Felicity as though she had already cost him a day's pay. "She's not to get away."

"Yes, yes, Cobby. Go on up, now. I'll take care of everything." Mrs. Cobson locked the door and stuffed the key into her pillowy cleavage. She patted Felicity's arm. "You're lucky, dearie. We've an empty room tonight. Cobby, I put Rawley and Horville in the dormer."

Cobson turned on the stairs. "What about that bloody draper and his whimpering family?"

"They're gone." Mrs. Cobson grinned and shook the purse that dangled from her sash. "His cousin paid his charges to us, as well as his debt to Mr. Nash. Left us before supper, so we got another day's take without even havin' to feed them."

"Good." Cobson's clomping boots disappeared into the darkness abovestairs.

"Come along to your room, Miss Mayfield."

"I'll stay down here, if you please." Felicity pointed to the parlor, a simple room that wouldn't feel so much like a prison cell.

"Mr. Claybourne wouldn't be pleased at all if you were gone when he come back. He paid extra for Cobby to fetch you in from the country. And I'll not be spending our own good money to fetch you back. Come along now." Mrs. Cobson took a fingerhold of Felicity's sleeve.

"He can't make me marry him."

"Probably not. But, dearie, he's a very rich man, is Claybourne, and very powerful. A fair-enough catch for a woman in such dire circumstances." Mrs. Cobson took in a breath and started up the stairs, towing Felicity behind her.

"I'd rather go to prison."

"Suit yourself, m'dearie, but I'd think on it. Five years can be a very long time in the Queen's Bench."

A single night at Cobson's Rest had seemed an eternity. Felicity hadn't slept a moment and now sat on the edge of the sagging bed, watching the early morning ooze its grayness into the darkened corners of the tiny attic room. She had listened all night to rats scratching their way along the baseboard inside the walls, and to the sawtooth snoring from the rooms on either side of her. The Knotted Mazel would have been sweet heaven compared to this sponging house.

"What happens now?" Fearing she'd start answering

herself, Felicity tried the low-slung attic door. It was locked, as it had been all night. She gave the panel a good smack with the heel of her hand, then turned back to the bed. She'd given up pacing. The ceiling hung so low and sloped so steeply that her neck had a crick in it. She was hungry and cold, and so deeply in debt she might not see another inn until the middle of the next decade.

"Uncle Foley, what have you done to me?" she wailed. He couldn't have known what trouble his enterprise would cause her. He'd invariably been there when her father had needed him. His business dealings hadn't always been sound, but without exception he'd been honest. And his scheme to take tools and supplies to the gold country had been brilliant. When he'd come to her with the idea of selling off her shares in the railway, she'd agreed in an instant. But he *couldn't* have known about the rider to her father's will. He wouldn't do that to her.

Felicity was certain Uncle Foley would return in a year, with more than enough money to repay Claybourne. Then she'd be free of debtor's prison without having to marry the merciless monster in the process. Surely she could bear up in debtor's prison for a year. Just one year, one year without trees and meadows, without the rumble of the rails beneath her feet . . .

And what about the *Hearth and Heath!* Her readers would soon forget her entirely if she couldn't report regularly on the quaint places she traveled to. Then Mr. Dolan would fire her! She'd have no money at all. How could she live?

"Miss Mayfield? Are you there, girl?" Mrs. Cobson's voice from the other side of the door seemed almost friendly in the gloom. Felicity hoped for at least a chunk of bread to deaden the noise squeezing out of her stomach.

"Where would I have gone, Mrs. Cobson?" Felicity asked through the keyhole.

The lock rattled and the tiny door opened. Mrs.

Cobson entered in a shuffling crouch, then straightened when the ceiling allowed.

"You're to come with me," she said.

"Is he here? Has he come back?"

"Mister Claybourne? No. He's sent for you. There's a carriage downstairs."

"Where is he taking me? I have the right to a trial, and to speak with my solicitor. He'll know what to do. Claybourne can't just throw me into prison!"

"With his kind of money, he can do anything he wants." Mrs. Cobson snorted. "But Mr. Claybourne isn't going to hurt you. His ways are a bit odd, but he's not a murderer. Leastwise I don't think he is. Come along, Miss Mayfield." Mrs. Cobson shook her ring of keys like a dinner bell.

"I'm not going to marry him."

Mrs. Cobson set her fists against her apple-round hips. "Then he'll probably drop you off at the Queen's Bench when he's done with you. He's paid your charges to us for your time at Cobson's Rest, and now you're to be put into his brougham. Where you go from there, I don't know, and I can't waste my time caring. Now, do you come with me peaceably, or do I get Mr. Cobson to haul you downstairs like a sack of potatoes?"

Thinking there might be a way to escape once she was outside, Felicity ducked her head and followed Mrs. Cobson through the tiny door and down the canted, squealing stairs.

But before she had time to plan her escape, she was escorted out the front door, flanked by both Cobsons, and then handed up into the brougham. The carriage door slammed behind her and was locked down tightly from the outside, a frightening realization that could only mean that Claybourne did this sort of thing regularly.

Before she could protest, her mobile prison cell shuddered forward into the smoke-bound fog.

"Blast the man!" He couldn't just deliver her to a

prison without a trial; there were laws against such things. And yet she had the sinking feeling that Hunter Claybourne could and would do anything he wanted without the slightest twinge of conscience.

But the brougham turned away from the Queen's Bench, crossed London Bridge, rolled up King William Street, and finally stopped in Cornhill Street opposite the majestic edifices of the Royal Exchange and the Bank of England.

The Bank of England? Had Claybourne learned of the thousand pounds her uncle had put into the bank for her? Did the piggish lout think to make her entirely penniless?

The door opened and Felicity quickly found herself in a cavernous lobby. What wasn't icy-white marble was severe mahogany or excessively polished brass. She felt altogether drab and powerless in her durable, pale-blue traveling suit.

"Where have you brought me, sir?" she asked the stone-faced footman, who'd taken over as her jailer.

"The Claybourne Exchange, miss," he said.

Claybourne. She might have known. Cold, lifeless, pretentious. Claybourne's signature—down to the thin-lipped doorman. Her courage fueled by a rising outrage, Felicity followed a crisp-collared clerk up the wide marble stairs and through a set of double doors.

"This way," he said, striding past a large desk toward another set of doors. He rapped twice, then waited.

"Come."

Felicity knew the voice; its rumbling, cool disdain reached past the lock and the brass hinges and angered her all the more.

The clerk swung the door open to a dimly lit office. Dark drapes hung heavily against the windows, shutting off any light that might filter in from the foggy morning, an effect no doubt fashioned by Claybourne to beat down the spirit of his victims.

"Go right in, miss."

Claybourne was standing behind his desk, glaring at her as if he had heard her thoughts through the mahogany door. Gone were the greatcoat and cape, replaced by an expensively tailored frock coat of the finest wool. The white of his shirt darkened his features by contrast; his hair curled willfully against his high collar and across his forehead. Yet for all Claybourne's frosted glaring, Felicity felt a breathy warmth rise up into her collar. His mouth was too perfectly formed and perilously fascinating.

"Come here, Miss Mayfield." His command rolled across the room at her, buffeting her courage like a winter wind.

"Felicity's here?"

She finally noticed the withered figure hunched over the desk in front of Claybourne. The tousled-gray head lifted, and the man looked up at her through watery red eyes.

"Mr. Biddle!"

"D-Dear Felicity . . ." he stammered, as he gathered himself up on a pair of wobbling legs.

Felicity dropped her portmanteau and her shawl and ran to him, throwing her arms around his startlingly insubstantial frame. He smelled of stale cigar and even staler beer. "You've come to save me from this cruel man and his falsehoods! I knew you would."

"Yes, yes, my girl," Mr. Biddle muttered and hid his brow against her shoulder.

Although she hadn't seen him for a few months, Felicity had remembered Mr. Biddle as being taller and more solid. He trembled now as she patted him on the back and glared up at Claybourne, who had stepped away to stand like a monolith in front of the green-tiled room heater. He didn't look at all contrite for scaring the poor man speechless.

"Dear Mr. Biddle," she said, seizing his bony arms and straightening him so she could look into his eyes. "You've come all the way to London to help me. How can I thank you?"

Claybourne snorted. "Your Mr. Biddle answered my summons, Miss Mayfield."

"I suppose you summoned him the way you summoned me." Felicity released her hold on Biddle to take a more square-jawed stance against Claybourne's imperiousness. "Mr. Claybourne, I gave you my answer last night. I will not marry you. Put me into debtor's prison; pluck out my fingernails one by one; I don't care. I have not changed my mind. Nor can you change it for me."

He took two deliberate steps toward her, making him all the more impossible to ignore. "I brought your Mr. Biddle here to ensure that you *do* change your mind."

Felicity hoped her laughter sounded unconcerned as she leaned against the desktop, trying to steady her breathing. "Mr. Biddle will have no better luck convincing me to marry you than you did yourself. He is our family solicitor, nothing more. His opinions have no bearing on mine."

"Felicity . . ." Mr. Biddle's wheedling voice could barely support her name. He was frightened to death by Claybourne and wasn't going to be any help at all.

"It's no use trying to change my mind, Mr. Biddle. I'll take my chances in prison."

"Felicity, you can't—"

"Nonsense. Uncle Foley will be home within a year, and we will use his new fortune to pay off the debt to Mr. Claybourne, with interest, and then I will be set free. The matter will be settled without me having to marry anyone."

Claybourne stirred again, an avalanche poised to descend.

"That won't do, Miss Mayfield." The oppressively tall man took another of his studied strides toward her, and she held her breath. "I am no longer interested in the money you owe me. Nothing will satisfy me, unless it's your shares and the full ownership in the

Drayhill-Starlington. I will have them by whatever means."

"You can't have them, Mr. Claybourne! Not now. Not ever! You'll have to settle for repayment in cash when my uncle returns."

Mr. Biddle was tugging at her sleeve, whimpering like a child. But Claybourne was bearing down on her, his voice a rumbling in her chest, and roaring through her veins.

"I will have the shares, woman, or you, and your uncle, and that cowardly little man hiding behind you will find your carcasses in prison for the rest of your lives!"

Chapter 3

"You can't do that!" Felicity planted herself squarely between Claybourne and Mr. Biddle. And it was a very good thing, because Claybourne began to advance on them with his next breath.

"Biddle cheated me, Miss Mayfield."

"He did not! Did you, Mr. Biddle?"

"Well, I—"

Felicity shoved Mr. Biddle behind her and continued backing away from Claybourne's seething, courage-stunting glare.

"And your uncle cheated me, Miss Mayfield."

She put her hand out to hold Claybourne in check, but she met a wall of shifting brawn, one that was moving ever forward.

"He did not cheat you! At least, if he did, I'm sure he didn't mean to. Did he, Mr. Biddle?"

"Well, he—"

"And now, *you*, Miss Mayfield, have cheated me."

Claybourne had driven them all the way around the desk. Mr. Biddle grunted as he plopped down in the chair. Another step backward and Felicity would be sitting in his frail lap.

"I have never cheated anyone, Mr. Claybourne, at any time in my life!" Feeling hugely overpowered and wishing for at least a hint of support, Felicity stepped around the chair and turned Biddle's scratchy chin toward Claybourne. "Tell him, Mr. Biddle!"

Claybourne looked fiercely smug as he stared unwaveringly back at her. "Yes, Biddle, do tell me."

Mr. Biddle withered and whined, then dropped his arms onto the desktop and his head into his hands. "Dear, dear Felicity. Please forgive me."

"Forgive you, Mr. Biddle?" Felicity got down on her knees to be closer to the old man and his disturbing weeping. He was her father's trusted solicitor. He was supposed to be strong for her, not the other way around. "Forgive you for what? Tell me!"

"Yes, tell her, Biddle," Claybourne said with a malicious sneer.

Biddle whined again but hurried on, his soggy words muffled by his coat. "Well . . . Felicity, I . . . I knew about your father's stipulations about selling the shares."

Felicity felt as if she'd been kicked in the stomach, but she refused to beg quarter and look up at Claybourne. "You couldn't have known about it, Mr. Biddle."

"But I did. And Foley knew as well. We were partners." Biddle rocked his head back and forth across his folded arms, and his whining turned to keening. "I'm sorry, Felicity. I'm so sorry."

Whatever misty ray of hope Felicity had held out for Mr. Biddle's intervention evaporated. She'd never felt so forsaken in all her life.

"You and Uncle knew you were cheating Mr. Claybourne!"

Claybourne shifted, the rigid stretching of boot leather, the whisper of wool against wool, a mountain settling back into place following an earthquake. For once he restrained himself from speaking.

Biddle lifted his chalky face to hers. "We did it for you, Felicity."

"For me? You and my uncle committed a felony for *me*? Well, why stop at larceny? Why not murder and treason while you're at it?"

"Felicity, please listen. Foley needed a lot of money, and he needed it quickly. He had a chance to buy a cache of mining tools and sell them in the gold country. It's a sure thing. My own money's tied up in this, too."

"So you thought you'd help Uncle Foley steal from someone to finance your scheme. Mr. Biddle, my father would be outraged! I am outraged! We trusted you!" Too disgusted to continue looking at him, Felicity took refuge in pacing in front of the desk. "Do you know what you've done to me?"

"I'm sorry. I know it was wrong. But we thought that once Claybourne discovered that he couldn't get the shares from the Bank, he'd be pleased to take on a partnership with us. He could have the railway and a profit on his money!"

"A fool's profit." Claybourne's teeth shone white in his scorn. "I don't risk my money or my reputation on untested speculation."

"Oh, don't you, Mr. Claybourne?" Felicity asked, leveling a finger at him, wondering where her fearlessness had come from. "You are at fault here, too!"

"I'm at fault?" Claybourne's face darkened, and he grew as still as a frozen pond.

"If you were duped by my uncle and Mr. Biddle, it happened because of your own sightless greed. You risked thirty thousand pounds of your precious money on a mere promissory note. Shouldn't you have had the ownership certificate in your hands before surrendering the money? Why take such a risk, Mr. Claybourne? Even I know better than to exchange bank notes for a worthless piece of paper."

Claybourne suddenly had her by the ribbons again. This time he'd planted his other hand in the middle of her back and trapped her against the desk, his face so near she could smell the lime of his shaving soap, could feel the startling, rock-hard press of his thigh through her skirts. She was scandalized and frightened and utterly bewitched by his simmering strength.

"My reasons are not your concern, Miss Mayfield. You and I will wed, or you and Biddle and that thieving uncle of yours will spend the next twenty-five years in prison."

"You can't do that! There are laws—"

"Yes, there are laws against felony fraud, punishable by long prison terms. I have the right, and the means, to prosecute. And I have every intention of doing so. Do you understand me, Miss Mayfield?"

He was so powerfully close, was such a breath-stealing presence, she could barely hear for the thundering in her ears. Yet Felicity understood him very well, was sure she would remember his heat and her terror till her dying breath. Twenty-five years meant that her uncle and Mr. Biddle would die in prison. She couldn't let that happen. A year and a day married to Claybourne couldn't be any worse than that.

"Unhand me, Mr. Claybourne."

"Your answer, woman."

She lowered her gaze from his impossibly dark eyes and watched the muscles tighten beneath his clean-shaved jaw. Marriage to Hunter Claybourne? What kind of life would that be? Waiting at home for a bleak winter storm to blow through the house and freeze her to death. Hiding from him and his ever-present wrath, from this reeling sensation.

But what choice did she have? None that she could see from the vantage point of his snarl. Still, there must be a way to protect herself and her family, to see that he didn't grind her into gravel. She'd learned a very long time ago that with the right amount of leverage, she could move whole mountains.

"My answer, Mr. Claybourne, depends upon two things." When he didn't speak, or move to release her from his too-private embrace, Felicity continued, trying to ignore the compelling sensation of his sultry wrath skiffing across the bridge of her nose. "If I consent to this . . . marriage, you will indemnify my uncle and Mr. Biddle against this felony. And we will agree upon a marriage settlement, set down in a legally binding document, drawn up by Mr. Biddle. What do you say to this, Mr. Claybourne?"

Hunter wanted nothing more than to order the vexing woman out of his office and out of his life, and yet he could not even bring himself to release her. She was lithe curves and warm, indignant sighs. She was a summer day, the sunlight on his cheek. He had imagined she would be a faded copy of her uncle; ungainly limbed and overly adorned; instead, she was unstudied grace and accidental elegance. She regarded him steadily, her mouth newly moist and altogether too rosy. Oh, the ice was thin here, and slippery. He'd been too long without a woman, and this one was too near.

"Well, Mr. Claybourne?" she asked, with a fractious lift of her delicate chin.

Hunter released her abruptly, and stepped to safety behind his desk. "Stay here, Biddle," he said, clamping his hand down on the old man's bony shoulder to keep the bumbling bastard from scrambling out of the chair.

"Yes, sir?" Biddle asked, looking up at him with those watery blank eyes. Hunter slid a sheet of paper onto the blotter.

"You will write out this settlement, Mr. Biddle." Hunter met the young woman's eyes, intending to send her a silent challenge, but finding meadow-green fire that set his pulse to racing. "Your first article, Miss Mayfield?"

"Now?" She looked convincingly startled, touched her slender fingers to her ivory throat, then slipped them through the loops of the untidy bow at her neckline. "Mr. Claybourne, I need time to think this through."

"You have one half-hour."

"Before what?"

"Before I call the bailiff," Hunter snapped, welcoming the throbbing that had come to play against his temples. The woman was no more than a headache to him, and it was best to be so starkly reminded of the fact. "Your first article, Miss Mayfield. What is it to be?"

She straightened and primly laced her fingers together among the soft folds of her skirts. "Firstly, Mr. Claybourne, this marriage will last one year and one day, and will end abruptly in divorce the moment my shares in the Drayhill-Starlington Railway become yours."

"Done. Write it, Biddle."

But Biddle was already scrawling his way through the first line, flinching each time Hunter moved a muscle. The man had been a cowering wreck from the moment he had arrived and now looked like a dog awaiting a well-deserved beating.

"Secondly, Mr. Claybourne," she said, pacing away from the desk toward the window, her hips swaying slightly until she turned to him, "since I make my living writing travel articles for the *Hearth and Heath*, I must be free to travel as I see fit."

Hunter had been prepared to agree to most any of the woman's pointless requests, but he paused, unable to imagine such an occupation. "And this travel takes you where?"

"To the very type of place you had me kidnapped from yesterday. To inns and oddities along the railway lines."

Hunter had no idea where Cobson had found her, and cared not at all. And yet now that she'd mentioned this traveling, riding trains into the countryside— "Do you travel alone?"

"Certainly alone, Mr. Claybourne." Impatience flecked gold in the crystal green of her eyes. "But it's no use questioning me on the subject. My freedom to travel is not negotiable—"

"Done," he said, cutting off her argument, and any

thought beyond the completion of this damnable settlement. "Your third article, Miss Mayfield?"

She cleared her throat twice. "My third article regards your behavior in public."

"My behavior?" Hunter would have laughed, but the woman looked ready to throttle him, her jaw set in stone, her mouth drawn tightly as if he'd already committed some indecent act.

"You, sir, are to keep your women out of the public eye."

"My women?" Hunter did laugh then—for all the women who had presumptuously taken his arm after dinner, who had smiled and hinted, who'd made him burn—

"I won't be laughed at, Mr. Claybourne. I realize you are a man of great social and financial importance, but I will not be embarrassed by your flaunting your mistresses where I might hear about them, or read about them in the news. I have my pride."

And Hunter had his own. "I can assure you, Miss Mayfield, you'll read nothing of me in the newspapers."

"And if your social life demands your attendance at a function, you will go alone, or if you must have a partner, we will attend together."

A partner. The idea had some merit. "I agree."

"Good, because—"

"And I demand the same courtesy from you, Miss Mayfield."

"From me?"

Now her cheeks were burning brightly, and Hunter felt his own blood rising, wondering who she was thinking of, which man in her life could coax such a flame of color. "You'll keep your parade of gentlemen out of my house and out of the newspapers."

"I have no such parade, Mr. Claybourne! Nor do I intend to arrange one."

"Fine. Article Four, Miss Mayfield."

"Article Four."

Felicity endured Claybourne's insolent glare as she went to the desk and looked over Mr. Biddle's shoulder to read the earlier articles. Imagine, thinking that she had a parade of men following her. Claybourne obviously harbored a guilty conscience. A man of his dark charms must attract women of the lowest sort. "Let's see, we will divorce at the end of one year; I may travel; you will keep your mistresses in seclusion, and . . ."

And the wedding night? A flush leaped like a forest fire out of her bodice and dashed up her neck to lick at her earlobes.

"And what?" Claybourne asked slowly, his curiosity at her sudden embarrassment far too apparent.

Marriage held certain physical responsibilities for a woman. Had she been marrying a man she loved, Felicity was sure she would be eager to share his bed. But the very thought of sharing anything with Hunter Claybourne made her head go light. As it had last week as she'd ridden over the Yorkshire moors in a hot-air balloon, soaring into the gladness of the day. The thought of sharing a marriage bed with Claybourne evoked the same kind of fear, born of the unknown and a feeling of falling from great heights. His hovering darkness descended on her, his mouth softened by the gilding of the gaslight above.

She turned to Mr. Biddle. "Will you leave us for a moment, sir?"

Biddle nodded and sped out the door, followed by Claybourne's bark of warning not to leave the building.

"Time is wasting, Miss Mayfield. What part of our marriage settlement couldn't you discuss in front of Biddle?"

Claybourne stood at the edge of the desk, his gaze efficiently charting her face, his arms linked across his chest.

"A personal part."

"Personal, Miss Mayfield?"

"Yes. Article Four involves . . . well, I don't know

how to put this properly without sounding . . ." Unable to face the man, Felicity shifted her interest to the brass rail that edged the desk, and ran her fingers along it.

"Without sounding what, woman?"

"Without sounding vulgar. Mr. Claybourne, since ours will be a marriage in name only . . ." Felicity looked back at Claybourne, hoping he would understand the source of her hesitancy so she wouldn't have to lay bare her fears in front of him. But he merely stared at her with those obsidian eyes. A curse on his rock-headedness, and the giddiness in her chest.

"Go on, Miss Mayfield." Now the monster seemed amused.

"I assume, Mr. Claybourne, that our marriage is to remain . . . unconsummated."

"It is," he said too casually, too quickly, leaving Felicity feeling exposed and thoroughly repudiated. Not worth his slightest temptation. Not that it mattered; she found him not at all interesting. Too towering, too darkly dangerous, too arrogant—

"Good," she said. "Then my fourth article is irrelevant. However, I shall write it down anyway."

Felicity sat in the desk chair and was just about to write the number four on the settlement when Claybourne's hand clamped around hers. It was very warm and very large.

And his voice was very near her ear. "What is it you plan to write, Miss Mayfield?"

His breath lifted the curls along the nape of her neck, making them dance lightly there. That balloon-soaring fear returned and nudged her off course for a moment. She went willingly—floated across patchwork fields, caught his updrafts and touched the clouds.

"Your plan, Miss Mayfield."

Felicity shook off the peculiar dizziness and forced herself to focus on the tip of the pen, which was nearly obscured beneath Claybourne's hand.

"I'm writing Article Four, Mr. Claybourne."

"Which is?"

He smelled of fog and exotic spices. His fingernails were clean and neatly trimmed, the back of his hand tanned and lightly haired, but striped with prominent white scars on two of his knuckles. The contrast between pampered gentleman and street fighter was so great, she almost asked about the cause. But she didn't want to know. He was a moment in her life, no more. She turned her head slightly to see him better.

"Mr. Claybourne, I want the settlement to address the issue of dealing with the result of an error in judgment between us—"

"What possible error in judgment?" He looked affronted, as if he had already considered every possible issue and she need not waste his valuable time considering any other.

"I mean to say that, should we find ourselves overcome with . . . you know."

"No, I don't know. Tell me."

She shook off his hand and stood up to get away from him. "Please listen to me, Mr. Claybourne. This is very important."

"I'm listening, Miss Mayfield."

She stepped around to the front of the desk. "You'll pardon the crudeness of my language, Mr. Claybourne, but, just in case our marriage *is* consummated . . . by some miscalculation—"

"Miscalculation?"

"Whether it be on your part or mine—"

"Yours?"

"*And* should a child come of this . . . miscalculation—" She glanced up at Claybourne. He was looking across the room at the wall of drape-shrouded window, into some unseen distance. He probably wasn't listening, but she continued anyway, knowing she'd never be able to broach this conversation again with any kind of confidence. He was so very large, and his hand had been so very warm, his pulse so strong. . . . "If we should conceive a child between us, for whatever reason, I want to be assured that he or she will live with me at the end of our marriage. That you won't fight me for custody."

He said nothing. Perhaps he hadn't heard her.

"Well, Mr. Claybourne? You don't appear the sort of man who'd want to bother with children. And I couldn't bear to part with any of my own. Do you agree?"

"There will be no children between us."

"Then you agree with Article Four."

"Yes."

"Good." Felicity felt his gaze follow every stroke of the pen until she finished the clause. As she fit the pen into its holder, her arms seemed made of lead. "Time to call in Mr. Biddle."

"Not quite yet, Miss Mayfield." He slipped the paper from beneath her hand, smearing the final line and taking up the pen. "I have an article of my own."

"Only one?" Felicity scrubbed at the ink he'd left on her fingertip. "You surprise me. This idea of marriage is yours, Mr. Claybourne. I would have thought a financially astute man like you would have drawn up a settlement of your own ahead of time."

He sighed as he studied the page, obviously feigning interest in its clauses. "An unnecessary effort, Miss Mayfield. According to law and tradition, you and everything you own become mine when we marry. Your debts become mine. Your actions, your income, and your possessions will belong to me without question."

"Then I present to you the rest of your property, Mr. Claybourne." Felicity pointed to the sad-face portmanteau she'd been toting for the last year. "I hope you are dreadfully happy with it. Though I'll need it in my work. Perhaps I can rent it back from you on a weekly basis?"

"Don't be insolent with me, Miss Mayfield. I don't want your portmanteau."

"I only want to know where I stand." She thanked God that Claybourne didn't know of her emergency fund in the Bank across the street.

"Where you go during this year of our marriage is unimportant to me." He dropped the settlement onto the desk.

"You'll hardly know we're married, Mr. Claybourne. I shall travel extensively, as indicated in Article Two of our settlement. You needn't concern yourself over my actions."

"I'll not concern myself as long as your actions never reflect badly upon my name. I'll not be made the subject of your penny magazines, nor find my name linked to your exploits in any way. Should you sully my reputation or my name—"

"Sir, if your name is sullied during the season of our marriage, it will be by your own hand." His face hardened, and she was instantly reminded of who she was taking on as a husband.

"Let it be known from this moment that Article Two of our settlement—your freedom to travel—depends entirely upon your actions. Should my name enter the newspapers for any reason, you'll wish you'd been sent to prison instead."

You'll have to find me first, she thought.

"Do you understand me on this point?" When she nodded, Claybourne scrawled the addition onto the settlement. "Sign here," he said, consulting his pocket watch.

Felicity read his article and then signed her name beneath his own, glad and grateful to be done with his inquisition.

"I shall have my clerk make a copy of this for you."

"And I'll have my solicitor keep it safe, sir." It was probably safer in her portmanteau with her gazette articles, since Biddle would probably use it for a handkerchief. But Claybourne didn't need to know her plans.

He yanked on the bell rope behind his desk. "It is time, Miss Mayfield."

"Time for what?"

"You and I will be married today."

"Today?" Claybourne's pronouncement had all the force of a blow to the stomach. "What of a license?"

"A civil ceremony will suffice. Did you expect a reading of the banns and a stroll down the aisle at St. Paul's?"

"Frankly, Mr. Claybourne, I had assumed that when I did marry, the reason would be to love and to cherish till death did my husband and I part. But this is no marriage; it's a business transaction. I don't care where or how it happens. In fact, why not seal the bargain at a clerk's stall in the lobby of the Bank?"

Claybourne arched a skeptical brow. "What a ridiculous idea."

So, the man lacked a sense of humor as well as a sense of humanity.

The office door opened. "Yes, Mr. Claybourne?"

"Bring in Biddle and Mr. Denning, then remain here yourself, Tilson. I'll need you as witness."

Tilson was brushed aside by an angular man who tossed his hat and cane onto a chair as he breezed into the center of the room, and met Claybourne with a hearty handshake.

"Hunter Claybourne, you old dog! Getting married—I never would have thought it."

The man's attention darted toward Felicity, and a huge grin brightened his already florid face. "Ah, but now I understand your reasons. She's a beauty!"

"That's enough, Denning," Claybourne said with enough distaste to include the entire room.

But Denning had already lifted Felicity's hand to his lips. "Tell me your name, miss, and I will ever treasure the privilege of knowing it."

Before Felicity could respond beyond a simple blush, Claybourne stepped between them, presented his broad back to her, and growled something unintelligible at Denning.

Denning laughed and went briskly to the desk. "In a hurry, old man? I shouldn't wonder why."

Claybourne ignored the man as he would a fly.

"Who is this, Mr. Claybourne?" Felicity asked, not really expecting him to answer.

"Madam, I am Gordon Denning, the superintendent-registrar. I record all of Claybourne's business transactions."

"Denning is here to marry us," Claybourne said offhandedly, as if he did this sort of thing on a weekly basis.

"A business transaction. You are very sure of yourself, Mr. Claybourne, and very sure of my answer!"

"Stand over here, Miss Mayfield," he said, pointing to the floor beside him.

Felicity frowned at the unyielding edge in Claybourne's voice. He looked thunderous, this future, if fleeting, husband of hers.

"Trouble, Claybourne?" Denning asked through a half-smile. He seemed to be enjoying himself enormously at Claybourne's expense, which didn't seem to be a wise thing to do.

"Mr. Denning," Felicity said, moving toward the windows, and away from Claybourne. "Is there any law that governs the proximity of the bride to the groom during the ceremony?"

Denning studied Claybourne for a moment, then lifted his shoulders in an exaggerated shrug. "None that I know of, Miss Mayfield. As long as the bride and groom are in the same room. Unless, of course, the deed is done by proxy, and then—"

"Then I choose to stand here by the—" But Claybourne had taken two long strides and grabbed her elbow.

"You will stand here," he said, drawing her with him to the desk, leaving Felicity to feel completely possessed by the man. "We will do this correctly, Miss Mayfield. There will be no question as to the legality of our union. Does the State require anything else, Denning?"

Denning looked even more amused as he peered around Claybourne at Biddle and Tilson, and then counted with a finger, "Two witnesses, a bride, a groom, and a registrar." He smiled brightly. "Everything seems to be in place."

"Then proceed. I haven't got all day." Claybourne cleared his throat and straightened. His fingers brushed past hers, then fled to the folds of his coat.

His fleeting touch aroused a measureless yearning inside Felicity, for want of something warm to hold on to. This ought to be a joyous moment in her life. She was getting married. The room ought to smell of roses and heather, not of book leather and ledger paper. The man standing beside her ought to be the treasure of her heart, not a prison warden. But this wasn't a true marriage, and she set the discomfort from her mind, hoping that Claybourne wouldn't notice the absurd tears gathering in her eyes.

Fewer than a hundred words later, Felicity found herself married to Hunter Claybourne and signing her name in Denning's marriage registry. Her temporary husband hovered over her, making sure she signed correctly.

He'd made no move to kiss her, had even scowled at Denning when the man had begun to mention the fact. And now she felt more than a little brazen for even thinking about such a thing. A kiss? Felicity tried to dredge up a measure of disgust, but instead found herself following his capable hand as he wrote his name above hers.

"Done," he said, jamming the pen back into its holder and straightening to his full height. He smiled down on her in stark animosity, firing off the opening salvo.

Living with Claybourne would be like living inside a storm cloud: she'd be constantly dodging his lightning strikes and his drenching moods. With any luck at all, and a creative travel schedule, she would rarely see the man.

"Thank you, Mr. Denning," Felicity said, as she picked up her portmanteau and shawl.

"The pleasure was mine, Miss Mayf . . . excuse me . . ." He beamed a goading smile at Claybourne. "I mean, Mrs. Claybourne."

Felicity shot a glance toward Claybourne and caught his forbidding frown. She was pleased to see that his mood matched her own.

But at least now she was free of his threats; she had fulfilled her part of the bargain. She'd go back to Beacon Chase today and try to make it up to Mrs. Duffle, to spend a few days of quiet while she polished this month's gazette articles, and still have plenty of time to meet her Friday deadline to Mr. Dolan.

Felicity stuck out her hand toward Claybourne. When the lout didn't take her it, she shrugged and started toward the door. "I'll be in touch."

She couldn't think of a single agreeable thing to say to Mr. Biddle, so she walked past him and through the outer office to the mezzanine, feeling no more married than she had when she arrived.

Which was a very good thing, because she had no intention of actually getting married to anyone, any time soon. She was immensely happy in her life, and felt her very best when she was traveling.

Felicity stopped long enough at the top of the stairs to slip her shawl over her shoulders and take the bonnet from her portmanteau. She touched the purse at her waist and decided to make a quick visit to her emergency funds while she was so close by the Bank of England. Her uncle had only deposited the money there the day before he left, and she wanted to assure herself that it was still safe.

And that Claybourne couldn't reach it.

Claybourne. Felicity hurried down the stairs, chilled by the startling realization that her new husband hadn't shaken her hand in farewell, because he was a man who never let go of anything.

Chapter 4

"Take care of the matter, Tilson," Hunter said, dizzied still by the scent of the woman's unwelcome sunlight. "Miss Mayfield and I have business at the bank. As for you, Biddle, get out of my office."

The still-quivering solicitor had retreated to the farthest reaches of the room. Another two steps and the man would have cocooned himself in the drapes.

"This way, sir," Tilson said firmly, handing Biddle his coat as he ushered him through the door to the outer office.

Hunter cursed himself for being a damn fool. He had expected a damp-browed, wilted wildflower, but Miss Mayfield had defied him outright. She had weakened his judgment just as artfully as her uncle's simplicity had swindled him.

And now he was married to the chit.

"'I'll be in touch?'" Denning sputtered, then pointed toward the door like a baboon. "Egad, man! You just married the woman! And now she's leaving you?"

Hunter had forgotten Denning was even in the room. Damn the woman for her distractions, for the gold of her hair and the changeable green insolence of her stare. At least he hadn't forgotten the other business of the morning, Lucius Treadmore's failed shipping concern. "Did you bring me a copy of Treadmore's deed?"

"As you requested, Claybourne. But where is your wife going? You should be with her! What about the wedding breakfast?"

Hunter ignored Denning, tolerating him only because he was forced to do so in the course of his work.

"Who is she, Hunter?"

"Forget it, Denning. Give me the deed. Or do I have to turn you upside down and shake it out of you?"

Denning's insufferable grin collapsed, and he presented the deed with a snort. "Registering your marriage and a foreclosure in the same day? Your new wife obviously approves, Claybourne, or she'd have protested your doing business on her wedding morn. She certainly seems the sort to raise up in defiance."

Denning walked to the window and lifted aside the drapes, allowing a shaft of morning sunlight to spear the carpet.

Hunter turned from the sudden brightness and unfolded the deed to be sure all was in order. The property was a fine dockland holding that he'd purchased years before. What a pity Treadmore had no sense of enterprise. But no harm done—after this morning, Fanno Pier would belong again to the Claybourne empire, and he would sell it to another, hopefully wiser, investor.

"Is she an heiress, Claybourne? Is that why you can't tell me who she is?"

Hunter didn't like this man, or his prying. His marriage to Miss Mayfield was a private, personal item of business, and he refused to speak of her to anyone.

"Whom I marry is none of your business, Denning."

"It is when you register your marriage in my book." Denning squared his shoulders. "I'm an officer of the court, Claybourne. I can ask any question I please."

"Have I made an illegal breach?"

Denning gave him the once over, then went back to his window gazing. "I don't know. Have you?"

Hunter dropped the deed on his desk and picked up the marriage settlement. The document was frivolous and impotent, but Miss Mayfield's demands had been sound in the glaring light of her situation: her freedom, her future, her preposterous concern over the lot of any children they might conceive. But Hunter hadn't figured her stunning beauty into the equation, any more than he had her bullheadedness. Damn it all, what had he brought down upon himself?

"There she is now, Hunter! Tying a hideous bonnet over that magnificent hair." Denning thumped twice on the pane with his fingertip. "Damn the bonnet, she's beautiful! And she's getting away from you, Claybourne. Your bride is escaping!"

Hunter stopped himself from going to the window. He'd wasted enough of the day on the woman, would waste enough of his life in the next year. "And is she getting into a carriage?"

"Yes."

"And is that carriage mine?"

Denning turned slowly and studied him, obviously looking for a cleft in his certainty. "What if I said it wasn't?"

Hunter lifted a shoulder. "I'd be damned surprised, and Tilson would be unemployed."

Denning vented a grunt and dropped the curtain into place. "Tilson can relax."

"And you may leave, Denning. I'm finished with you. Here." Hunter shoved the register under Denning's arm and sent him toward the door.

"You're not going to tell me who she is, are you?" Denning waited a beat for an answer, then sighed as he retrieved his hat and cane. "Stephie will murder me in my sleep when she learns that I married you to your mystery bride and didn't confess it to her. You'll find your match in that wife of yours, Claybourne."

"Good afternoon, Denning."

"And a good wedding day to you, Claybourne."
Denning offered one last grin and then let himself out.

Wedding day. Now there was a preposterous notion.
And yet Hunter found himself imagining her hair
tugged free of its bindings, a halo of gold, rumpled
bedclothes—Damnation!

Hunter yanked on the bell rope.

"Sir?" Tilson said, brushing a fall of crumbs from his
chin as he entered. "Sorry," he mumbled.

Tilson was a capable young man with a growing
family, the perfect amalgamation of pluck and anxiety
to make for a loyal clerk. He asked few questions and
offered fewer opinions, but his wife coddled the man
like a babe, sending scones and jam with him every
morning, and having a box lunch delivered promptly
every half-noon. She treated her husband like a
monied merchant, then complained at the state of the
family finances. Hunter had often overheard her
heated whispers through the office door, bleating at
Tilson to beg a raise in pay.

But Hunter had studied Tilson's household finances
and had judged the salary he offered suitable for a
married man with two children. The woman still
hadn't forgiven him for throwing open his office door
on one such argument and presenting these fiscal facts
to her in black and white. Mrs. Tilson had sped from
the office in a veil of weeping, leaving Tilson to decide
between rushing after her and staying at his desk
during work hours. Tilson had wisely chosen to stay,
but looked much the worse the next morning for what
must have been a long night's battle under the barrage
of his wife's ignorance of business.

Wife.

Hunter wondered what sort of mood his own was in
at the moment.

"Sir?" Tilson repeated.

"Ah, yes." Hunter shrugged into his coat, annoyed
at the recent lapses in his thinking—lapses which had
begun late last night, and in the confounding presence

of Miss Mayfield. And in her absence, sleep had been elusive. "I'll be lunching with Lord Spurling at Hammershaw's, then attending a meeting of the Committee at Lloyd's. Should last the afternoon."

"Yessir."

"See that the notice of foreclosure is delivered to Treadmore. He's had his last warning. I want him out by morning. And . . ." Hunter began, remembering the marriage settlement on his desk. He'd promised a copy for Miss Mayfield, but the meaning of the clauses was still too unsettling for others eyes to see.

"Yessir?"

"Nothing more." Hunter folded the settlement and locked it in the safe. "I take it that Miss Mayf . . . my . . . wife is waiting for me?"

"As you required, sir." Tilson lowered his gaze for a moment, toeing his shoe along an arc of gold in the carpet. "Though Mrs. Claybourne didn't seem at all happy about it, sir, if I may say so."

"No, Tilson, you may not say so. Ever."

"Yessir. Thank you, sir." Tilson started to retreat, but stopped and brightened a degree. "Oh, and . . . congratulations, sir, on your, uh . . . recent—"

"Good day, Tilson." Hunter lifted his hat from the coat tree and let himself into the mezzanine.

The spectacle of marble and mahogany and brilliant brass stirred joy and satisfaction in the center of him, just as it always did—aromatic of beeswax polish and the fragrant spices from the India traders, and ringing with the sounds of pristine heels upon gleaming stone.

This was his kingdom, his impregnable fortress. The Claybourne Exchange. Rival to the almighty Royal Exchange in its influence on the country's wealth, but far more capable of overcoming the vagaries of the world's markets than that ponderous behemoth across the street. Kings, counts, and foreign governments crossed Cornhill Street to trade in the Claybourne Exchange. None could doubt his supremacy and none dared challenge him.

Not even Miss Mayfield and her felonious uncle. A year was a long time to wait for the Drayhill-Starlington shares to finally become his, but he'd already begun to redesign his plans to fit the new schedule. In time, he would cause the delay to work to his advantage.

Turning flotsam into cold, countable cash: that was his strength.

Hunter greeted a stream of lords as he passed them on his way down the stairs. He'd made a dozen fortunes for these men; without his guidance they would lose them again, and so they stayed on as clients. Some even sought his friendship, but he always declined. Friendship and business didn't mix, so he avoided friendships entirely. Uncomplicated acquaintances provided him with the contacts he needed for success. Beyond that, he needed no one.

Especially not a wife.

"A glorious day, Claybourne, wouldn't you say?"

Hunter turned on the stairs and stared up at Lord Vincent, wondering for an awkward instant if the grinning fellow had somehow heard of his recent marriage. Not that it mattered. The marriage wasn't a secret; he had just planned to keep the fact of it private.

"Yes, it's a fine day, Lord Vincent," Hunter said, offering his most pleasant smile, searching the man's face for a trace of such news of his marriage. "You gentlemen seem in grand spirits."

"Of course we are!" Lord Vincent laughed and bounced the two steps down the stairs to sling a hail-fellow's arm over Hunter's shoulder. "And you're the cause, man! Right, gentlemen?"

They rumbled "ayes" and "hurrahs" from the top of the stairs.

"Am I?" Hunter asked slowly, casting a glance to the other faces, each flushed and damp in some kind of excitement. No, this wasn't about his marriage.

"Brakestowe Iron Works, Claybourne!"

"Ah, yes." Hunter had forgotten. More evidence of

Miss Mayfield's distractions from his day; he should have remembered that Brakestowe's quarterly profits were to be announced. Instead, he'd spent his morning marrying himself to a thief.

"The shares have sold out, and are now worth half-again as much as we paid for them. Just as you said they would be, Claybourne. You've made us all very happy."

"And very rich," added Lord Haverstone.

Hunter offered a benevolent smile and patted Vincent on the arm. "Did you think I would misadvise you, Lord Vincent?"

"Never!" the man bellowed, raising a fist in salute. "Hurrah!"

The others followed suit, and Hunter continued down the stairs to a satisfying round of cheers. He counted bishops, peers, and members of the royal family among the most prestigious of his clients. Yet he never revealed to anyone the names or the substance of his dealings with them. Privacy and security were the bywords of the Claybourne Exchange. Hunter's good name was his fortune.

His footman greeted him at the curb, looking warily toward the fiercely frowning woman who glowered from the window of the brougham. A wet cat locked in a wire cage.

"Good luck, sir," Branson said, stepping away.

Hunter opened the door himself, expecting his wife to spring on him. Instead, she continued her murderous glower and leaned deeper against the seat, her arms folded across the ugly portmanteau that dwarfed her lap. He wondered for an unsettling moment if she might be armed with pistol or knife.

"Do you find great joy in imprisoning me, Mr. Claybourne?" she asked sharply, as he took the seat opposite her.

"I have no opinion at all, Miss Mayfield. We're going to the Bank of England. Drive on!" he said with a rap to the roof. The carriage entered the traffic.

"To the bank? Why? I thought we were finished with each other for the moment. I have work to do, Mr. Claybourne." She lifted up the sleeve of a writing portfolio. "Do you see this? My travel articles for the *Hearth and Heath.* I have deadlines to meet—"

"One final detail, Miss Mayfield. A paper to sign."

She peered out the window and added another fret to her brow. "Why travel in a carriage, Mr. Claybourne? Why not walk? The bank is right there, across Threadneedle Street. Is your station so lofty you'd rather not brush shoulders with the rabble, or dirty your boots on the street?"

"Cease your comments, Miss Mayfield."

The short ride was punctuated by a grisly growling coming from his wife's stomach. The Cobsons weren't known for their generosity; she probably hadn't gotten a crumb from them this morning. He supposed he ought to feed her. He didn't want rumors to spread that he'd let his own wife starve. That wouldn't do at all.

"Come, Miss Mayfield." Hunter stepped from the carriage onto the crowded walk in front of the Bank of England.

Branson moved in to help her down the step, but Hunter stuck his gloved hand out and she allowed him to help her down. Her own gloves were worn and fawn colored, and looked small inside the black leather prison he'd made of his own hand. She lifted her gaze to him for the briefest moment, and he was transported suddenly to a misty meadow. He missed the pressure of her touch when she pulled her hand away.

She stood on the curb and chewed on her lower lip as she surveyed the block. She set her ever-present portmanteau on the ground and adjusted her bonnet. "How long will this take, Mr. Claybourne? I have business in Fleet Street."

"You'll leave when we are finished. Come," he said, taking her elbow as she stared up at the edifice.

He'd taken only a half-step when she gave a shout,

then bolted from him into the oncoming crowd. Her uncle had escaped him, but he damn well wasn't going to let her get away. Hunter caught her before she'd passed another lamp post and held fast to her waist, a tantalizing expanse made more so by her rapid breathing.

"Let me go, Claybourne!" She squirmed and tried to twist out of his hands.

"You can't run from me, woman."

"I'm not, you blockhead! Someone stole my bag!"

Hunter glanced up from her anger and saw the thief shifting through the crowd, trying to look like a part of the noontime foot traffic. Damned parasite.

Felicity watched in amazement as Claybourne handed her his hat, then adroitly zigzagged through the oncoming press of people. His progress was easy to follow; he was a full head taller than anyone else, his raven hair darker than rail iron. She wouldn't have expected such agility from a man of his temperament. But it was brawn, not neglected muscle, that flexed beneath his coat. She wondered witlessly how that supple strength would play against his linen shirt. She was in the midst of chastising herself for thinking such things about a stranger, when the fact dawned on her that he was her husband now. And that it was probably quite all right for her to wonder what he looked like without his shirt.

Felicity felt that same flush creep out of her neckline and quickly changed the direction of her thoughts to the subject at hand. There had been two ragged boys, one nearly grown and the other not more than ten or eleven years old. The larger had elbowed her out of the way and the smaller had sped away with her bag. Her paltry stash of ready money was still in the purse dangling at her waist, but her portmanteau contained all of her clothes and all her writing from the last month of travel. She hoped Claybourne would catch at least one of the little thieves, but she hoped most of all that he wouldn't hurt them. He seemed capable of any kind of violence.

At last she caught sight of Claybourne striding toward her, wrestling with something, frowning ruthlessly and parting the sea of people as easily as a steamship cuts through water.

"Is this the one?" he asked, shoving a ragged boy to the ground at her feet, tearing the already tattered sleeve with his carelessness. The boy cowered dramatically and a space grew like a desert island around them as the crowd gathered quickly for the spectacle.

"Well, is this the thief, madam?" Claybourne repeated, his dark eyes glittering in misbegotten triumph, his breathing steady but outraged.

"I don't know . . ." Felicity said, not at all pleased with Claybourne's rancor. She'd been the man's victim for the last twenty-four hours and knew exactly how the lad must feel. "You needn't frighten him, Mr. Claybourne. He's just a boy."

"Look up . . . *boy*." Claybourne lifted him by the upper arms to Felicity's level.

"Mr. Claybourne, you've torn his shirt."

"And he has stolen your portmanteau." Claybourne held him off the ground as if the boy weighed no more than a scrap of yellowed newsprint that had blown past in the wind.

The woeful lad's eyes glistened gray as a stormy sea; his blond hair bristled with caked mud. He smelled like he hadn't been near a hot bath in years, if ever. Belligerent pride worked the guileless bow of his mouth, but stark terror seemed to keep it shut.

Felicity shifted her gaze to Claybourne's face and was disgusted by the open loathing she found there. He held the boy as he would a bundle of stinking rubbish.

"Look closely at him, madam," Claybourne barked, giving the boy a teeth-rattling shake. "Yes or no, is this your thief?"

It was, but she'd never confess it to Claybourne. The lad probably hadn't eaten in a week. Everything she owned had been in her portmanteau, but she was a very wealthy and lucky woman compared to the child dangling from Claybourne's malevolent hands.

"No, Mr. Claybourne, this is not the boy who ran off with my bag." Felicity was pleased to see impotent anger blaze in Claybourne's eyes. "You've imprisoned the wrong person. Again. You seem to be very good at that, sir."

He set the boy hard on his feet, but held fast to his shirt collar, his fist wound so tightly, Felicity feared the boy would be strangled.

"Take care, sir," she said, loosening Claybourne's grip with a slap at his hand. "You'll hurt him."

"He's as guilty as sin, Miss Mayfield," Claybourne said, taking a tighter hold on the frail shirt and tearing it even further. "He's one of a pack of young thieves that preys upon people along Threadneedle Street. He must be dealt with to the full extent of the law."

Claybourne started dragging the boy up the bank stairs, but Felicity ran ahead and stopped him with a hand to his chest, a very solid and uncompromising barrier.

"Out of my way, Miss Mayfield."

"Where are you taking him?"

He brushed her aside, but she clung to his arm and stopped him again, planting herself between the boy and his immoveable judge. Her efforts brought her chest against Claybourne's belt, and even as he bent his angry face to hers, Felicity found herself marveling at his strength.

"I'm taking the little bandit to a bank guard, who'll then take him to the police, who will then lock him up." He bent closer, if that was possible, and the obsidian of his eyes turned to molten scarlet. "It's what I do with thieves."

"This boy is not a thief, Mr. Claybourne. The real

thief was taller and . . . wore a green shirt. This boy's shirt is brown. What's left of it." She stepped out from under Claybourne's ill-tasting doubt and looked directly into the boy's upturned face. "Isn't your shirt brown, lad?"

He nodded his head slowly, never dropping his gaze from hers. The boy hadn't spoken at all, seemed incapable at the moment, with his mouth gaping and his eyes as wide as the sky. She wondered if he wasn't a mute. In any case, Claybourne had no right to beleaguer anyone without proof.

"He's completely innocent of the crime."

"An innocent doesn't run," Claybourne said, growling as if he'd rather throw the boy off London Bridge.

"If you were being chased along Threadneedle by an enraged giant, Mr. Claybourne, wouldn't you run, too?"

Claybourne's eyes shifted to the street, then back to her. His anger paled his brow and then his neck. He let go his grip on the boy's collar with a snap and then looked down at his own hand as he closed his fist.

The boy scampered to her side. "Thank you ever so kindly, miss," he said.

"You're very welcome," Felicity said, straightening the torn and rumpled shirt. The poor child. Motherless, no doubt, and grateful for her gentle encouragement. "What's your name, lad?"

"Pepperpot, miss. Giles Pepperpot." He smiled grandly at her and slipped his warm, calloused hand inside hers, letting it hang there among the folds of her skirt.

Claybourne muttered a curse and grabbed his hat from her other hand. "You've let yourself be taken in, Miss Mayfield."

"Have a heart, Mr. Claybourne, and let him go. We'll finish our business at the Bank and then part as we planned. Away with you, lad, before the great man can catch you." She patted the boy's matted head and he sped away, tucking in his shirt, his filthy bare feet slapping the pavement. The crowd muttered its disappointment and dispersed as soon as he was gone.

"You're a fool, Miss Mayfield."

"If granting a kind word to an unfortunate child makes me a fool, then I wear the label proudly. You, on the other hand, are miserly and cruel, Mr. Claybourne. Not that it surprises me. I knew it by inference before, and now you've shown me in vivid detail."

"Thank you. And where do you suppose your bag is now, Miss Mayfield?" he asked, taking her elbow and starting up the steps toward the Bank.

"I couldn't even imagine. It was probably taken from little Giles by the older boy—"

Claybourne stopped on the step above and bore down on her like a thunder-heavy cloud. "Damnation, woman! You knew it was he! That little thief stole your good sense as well as your bag! You let him escape when I had him by the nape."

"Yes, I did. The bag was long gone. Taken by the other. There was nothing to be done. Giles Pepperpot is a poor little boy—"

"He's a thief, madam. He'd rather slit your throat for a ha'penny than to look at you."

"You may be a cutthroat, Mr. Claybourne, but that doesn't mean that everyone is. Children like Giles need care and comfort and a good home. In fact, if I had thought about it in all the commotion, I'd have given Giles money to buy himself a new shirt to replace the one you tore." Felicity reached for the purse that hung from her belt, prepared to shake the coins in Claybourne's face.

"My purse—"

It was gone. Nothing remained but the short length of cording.

Claybourne's growling anger smoothed into the rumble of insolent laughter. "Stolen by your wretched little angel?" he asked, lifting a diabolical eyebrow, knowing the answer as clearly as she did. "Who'd have thought it possible?"

Heat rose in her cheeks. The boy's gratitude and need for affection had only been a ruse for cutting her purse from her belt. The little imp. The thought was strangely comforting. With a bit of luck, a clever lad like Pepperpot might survive his poverty to become a ruthless financier like Claybourne.

She didn't even try to disguise her laughter, because she knew it would gall Claybourne. "Crafty little devil, wasn't he?"

Claybourne grunted and captured her hand to fit it into the crook of his stone-rigid arm. His long legs took the steps two at a time and sent her running to keep up with him.

"You married Mayfield's daughter?"

"Less than an hour ago, Lanford." Hunter handed him the note that changed Miss Mayfield's address to his own. That change now seemed so much more significant than simply a new address. He was married—to that green-eyed, willowy bit of opinions waiting for him in Lanford's reception room. "I'll have a copy of the registry sent to you tomorrow."

"Is she pretty?" Lanford raised his eyebrows and smiled too broadly.

Hunter didn't answer; the man didn't need to know that his new bride was somewhat more attractive than he'd reckoned for, somewhat less insignificant.

"No, I suppose looks wouldn't matter, would it? You'd have married a goose if it would have brought you that railway."

"Good day, Lanford." Hunter left him behind his desk and strode deliberately to the door, tired of the banker's society.

Lanford followed him like a puppy. "I knew you'd come up with something, Claybourne. But I never really thought you'd marry the woman."

Hunter turned as he caught the door latch. "Think what you will. I came here only to inform the Bank of England that Miss Mayfield and I are now legally wed, and that her shares in the Drayhill-Starlington Railway will revert to her one year from today."

"And, by way of marriage, they will become yours at the same time. A bold step, Claybourne. Though I don't know why you would want those shares—you'll become sole owner of a five-mile line of iron track that begins in a bog, leagues from any town, and then dead-ends at the foot of a chalky cliff. I don't understand it, myself. But you are a man of unerring judgment where finance is concerned. You must know what you are doing."

"You and the Bank have benefited countless times from my advice, Lanford."

"Yes, we have. And I suspect we will again. Along that same course, are you, by any chance, looking for investors in the Drayhill-Starlington?"

Hunter had never felt quite so absurdly possessive, as if the railway was the woman herself and he craved some claim on her. "No investors, Lanford. I'm in this alone."

"Let me know if you change your mind."

"I never change my mind. Good day, Lanford." Hunter threw open the door, wondering if his wife would still be waiting for him.

She wasn't.

Chapter 5

〜〜❦〜〜

"What do you mean I haven't an account here at the Bank of England?" Felicity held fast to her temper; her heart had taken off on its own at the teller's outrageous statement. "You're quite wrong! My uncle, Foley Mayfield, put one thousand pounds into an account for me just three days ago! Have you spent it already?"

"I can assure you, miss, the bank does not spend your money for you. But I must repeat: there is no account here in the name of Felicity Mayfield, or Foley Mayfield, or even in your father's name. I'm sorry."

"But Uncle Foley said——" Oh, but he'd said a good too many things that day, that very singular day when he'd sold her to Hunter Claybourne.

"Would you care for a cup of water, Miss Mayfield?"

"No. Unless you want it dashed into your face, sir." Felicity was instantly sorry. It wasn't like her to take out her troubles on the innocent. "Please forgive me. It's just that I'm . . ."

She was penniless, homeless. And all her irreplaceable work had been stolen!

Felicity pushed away from the teller's stall and crossed the lobby to the lofty windows that looked out onto the street. Perhaps Uncle Foley had forgotten to put the money into the bank. He had been in a devilish hurry to sail that day.

No. She was just making excuses for him. He'd failed her, as no other could have done.

Hunter found his wife in the lobby, staring out the window, her bonnet sitting askew. No doubt searching for that grimy urchin who had just stolen her blind. Probably looking to reward him with a basket of cakes. He curbed his anger. He couldn't very well make a scene in the bank lobby. He knew far too many people here.

"Where have you been, Miss Mayfield?" he asked at her elbow.

She turned sharply. Her eyes were liquid and angry, and Hunter felt a moment's guilt for the day's business.

"I've been busy falling off the turnip wagon, Mr. Claybourne," she said, righting her bonnet with a yank. "I would like to leave now. It seems I have pressing business at the *Hearth and Heath* in Fleet Street."

The reckless woman had no sense of her own helplessness. "Have you any money, Miss Mayfield?"

She opened her mouth to answer at the same time her hand unconsciously touched the empty place where her purse had once hung. She sent a look of impatience toward the teller stalls, then shook her head at him.

"I'm momentarily without funds," she said, raising her chin, quite proud of her loss, it seemed. As if she'd just donated a million pounds to a worthy charity, instead of losing her last penny to a thief.

"And what do you plan to do about your lack of funds?" he asked.

"I . . ." She seemed to look for an answer in the cavernous ceiling of the bank lobby. She had caught up her lower lip between her teeth, deepening the rose tint of her mouth and lighting a spark in the center of his chest that burned an instant path to his loins. He took a sharp breath as it hit, but hid the sound inside a growl.

"Where do you live, Miss Mayfield?" he asked sharply, wishing away this damnable attraction to her.

But she tilted a slender hip into her palm and cocked her head in open defiance, tipping her bonnet off-center once again. "I live wherever I please."

Hunter didn't like this all of a sudden. His legal wife, let loose on the city. He hadn't considered the ramifications. He could see the headlines in the *Times:* "Hunter Claybourne's wife found sleeping in a railway station." That wouldn't do at all.

"Have you no rooms anywhere?" He hadn't considered the living arrangements between them. Hadn't thought it necessary.

"Why should I pay rent all the month, when I'm gone for days at a time? I live in a boardinghouse when I'm in London and take my rent in kind when I'm traveling."

"In kind?" Hunter was stunned by the implication. He imagined beady-eyed innkeepers and seedy bedrooms, sweaty hands reaching for the private curve at the base of her breast. His own hand ached for the same. "What the hell do you mean by 'in kind'?"

She gave him a look of annoyance, as if he were out of his league and she was too busy to explain. "Innkeepers are quite happy to exchange meals and lodging for listing their inns in my travel gazette."

Hunter hadn't realized that he'd been holding his breath until he blew it out of his chest in a storm. "You live by that means? By barter? For mention in a gazette?" Good God, he'd married a gypsy!

"By bartering, and by selling my articles to the *Hearth and Heath.* What did you think I meant, Mr. Claybourne?"

Hunter frowned and led her out of the bank into the

gray blanket glare of noon. They had just reached the bottom step when a young man in a moth-eaten tweed suit rushed in between them.

"Felicity!" the man shouted. Then he yanked the woman into his embrace, causing the hair to bristle on Hunter's neck and a spot of coal-hot anger to blossom in his gut.

"Adam Skinner!" Miss Mayfield hugged the man even more fiercely in return. She finally pulled away from him and stood back to gaze on him in too-obvious admiration.

The Skinner person swabbed his hat from his head and beamed at her. "You're a sight for sore eyes, Felicity!"

"What are you doing here, Adam? Last I knew, Mr. Dolan had sent you to Cardiff to report on the auctions."

"I left Dolan's weeklies for the *Times.* I'm working here in Threadneedle now! Special reporter to the Bank. Reporting on the great Hudson's demise."

"Special reporter! How wonderful!" She hugged the giddy-faced man again, and Hunter wanted to toss him under a speeding dray.

Instead, he reached down and separated them. "You'd best be on your way, boy."

The man looked like a chicken whose feathers had been stroked backward. "Who is this fellow, Felicity?"

She sent Hunter a damning glare and fluttered her hand as if she were explaining away a stray dog. "He's just my husband."

"Your husband?" Skinner's mouth sagged, and he took a long step backward. "You got married?"

"Well, I . . ." She seemed abruptly awkward and unsure of herself, casting Hunter a stammering glance.

"Enough, wife." Hunter would have led her immediately to the carriage, but he looked up from her wrathful displeasure into the white-browed, laughing eyes of Lord Meath. Damnation, but there were too many people about this morning.

"What's this?" Meath said, his forehead furrowed in genuine concern. "You've gotten yourself married, Claybourne?"

"Lord Meath," Hunter said, taking his lordship's outstretched hand. "Good to see you, sir."

Meath shook Hunter's hand, but ignored the greeting. "Is it true, Claybourne? Have you married at last?"

Meath was a member of the Board of Trade, a man whose reputation and goodwill meant more to Hunter than any man's in the city. He seemed quite pleased at the moment, but a single stray word from Hunter's scowling bride could ruin it all.

Skinner watched the exchange with far too much reporterly interest, his notepad and pencil at the ready.

Hunter pulled his wife against him and settled her beneath his shoulder. Fortunately, she fit perfectly. "Lord Meath, I present to you my wife, Miss—"

"Mrs.—" she corrected, boring a sharp, but ineffectual, fingertip into his ribs.

"Mrs. Claybourne," Hunter continued, realizing that he must work on this breach in his thinking, and on his wife's behavior in the presence of a lord. "Mrs. Claybourne, Lord Meath."

Meath smiled down on her and took her hand. "I am charmed, my dear. When was the happy event?"

"An hour ago," she said quickly.

Lord Meath laughed and patted her hand. "You have snared a very eligible jackrabbit, Mrs. Claybourne. Many women have tried. However did you do it?"

Felicity tipped her head up toward her intolerable husband and considered telling the absolute truth: blackmail. Claybourne had narrowed his eyes to slits, looking very much like an ill-humored dragon disturbed from its afternoon nap. She decided against the absolute truth; the explanation would take all day and she didn't trust Claybourne's reaction, not after his treatment of Adam.

"Dear, sweet, Mr. Claybourne *insisted* that I marry him," Felicity said instead, settling a false smile on her face. Claybourne must have approved; he seemed to start breathing again. But would he breathe as easily if he knew she had noticed that weakness in his defenses? He was much impressed with himself and seemed determined to have others return his good opinion.

"Ah, ha!" Lord Meath said, beaming at Claybourne. "Your heart stolen away by true love. Good. Good. Should happen more often these days. Congratulations, Claybourne."

"Thank you, sir." Claybourne nodded respectfully to his lordship.

"You and your lovely wife must come to dinner sometime next month."

Felicity opened her mouth to decline, but Claybourne grabbed her hand and placed it on his arm, then clamped his own hand down on top of hers.

"We would be delighted, your lordship," Claybourne said, his white teeth gleaming in the afternoon sun.

It seemed strange to her that the beastly man could transform himself in the daylight into quite a handsome figure, his primitive darkness turned to dignity, his blunt-shouldered hugeness turned to a nearly charming presence. And strange indeed that her heart fluttered wildly when she studied his face in search of some kind of virtue. A fruitless venture, to be sure.

"Good to see you, Claybourne." Lord Meath was glancing down Threadneedle Street, kneading his gloved palms together. "Well, I'm off to the club to rub some salt into some very sore wounds. George Hudson is going to hit rock bottom in the next few days."

"So I understand." Claybourne seemed relieved to be talking business. Felicity wanted to be done with the man and his overwhelming presence, wanted most of all to pursue her own business at the *Hearth and Heath*. How else was she to live? Bartering for food and lodging only succeeded half the time; she often had to pay her own way. And now that Giles had run off with her purse and her writing, and her uncle had left her penniless, she needed to explain the delay to Mr. Dolan, and then somehow recreate her articles as soon as she could manage.

But this Lord Meath fellow seemed to have Claybourne's full attention.

"You were quite right about Hudson, Claybourne. There will be resignations among the board members. Your timely warning saved my fortune and my name. I thank you. Again."

"Glad to be of service, Lord Meath." Funny how Claybourne could be downright engaging when high finance was involved.

"I'm not likely to forget such things, Claybourne." Meath tapped the brim of his top hat with a finger and waved as he stepped around them and started down Threadneedle.

Felicity winked at Adam as the wily reporter followed on Meath's heels.

Claybourne stared down at her, unblinking. "Who was that young man?" he asked.

"A reporter friend of mine."

"You'll have no reporter friends while you're married to me."

Felicity laughed at his frown and at his unenforceable, uncontracted-for demand. "I'll have any friend I want, Mr. Claybourne. And as for next month, I plan to be in Northumberland. I doubt I will have time in my schedule for a soiree at his lordship's."

"You'll make the time, wife, or I'll make it for you."

Then Claybourne wrapped his big hands around her waist and lifted her into his carriage.

"Curse you for a liar, Claybourne!" Felicity made a grab for the doorjamb, but he'd taken her by surprise and she stumbled to the seat as he locked the door behind her. She righted herself, reached through the window, and took hold of his wrist.

"Let me out of here! We made a bargain! You said I could leave. And unless you're sending me to the

Hearth and Heath in Fleet Street, I want out of this carriage immediately."

"Without money, where will you sleep tonight?" He cocked his know-it-all eyebrow. "In Waterloo Station?"

"I've slept in worse places."

"You won't while you're married to me."

"Is that going to be your standard answer to my every request for the next year?"

"Be prepared to hear it, or you'll take up residence at my house for the duration of our marriage."

"I will not! Damn you!" Felicity rattled the door handle, hoping for a means to escape the madman she'd married. "You promised I could travel. You signed your name to our settlement! Is that what your name is worth, Mr. Claybourne? Nothing?"

"We'll speak of it later," he said coolly.

"Later when? I have to explain to Mr. Dolan that all my work was stolen. He needs to know!"

"You should have thought of that when you insisted on releasing that little thief. Home to Hampstead, Branson!"

The force of the carriage threw Felicity back against the padded seat.

"Blazes!"

She scrambled to the rear window, hoping to wound Claybourne with a glare. He stood shoulders above the stream of foot traffic, his attention intent upon her departure. He looked utterly out of place, a siege-built castle erected midriver, buffeted by tree trunks and rising water. And yet he managed to remain unjostled, founded in the bedrock.

The arrogant blockhead!

The carriage door was locked again from the outside, and the windows were far too small to climb out of without getting stuck. She had a pair of scissors in her portmanteau that she could have used to jimmy the lock, but she'd donated them along with all her clothes and her writings to young Mr. Pepperpot and his associate.

Where would I go anyway? The boardinghouse was out
of the question. Without ready cash, she'd be turned
away at the door. Mrs. Wright and Mrs. Cobson could
have been twin spirits separated at birth for all their
natural-born charity.

Right now, Felicity was so hungry she could eat the
batting out of the carriage seat. So, if Claybourne was
offering hospitality for a while, she might as well take
him up on it, as long as he was willing to let her keep
her appointment with Mr. Dolan and would allow her
to write. She would merely consider him a peevish
innkeeper, forced to provide food and lodging for a
year. He could well afford it. Judging by the grandeur
of his office, his estate must rival Windsor Castle. She
was certain to find elegant, well-kept gardens, a large
stable and paddock, liveried servants, a stately gallery
of gilt-framed ancestors, and a well-stocked kitchen
complete with a French chef.

Her stomach growled.

Felicity leaned back against the seat and sighed as
she imagined the dining room at Claybourne's estate,
bright with candles, a block-long table sagging under
the weight of succulent meats, creamy desserts, and
candied vegetables.

"Another helping of Yorkshire pudding, Miss Mayfield?" she said in his basso voice.

"Make that two, Mr. Claybourne."

Felicity sighed. A day or two of splendor might do
wonders for her spirits while she straightened out her
finances and made sense of the coming year. Her
deadline to Mr. Dolan was the end of the week;
perhaps she could re-create her travels in the meantime. She wouldn't have to wonder where her next
meal would come from, or where she would sleep the
night. And Mrs. Wright wouldn't be poking her head
into her business every other moment.

But there was Claybourne himself to consider. All of
him: the searing heat and the bone-breaking chill, his
arrogance and his greed. And the stark realization that

when he hadn't kissed her at the end of their oh-so-brief wedding, she'd felt cheated. Cheated! The insatiable blackguard had stolen her railway from her!

The brougham rose up with the road as it carried her through Hampstead and soon turned off the rutted thoroughfare into a narrow lane. Another ten minutes and the lane ended entirely, blocked off by a pair of rusted gates that squealed as the footman opened them, and squealed again after he'd pulled through the gates and closed them.

The carriage sped along inside a shaded tunnel of overgrown yew and dogwood. Branches whipped past, slapping at the windows. Felicity kept waiting for a break in the oppressive tunnel, but the green went on for a quarter mile until the road crested and then hurdled downward and opened into a broad glade.

She saw the roofline first, vast and crenelated like a fortress, stubbled with odd-lot chimneys and twisted towers. A pitifully lonely-looking sight.

Claybourne's house grew out of an island of bramble and weeds that reached nearly to the second floor. If there had ever been a hedged and clipped garden, it had long since been overtaken. The wildness crowded against the courtyard, held in check by an iron fence.

Pallid faces peered down at her through the dark windows as the brougham clattered to a halt in front of the stone porch, and Felicity felt her heart sink. What sort of man had she married? What sort of greed was this?

A stick-thin man came flying out the front door, frantically flapping his elbows as he tried to fasten the front of his coat.

"Hell and be damned!" he hissed to the footman. "What's the master doin' home at this hour?"

"Easy now, Earnest," the footman said as he slipped down from his seat, "I haven't got the master with me."

The stark terror melted from Earnest's face, replaced

by the grace found in a reprieve from death. "Ah, it's just you, then, Branson—"

"No." Branson brushed aside Earnest's worthless efforts at buttoning the livery coat and finished the job himself. "I've brought the master's wife."

Felicity heard a chorus of gasps but couldn't place its source until she saw the drapes swing back into place in the ground-floor windows. She could well understand their skittish anxiety. Claybourne was abrupt and disdainful in public; what kind of demon was he in the privacy of his own isolated estate?

"Did I hear you say 'wife,' Mr. Branson?" Earnest peered into Branson's face and waited for his answer as a dog awaits a bone.

"You heard right, Earnest. Now let's get the little thing out of the carriage and settled into the house. Take care, though. She might have a mind to bolt."

"I won't bolt, Mr. Branson," Felicity said as the footman opened the carriage door. Where would she go in this godforsaken landscape? "I'm too hungry to do anything more active than faint."

"We'll see about a meal, then," he said as he handed her down the steps to the gravel walk.

"Afternoon, ma'am." Earnest's smile started on one side of his mouth and traveled quickly to the other side.

Felicity had to smile back at his eagerness to please, more certain than ever that Claybourne was an overbearing, ungrateful taskmaster.

"I'll get her bags, Mr. Branson," he said, vaulting the rear carriage wheel to the luggage boot.

"I haven't any bags, Mr. Earnest," Felicity said over her shoulder as she followed Branson toward the gloomy house.

How could this woebegone property belong to Hunter Claybourne? The Claybourne Exchange outshone any other building in the City. His office spoke of careful design and limitless finances. His home looked utterly forgotten.

A wicked beast, enchanted servants, a hoary old manor house; the tale had frightened her as a child, and now she come to live it. Dear God, what had she gotten herself into?

"Does Mr. Claybourne actually live here, Mr. Branson?"

"He does, indeed," Branson said as they passed beneath the palladian entry and into the jail-dreary foyer. "Mrs. Sweeney!"

The shout echoed off the walls and tumbled up the massive stone staircase that clung to the central tower. The scene was bleak and uninviting. Where the Claybourne Exchange overwhelmed the senses with marble and brass, the gray stone of Claybourne's home dampened and dulled. Felicity thought of prison, and her old fears returned. Who would know where she'd been taken? Was there a dungeon waiting, one designed for Claybourne's more stubborn debtors?

Branson lost no time waiting for this Mrs. Sweeney to show Felicity her new home. Felicity ran to keep up with him, managing a racing tour of the ground floor of the eastern wing—what little she could see of it in the near-dark—trying to memorize all the exits, just in case.

Opaque drapes hung heavily over the enormous windows in the long gallery. Crates and boxes and barrels lined every wall and clogged every corner. The few pieces of furniture boasted elegance and taste, but there was so little of it: a gilded settee keeping solitary watch by a cold hearth in the drawing room, a chair and a small table in the dining room. Everything looked so temporary.

"Is Mr. Claybourne in the process of moving?" Felicity asked, trailing a finger along a bank of packing crates. Her glove came away caked in dust.

"No, no. The master's lived here five years now, and I imagine they'll have to carry out his cold carcass when he dies. He doesn't fancy change."

Rabidly curious, in spite of the dim shadows and the

unknown terrors of the year to come, Felicity stopped in the middle of the corridor to examine the lid of a crate. A fine coating of dust dulled the label. Erebus Glass Works, London. Deliver to Claybourne Manor, Hampstead.

Erebus Glass. Only the best for the master.

"But if Mr. Claybourne isn't planning to move, why is everything boxed up?"

"You'll have to ask the master, Mrs. Claybourne." Branson continued his stride and Felicity followed, drawn down another corridor by the smell of an unnameable food.

"Here we are," Branson said, breezing through the butler's pantry to the whitewashed kitchen at the back of the house.

A tall, broad-shouldered woman hunkered over a huge steaming pot, wielding her stirring stick, doing battle with the contents for the sovereignty of the stove. Droplets of steam clung to the ends of the steely hair bristling from under her cap. A mist clouded her spectacles.

"Mrs. Sweeney, didn't you hear me calling?"

The woman looked up and squinted. "Mr. Branson! Is that you?" She stopped her struggles and pinched the tiny lenses off her face.

"Yes, it's me, Mrs. Sweeney. And I've brought the master's new missus."

"What? Now you wait a hardy minute, Mr. Branson." Mrs. Sweeney scrubbed at her lenses with her apron hem, then pinched the frail frames back onto the end of her nose. "There, now I can hear. Speak it again, sir." She laughed. "I thought you said you'd brought the master's new missus."

"Mrs. Claybourne," Branson said with a well-practiced tone of irritation, "this is Mrs. Sweeney, the cook."

"*Mrs.* Claybourne?" the woman yipped, adding a snort.

"I'm very glad to meet you, Mrs. Sweeney." Felicity

felt like a newly plucked chicken on the way to the stew pot as Mrs. Sweeney walked a circuit around her.

"Too skinny," she said, dismissing her with a wave of her hand. "Won't eat more than a raisin a day, I warrant."

Felicity followed the woman, her misgivings dismissed for the moment and her mouth watering as she approached the darkly bubbling concoction on the stove. The food didn't look at all edible, but at this point she was willing to try anything.

"I'm a very good eater, Mrs. Sweeney! I promise! In fact, I'd like a big bowl of this soup . . . or whatever it is."

"Would you now?" Mrs. Sweeney laughed, a very girlish sound coming from a woman built of brick and timber. She was missing all of her back teeth, the lack made prominent by her wide grin.

"Yes, ma'am, it smells heavenly."

Mrs. Sweeney stuck her long spoon into the watery blackness and dragged out a length of wool sacking. "Dearie me, Mr. Branson," she said, "if the master's new bride likes the taste of my dye works, think how much she'll like my stew!"

Branson joined Mrs. Sweeney in a hearty bout of laughter.

Felicity felt foolish only for a moment; then her stomach let out a howl, and she had to laugh, too. Claybourne's servants seemed as harmless and friendly as he was threatening. At least her days here might be untroubled. The nights would be another matter all together.

They refused to let her eat in the kitchen. Branson set her at the dismal little table in the cavernous dining room, proudly pulling aside the single chair and lighting the single candle against the darkness, even though God's bright sunlight shone just outside the draped windows.

Earnest bobbed and chattered as he served her a bowl of hearty stew and a chunk of dried bread. After he was gone, Felicity moved her chair to the window, intending to push aside the drapes and enjoy her meal in the daylight. But a hedge of arborvitae obscured the view entirely, grown so close to the panes that the brown and denuded interior of the bushes was laid bare. An abandoned bird's nest hung askew among the branches, a long-dried yolk and delicate blue-green shell preserved among the twigs just below it.

A deep melancholy settled over her. Oh, what a terrible year to come. Felicity closed the drape, then retreated to the table and its feeble candlelight.

To busy herself through the afternoon, she found paper and pencil in one of the crates marked DOVE AND SONS STATIONERS, then set to work trying to re-create the half-dozen entries she had lost to Mr. Pepperpot's light-fingeredness.

When Claybourne didn't return by dinner, Felicity took that meal alone in the dining room as well. Stew again, filling but not exactly the fine French cuisine she'd dreamed about. Earnest seemed intent upon speaking, but unable to loosen the words. He stood over her table, his hands drumming against each other and Felicity's nerves.

"Is there anything I can help you with, Earnest?"

"Ah, well . . . yes. You see, the master didn't send us instructions as to what to do with you, Mrs. Claybourne. And neither did Branson. I mean as far as . . . where you're to—"

"Sleep?"

"Precisely." Earnest cleared his throat. "Did he, or Branson, by any chance, discuss the matter with you? Will you be taking the master's suite—"

"Actually, Earnest, it had been my assumption, and my hope, that Mr. Claybourne would be sleeping tonight in Hampstead and that I would be sleeping in an altogether different county, but that doesn't seem to be the case."

The poor man seemed shocked to the marrow.

"Put me wherever you wish, Earnest. This house is

the size of a castle. Surely there must be a guest room to spare."

"Plenty of rooms, Mrs. Claybourne. But just enough beds for those of us who've been here awhile."

"Oh, I see." She glanced at the crates of Wedgewood stacked near the pantry door and understood completely. No one had ever been invited to Claybourne Manor. And it was clear that the master preferred it that way.

"I'm awfully sorry, Mrs. Claybourne. You could have my bed, but I share a room with the gamekeeper. He snores. If I can do anything—"

"A bath and some nightwear, and then some bedding will do for now. I'll discuss the details with Mr. Claybourne as soon as he comes home. Which is usually when, Earnest?"

Earnest frowned and shook his head. "Late, Mrs. Claybourne, ma'am. Branson has gone back to the City to fetch him. Sometimes they don't come home till well after midnight."

"I'll wait up."

Chapter 6

As Hunter had watched his carriage cut into the traffic and wheel away that afternoon, he knew that his wife wasn't at all happy. But the fool would have actually spent the night sleeping on a bench in a train station if he'd allowed it. The scandal would have rocked the foundations of the Claybourne Exchange. The woman hadn't the sense God gave a lump of coal! Allowing herself to be advised by an incompetent attorney, then deserted by a scheming uncle, conned out of her worldly goods by a filthy urchin . . .

And now married to you, Claybourne?

Yes, and after less than two hours of marriage, he felt as if it had been a lifetime. How long was the coming year to feel?

Lunch with Lord Spurling had proved ripe with impending opportunity. The man had hinted at a nomination to a committee of the Board of Trade as soon as an opening occurred. Hudson's fall would surely take two members with him. Hunter was not quite thirty; his reputation was spotless. Time was on his side. And so, it seemed, was Lord Meath.

Meath had been unduly charmed by his wife. Hunter wouldn't exactly call Miss Mayfield an asset, but like any other bit of flotsam that floated his way, he would

orchestrate her talents to their fullest potential. Yes, he
could see her on his arm in Lord Meath's parlor,
clothed in satin, her wild hair tamed somehow, and
piled atop her head, exposing that long neck of hers. A
necklace of pearls would flatter her throat and bring
every eye in the room to the woman he'd married.
Another reason for envy. Another reason to keep
himself well apart from her.

He had spent the early evening in his office, analyz-
ing the prospectus for a small company that was
developing a new, more economical steel-making
process, then had taken a late dinner with two members of the prime minister's cabinet. It wasn't until his
carriage arrived in the courtyard of Claybourne Manor
that Hunter realized his wife would be somewhere
inside.

"She was delivered safely, Mr. Claybourne."

Hunter glanced at Branson and wondered when the
man's mustache had gone gray. "Of course," he said.

Hunter stomped up the front steps of the manor and
into the foyer. The staircase was blue-dark and free of
shadows, silent and immense. And all of it was his.

"Where did you put her?"

"Put her?" Branson asked, his steps halting
abruptly.

Hunter turned. "Where did you put Miss Mayfield?"
he asked, wondering if Branson's hearing had aged as
rapidly as his close-cropped temples.

"Sir," Branson said, brimming his hat through his
fingers, "do you mean to say Mrs. Claybourne?"

"Yes, yes, Branson. Mrs. Claybourne. Where did you
put her?"

"I don't know, sir."

"You don't know?"

"That hadn't been settled when I left."

"See to it that you find out. I want to be sure she
hasn't bolted."

"She promised she would stay. Ate like a black-
smith, then sat down to her writing. Before I left, I told

Earnest to send word if he had any trouble. There's been no word, sir."

"I'm pleased to hear it. Good night, Branson."

The day had been long and Hunter craved the solace of his chamber, where he could shut the door against the everlasting tension. His footfalls rang against the stone walls as he climbed the wide staircase to the upper floor.

He turned at the top of the stairs and glanced down the western corridor. She would be there somewhere, behind one of those doors, sleeping, dreaming of her uncle and his fool's-gold fortune. Her hair would be slumber-tossed against one of his pillows, her defiant chin tucked beneath his counterpane.

Wife. A damned odd circumstance. He thought to check on her himself, but decided he would speak with her tomorrow, to lay down the rules.

All was as it should be in his chamber: the fire lit and his brandy heating on the hob, his bed turned down.

And something else.

The vanilla scent of soap, a lightness behind him where there ought to be shadow.

"Good evening husband—darling. Did you miss me?"

Miss Mayfield was sitting in his chair beside the bed, her legs tucked beneath her, a book resting open across the enticing rise of her thigh. She'd loosened her hair from its ribbons, and now great cascades of gold clouded her shoulders, as wildly as she had clouded his senses.

Hunter steadied his breathing and lifted the brandy to let the shimmering fumes rise against his nose. Her robe was russet velvet and heavy, the cuffs rolled, and the shoulders drooped to her elbows. The damn thing was his.

"What are you doing here?" he asked, trying to ignore the unnamed stirring in his chest, the hollow burning that spread downward to his knees, that deepened his breathing and leadened his arms.

"What am I doing here, Mr. Claybourne?" Felicity abandoned her vow to keep her temper and flung herself out of the chair. She'd planned all day to be cooler than he, but that would be impossible unless she were an iceberg. "I'm here because you threw me into your carriage and had me dragged here to your very charming estate in the wilds of Hampstead."

"This may be your home for the next year, Miss Mayfield. That doesn't give you leave to enter my chamber uninvited."

"Uninvited, sir? But isn't this the master's chamber? Aren't we married, Mr. Claybourne? And isn't this our wedding night?"

"Is that why you've claimed my robe?"

"I had nothing else to wear," she said, refusing to be embarrassed by the heat plaguing her cheeks again, confused that the heat should find its way to her chest.

"And you think this is my fault?" He tipped his brandy to his mouth and sipped slowly. He had a wicked way of looking at her—through her; and through her robe—his robe.

She stuck her fingers into the sash wrapping and flicked open the front of it. The cold hit her like a slap, but she shrugged out of the sleeves and tossed the robe onto the end of the bed.

"There," she said, closing her arms across the cotton nightshirt that seemed as slight as a cobweb. Her feet were bare against the polished wood floor, and she stepped in front of the fire to keep her teeth from chattering.

"Whose nightshirt is that?" he asked, his eyes narrowed in his shadowy assessment.

"I don't know. I found it with a towel in the bathing closet next to your chamber." Claybourne was frowning. "I suspect it belongs to Earnest." That explanation didn't seem to make him any happier.

"We'll discuss this in the morning. Go to bed."

"Mr. Claybourne, I've decided to treat you as an innkeeper."

"You have?" He seemed vainly amused.

"And in the morning, I might just decide to be gone from here. I can't afford to stay long; I haven't written a coherent word about my travels all day. Claybourne Manor doesn't lend itself to creativity, nor does the idea of being entirely dependent upon you. Article Two of our marriage settlement allows me to decide when and where I travel."

"And the very fact of our marriage allows me the legal right to nullify that decision, and any other you should make in the coming year."

He was so very calm, his voice even and precise. Felicity wanted to scream, but she matched his composure and spoke through her clenched teeth.

"So I've exchanged a sentence in the Queen's Bench Prison for a more hideous one in the Claybourne Manor? That explains the gray walls and the gruel."

"We'll speak of this tomorrow."

"We'll speak of it now." She was cold despite the fire at her back, and the one in the pit of her stomach.

"Madam, my home is a quiet place."

"A tomb. I've noticed."

"And I plan to keep it that way." Claybourne set his empty glass on the washstand, his manner turned perilously benign. "This arrangement of ours is . . . unconventional at best. It's ill-fitting and uncomfortable, and as new to me as it is to you. But we are now connected, and I have a reputation to consider. You, madam, have no money, and no place to stay. I cannot have that in a wife. Therefore, you need only prove to me that you have sense enough not to disturb my life any more than you already have, after which you may, with my most sincere blessing, leave on your travels."

"And how am I to prove this?"

"You can start by going to bed."

Felicity chided herself for the glance she aimed at Claybourne's bed. The huge man's gaze followed hers and lingered like a fragrance among the pillows, sending her into another fit of blushing.

"You have nothing to fear from me, Miss Mayfield." His face was as blank as a slate; yet his mouth remained every bit as fascinating to her, well-planed and improvident. "Article Four states that our marriage will remain unconsummated. I have no salacious designs on you."

Felicity blotted up his scorn and used it against him. "Good. For I plan to have a real husband someday, and will go to his bed chaste."

"My best to you both. Now, go to bed, Miss Mayfield," he said quietly.

"Go to hell, Mr. Claybourne."

He frowned, took her gently by the elbow, and swept her out into the corridor, then shut the door in her face.

"Pinchfist!" she shouted. The word multiplied itself and bounced away from her, leaving a bleak silence in its wake. He was the rudest man she had ever met. Rude to everyone it seemed. But at least she'd been locked out, instead of in.

She was cold to the bone and hungry again. She had left her blanket in Claybourne's chamber, but she wasn't about to return for it. And she'd forgotten to ask about a bed. At least one that wasn't his.

Felicity hurried to the kitchen and huddled beside the still-warm stove. Mrs. Sweeney hadn't left so much as a crumb of food anywhere, and the larder was locked down tightly. A stuttering oil lamp kept the room from total darkness. The only difference between this night and the previous one at Cobson's Rest was space.

Her one and only skirt and shirtwaist were drying on a rack near the stove. She hadn't known Mrs. Sweeney was going to wash until her clothes disappeared from the bathing closet. Now they seemed to have lost some of the blue and gained a tinge of black along the seams, from the woman's dye pot.

With the exception of Claybourne's chamber, this was the warmest room in the house—certainly warm-er and more quiet than Waterloo Station—and Mrs. Sweeney's rocking chair would do just fine as a bed. Tomorrow she would demand to be taken to London for the day, else she would walk there herself.

Felicity dragged the rocker out of the corner, dislodging a bundle of rags from behind it. The bundle teetered and rolled to the center of the room, and a small, grimy face appeared among the folds.

She would have jumped out of her skin, but that little face was far too familiar.

"Giles Pepperpot!" she hissed, catching and holding the boy by the ear. "So we meet again!"

"Ouch, miss! Let go, please! Owwww!" His arms whirled and his eyes pinched closed as she dragged him toward the light. "You're hurting me."

"Good. I ought to throw you to Claybourne's dogs. They'd like a tender little morsel to chew on."

"Leave off!"

"You stole everything I own, Mr. Pepperpot. There's nothing left to steal. And you're a bloody little fool if you've come here to rob from Claybourne!"

"But I didn't come for nothing like that! I come to settle with you."

"To settle with me?" Felicity tapped his bony chest and he fell, panic-stricken, backward into the rocking chair. The dark circles under his eyes made him look older than Claybourne, but she wasn't about to feel sorry for the little larcenist. "I won't be made a fool of twice, Mr. Pepperpot. Today on the street I was being generous. Now you've come to take advantage. That makes me angry, and very dangerous to a sneak thief!"

"I haven't come to take advantage! I haven't come to take anything." Giles drew his scrawny, threadbare knees against his chest and clung to them.

"How did you get here?"

"In the carriage boot. I saw the big man send you away this noon, and I kenned the brougham would come back for him sometime, so I waited. When it come, I slipped inside and waited some more. Then I come here and hid out in the stables till I thought it safe to come into the house."

"Why, Mr. Pepperpot?" Felicity grasped the rocker arms and leaned forward. The reek of poverty nearly gagged her; Giles Pepperpot was the sewers of London made flesh. She closed her nose against the horrible smell and pressed him for the truth. He owed her that much. "Why did you come here if it wasn't to practice your nefarious trade?"

"I come to give this back to you."

He drew a folio of papers out of his shirt.

"You brought my writing!" Felicity grabbed the folio and hugged it against her, wanting to whoop with joy. This was her ticket to ultimate independence from Claybourne. "Thank you!"

"It was the only thing I could bring you." The boy's head was cocked, and a ripe new bruise bulged his brow.

"You did this for me? Came all the way to Hampstead in the boot of a carriage to return my writing?"

He shrugged. "I owed you."

Grateful beyond words, Felicity leaned down and kissed his cheek, trying to ignore the grime there. "Thank you, Mr. Pepperpot."

The boy laid his hand across the kiss and his eyes seemed to grow liquid. "I'd return your money, miss, but I don't have it anymore."

"Never mind about that. I should have given you the coins to pay for your shirt. I hope you bought something with the money to keep you warm."

He shook his head. "Harry kept it."

"Harry—the other boy? He kept the money?"

Giles nodded and rubbed the bruise on his forehead.

"He shared nothing with you?"

"I work for him. Why should he?"

"Ah, then Mr. Claybourne was right. You are a member of the gang of boys that works Threadneedle."

"And we also work Chancery when Threadneedle

gets too close with police." He unwound his legs and arms as his hesitancy slipped off him like a too-big coat. His bristling courage reminded her of a young eagle whose feathers have only just begun to sprout. "I've never been caught before. You saved me from the workhouse. And I'd rather die than go back there."

"A terrible place?"

The boy wouldn't elaborate; he only nodded.

"Well, Mr. Pepperpot, I don't condone your trade, but you're very good at it. You cut my purse and I didn't discover it missing until you were long gone."

"I cut it with your own scissors."

"How?" Felicity laughed for the first time all day. "Never mind! I don't want to know. Slicker than a railway baron. You'll go far, Mr. Pepperpot."

The boy didn't take well to the compliment. He blushed like a beet, clear through the grime. His smile sloughed its hard-edged cynicism and softened in innocence.

"Well, miss, I come here to return your papers and I done that, so I'd best be leaving."

"Where do you live?" But, of course, he wasn't going to tell her that! She could tell by the set of his jaw. What would he think if he knew she hadn't much of a home herself? "How will you get back to London?"

"I'll walk."

"No. Wait. Stay the night in the stables, and you can return in the carriage boot tomorrow without Claybourne or his footman ever being the wiser."

"What if I'm caught?" The boy's stomach let out a howl much like her own had done earlier that day. He didn't seem to notice.

"You won't be caught. Let's steal us a late night feast, and then we'll put you up where no one will find you." Felicity went to work on the larder lock, hoping to find a breach in Mrs. Sweeney's defenses.

"Allow me, miss." Giles brushed her hands from the lock, then slipped a thin wire into the keyhole. "Do you work for him, miss? Are you his housekeeper?"

Felicity smiled. "If you mean Mr. Claybourne, then no, Mr. Pepperpot. I'm his wife."

The lock popped open.

So did Mr. Pepperpot's mouth.

Miss Mayfield had called him a pinchfist. Probably the best she could manage; he'd been called far more colorful things in his life. A man in his business acquired epithets and enemies by the bushelful. The word had just seemed more jagged and empty when she said it.

Hunter picked up the robe she'd thrown across his bed and hung it in the closet. She'd left her warmth and the scent of vanilla draped among the heavy folds. She'd also left an unblinking image of soft angles and spun gold. He shouldn't have mentioned the damn robe; he had others. But he hadn't reckoned she would throw it off and stand nearly naked in front of the fire in his valet's nightwear.

On his wedding night.

The ache was deep and progressive; it rose out of his chest and curled like a thrashing fever through his groin, leaving his heart to beat a hollow, hollow thrum.

His wedding night.

Willing his new wife from his thoughts, Hunter shrugged out of his jacket and planted himself in his chair, to watch the fire and read. He'd been spared only a moment's calm when heavy footsteps slogged up the corridor toward his room.

He was out of the chair and opening the door even before the knock sounded. Branson's fist hung in the air, unused.

"What is it Branson?" His pulse was racing; the threat born in the woman he'd so recently married.

"She's gone, sir."

Hunter didn't have to ask who *she* was. "Gone where? She was just here."

"Here, sir? In your chamber?" Branson looked befuddled and peered past him into the room. "But I thought you weren't—"

"Did you look in her room?" Hunter blocked the way.

"Her room, sir?"

"She left here not five minutes ago. I sent her to her room."

Branson looked at him as if he'd been speaking Greek. "Ah, then, that just might be the problem, sir. She doesn't have one."

"She doesn't have what? Quit speaking in riddles."

"A room, sir. Mrs. Claybourne doesn't have a room. You neglected to give instructions to—"

"Damn it, Branson. Do I need to give such instructions? I have a wife now, Branson, see that she has a chamber with a bed."

"Yes, well, that was the crux of the problem, sir. All the beds at Claybourne Manor are used up."

Hunter opened his mouth to protest the idiocy of Branson's argument, but he knew the fact to be true. Ten servants, ten cots, and his own tester bed. There were no more beds. He'd never needed more, because he never expected overnight guests. Or any other kind of guest, for that matter.

"Fix it, Branson. Find her. Search the upstairs rooms, every closet—"

"Earnest is looking—"

"Oh, for God's sake!" Hunter left Branson to his excuses and set off down the stairs. She could be halfway to Hampstead by now, gone like a wood nymph to roam the heath. He'd take his horse and follow the road. As he passed the dining-room door, he thought of her howling stomach and wondered if his half-witted staff had forgotten to feed her. Miss Mayfield wasn't one to wait around for room service.

A faint light limned the kitchen door as he stepped through the butler's pantry. He caught the murmur of a feather soft voice and the rattle of a cabinet. He'd found her.

Felicity heard the footsteps slow to a stop on the other side of the pantry door. She turned to motion Giles to hide, but he was already there behind the plate rack, bunched up among a bank of aprons, poking cheese into his already bulging mouth. The child had eaten as if he intended on stocking up for his next spurt of growth.

Claybourne burst through the door as she was fitting the lock back into the hasp. His hair drooped against his forehead, his shirt sleeves were rolled to his elbows, and his collar and stock were missing entirely. The brawn she had imagined beneath his coat was an extraordinary fact.

"Hungry?" he asked.

Felicity lifted her gaze to his and found a carefully banked flame. Dear God, had he seen her looking?

He left the doorway and came toward her in that deliberate, overbearing stride of his. "Did she feed you?"

"She? Mrs. Sweeney, you mean?"

He looked exasperated and charmingly rumpled. "My servants neglected to find you a bed. I thought perhaps they'd neglected to feed you as well."

"No. I was fed well, thank you."

"But you haven't a bed."

Giles poked his face out from behind the bank of aprons. Felicity frowned at him in a warning to stay hidden.

"It's no bother, Mr. Claybourne. I was going to sleep here, next to the fire."

"Why didn't you tell me you hadn't a chamber when I ordered you to bed?"

"I didn't think you'd be interested. You seemed occupied. And there's no need to disturb your household. I don't plan to stay long. The kitchen will be fine with me."

"But not with me."

"Then where shall I sleep, Mr. Claybourne? On top of one of your everlasting crates? Give me back my bedding and I will."

"You'll sleep in a bed."

"I won't have you evict one of your hard-pressed servants from their own bed—"

"You'll sleep in mine."

Tangled in the bedclothes, wrapped in the searing kind of heat he was throwing off at the moment— "I will not, Mr. Claybourne!"

"You're my wife. You'll sleep in my bed. This way, Miss Mayfield." He turned away just as Giles took the fool notion to race toward the garden door.

"No!" she said, unsure who she was talking to.

Giles made it as far as the rocker before Claybourne whirled back on her.

"No?" he asked. But the rustling of Giles's dive for cover drew Claybourne's eyes as the flicking tail of a rabbit draws a wolf. He looked past her, scanning the room. She fancied him sniffing the air. The only sound was the rasp of the rocker runners against the floor. Her folio lay exposed on the butcher's block. If Claybourne found it, he would quiz her without mercy to learn how it had been returned.

Felicity tapped on Claybourne's chest and drew his gaze back to her. Now she was the rabbit, caught in the wolf's cold gleam.

"All right, I'll sleep in your bed, Mr. Claybourne, as long as *you* don't."

He snorted. "You have my word."

Feeling roundly displaced by the conviction in his voice, Felicity followed him through the pantry into the dining room. Needing to return for her folio and for one last word to Giles, she stopped abruptly.

"My clothes," she said, backing toward the pantry. "They're drying in the kitchen. I'll need them in the morning."

He seemed skeptical, but Branson chose that moment to enter the dining room, nearly dragging Earnest behind him.

"Be quick," Claybourne said to her. "See, Branson, I've located Miss Mayfield. No thanks to you."

"Mayfield?" Felicity heard Earnest ask innocently as she dashed back into the kitchen. If Giles was still in the room, he'd hidden himself well.

"Eat your fill from the larder, Mr. Pepperpot," she whispered to the dimness, wondering if she spoke in vain, "then sleep in the stables tonight. I'll come find you in the morning."

"Thank you, Mrs. Claybourne." The whisper came from behind the stove.

Yes, the lad would survive. She hoped he wouldn't steal too much from the house.

"And I thank you, Mr. Pepperpot." She wrapped the folio in the folds of her still-damp skirt and hurried back to the dining room.

"But I swear to you, Branson," Earnest said, "I heard something in the stable. That's why we were awake when you come in. Willis heard it, too."

Probably Giles, sneaking around, trying to find a place to hide.

"Hire a rat catcher, Branson," Claybourne said. "Do it tomorrow. I'll have no vermin living in my stables."

"Yessir."

Giles would be safely gone by then. She could feel Claybourne's gaze shift between her nightshirt and Earnest's matching one, and knew the sight wasn't sitting well with him. The man was very possessive. Her feet were cold, her calves cramping, and she lifted each in its turn.

"To bed with you, Miss Mayfield," Claybourne said with a jerk of his head.

She wanted to ask where he would be sleeping, but the question would answer itself come morning. And she was weary enough not to care. "Good night, Mr. Claybourne," she said.

His chamber was warm; his sheets were fresh and

smelled of lime and folded sunlight. She'd just gotten settled in the mound of pillows when the door opened.

Claybourne paused in the doorway and studied her for a moment before tossing an armful of blankets onto the bed.

"I have plenty of blankets, Mr. Claybourne."

"I see that."

He sounded utterly disgusted, and growled something beneath his breath as he sat down on the edge of the bed. The mattress dipped with his weight, a compelling force that tried its best to draw her toward him. When his first shoe hit the floor, Felicity started, the sinister sound sending her heart up into her throat.

"What do you think you are doing, Mr. Claybourne?"

The other shoe hit the floor and he grabbed a handful of the blankets he'd brought in.

"I'm going to sleep." His voice drowned in a groan as he lay back against the bank of pillows.

Felicity pushed herself up against the headboard. "You're sleeping here? With me?"

"No, Miss Mayfield. You are sleeping with *me*."

"You gave your word that you wouldn't sleep in your bed."

"I'm sleeping *on* my bed, not in it."

"This isn't proper."

"It's our wedding night, if you recall. Go to sleep."

"But . . ." The man had a point. They *were* married, and sharing a bed on this night, of all the nights in a marriage, was altogether proper, if not expected. She wasn't sure what would have been expected of her in an ordinary marriage bed. More than a kiss, certainly. But theirs wasn't to be an ordinary marriage, and gave no hint that it would be. Her husband lay atop the counterpane, still in his clothes and covered by an entirely different pile of blankets. And he didn't seem at all interested in her.

Not at all. That disappointed her more than she had first admitted. She had been fighting an unreasonable urge to touch him, one that had stirred when he'd come back into the room just now. The same kind of stirring that she'd felt at the Cobson's, when he had pulled her close—stark terror and a superb sort of singing in her pulse. And it had come again, just after she had signed her name in the marriage registry: she had seen his gaze flit to her mouth and then away, saw the marriage kiss evaporate with his disinterest. Which had been all for the best.

But still, there was that odd whirlpooling commotion that seemed intent upon dragging her toward him. He didn't seem to be affected by it in the least. He lay on his side, facing away from her, his hair dark against the pillow, his shoulder a wall.

He was handsome in a frightening sort of way, like the dizzying view from atop a sheer cliff, like the terrible beauty of a dangerous storm. No, beauty wasn't the right word; beauty was the bliss that happiness brought to a smile; it was the hope shining up from a fearless soul. Hunter Claybourne was sorrow and despair and bone-chilling dread. He seemed to thrive on this bleakness, proud of his ruthless ways, of taking advantage of his power.

"Mr. Claybourne, did you know my father?"

He didn't answer, and she was about to give up and settle in for the night when his voice rumbled through the mattress, settling low in her chest and making her a little breathless.

"I knew him only from a distance."

"He was a great railway engineer."

"He was a miserable business man." Claybourne shifted his weight and stuffed his blanket beneath his folded arms.

"That doesn't matter in the least, Mr. Claybourne. The railways he designed and built will last through the millennium. He made me very proud."

"Your imprudent father left you with nothing but a bankrupt railway—"

"Which you then stole from me." Felicity sat up again and stared down at him.

"The opportunity presented itself to me. Your uncle approached me—"

"And you thought him quite the pigeon, didn't you? Easy to pluck, ready to spit and roast. Didn't expect a mouthful of feathers, did you?"

Claybourne rolled over onto his elbow and glared at her through weary-lidded eyes, their color gone to silky black smoke.

"It was business, Miss Mayfield. I wanted the Drayhill-Starlington and it became available. If I hadn't purchased it, then another man would have. And your fate would have been the same."

"Except, Mr. Claybourne, that I'd be married to someone else instead of to you."

The fire popped at the end of her statement, then fell to hissing.

"Or you'd be in jail." He snorted and presented his broad-shouldered back.

Felicity felt entirely deserted, and yet there it was again, that immodest urge to have him kiss her, to finish off the business of their wedding ceremony. The urge would soon pass, and she certainly wasn't about to rekindle it when it did.

"Good night, Mr. Claybourne." Felicity settled into the pillows and pulled the counterpane to her chin. Claybourne didn't move, but his breathing eased after a time.

Her wedding night. Felicity tried to imagine herself lying next to another man: someone who might smile now and then, someone less imposing, less baffling.

But no matter the strength of their character, they all seemed to have one thing in common—the face of Hunter Claybourne.

Chapter 7

⦿⟨◦◦◦⟩⦿

Hunter lay awake all night, waiting. He wasn't sure what exactly he was waiting for, but he knew it had a great deal to do with the young woman lying beside him in his bed.

His wife.

His bedmate—one who roamed the mattress in search of the best place to nest. He had suffered the brush of her hand across his temple, and her soft breathing against his arm. He'd spent most of the night aroused by the scent of her and by the very real fact of her alliance with him, and by that damned nightshirt, which was too thin and too big and belonged to Earnest.

Giving up on the notion of sleep, Hunter bathed, dressed in his crispest linen, put on his coat, and hurried downstairs to his breakfast.

Earnest met him at the dining-room table with the usual dry toast, a plate of stew, and a steaming pot of tea. The young man seemed even more skittish than usual.

"Uhm, sir . . ."

"Yes, Earnest. Speak."

"Will she . . . join you, sir? I mean your wife . . . I mean Mrs. Claybourne—"

"I have no idea what my wife will do for her breakfast."

"Thank you, sir." Earnest bowed and started for the pantry.

"Earnest, come back here."

"Yessir?" Earnest skidded to attention, shielding his chest with the tarnished tray.

"Whose nightshirt is my wife wearing?"

"Nightshirt? Oh, God!" Earnest's knees turned toward each other and began to knock together. "Curse me, sir—I didn't mean anything by it! She needed . . . It was the only . . ."

Hunter should have fired Earnest years ago. Loud noises seemed to send him over the edge. "Never mind, Earnest. Just see that it doesn't happen again."

Earnest's eyes nearly popped out of his head; indignation stained his cheeks. "Sir, I would never presume to—"

"To the kitchen, Earnest." He watched his young valet plow through the pantry, nearly taking the door off its hinges. When Hunter turned back to his breakfast, his wife was standing across from him on the other side of the table. She looked fresh as the day, her hair tucked into a springy bundle, her eyes sparkling with the same kind of mischief that had mocked him in his half-awake dreaming.

"Good morning, Mr. Claybourne."

"Good morning."

"Did you sleep well?"

"Like a rock."

"Good. Mr. Claybourne, I need a loan."

Hunter was in the midst of swallowing a mouthful of tea when she threw this challenge at him, and the tea went down the wrong way. He spun out of his chair to deal with his fit of coughing, and when he finally recovered she was kneeling at the table, ladling blackberry preserves onto a square of his toast.

"I'm sorry to have startled you, Mr. Claybourne. But, as you rightly pointed out to me yesterday, I was blindsided by an enterprising young urchin and now I haven't a penny to my name."

"And you want a loan? From me?"

"Ten pounds should do it." She rose from her kneeling and studied the stack of crates along the pantry wall.

"Ten pounds?"

"I have only this dress, Mr. Claybourne." She fingered the dingy blue folds of her skirt. "And it will fall to shreds long before this year is out if I don't have others to wear." She carried a small crate to the table, placed it on the floor, then sat down on it. "What would your business associates say, if your wife was discovered in such a threadbare state? Not terribly good for your precious reputation."

"Go on," Hunter said as he sat down to study this wifely logic of hers.

"And I'll need travel money to cover my expenses should I find myself unable to pay in kind."

If he hadn't been looking so closely at her, he'd never have seen it: a glossy piece of straw poking out of the curls just behind her ear and above her collar. Where the devil had she been this morning? And when? She'd been asleep in his bed when he left her not a half-hour ago.

"You'll not be traveling soon," he said more sharply than he'd meant.

"Then how can I ever hope to repay the loan of ten pounds? You are a businessman, Mr. Claybourne. You do understand that my business is reporting on interesting travel spots. In order to practice my business, and make money, I must travel to various locations across Britain—"

"Why?" The only place she could have gotten a piece of straw in her hair was in his stable.

"Why do I need to travel? So that I can convey to my readers the full experience of staying at country inns, and describe the joys of eating local food and visiting colorful festivals."

"Why would anyone want to read about such things?" And why had she gone to his stable? To meet someone? Whom? Earnest? Or that skinny reporter fellow? A shaft of pure jealousy pierced him; the shock of it set his head spinning.

"Two reasons, Mr. Claybourne. The first being so the readers can decide for themselves if they would like to experience the same food or inn or festival. The second reason is to allow those who can't travel for themselves a way to see the world without leaving the safety of their own parlors."

"Ridiculous." As was his jealousy. She meant less than nothing to him.

"Do you ever travel, Mr. Claybourne?"

"Only when my business forces me to." His fingers itched to pluck the straw from her hair and present the evidence to her. He wanted most of all to know how it got there.

"Have you ever taken lodging in a comfortable-looking inn, but discovered upon retiring that the beds are saggy and the food indigestible?"

"I learned a long time ago which places to avoid."

"Exactly. And my job is to see that the traveler doesn't make that mistake in the first place. Do you see the logic?"

"Barely." All he could image was blended laugher and heaps of straw tossed around the loft and a tangle of blue skirts.

"In any case, I'll be going to London today."

"Why were you in my stable this morning?"

"In the stable?" Her headlong confidence faded; her gaze flitted its gold across his face, then flew off to appraise the ceiling.

"Why were you in my stable?" he repeated, his hand shaking as he reached for the straw.

She dodged his hand, then glared at him. "What are you doing?"

"Fetching this."

"Fetching what, Mr. Claybourne?"

Hunter steadied her with a hand to her shoulder, and then worked the stiff piece of straw from its refuge among the softly curling silk.

Hunter would have tarried there if he could, would have run his fingers through it and touched it to his cheek to study its textures and ease the burning in his chest. But he took a steadying breath and produced the length of straw.

"Now, Miss Mayfield, why were you in my stable this morning? You didn't get this from my bed. My mattress is made of fine French wool."

A frown of concentration touched the corners of her captivating mouth. Whatever she was about to say was going to be a lie, carefully prepared to deceive him. He watched her lips part, watched her moisten them with the tip of her tongue. The heat left his chest, headed for his belly, and lodged in his groin.

"I took a walk around the estate yesterday, Mr. Claybourne, after my bath. And I soon found myself in the stable, looking at your horses. They're very nice. I must have gotten straw on my bonnet." She crunched down on her toast and came away with a dab of preserves on her upper lip. She wiped it off with a fingertip, licked the dab from her finger, then looked up at him.

"Well, Mr. Claybourne, do I get my loan?"

Hunter heard her question, but he'd begun to imagine his mouth on the end of that finger, and on her lips, and wasn't sure he was prepared to answer. His throat had gone dry.

"Ten pounds, Mr. Claybourne. Do you agree to it?"

Hunter was about to mindlessly agree to anything, but he caught himself in time. Damn the woman for keeping him from beginning his day! And damn her for being right. She needed clothes. He couldn't very well have a wife traipsing around London in threadbare fashions, looking no better than a Ragged School missionary.

Hunter stood up from his congealed, uneaten breakfast. "I'll have a letter of credit drawn up for one of London's best dressmakers."

Now the chit had the gall to look annoyed. "Sir, there's no need to force me more into debt. I'll never be able to repay you. And I will not spend the rest of my life owing you."

"What about that fortune your enterprising uncle is to return with? Or have you come to doubt his chances?"

She glowered at him. "Uncle will return with plenty of profits, Mr. Claybourne. In the meantime, three simple, ready-to-wear dresses will suit me and my finances just fine."

"You'll see the dressmakers, or you'll get no money from me at all. You've a role to play, Miss Mayfield, and you'll play it in the correct costume."

"I can't afford it, Mr. Claybourne."

"When our year together has ended, Miss Mayfield, and I own the Drayhill-Starlington railway outright, then I will consider the dressmaker's bills paid in full. You will owe me nothing."

"At which time I shall donate my entire wardrobe to some charitable union for the benefit of impoverished women, who wish only to clothe themselves in a bit of dignity."

The room became stifling to Hunter. He wasn't offering anything like charity. This was a business decision, nothing more. "When the time comes, you may burn them for all I care."

"Very well, then. I'll see the dressmakers."

"Do it today. Branson!" Hunter shouted, feeling the sweat beading at his temple. "We're late!"

"Sir." Branson entered and handed Hunter his case and his hat. "The carriage is outside, sir."

Miss Mayfield beat him to the dining-room door and blocked his way. "I'm coming with you, Mr. Claybourne. I must talk with Mr. Dolan, today."

The woman could pierce solid rock with her determination.

"You will see a dressmaker, Miss Mayfield. If there is time, Branson, you may take her to this Dolan character."

"Yessir."

"And what about a bed, Mr. Claybourne?" she asked, her eyes blazing with unwarranted triumph. "I can't very well keep using yours, can I?"

"Purchase a new mattress and bed, Branson," Hunter said, braving another moment of unspent, inconceivable yearning. "And see that a chamber is arranged for Mrs. Claybourne."

She smiled grandly and moved out of his way. He strode past her down the hallway as he shrugged into his top coat.

He hoped the rest of his day wasn't the contest his morning had been.

Felicity thought Claybourne a very closed-off man as he sat silently at an obtuse angle beside her, hidden behind the crinkled wall of the *Times*, all the way to Cornhill Street. He muttered occasionally, shifted in his seat, shook out the crease a dozen times, and finally folded the newspaper only as the carriage came to rest in front of the Claybourne Exchange.

"See that your business is finished by noon," Claybourne said.

Felicity felt the rear of the carriage shudder, and hoped that Mr. Pepperpot's escape from the luggage boot had gone unnoticed. She also hoped he'd been discreet in his thievery at the manor. Not that anything would be missed from among the crates.

"Why noon, Mr. Claybourne? Are you taking me to lunch at your club? If so, please remember to shave before we go." In jest she flicked a finger along the stubble of his chin. His jaw tightened, a tremendously solid edifice. "You look a bit scruffy this morning."

Claybourne scrubbed his hand across his cheek, then sent her a look that promised murder. "You should have said."

"Reminding you to shave isn't among the articles of our marriage settlement, Mr. Claybourne."

He looked thunderous and turned to his footman. "Keep her out of trouble, Branson. Here is a letter of credit that will send the bills my way. Good day." Claybourne left Branson standing beside the carriage, and Felicity glaring after him.

"Do you know Fleet Street, Branson?" she asked, watching Claybourne's doorman greet her husband and grovel as if Claybourne were king.

"Enough to know that you'll find no dressmakers there." He started to close the carriage door, but Felicity held it open with the toe of her shoe.

"Please, Branson. Let me see Mr. Dolan first. It's urgent."

"Impossible. Mr. Claybourne gave strict orders to—"

"Mr. Claybourne can sit on a tack. Let me see to my business with Mr. Dolan, and then I'll quite happily visit the dressmaker."

"I'm afraid I can't do that, miss. Please don't ask again." Branson seemed terribly distressed and Felicity relented. The footman and all his staff seemed frightened to death of Claybourne; she didn't want them thinking the same of her.

"To the dressmaker's, then, as quickly as possible."

The ordeal at Madame Deverie's Apparel Shoppe took hours and hours, and promised even more hours of torture when she returned for fittings and to choose accessories. Felicity felt flayed and punctured. Claybourne's letter of credit included instructions to outfit his wife for every eventuality. Felicity stressed comfort and durability, and gave in to elegance only on a few items that she might wear to one of Claybourne's financial events. Such a waste of money. Such a waste of time.

She could be walking the sheep trails above Conniston Lake right now, or sitting in a Shropshire tea room, chatting with the proprietress about the upcoming village cycle play, or about Founder's Day. In any case, she wouldn't be in London right now, with her arms stuck full of pins, and her ears full up with advice about how her curls might be better harnessed by the proper use of lacquer and wire mesh.

Her father would be dismayed. He'd never had any use for society. What would he think of this muck she'd become mired in? He would surely be blazing angry with Uncle Foley, and he'd probably have changed his will to keep her from finding her way into such a marriage.

But she was anxious to see Mr. Dolan and explain her new situation. She would then present him with her grand idea for a new kind of travel guide, and be gone from Claybourne Manor on a new adventure.

After what seemed hours, she was finally free of the pins and Madame Deverie's chattering, and on her way to Mr. Dolan's office.

"You've married Hunter Claybourne?" Thomas Dolan gripped the arms of his chair and held on as if he thought he would be tossed from it headfirst. "*The* Hunter Claybourne?"

"Yes, that's the one, Mr. Dolan, but—"

"The richest man in all England?"

"He's not *the* richest man, Mr. Dolan. At least, I don't think he is. But that's not why I came."

Felicity had known Mr. Dolan for nearly a year, but had never seen him in such a state.

"You might have told me that you planned to marry him, Felicity."

"I would have. But I didn't even know the man till two days ago."

Dolan propped his elbows on his desk. "You met and married in two days? That much in love? What the hell are you doing here, then? You ought to be on your honeymoon!"

"Mr. Claybourne isn't the honeymooning type."

"How did you meet him?"

"It doesn't matter."

"Oooo . . . The man himself is a mystery, and now he's got himself embroiled in a mystery courtship. What have you gotten yourself into Felicity?"

Felicity sighed and sat down opposite the man. How many times had she wondered that same thing in the last two days? Married to a madman; living in a tomb.

"Never mind that, Mr. Dolan. I came about next month's gazette piece. I'm nearly finished with the piece on the Bennington Post."

"Bosh the gazette, girl. I want stories about dinner parties and soirees. I want bejeweled matrons and scandalous barons, licentious cabinet ministers and their mistresses! Bring me gossip, my dear!"

Felicity stood again. "Gossip? I will not."

Dolan jumped to his feet. "Oh, but don't you see the opportunity? You'll be sharing the salt with society! You'll be my fly on the wall."

"I'll be nothing of the sort, Mr. Dolan. I'll write my gazette pieces and that is all. This is the last of the Bennington Post series." She propped the end of the folio on top of his desk. "Take it or leave it," she said, feeling very much like the devious Hunter Claybourne at the moment.

Dolan studied her for a long moment then frowned. "All right. I'll take it."

"And what would you say to taking all of the Bennington Post entries, binding them together, and making a single book of it?"

"Hmmm. Easy to carry in one's travel case—"

"Exactly, Mr. Dolan. And what if we promised one bound-together travel guide for every railway line in the country? Each would cater to the needs of the modern female traveler."

He sat forward, nearly licking his chops. "And you'd be writing under the name Mrs. Hunter Claybourne?"

"Who else?"

Dolan clapped his palms together. "You're a shrewd woman, Felicity Mayfield."

"Felicity Claybourne. And I want a raise in salary."

"A raise?"

"And an advance."

"I already pay you twice what you're worth. And now you're married to a man who could buy up all the papers in London with the change that collects in his trouser cuffs." He sat down. "Hell no, there'll be no raise, and no advance."

"That's your choice, Mr. Dolan." Felicity picked up her folio and turned to leave, stopping long enough to brush an imaginary bit of fluff off her very dingy skirt. "Perhaps the *Lady's Day* would be interested in employing the wife of Hunter Claybourne."

"You wouldn't—"

"Let's see, the *Lady's Day* is two buildings down, and above the *Record,* I believe . . ."

Dolan growled. "How much of a raise, Felicity?"

She thought of young Giles and decided to use her raise to buy him a new shirt—no, *three* new shirts to replace the one that Claybourne ruined with his vile temper.

"Another guinea per story will do, the next installment in advance."

"Not on your life!" Dolan held his breath and vigorously shook his head.

Felicity shrugged and started toward the door. "Good-bye, Mr. Dolan."

"Oh, all right!" He threw himself out of his chair and made the door before she did. "But that means I'll have to drag in another advertiser."

Felicity smiled pleasantly and tapped on his lapel, exceedingly pleased with herself. "Try the Claybourne Exchange, Mr. Dolan. The management might be inclined to send some trade your way."

Dolan brightened like a beacon; his mustache twitched with the possibilities. "Brilliant, Mrs. Claybourne!"

"Now, Mr. Dolan, about binding my travel articles . . ."

Half an hour later, Felicity descended the stairs with three guineas in her pocket, her folio of the Bennington Post Railway under her arm, and a promise from Dolan that he would print her first complete travel guide as soon as she could edit the entries into a single book. When that was done, she would begin researching a new guide: perhaps somewhere in Northumberland— somewhere far away from Hunter Claybourne.

She arrived back at Claybourne Manor in time to down another bowl of Mrs. Sweeney's stew. Four meals in a row of carrots, potatoes, and chunks of beef. Perhaps she would speak with the woman in the morning.

Earnest was in the process of trying to furnish her new chamber. The crates that had once packed the room now lined the corridor. The only piece of furniture in sight was a dusty wardrobe, and the entire effect was lit by candles instead of by the sunlight that beat hard against the windows.

"This darkness will never do." Felicity drew the drapes aside, flooding the room with light. "Douse those candles, Earnest. Daylight is good for the eyes and the spirit, and candles are expensive."

"Yes ma'am." Earnest pinched out the flames and rubbed the wax into his palms. "Your bed hasn't come, Mrs. Claybourne. Branson said it was due any time. As for the rest of the room . . . I don't know. I've never done this before."

"Come, then, Earnest. We'll search through this warehouse that Mr. Claybourne calls home and see what else we can find."

Felicity and Earnest quickly uncovered a dresser and a side table in a room under the stairs. They rescued a writing desk from the cellar, and a comfortable chair from beneath the mounted head of a surly-looking boar.

The bed arrived in midafternoon and soon stood against the wall, centered between two pastoral paintings. She found lamps packed away in crates, their

beautifully etched and prismed globes wrapped in
cotton and never disturbed. No one at the manor
seemed to know why, or for what eventuality, Claybourne was saving his treasures. According to Earnest,
packages arrived regularly, authorized and purchased
by Claybourne himself. Yet the master never seemed
interested once the goods arrived. He would merely
point to a corner, wave a careless hand, and instruct
the crate or barrel to be put with the rest.

Convinced that she couldn't very well live like that
for the next year, Felicity vowed to fashion her own
haven in the midst of Claybourne's mausoleum.

Dismissing her husband and his odd behavior from
her thoughts, Felicity swept and dusted her chamber
and had the windows washed. She took the drapes
outside and beat them until the air cleared of the dust
clouds, then had Earnest rehang them with tiebacks.

Finally, she directed her bath to be set up between
the bed and the window, so that she could watch the
fading sun on its way toward the distant hills. She was
sore all over and coated with dust. The warm water
seemed to soak right into her bones.

Ah, this was much better than the Queen's Bench,
better even than a bench in Waterloo Station, or Mrs.
Wright's Boarding House for Genteel Ladies. Once she
finished negotiating the thorny details with her foul-
tempered innkeeper, Claybourne Manor might work
out very nicely for a base of operations. She could
close herself up in her chamber when she needed to
write; travel when she needed to augment her
research—and when she needed to get away.

And with any luck, she would only occasionally pass
her irascible husband in the halls.

Chapter 8

Hunter crossed his own threshold and followed his wife's vanilla scent up the stairs to her chamber door. He had business to discuss with her. Married only a day, and she was already costing him. He would have knocked, but the house belonged to him.

He threw open the door and met with dazzling sunshine. "Damnation! What the hell have you done here?"

"Mr. Claybourne, I'll thank you to leave immediately!" Her bristling indignation came from somewhere across the room, beyond the bed and all its gauzy drapings. "How dare you burst into my chamber!"

Then he caught the faint plash of water. She was bathing.

"Out, Mr. Claybourne!"

She was his wife.

"And next time, knock."

But this was his home, though at the moment it looked anything but. Hunter stayed, and slammed the door shut.

"And good riddance, you swollen-headed, penny-pinching barbarian!" A hairpin landed with a click at his feet.

"Well," Hunter said quietly, "at least I know your true opinion of me."

The splashing stopped, but the water kept sloshing. She harrumphed. "I asked you to leave, Mr. Claybourne. Can't you see that I'm bathing?"

He could see only that she'd drawn her hair to the top of her head into a loosely ribboned cloud. A stream of afternoon sunlight fanned through the watery windowpanes, lighting her hair like a spun-gold explosion. But the bed and the brightness obscured more detail than that; and he was better off blinded. She had diverted his intention too deeply already.

"You spent seven hundred seventy pounds at Madame Deverie's today."

"That much, Mr. Claybourne? I had no idea a wardrobe cost so much. You should have loaned me that ten pounds, and saved yourself the entire seven hundred seventy."

"And you should have been mindful of the cost."

"What would I know of the price of fashion? You wanted me dressed for every eventuality. Madame Deverie saw to that task quite thoroughly. I would have preferred the simpler fabrics and styles, but the woman insisted on the best. But fear not, Mr. Claybourne: should we ever be invited to a duck hunt, I have the perfect shooting costume."

"Damn the ducks!"

"And why haven't you gone, sir? This is my chamber."

"This is my house."

"Except for this room, at the moment. It is mine!"

"I can see that."

"You should be pleased with the change. Amazing what an open drape and a clean window will do to eliminate the gloom. I borrowed a few things from other parts of the house; I hope you don't mind."

The woman had strewn all sorts of objects about her

chamber: a bandy-legged table, a black-and-gilt lacquered screen, lamps and pastoral paintings—and he couldn't recall a single item. The objects were of little value to him, meant nothing more than the fact of their existence.

"You have expensive taste in lamps, Mr. Claybourne."

He snorted in frustration. "And in wives."

She laughed suddenly, brightly, and turned toward him. Her arm was lithe and damp, and circled the lip of the brass tub. She looked a little surprised, and then sent a disappointed sigh into the air between them.

"Ah, you weren't joking, Mr. Claybourne." She turned away again and sank deeper into the water. "I thought you had discovered your sense of humor. I was about to compliment you on its depth, but I shall have to refrain."

"I have a sense of humor, Miss Mayfield!" He hadn't meant to defend himself on so insignificant a point, but he refused to be dismissed for lack by this thieving travel writer.

"Oh, I'm sure you do have a sense of humor. It just needs exercising."

"It needs a reason."

"Then look no further than the end of your nose."

"You find the end of my nose to be humorous?" Insulted to the marrow, Hunter stalked to the foot of the bed, but found it a precarious place to stand. She was too lovely and he was too close. Her back was to him, bare to the nape, where stray curls clung damply to her shoulders.

"Stand away, sir." She quickly drew her knees to her chest and tented the *Times* over the opening in the tub, leaving only her bare shoulders and her fierce gaze to entice him. "You are husband in name only, Mr. Claybourne. This is my bath, sir, my private chamber. Now, turn your back and stay turned while I escape to the dressing screen."

He did as directed, though he wanted to linger. He

stared at the door and gripped the bed pole to rid himself of the aching need to slide his hand down the sleek column of her neck and across her shoulders. He heard her stand, heard the caressing sluice of water. Every sinew and fiber urged him to turn.

And now her earthy voice came unmuffled from behind the screen. "And regarding the end of your nose, Mr. Claybourne, I used it as a figure of speech. Your nose is quite adequate for the size and shape of your face. What I meant was that our situation is fraught with humor."

"Is it?"

"It's all around us. You may turn now, Mr. Claybourne."

He already had. Her watery footprints led across the unpolished floor toward the screen. He wondered if her bare feet matched the shape of the small imprints.

But damn the woman! She had distracted him again from his purpose. "You are dancing around this dressmaker's bill, Mrs. Claybourne."

"Then cancel the order if you think it's too much!" Felicity wished the man would make up his mind. "I don't want to argue about it. It just seems that dressing the wife of Hunter Claybourne is an expensive endeavor. I'm truly sorry, but I don't know what I can do about the expense, or the fact that, at the moment, I am your wife. Whether we like it or not, we seem to be stuck with each other, like a train unable to move forward or backward without its track. And please don't ask which of us is which."

Felicity waited for his reply as she slipped into her new set of petticoats and one of the day dresses Madame Deverie had sold to her ready-made. It was a bit too spriggy and yellow for her tastes, and the sleeves were too full for traveling, but it would do for now.

She found herself wondering if Claybourne would like it, if he would find her at all attractive. He'd looked momentarily harmless standing near the door when he'd first come in, peering at her as if she were out of focus. She'd been angry at the time, and amused as well. And even a little charmed.

Yet, he'd been too quiet in the last few minutes. . . . She came around the screen, stockingless and without slippers. "Mr. Claybourne?"

The meddlesome scoundrel was bent over her writing table, leafing through her travel folio! The very folio that Giles had stolen and returned to her. If Claybourne had enough sense to put the loss and the return together, he might—

"Put that down, Mr. Claybourne!"

"'The weary traveler should keep in mind the security of his or her baggage.' If I'm not mistaken, Miss Mayfield, this is your . . ."

He looked up at her and his words trailed off. He seemed startled, not that she'd caught him reading, but by something else, something that softened his face and brought color to his brow. His fine mouth reshaped itself as he swallowed. When he continued to stare without comment, Felicity touched the back of her hair to see that it wasn't standing on end.

It wasn't.

So she dashed over to him and yanked the folio out of his hands. "Keep your fingers off my belongings, Mr. Claybourne."

He looked down the length of his nose at her, and followed her every movement as she straightened the stack of pages. "I thought your little bandit had stolen your gazette when he stole your portmanteau. What's it doing here?"

Felicity's thoughts clambered over a slippery hillside of possibilities and came up with the perfect explanation, one that bore a great deal of truth.

"It's been returned to me." She tucked the folio into its sleeve. "Miraculously!"

"Here at the house?" he asked. Felicity tried to ignore the heat of guilt rimming her ears as he studied her profile in conspicuous detail.

"Mr. Dolan had it," she said quickly. One small lie wouldn't hurt anyone. And it was certainly better for Giles than the full truth. If Claybourne knew that the boy had been here at the manor—

"How did this Dolan fellow come by your stolen gazette?" He sat on the edge of the table and watched her every move, watched her straighten her desktop. Yet all the while she imagined his gaze on her mouth, watching for something only he could see, though she could feel his interest as if he were drawing his fingertips across her bare nape.

"I guess the envelope was found by someone and returned to the office of the *Hearth and Heath.* You see the address here." Felicity pointed to the evidence on the front of the folio sleeve. "Anyone could have slipped it through the editor's mail slot outside the building and gone about their business."

That seemed the hardest for him to swallow; he exhaled as if she'd worn out his patience. "Which person in all of London would have gone out of their way to perform such a charitable act?"

Here was a perfect place to advertise the merits of her new little friend without giving him away. She tried to look casual and speculative. "Perhaps little Giles Pepperpot had a change of heart."

Claybourne's broad shoulders lifted with a single grunt. "You expect me to believe that the boy has a conscience, *and* that he can read?"

This wasn't going badly, she thought. "Giles might be able to read. He told me that he'd once been committed to a workhouse and that he hated—"

Felicity clamped her hand over her mouth, hoping to muffle the words she'd just said. But Claybourne had heard them quite clearly. He leaned forward and tilted her chin so that she was forced to look directly into those opaque eyes.

"You've seen that little thief again, haven't you?"

"Briefly."

"Where?" Felicity twisted out of his way, but he

followed and turned her, holding fast to her arms.
"Where? You haven't had any free time."

She took a long breath while she concocted a logical
answer, one she could back up with the lies she'd
already spun. "I saw him with Mr. Dolan. Giles had
arrived just before I did."

"Had he now?"

She might as well make the lie enormous. "He was
trying to get money from Mr. Dolan."

The obsidian in Claybourne eyes glinted. "He was?"

"The silly child wanted payment for my gazettes."
She tossed her head for effect and tried to sound
scandalized. "Imagine the audacity! He's a lot like you,
Mr. Claybourne, willing to make money any way he
can."

"I don't steal."

"Never?"

He released her arms. "So once again, you let the
little thief go when you could have given him over to
the police?"

"Yes, I let him go, and if I see him again, I plan to
buy him a shirt—to replace the one you tore."

"Not with my money."

"No, Mr. Claybourne, with my own." Her miserly
husband wouldn't even spring for a three-penny shirt
for an unfortunate child.

"So you've struck a vein of gold, have you?" Claybourne planted himself on the blanket chest at the end
of her bed and stuck his heels into the carpet. His legs
were long and as well-muscled as his shoulders, fashioned of the same tethered strength. "And to think,
Miss Mayfield, your uncle had to go all the way to San
Francisco to find one."

Felicity picked her three guineas off the table and
dropped them into her palm one by one, pleased at the
satisfying clink as they hit against each other. "I've
been paid in advance for my travel guide of the
Bennington Post Railway."

"All of three guineas? How can you carry the weight?"

His snort of laughter took a jab at her pride, but she dodged it with growing sense of resolution, relieved that she had successfully led him away from the subject of Giles Pepperpot.

"This is a goodly amount of money by my standards. I'm not accustomed to earning it by the bushelful like you are."

"No doubt you'll waste it all on that boy, and have nothing to show for it."

"I suppose you would have me invest my three guineas in one of your schemes?"

"A wise man looks always to the future."

Felicity stood eye-level with Claybourne for the first time, and felt equal to his smugness—though a bit dismayed by the fluttering in her chest as he stared at her from beneath his lowering brow. She had her future planned; she didn't need his advice. She would find Giles in the next few days, settle her husband's debt with him, and then set out on her travels.

"And what is it you see in your future, Mr. Claybourne?"

He straightened, clamped his hands over the edge of the blanket chest. "What do you mean, Miss Mayfield?"

"Oh, I know that the Bank of England would collapse on itself if you should desert it. And that you are the bedrock of the financial district. But I can't help suspect that you anticipate a time when you'll have to pack up all your things and leave Hampstead in a great hurry."

The accusation drew a growl from him. "Leave Hampstead in a hurry? Why? What brings that fool question to mind?"

"Come with me, Mr. Claybourne." Felicity deposited the three guineas in the lotus bowl on her writing table, then went to the door.

Claybourne stayed put on the chest, looking too handsome in his dark suspicions.

She stretched out her hand and beckoned him. "Come, come, Mr. Claybourne."

Hunter thought his wife seemed far too resourceful at the moment, and far too inviting with her hair drying in curling wisps around her face. And she was barefooted. It was strange enough having a guest in his house; the fact that this particular guest was his wife unsettled him completely. His moods had become mercurial and unreliable, from irritation with the woman's self-assured independence, to an unwelcome response that bordered on lust—and all this could manifest itself in a matter of seconds. It would not do.

"This way, Mr. Claybourne."

Hunter reluctantly followed her out of the chamber into the hallway, keeping his hands stuffed safely into his coat pockets, and away from the undone button in the middle of her back.

"What is this, Mr. Claybourne?" She was pointing impatiently at the crates lining the walls on either side of the corridor.

"What is what?" he asked, confused by her question, and wondering why the passage seemed suddenly so shadowed.

"When I arrived here yesterday, I asked Branson if you were in the process of moving. He said no, that you've lived here for five years."

"Five years, three months. Why?"

"Well, I've been here for less than two days, Mr. Claybourne. And, granted, I only brought with me a folio of papers and the clothes on my back, but I have moved in." She bent and blew dust off a crate. "It appears that you have no intention of doing so."

He bristled. "I am here to stay."

"Then why all the boxes, if you don't plan to move at a moment's notice?"

He didn't like this kind of breezy banter, wouldn't allow it but for the way her laughter brightened the hallway. "Claybourne Manor will be my house until the day I die."

"Let's hope the undertakers remember which crate they put you in before they cart you off to be buried."

He laughed ruefully. "It won't matter then, will it?"

She dusted at another label. "It certainly will matter to your heirs and your family."

"I haven't any."

"Well, you have me. . . ." She stopped her dusting and lifted her startled gaze to his.

Her words had come so easily, Hunter knew she hadn't meant them for him. They were something she would say, and mean, to that uncle of hers or to her feckless father. But they pricked him, as a casual glance in the mirror reveals an uncomfortable truth.

She seemed embarrassed and brushed her palms together as if to dislodge the dust. "Most of these crates were in my chamber, Mr. Claybourne. Dozens and dozens of them."

"I'll have Earnest remove them from the corridor."

"That's not my point." She looked exasperated, as if he had spoken another language and she didn't understand him. "I merely wondered what you expect to do with all of it."

"Do?" He certainly didn't understand her.

"Yes, do. The label on this crate, for example, indicates that it's come all the way from Turkey, and claims to contain carpet runners."

"And?"

She lifted the hem of her soft yellow skirts a few inches, and wriggled her bare toes against the floor. "This very cold and dank hallway could stand a carpet runner, Mr. Claybourne. Why not open the crate and lay it out here?"

"I'll have Branson see to it come morning." Hunter nodded and started down the hall, satisfied that he had survived another of her questions, and that he hadn't acted on the urge to thread his fingers through her hair.

"Mr. Claybourne, this barrel holds six copper cook pots."

Hunter stopped and turned. Her hands were stuck against her hips, her toes showing again. "And?" he asked, unable to read a meaning beyond her simple irritation with him.

"Mrs. Sweeney could use them to cook that delectable stew you seem so very fond of."

"Then I'll have Earnest deliver the pots to her in the morning."

"And what about all these the other crates and barrels?" She lifted arms that seemed to encompass the entire county, then went back to scrubbing her fist across the labels. "Here are linens, and an umbrella stand, and more drapery, though God knows why you think you need more protection from the sun inside this house. And here is a cylinder lawn mower. Why do you keep garden equipment in an upstairs bedroom?"

"I haven't got a gardener."

She blew a puff of air into her hair. "That's quite obvious. But what do you plan to do with it? What are you saving it for, Mr. Claybourne? More's the point, why purchase a lawn mower or an umbrella stand if you're not going to use them?"

Hunter hadn't a single answer for her, so he gave her none. Which ought to leave her silent and hanging onto her last question long enough for him to gain the quiet of his library.

He started down the stairs, and was surprised and strangely disappointed not to hear her quick footsteps following him. He found himself straining for the soft pad of her tread as he walked the distance of the hall to the end of the west wing.

Hunter had located his library in a room which he knew to have once been a grand ballroom. He'd purchased the house from a man who'd made his fortune in canalways, a foolish man who hadn't had the sense to see that trains would soon replace post

roads. Hunter himself had advised him to invest in the
rails, made repeated offers to assist. But the man was
too proud and, in the end, too late. Hunter bought the
house and the grounds in a rare act of charity, and
because it was isolated yet close enough to commute to
the Claybourne Exchange every day.

A fire was newly set in the library grate, and two
lamps had been lit against the evening. Branson had
dutifully laid out Hunter's attaché on the desk alongside a stack of the day's newspapers.

He had decided he would pay his wife's dressmaker's bill without further comment. Lord Meath
would expect Mrs. Claybourne to look the part when
they dined at his house. Not that any man would
notice fashion, in the light of Miss Mayfield's distracting smile. He had only noticed the new dress she was
wearing because of the button that needed fastening at
her back. Which caused him to think of her dressing
behind the screen in her chamber, which made him
wonder if Madame Deverie thought to include suitable
nightwear in this very expensive wardrobe. He stood
up from his desk, intending to seek out Miss
Mayfield—

But she was standing in the doorway, taking in the
length and breadth of the library in a single, efficient
assessment. Absurdly, he wanted to know what she
thought. It was the only other room besides his bed-
chamber that he used with any frequency. The cases of
books reminded him that he'd read each one; the
exotic woods and works of art satisfied his sense of
order. The room smelled of solid, successful contentment.

But his wife frowned at the bookcases and the
statuary, and then turned her frown on him.

"Yes?" he asked, feeling roundly chastised without
knowing the offense.

"I'm sorry to disturb you, Mr. Claybourne, but two
of the crates contain dining-room chairs. May I have
them set out in the—"

"Put them anywhere you like."

She seemed to approve of his decision but remained in the doorway as if she were afraid of contracting some illness from the room. "You've more books upstairs in the hallway, Mr. Claybourne. At least, that's what the crate says they are. Shouldn't they be brought in here?"

"I'll speak to Branson—"

"In the morning. Yes, yes, I know. Why don't I take care of that? Set some of it aright. If I'm to call this place home for the next year, I'd prefer it to feel more like a home and less like a dockside warehouse."

Hunter hadn't thought much about uncrating the house. He didn't use many of the rooms, rarely needed anything. But he could think of no good reason to object to his wife's suggestion. And if it would keep her occupied . . .

"Uncrate it all, if you have a mind to."

She took in a breath of surprise. "Do you mean it, Mr. Claybourne?" She smiled as if the library had been transformed into a wonderland.

Hunter swallowed his own smile. "You see, Miss Mayfield, I'm not an illogical man. Your offer is sound and I accept it. And if you'll come in here out of the hallway, I'll finish buttoning your dress."

"My . . . ?" She leaned forward at the door.

Hunter stood up and came around his desk. "You've missed a button." She didn't move. "I'll fasten it if you'd like."

She seemed stunningly shy all of a sudden but came toward him with her chin held high. He made a turning gesture and she presented her back to him.

"I'm going into London again tomorrow, Mr. Claybourne."

"You think so?" The faint spray of honey-colored freckles across the rise of her shoulders caused him to wonder at the nature of her travels. Hours in the sun, perhaps?

"I need to spend some time in the British Museum

Reading Room. By latest count, it has nearly a half
million books." She swept her arm along her nape,
lifting the wildest of the escaped strands of hair off her
neck.

And there it was again, the urge to kiss her, to
unbutton where he ought to be buttoning, to slip his
hands inside her bodice and hold her against him, to
turn her in his arms and press his mouth against hers.

"And which of these books do you intend to read?"

When she spoke again her voice had grown silky
and low. "Anything about Northumberland. For my
next travel guide."

He thought he heard her sigh as he finally, reluctantly, fastened her dress closed. It was another moment before she dropped her arm and turned to him.
He thought she would flit away, but she looked up at
him, her lips newly moistened and lush. The high crest
of her cheeks had pinked, and the green of her eyes
had taken on the dappled hues of the forest.

"Your travel guide," he repeated for her, for himself.

"Ah, yes, Northumberland. I rarely travel there.
That's George Hudson's territory," she said, leaving
him for the wall of books opposite the windows. He
stood in the middle of the library while she studied the
titles, her back straight and her profile perfect. "Father
disliked and distrusted Hudson for the man's loyalty to
profit over safety. He'd be very happy to know that the
Railway King's reign is ending."

"You know about Hudson's imbroglio, then?" Hunter asked, fascinated and very much impressed that she
should know about such things.

"I know that he used capital to pay out dividends to
his shareholders, then paid a pauper's salary to his
staff. He always took the lowest bid in his construction
materials. And I know he spread rumors that my father
drank himself to death."

Hunter had heard the same, and now felt uncomfortable with the knowledge. "How was it he died?"

"The doctors said it was a cancer of the brain. Last

autumn, Father went blind in his right eye." She ran her hand along the back of a small, bronze buck. "Two months later he lost feeling in his leg on the same side. But he loved his railways, and worked until the week before he died."

When she looked up at him, her eyes were pooled with tears. "I miss him very much."

Hunter chided himself for having asked; he wasn't the comforting type. She seemed an island to him, or an elusive meadow, a place of native beauty that he could never reach, never fully comprehend. And he dare not try. In the name of his fortune, he had already risked a marriage with her; he would not risk anything deeper. George Hudson had failed because he had risked too much; Hunter wasn't such a fool. He would increase his vigil and keep his distance.

"I'm sorry for your loss, Miss Mayfield."

"Thank you, Mr. Claybourne. But that's why I need to go to the Reading Room. To learn about Northumberland."

"And you'll be home by afternoon?"

"If you insist." Felicity kept herself from sighing her impatience. Claybourne's head was immensely thick when it came to her independence. She held her breath and hoped.

"Very well. Branson will see to your transport in the morning." He sat down at his desk and picked up the newspaper.

"I appreciate your cooperation, Mr. Claybourne." Felicity reached the door and turned back to him. He was looking at her over the top of the *Times*.

"Mr. Claybourne, will you be taking dinner in the dining room tonight? Mrs. Sweeney is serving stew."

Felicity offered her most gracious smile, but he didn't move, and his eyes told her nothing at all until he lowered his gaze to the newspaper. "Not tonight, Miss Mayfield."

Feeling very much dismissed, Felicity shut the door over-hard as she left, then leaned against it.

"Miserable hermit!" she said, not caring who heard her, and hoping he had.

The *Times* rustled behind the thick panel of carved oak, and a chair scraped. Felicity jumped away from the door and watched the latch, thinking it would shift and then she'd be confronted with Claybourne's scowl. Anger. At least that would be something she could understand and rail against. It was his granite moods that disturbed her, the unpredictable times when his jaw would harden and his eyes shade over.

And even more disturbing was the way his gaze could alight on her mouth and linger like a kiss—a kiss she wasn't sure she would turn away from.

A moment passed and she heard him settle back into his chair.

Wretched man! Hunter Claybourne might have money to burn, but it certainly wouldn't keep him warm.

Chapter 9

Felicity left the British Museum Reading Room after just an hour, quite relieved not to find Branson hovering outside, ready to report her whereabouts. She had assured him that she wouldn't need his services until late in the afternoon. She found a shop nearby and bought three shirts for Giles, then took a hackney to Threadneedle Street, where she hoped to catch sight of him as he went about his daily thieving in front of the Bank of England.

She hadn't been there more than a quarter of an hour when she nearly crashed into Giles as he dodged past a coffee seller's rickety cart. He was in a guilty hurry, stuffing a pouch into his shirtfront. But he hadn't seen her.

She hurried after him and almost called out to him, but she suddenly wanted to know where he lived, where he laid his head at night. If she stopped him now to give him the shirts, he might turn her away. So when Giles went north at Bishopsgate, Felicity followed him all the way to the alleyways off Shoreditch Road.

Where she lost him in the blink of an eye.

"I'll see if Mr. Claybourne is in."

"Lanford," Hunter muttered as he heard the voices

on the other side of his office door. The man probably only wanted to gossip over George Hudson's troubles. It seemed the only subject of interest in Threadneedle these days.

"Show him in," Hunter said, before Tilson had gotten the door completely open.

"I thought you'd like to be the first to know," Lanford said, as he strode into the room. "Hudson's put the Blenwick Line and three other railways up for sale. Seems he needs some ready cash to settle a suit against him. One of his shareholders wants to know if you're interested."

"In one of Hudson's ventures? I think not."

"It's going for pennies on the pound."

"Not my pennies."

"The bank was considering it, but if you're not interested, Claybourne, perhaps we shouldn't be either. By the way, is your wife in the City today?"

Hunter hadn't paid much attention to the man until that moment. Miss Mayfield had been a plague upon his thoughts through the course of the morning. "She is, Lanford, though it's none of your business."

"Visiting somewhere nearby?" Lanford cocked his head toward the door.

"No. Why?"

"Because I just saw her in Threadneedle Street."

Hunter couldn't ignore the heavy stone that dropped into his stomach. Lanford was lying, or mistaken, or—

"Granted, I saw her only from my window, but she's not a woman easily mistaken . . ."

"When did you see her?" Hunter hoped his uneasiness didn't show; his pulse had come to a standstill.

"Most recently . . . maybe an hour ago."

"Most recently?" Hunter asked casually. "How many times did you see her?"

Lanford shrugged and smiled, seeming to dote on this clandestine information. "A dozen or more. She had a bundle under her arm."

"What kind of a bundle?"

"Couldn't tell. Though not a baby, surely. Too soon for that, eh, Claybourne?" Lanford lifted his brows.

"Go on," Hunter said, as evenly as he could manage, given the urge to toss the man from his office.

"A bundle wrapped in brown paper. And she walked up Threadneedle," Lanford said, tracing the air with his finger, "then down again, weaving in and out of the foot traffic as if she were looking for someone. I say! Where you off to in such a rush, Claybourne?"

But Hunter was already in the outer office. "Get Lanford out of my office, Tilson. Immediately. I don't know when I'll be back."

Damn the woman! She had confessed outright that she was going to give a shirt to that Pepperpot brat the very next time she saw him. And now he would bet the Drayhill-Starlington that she'd come to Threadneedle looking for the boy!

Hunter took the seat next to Branson, grabbed the reins, and launched the brougham into traffic.

Giles couldn't possibly live here; his eyes were too bright, his wit too quick! Felicity bit back her revulsion as she picked her way along a fetid and tightly curved lane that had led her off Shoreditch Road and into Bethnal Green.

She'd heard of the slum and its poverty, but she could never have imagined a wretchedness so deep as this. She stepped around a heap of withered vegetables and the dirt-colored man who guarded it as if it were a mountain of gold. A somber-faced child hung fast to his hand—boy or girl, she couldn't tell, for the matted hair and the ragged clothes. Broken crates and sprung barrels narrowed and twisted the passage, home to rats and a playground to more children.

She had eaten a currant cake in the brightness of Threadneedle Street, and now it threatened to rise in protest over the reek of offal and stagnant water that pooled beneath her shoes. And still she hurried deeper into Bethnal Green, ashamed of her disgust but more determined than ever to find Giles.

As Felicity rounded a corner into a crowded square, her feet slipped out from underneath her, laying her out flat on the cobbles.

"Careful, miss." A young woman with falsely rouged cheeks smiled down at Felicity, helped her to her feet, and handed her the bundle of shirts. " 'Fraid yer lovely dress is ruint f'good."

Felicity swallowed back her nausea. "It's all right. Thank you." Her elbow ached, but she had only wounded her pride and filthied the front of her skirt and bodice, pink linen turned to brown muck. "You've been very nice."

Felicity thought to ask about Giles, but the young woman was gone in the next moment. The street teemed with gin shops and old-clothes stores, and with people who wore one rag atop another.

Finding Giles wasn't going to be easy.

She tucked the bundle against her and tried not to look too closely at the odd characters huddled in the doorways, and leaning drunkenly against lamp posts.

The lane bent again and she found herself at the center of an intersection, facing a ramshackle building whose second floor listed against its neighbor.

THE BEGGAR'S ACADEMY. As tumbledown and dreary as it looked, it was her first sign of hope. If Giles lived here in Bethnal Green, and if he attended school at all, this was probably where she would most likely find word of him.

The rickety door hung open on a single iron hinge. She heard young voices beyond, and another older, more soothing one. The shadows weren't inviting, but the lack of an invitation rarely stopped Felicity. She stepped into the barren anteroom, and then deeper into the gloom.

An elderly woman sat in a chair at the far end of the long, narrow room, reading aloud by the light of a single candle and surrounded by bedraggled but enraptured children.

Such a forlorn place for a school. It wanted windows, and chinking for the walls. A coat of whitewash and a few more lanterns would help dispel some of the shadows. And food in the bellies of the lank-limbed children, and fresh country air in their lungs—

Wherever would one begin to put it right? Felicity swallowed hard against the currant cake and turned to leave.

"Do come in, miss." The old woman had risen on a cane. "I'm Gran McGilly. And you're welcome here at the Beggar's Academy. What is it we can help you with?"

"Oh . . . hello." Felicity tried not to stammer at being caught in midflight. "I'm Felicity Mayf . . . Felicity Claybourne. I'm sorry to interrupt. I was looking for someone—a young boy, about ten years old, I think. Giles Pepperpot. Do you know him?"

Gran McGilly laughed broadly and gathered an armload of boys and girls as she hobbled toward Felicity. "Everyone knows Giles. Don't they, loves?"

The children giggled and agreed as they swarmed around Felicity, small ones and some closer to her own height, every one of them dressed in castoffs.

"Is Giles here?" She looked for him among the upturned faces and cast a hopeful smile over them, ashamed at herself for wanting to run from the horrible smell of unwashed bodies and filthy clothes. She had an uncharitable thought about protecting her purse, but dismissed it entirely.

"Giles doesn't have time for us anymore." Gran McGilly grunted softly as she sat down at the worktable. A little girl scrambled onto her lap. "All full up with schooling, he says. He's a very busy lad, you know."

"Does he live nearby? He helped me recently, and

I'd like to pay him for it." Felicity felt idiotic still clutching the bundle to her chest.

"Like most of the boys around here, he lives where he pleases."

"Well, I just saw him . . . out on Shoreditch—"

Gran McGilly laughed fondly and pulled a gentle comb through the tangled hair of the little girl on her lap. "Oh, you'll not find Giles, unless he wants to be found. Keeps himself two steps ahead of the constabulary. But then that's the fortune of the clever boys in Bethnal Green. They either run ahead, or they'll be run down and crushed."

Felicity hadn't considered that Giles might not want to be found. She'd given him no reason not to trust her—except that she was an outsider. That had become quite clear in the last few minutes. She had no idea that he lived this way, that he had attended this very bleak school for beggars.

Beggars—it seemed such an incriminating word for the innocent, dark-eyed children who watched her and touched her muddied clothes as if she were an oddity at the circus.

"So is this the only classroom?"

"Room for eighty on a good day. We even board a few here at the academy as well, upstairs mostly—the orphans and the ones who've been forgotten."

Felicity moved farther into the room, trying not to imagine where the throat-thickening smell of the sewer was coming from. "How many children do you board?"

"That all depends upon the time of year, and the threat of cholera, the weather, how far the stores can be stretched. We've been here nearly thirty years. Begun by the Ladies League of Ragged School Reform, but they've long ago disbanded; and I'm afraid we're sadly overlooked, but for the occasional kind heart." Gran McGilly gathered up a hank of thin, dull-brown hair from the little girl on her lap and tried to tie it back with a too-short length of twine.

"Here, use this." Felicity started to untie a ribbon from the lacing at her throat, but the woman shook her head slightly, her glance encompassing all the other little girls.

"Oh, we like our hemp ties, don't we Floree? That way all my girls look alike. No fancy ribbons for us."

Felicity felt inadequate and even more out of place. She never thought a simple ribbon could have such meaning. Gran McGilly was a very practical woman. She would have to be, to run an ill-funded school.

"Are you the only teacher here, Mrs. McGilly?"

"Come, call me Gran, everyone does. There's four of us who do the regular work. Cooking, washing up, teaching. We make do."

The idea of leaving these children in the darkness seemed suddenly heartless and sinful. "Would more candles help?"

Gran raised her kindly blue eyes. "Candles would be much appreciated, Mrs. Claybourne."

A perilous thought came to Felicity. "And what about cook pots?"

"And soup!" little Floree said, rubbing her tummy and rolling her eyes. "Yum! I like ta'tato soup."

Gran hugged Floree. "Whatever you can do, Mrs. Claybourne."

"I'll be back. As soon as I can manage. But just now I need to try to find Giles." She hurried to the door, and Gran called back the children who wanted to cling. She felt terribly guilty leaving the frail old woman with all her charges, but she had no choice at the moment.

Felicity gave a feeble wave with her fingers, then rushed out of the Beggar's Academy into the congested square, thinking to take a less fetid breath. But the air had thickened with the stink of ale, and with the lewd comments from doorways of places she didn't want to think about. She must find Giles and give him the shirts as soon as possible; that would make her feel so much more charitable—and so much less like the callous Hunter Claybourne.

She hadn't gotten a half-block through the muck and the unflinching stares when her bundle was yanked out of her arms from behind.

"Hey!" She had come too far to deliver these shirts and, by God's grace, she was going to—

"Giles!" Felicity had never been so happy to see anyone. So much for Giles trying to avoid her! She reached for him, but he recoiled and backed away a step.

"Y' followed me!" he shouted, his face screwed into an angry landscape of grime. "Why, Mrs. Claybourne?"

Felicity hesitated, Gran McGilly's warning still sounding. "Well, I . . ." People were looking at them, looking at her, and murmuring. She felt their stares as she had felt each of Madame Deverie's pinpricks.

"Ooo! Another one of them missionary ladies, Giles?" The crackling voice came from behind her and ended in a croupy cough. "Taken a fancy to yer ugly mug, has she? Wha'd'ya say, Potter?"

"Shut it, Harry!" Giles said, without a glance at the other boy. "And you, Mrs. Claybourne, had best leave while y'can. We're an unsav'ry lot." He shoved the shirt bundle back into her arms with too much malice for a boy of ten.

"Please take them, Giles. I owe you." Felicity tried to press the bundle gently into his hands, but he crossed his arms over his tattered, too-short coat.

"No, you don't. I was paid fine," he said. "I stole a silver teapot and three knives. Now leave, Mrs. Claybourne. This is no place for th'likes of you."

Giles had grown taller in the last day, and tougher. Not a trace remained of the frightened little boy. But she wasn't going to let his blustering keep her from her mission.

"Where do you live, Mr. Pepperpot?"

"His name is Potter, lady."

"Shut yer gob, Harry!" Giles shook a fist at the other

boy, then turned that same anger back on Felicity. "It don't matter where I live."

"And your name is Potter, not Pepperpot?" Claybourne had been right, the boy had lied.

"Go, Mrs. Claybourne. Leave here, and don't come back," he said flatly. He dismissed her with a jerk of his head toward his chums, and started away.

"But the shirts, Giles."

Giles stopped short and returned. He took hold of her arm and started toward one of the shadowy passages. "This way, Mrs. Claybourne."

"I know the way out!" she said. But she followed him, easily committing the route to memory, resigned to today's failure but already planning her next foray. There were missionaries and charity homes all around London. She would see that Giles was entered into one of them, where he would be fed wholesome meals, where he would sleep on a clean mattress under warm blankets. He would get some schooling, and maybe work for Claybourne one day. Now, there was an idea that would take some clever negotiations!

"Do you have a family, Giles?"

He growled and stopped short in the midst of a rivulet of filth. She could feel it oozing past her shoes but refused to move.

"What are you trying to do to me, Mrs. Claybourne?" His face wasn't quite so red, and his voice had smoothed out some. Pride. That was the boy's obstacle.

"I'm just trying to set things right between us."

"Why? They're as right as they ought t' be."

"Because you were honest enough to bring me my writing materials, and I wanted to let you know that I care about what happens to you."

"I don't want ya t' care, Mrs. Claybourne. I don't know you, an' I don't want to. Y'come here tryin' out yer charity on me, and now y' have me chums thinkin' I'm a pulin' babe. Go back to Hampstead."

"But I want to help—"

His fury returned. "Then dump yer charity on someone 'at wants it!"

He took her arm and drove her faster through the twisting passages, dodging heaps of garbage and people as if he knew this alley blindfolded. Then she was thrust suddenly into the bright sunshine and traffic noise of Shoreditch Road.

"And stay away!" Giles shouted. Then his eyes narrowed, and Felicity followed his scowl as a dark and too-familiar brougham drew up beside the broken-down curbing.

Claybourne. And he was leaping at them from the driver's seat.

Felicity turned back to Giles to warn him, but he had vanished into the mean protection of his warren. She planted herself in front of the passage opening and stared down her husband.

"Too late, Mr. Claybourne, he's gone."

Claybourne's gaze settled hard on her, weighing her down with his livid revulsion. His jaw was etched in pale stone and sweat beaded at his temples, dampened his rigid collar. He glanced over her head into the dark passage and a disgusted shudder shook him. When he took hold of her wrist with biting fingers and dragged her to the curb, his bare hand was as cold and damp as a cave wall.

"You have no right, Mr. Claybourne. I'm a grown woman. I can go where I please."

"Take her." Claybourne propelled her roughly toward Branson, then dropped her wrist as if it would somehow contaminate him. He left them standing on the curb and threw open the cab door. The carriage rocked convulsively as he climbed inside and slammed the door shut behind him.

If she hadn't known better, if she hadn't smelled his aftershave instead of whiskey, she'd have thought him drunk.

"You'll have to sit up front with me, Mrs. Claybourne," Branson said, plainly uncomfortable.

Felicity sat down beside him on the driver's bench, more than ready to leave Shoreditch Road for the moment. Her shoes were sopping with filth, and her skirts caked in an unthinkably revolting muck. She had failed Giles and lost the bundle of shirts somewhere along the way, but next time she would come prepared for his rebuff, and with candles for the children of the Beggar's Academy.

"I'm coming back here, Branson."

"The master won't like it, Mrs. Claybourne."

"Good. Because I don't like him."

Hunter shuttered the carriage windows and pressed his head between his palms to contain the pounding. He would have this headache until sleep scrubbed it away, until he cleansed the stench from his nostrils and his lungs. He needed cool, unadulterated air, but he dared not open a window for the piercing sunlight and the stench.

The stench. He thought he had escaped it.

He rode in sweltering darkness the rest of the way home, roused from the reeling blackness by the carriage wheels grating against the gravel drive of Claybourne Manor. He was home.

She met him as he descended the cab, this wife of his who now stunk of the gutter, yet who stood ramrod straight in her outrage against him.

"I won't be treated like a child, Mr. Claybourne!"

His throat clogged and he couldn't breathe for the smell of her. He fought off the blackness that throbbed against his temples.

"Take her around back, Branson," he managed through airless lungs. "To the plow shed."

She looked suddenly and satisfyingly petrified, but seemed to gather her misspent courage an instant later.

"Do you plan to imprison me again, sir?"

He wanted to throttle her, but he balled his hands and left the courtyard for the clean, cold air of the foyer, closing off his ears to his wife's colorful tirade as it weakened to a single strand and then disappeared around the rear of the house.

Bile rose in his throat as he threw open his chamber door. He ripped his coat lining as he wrenched out of the clinging wool. It was soaked through to its buttons with sweat.

She had done this to him. She'd dragged him to that vile place with her insubordination. He'd warned her to leave the boy alone, not to get involved with his kind of corrupt filth. But disobeying his commands was what his wife seemed to do best.

His hands shook as he tore off his damp shirt, scattering buttons into the air as they fell victim to his fumbling struggle. He swabbed his face and chest with cold water from the pitcher.

Damn the woman! He would make his demands crystal clear to her this time. She would remember this warning.

Voices from below his window drew him to finger the curtains apart. Branson was leading Miss Mayfield along the overgrown path toward the plow shed hidden amongst the brambles in the ravine. She was giving the man an earful, shaking her fist at the house, and slapping at his hands.

Hunter's head still pounded, but he had passed through the worst of it. He couldn't let this woman, this transient wife, unstructure his days. He dressed in a clean shirt and coat, grabbed a blanket, then made his way to the rear of the house.

He could hear the rumble of his wife's angry fists thrumming against wooden walls even as he made his way through the undergrowth.

Branson was standing guard at the closed door and solemnly shook his head as Hunter approached. "She's angry, sir."

"So am I," Hunter said flatly. The thumping from

inside the shed echoed the pounding of his headache with remarkable precision.

"Frankly, sir," Branson said with a sniff, looking at the blanket Hunter carried but unwilling to look him in the eye, "I'm not too happy myself. At the moment."

Hunter had never seen Branson with his lower lip thrust out in such a sulk. The man had taken the wrong side in this war. "Don't forget who pays your salary, Branson. Leave now. And keep the staff away until I return to the house."

Branson gave him a suspicious glare and seemed to consider asking why, but nodded stiffly and disappeared through the tangle of brush.

"You're out there Claybourne, you bastard!" She emphasized his name and the epithet with another thunk against the wall. "I can smell you!"

Hunter yanked open the shed door. "I'm surprised you can smell anything but yourself!"

Her fist was raised to strike the wall again. Instead, she leaned against the doorframe and slanted him a belligerent smile. "Ah, you've brought me a blanket, I see. Is this lovely shed to be my new chamber?"

"You seem to favor the slums, Miss Mayfield. This is far better lodging than you'd find anywhere in Bethnal Green."

"As if you'd know or care!"

The woman had grown fierce in her ignorant defense of London's refuse. Filth sought its own kind— he'd learned that truth early in his life. It was time that his wife learned the lesson as well.

Even in the soft afternoon breeze, the stench on her clothes nearly felled him, threatened to send him reeling again. Couldn't she smell it? His stomach stood on end.

"Come with me, wife."

"I'll stay here in my new chamber, thank you. It's more airy than that depressing crypt you call home."

His patience at an end, he grabbed her by the scruff

of the neck and led her like a recalcitrant child into the
leafy bracken, away from the house.

"Where are you taking me?" Felicity panicked and
made a grab for a stand of willow. She missed, and
clung for a moment to Claybourne's coat sleeve to keep
from strangling herself. His broad strides never
changed. "If you kill me out here in the woods, Mr.
Claybourne, someone will miss me and come
looking."

"Who, Miss Mayfield? The ever faithful Mr. Biddle?
Now there's a man to trust."

"Well, I certainly don't trust you, Mr. Claybourne!
Let me go."

But he hurried her down an embankment, catching
her by the elbow when she slid, but otherwise keeping
her at a stiff-arm's distance as they trounced through
the nettles. He stopped abruptly at the edge of a wide
stream.

"Get in," he said.

"Get in?"

Felicity was standing on the brink of a crystal pool
that had been created from a clump of fallen birch. On
any other day this would be a rare place of sylvan
contentment, with its canopy of maple and beech, but
on this particular day, Claybourne held her by the
scruff of the neck and was threatening her life.

"What do you mean, Mr. Claybourne? You want me
to get into the water?"

"Get in and clean yourself up." He let go of her but
left no escape, except across the water.

"Clean up? Do you mean bathe? In here?"

"That's what I mean. Now, into the water."

Felicity laughed and stood her ground. "Sir, I have a
perfectly good bathtub in my chamber. Warm water, a
new lock, a screen—"

"You're not going back into my house until you've
cleansed yourself of Bethnal Green." Claybourne's
breath came and went in short bursts, out of propor-

tion with the energy he'd expended in his uncaring strides. He swabbed sweat from his face with the blanket he had dragged along.

"You can't be serious, Mr. Claybourne." So the front of her dress was caked in muck and looked like she'd used it for a doormat, and she smelled like a cesspit. Where was the man's sense of the absurd? "It's just a little mud. I'll launder it myself—"

"Get in," he repeated, growling as he took a sharp step toward her. "Now."

He was deranged. She had married a madman! Better to humor him and his blazing temper for the moment. She was an excellent swimmer; once in the water she could cross the pool, put the stream between them, and then add the rest of the county as well.

"And don't even consider running from me, Miss Mayfield. My hounds will find you."

Wonderful—a madman who read minds. Very well, wet or dry, she would find a way out of this. She bent to unlace her shoes.

"Leave the shoes," he said, dropping the blanket onto the mossy bank at his feet. He took another deliberate step in her direction, and Felicity stumbled a few yards into the stream until the icy water reached her knees.

"There, Mr. Claybourne," she said, swishing the hem of her skirt across the surface to lift out the worst of the grime. The water clouded as it eddied away from her. "Are you happy now?"

He must not have been. He yanked off his coat, and stalked into the stream toward her.

"What are you doing, sir?" Felicity backed away from the flaming determination in his eyes, but he kept coming. She was chest-deep in the middle of the stream when he put his hands on her shoulders, and shoved her down.

Dear God, he was going to drown her! Felicity held her breath as she went under. She grabbed at Claybourne's trouser legs and plucked at his hands, kicking out at him to get away. But then he grabbed a fistful of sleeve and yanked her to the surface.

Felicity came up splashing violently and sputtering. "Why not just use a washboard on me, Claybourne?"

"Too bad I didn't think of it, woman!" He caught her arms, and held her in front of him. His hair hung in midnight rivulets, and he was soaked to the skin. He looked like a village boy who'd gotten dressed up for Sunday, only to find the creek too inviting to resist.

"Now, Miss Mayfield, you'll take off your clothes."

"I'll do nothing of the sort!" Felicity stumbled backward a step, but he followed and caught her by the skirts.

The current tugged at her, and Claybourne held her against him lest she float away. The water eddied around him and picked up his warmth, gliding past her legs and across her chest.

"Then you'll stand here until you fall unconscious from the cold. You're filthy, and I won't have you in my house."

"So each time I return from the slums, you're going to try to drown me in the stream?"

Heat poured off him in billowing sheets and Felicity soaked it up greedily. "There won't be a next time!"

Felicity opened her mouth to contradict him but knew there was no point to it. She would fulfill her promise to the children of the Beggar's Academy, with or without Claybourne's consent.

"Why did you come after me, Mr. Claybourne? What does it matter to you if I want to spend a few of my own pennies to help a child? To repay him for the shirt *you* tore, I might add."

"I came after you because you're a fool, Miss Mayfield."

"*I'm* a fool? You're the one who is standing over his wife, forcing her to bathe in a frigid stream. Can I get out now?"

Claybourne released her. "Not until this dress and

any other piece of clothing that touched the streets of Bethnal Green are lying right there." He pointed to the bankside as he stalked out of the stream. "I'll give you three minutes to cover yourself with that blanket."

His shirt was wet and fascinatingly transparent against the well-carved back muscles beneath. She wondered how a man who spent his days holed up in an office like a mole could boast the brawn of a laborer. He turned, and she found the same definition in his chest. Well-worked, well-formed muscle. Planes and angles that begged her hand.

"Undress—wife."

She'd been staring, boldly. Had her mouth been hanging open, too? "You'll keep your back turned, Mr. Claybourne."

"For as long as I hear movement."

Felicity's legs were beginning to cramp; she needed to get out of the stream. She muttered as she worked her way out of the wet bodice and skirt, and the first of her petticoats. Her camisole and the other petticoats were clean and unmarked by the mud, but now her drawers threatened to fall off with the weight of the water. She slogged her way out of the stream.

Claybourne was staring at her when she raised her head.

"How long have you been watching, Mr. Claybourne?"

"Long enough." He'd been chewing on a shoot of sedge grass and now spat it into the brush. He took hold of her shoulders and turned her in a circuit.

"Do I pass inspection, sir?" Felicity followed his gaze down the front of her and immediately wished she had taken up wearing stays. Her camisole might as well have been window glass, for all the details it exposed. She could plainly see color and puckering definition at the tips of her breasts. Claybourne had seen, too. His hands blazed hot against her arms, and his breathing had gone ragged. She ought to run or find fault with his staring, but that bewildering urge to rise up on her toes and kiss him rooted her to the spot. His scowl darkened, and then the blanket came around her, warm from a patch of sunlight.

"Come with me," he said, starting away.

Feeling deserted and dismissed, Felicity followed after him, hobbled by the blanket that bunched at her ankles. When she didn't follow quickly enough, he came back for her, lifting her easily into his arms.

"I can walk, sir."

He didn't reply, but kept his gaze transfixed on the trail in front of him, and finally on the unkempt garden path. He strode with her past Mrs. Sweeney and Earnest, past Branson who was unpacking a crate of dishes, and up the stairs to her chamber. Someone had lit a fire in the grate.

Claybourne stood her upright in front of the hearth like one of the Egyptian mummies on display at the British Museum. Then he left the room without another word. She heard his chamber door slam across the hall.

At least he hadn't drowned her. Perhaps she wouldn't be so lucky next time. She unwound herself from the blanket, then wrapped herself in her nightrobe and made to the window just in time to see him step up into his carriage.

"Pompous, stiff-necked . . . miscreant!" she shouted against the pane.

But Branson was already pulling away with his surly, soggy-haired cargo. She hoped she had cost Claybourne a dozen of his bloody contracts.

But now she had a contract of her own to fulfill—her promise to the children of the Beggar's Academy.

Chapter 10

Felicity spent the rest of the week collecting candle stubs and worn-out china, all of which she replaced with the hoarded goods from the crates. As she unpacked a mountain of new blankets, she set aside a dozen ragged-edged ones for the children—and for Giles, if she could ever find him again.

Mrs. Sweeney squealed in delight at the sight of all the newly unpacked kitchen tools, and didn't seem to notice the dented pots and bent spoons disappearing into the plow shed with the rest of the contraband.

Felicity kept a careful accounting of everything she took. When Uncle Foley returned with her portion of the profits, she would pay Claybourne back for every candle stub and every chipped bowl.

The house no longer frightened her, and Claybourne and his blustering rarely did. She had set the staff to hacking away at the choke weeds that strangled off Claybourne Manor from the sunlight. Earnest took to the garden with enthusiasm, and soon became expert at maneuvering the new lawn mower around the hedges and trees.

If Claybourne noticed the taming of the wilderness into a nearly workable garden, he never said anything.

And neither did she, for fear that he would command her to stop. He allowed her the use of his library, and didn't seem to mind that she had peeled back the drapes in the dining room and taken down the dreary bushes that blocked the light. He occasionally engaged her in stilted conversations, usually about some minor domestic matter, sometimes about George Hudson.

She sometimes fancied that he enjoyed her company.

And she sometimes fancied that she enjoyed his.

The thought startled her one evening as she sat opposite him at the dining-room table, which had quadrupled in length and now had a dozen chairs stationed around it, awaiting guests who would probably never be invited.

He had arrived home in time to take dinner with her—nothing more than a coincidence, she was certain, since he had seemed startled to see her enter the dining room. But he now sat easily in his chair, unlike his posture outside Claybourne Manor, where his shoulders were always squared and his eyes always alert.

She liked him this way: his guard down, and his eyes gone to the milky gray of smoke instead of black obsidian. The back of her ears began to burn, and made her think of his wet shirt and the burnished muscle that had shown beneath.

"You were about to say, Miss Mayfield?"

Felicity caught herself staring at him again, and gave a quick glance at her bowl of stew before raising her chin again.

"I had been thinking about what you just said—the possibility of a telegraph cable being laid across the Atlantic. Imagine if such a thing existed right now: when my uncle landed in New York, he could just send me a telegram telling me that he had arrived safely."

"Yes, he could."

She saw him try to hide a smile with a finger to the

corner of his mouth, and wondered if he thought her an imbecile. She tried again.

"I've read about the plans to lay a cable between Dover and Calais—have you a financial interest in that, Mr. Claybourne?"

He lowered his brow at her as if she were his rival in business. "It's no secret. I have secured the contract to supply the cable, a design based upon the specifications of the project engineers. Whether the project succeeds or fails, I will have my profit."

"Why doesn't that surprise me, Mr. Claybourne?" He was so very sure of himself, born to the certainty of his wealth and privilege. "And what about the cable across the Atlantic? Will you be taking your profits from that as well?"

"Not for a few years yet."

"But you must be looking forward to such a grand achievement and its advantage to your business. You can decide to buy an American railway in the morning, telegraph your bid before lunch, and learn of the seller's acceptance before you go home that night to eat your plate of stew."

He laughed mutely and raised a brow, as if the thought of doing business by telegraph across the ocean hadn't yet occurred to him. "Yes," he said, gliding his forefinger around the edge of his glass.

"I will be going to London again tomorrow, Mr. Claybourne."

"For what reason?"

More half-truths, but they would have to serve.

"For many reasons. My Northumberland project for one, and to consult with Mr. Dolan. Also I need to see Madame Deverie. If I don't return for the final fitting, the wardrobe you spent so much of your money on will go to waste."

He hadn't moved a muscle. "If you come home stinking of—"

"I won't, Mr. Claybourne." Felicity touched her

napkin to her mouth. "You can be sure that you'll not smell Bethnal Green on me ever again. I prefer to bathe in my chamber—in warm water, thank you very much."

He scowled at that and left the table. His footfalls echoed on his way toward his library. He would probably be there all night.

Yet she had heard him leaving the library after dark, had seen him carrying a lantern away from the house, perhaps to wander the wilds of the estate. She'd caught him on the staircase the night before, after one of his wanderings—his waistcoat open, his shirt stuck to his damp skin, and bits of wood splinters caught up in his hair and on his trousers.

He had grunted and passed by her without a comment.

He was a strange man. And too handsome by far.

But he had accepted her reasons for going to London. And every morning for the next full week, Felicity loaded up her new portmanteau with as much as she could carry, stuffed it into the boot of the carriage, and rode with her husband into the City.

She hadn't promised not to go to Bethnal Green; she'd only promised not to smell of it.

"Christmastide in May!"

The boys and girls of the Beggar's Academy shrieked in perfect delight over each and every item Felicity unpacked. Chipped bowls, broken bits of candle, socks with holes—

"Blankets, this time!" Gran McGilly clapped her craggy hands against her withered cheeks and sighed. "And more candles! Dear child, every day you come bearing the treasures of Solomon! The Beggar's Academy thanks you, each and every one of us."

Blankets and pots and candle stubs could never take the place of fragrant meadowlands and pure sunlight. How could she hope to bring the children what they truly needed?

"It's my pleasure, Gran." Felicity would have to explain later that this would be the last of it for a while. Until she could earn some money of her own.

Hardly Christmas.

She lifted little Jonathan onto the table to put clean socks on his filthy feet. The socks were too big, and without shoes would last only a day, but for the moment his little toes would be warm. He winced as she lifted his foot.

"I'm sorry, Jonathan. Have you got yourself a sore here?" More than a sore, the boy's foot was covered with cuts in various stages of healing, and a few long, pink scars. "What happened?"

"Jonathan is a mudlark," Gran said, from her pot at the cookstove.

"A mudlark?" Felicity had heard the term but didn't really know its meaning.

Jonathan sighed, obviously impatient with these adult anxieties. "It's nothin'. I get cut steppin' on glass buried in the mud, miss." He hooked his foot with his hands and inspected the sole. "Looks good compared t' some days."

"In the mud? Where?"

"The Thames, mostly," he said, letting Felicity peer at his feet. "Coal is m' biggest business. I gets the stuff what falls from the barges."

"The Thames is a sewer," Felicity said, trying not to let her horror show. "You shouldn't be walking in it."

"I don't mind, miss. Glass sells good. When it cuts me, I find it, then I sells it. A fair trade, I warrant."

"Why don't you wear shoes?"

He shrugged and picked a dark thing from beneath his jagged fingernail. "Haven't any. 'Sides, they don't last long, being wet and muddy all a'time."

Felicity made a mental note to acquire a steady supply of ointments and thick-soled boots. The list was dreadfully long, and her time was so short. If she was to make a success of her new travel guide, and earn the money for it, she would need to spend a few weeks traveling through Northumberland. And then there was always Giles. She hadn't given up trying to find him again.

She stayed through the late afternoon, unpacking, helping with supper, and finally reading aloud from a book she had discovered among Claybourne's things. *Robin Hood.* They seemed to love that the best.

As she read, she became as enchanted as the children. Not with the valiant man who shunned his wealth and station to ease the plight of the downtrodden, but with the settledness of the school, the sense of home she had found there among the children. She'd never really had a home, and this one felt very good.

But the afternoon was lengthening, and she needed to spend some time looking for Giles before she had to race home ahead of Claybourne and scrub her skin raw and her clothes threadbare, just to keep his prickly sense of smell appeased. So far, he didn't suspect a thing.

She said good-bye to the children, then turned to Mrs. McGilly. "I must go look for Giles. He's eluded me—"

"Mrs. Claybourne," Gran whispered. Her face looked terribly solemn. "You won't find Giles."

"Why not? Is he ill?"

"The fool was caught in Chancery Lane a few days ago, cutting a purse, it seems. The police have him."

"The police?" Felicity's heart sank. She had saved him from Claybourne, only to lose him to the magistrates. "Where was he taken?"

Gran shook her head and sighed. "No one seems to know. The poor boy could be in Newgate by now."

"But he's just a child!"

"That doesn't matter a whit to the magistrates."

"Well, it matters to me!" She kissed Gran on her leathery cheek. "I'll be back tomorrow."

Felicity found a hackney on Shoreditch and hired it to Chancery Lane. The station house was small and crammed with every kind of person. She worked her way to the counter, and finally gained the attention of a stiff-coated officer.

"Excuse me, sir. I'm looking for information about a pickpocket."

He didn't look up. "Had your purse snatched, miss?"

"No. I want to know where a young prisoner might have been taken. He was arrested a few days ago on Chancery Lane."

"We get 'em in dozens, miss." The man seemed thoroughly bored. "Do ya have a name?"

"Giles Pepperpot, or Potter, perhaps."

The officer muttered about long hours and low pay as he leafed backward through a book of names and dates. "Yes, here it is. Pepperpot."

Well, at least she'd found him. "What's to be done with him?"

The officer studied the page and then consulted another book. "Looks like it's already been done."

"Done! What has been done? Dear God, he's only a boy."

"Convicted of theft and . . ." The officer fumbled with a pair of spectacles as Felicity rode out her fears, waiting to hear the worst. "Hmmm. Sent north to—"

Felicity slapped the countertop and drew a dozen stares. "To where, sir?"

The officer peered at her over the top of his rims, his opinion of her station in life having drooped along with his frown. "To an apprentice school. Are you his mother?"

"To a school?" Felicity's heart lightened. Giles wasn't in prison after all; he was in a school. He would learn a trade, just as she had hoped for him.

"Does it say where the school is?" Feeling quite charitable, Felicity smiled and peered over the counter, trying to read the name upside down.

"Blenwick."

"Wonderful!" Felicity couldn't believe her luck. Blenwick was on her way to Northumberland. She would take Giles a package of sweets to share among his schoolmates, and maybe slip him another shirt. Surely a young man at school could find a use for a bag of treats from a friend.

"I'm leaving, Mr. Claybourne."

Hunter looked up from his accounts and found his wife dressed for travel in a functional brown suit done up to her neck. He liked her better in wet linen, but he couldn't very well tell her that. She dropped her new portmanteau on the floor. It gave a decisively leaden thud meant entirely for him.

"You're not going anywhere," he said flatly, returning to his figures. He'd come home at noon to finish his work in the quiet coolness of his library, but peace and quiet were nearly impossible anymore. And then there was her scent, that faint coiling of vanilla that could stop him dead in his thoughts and dangle him over a cliffside.

Crinoline whispered from beneath her skirt as she crossed the carpet to his desk. He refused to look up again. He'd given his order. She was staying.

"I'm leaving," she said. "Today. There's a running of the cheese in Brimsleigh in the morning, and I want to be there to report on it firsthand."

"What the hell is a running of the . . . never mind." Tired of this argument, Hunter was about to repeat his denial and send her to her chamber when she plucked the pen out of his fingers.

"I'm a pest, aren't I, Mr. Claybourne?"

"A plague," he said, grabbing for the pen but finding a drop of ink dangling from his fingertip instead.

"You resent my existence." She replaced the pen in the holder.

"Entirely." Hunter wiped the ink off his finger and watched her saunter toward the windows.

"Then why keep me here under your roof? So dangerously near London, where I might sully your name. Why not send me out of town where no one knows our connection? Be rid of me."

"No."

She seemed to ignore him and gave a yank to the drapes. He kept them closed for the lack of a view through the tangled bushes that had always pressed at the windows. But now the sun leaped through the clean panes to wash the room in glorious brightness. It launched gilded shafts across the carpet, and caught at her smile.

"Are you so fond of me then, Mr. Claybourne?" She threw open another set of drapes and the library brightened further, warming the dark wood and touching off the rich colors of the book bindings.

"I'm fond of order."

"Then you cannot possibly be fond of me." She opened the last set of drapes and turned to him, her gaze steady and clear, her hair brighter still. "I've brought nothing but disorder to your life, haven't I?"

"Yes."

"And that is the way I am. I cannot change my behavior any more than you can change yours."

"I have no reason to change mine."

Her laughter seemed too indulgent. "No, of course not. You are in perfect control of everything and I am perfectly out of control."

"Exactly."

"Then why keep me underfoot? Let me do what I do best—quietly explore the byways of Britain—while you do whatever it is you do. We had never heard of each other before this mess began, and we were both perfectly happy. I see no reason why we can't return to that state."

"You're married to me now."

"But not for long. I need this work, Mr. Claybourne. I need to keep my travel gazettes popular and in the public eye. Come next May, when you and I are officially divorced, I'll be destitute if I can't find a job. And I'd rather not take up work as a needlewoman in one of those Southwark slopshops, working for six pennies a day. Now there would be a scandal for you: Hunter Claybourne's ex-wife reduced to poverty, dying horribly of septic fingers from sewing men's trousers."

Hunter hadn't thought of that: what his wife would do once she was no longer his wife. God knows she couldn't count on that uncle of hers.

"And, if I can't pursue my living, I'll have to return to Bethnal Green whenever I can, to make a friend or two who might put me up when I'm reduced to living on the street. You wouldn't want that, would you?"

Her argument held a certain amount of logic. She *would* be on her own again at the end of their marriage, left to her own devices. He couldn't very well let her end up as she described, as bait for his critics. And he desired not to think of her living the life of a needlewoman, her luminous eyes dulled by fatigue, never getting the stink of her impoverishment out of her hair. His stomach flipped; a sheen of sweat broke out across his upper lip.

He wiped it away and stood up, restless with the persistent image of his wife dressed in tatters. "You may leave tonight," he said.

"I can?" Her eyes lit up and she threw her arms around his neck. And was that her mouth that brushed the underside of his jaw, just beneath his ear?

There was something unsettlingly right in her spontaneity. Had she been a real wife, she might have done the same if she'd been pleased about a new hat or a night at the theater. Had he been a real husband, he might have been just as pleased to receive such an embrace. As it was, he couldn't let his arms fit too naturally around her—there was great risk in that kind of contact—so he let them hang at his side. She drew away quickly, looking every bit as uncomfortable as he felt.

Her forehead crinkled like a flight of wary geese. "This isn't a trick, Mr. Claybourne?"

"No trick. You have my permission. But I insist you leave me an itinerary."

"Gladly, Mr. Claybourne." She grabbed the pen and a sheet of paper and began to scribble. "I expect to spend tonight in Peterborough . . ."

Hunter sat down and straightened the pen holder. It was a different one than he'd always used, made of burled wood instead of pewter. But he'd found it on his desk one day—the same day he'd found the first bowl of flowers sitting on the library hearth—and so he'd begun to use it. He knew that she had brought it, but hadn't found the right moment to mention it. Not that he needed to.

"You're not to sleep on benches, or barter for food and lodging, and I want a telegram every day stating where you are and where you expect to be the next day."

"Every day?" She was frowning again and replaced the pen with a clunk. "Then that's the trick—I knew you'd snag me with something. I haven't the money for all that, Mr. Claybourne. I have barely enough for food."

"Give me your purse."

She eyed him over the bridge of her nose, but finally settled the bag on the blotter. He carefully counted out ten pounds from his desk drawer, then poured the coins into her drawstring bag and handed it back to her. "This should last two weeks—if you're careful not to give it away."

She peered into her purse as if he'd just filled it with poisonous snakes.

"No, Miss Mayfield. This isn't a loan. It's just another expense. See. You've become a column in my ledger." He pointed to a column of numbers whose sum had grown faster than its length. He had titled the column *Miss M.*

"That's me?" she asked, coming around the side of his desk.

"Added to what I just gave you . . ." He entered the

expense as *Travels to Northumberland*, trying all the while to ignore her warmth as she stood beside him, peering over his arm. The effort drained the blood from his fingers and sent it rushing elsewhere. "The total comes to eight hundred and ten."

"Well! I never thought I'd be reduced to a column of numbers, Mr. Claybourne. But I do appreciate your taking on my expenses. And I do consider this outlay, and all the rest of the money you've spent on me, a loan; I plan to repay you as soon as Uncle Foley returns—"

"From the gold fields. Yes, yes, I'm sure you will."

She lifted a defiant chin. "He'll come back, Mr. Claybourne."

Hunter felt an odd twinge of conscience and regretted his comment, as well as the sarcasm he'd injected into it. "Another few months, Miss Mayfield, and you may hear from him."

"Yes, Mr. Claybourne. May I go now? I need to catch the train."

Hunter was struck by the starkness of her simple declaration. Oddly, he thought of her chamber, and the island of abundance she would leave behind; and the dining room with its too-long table and all those chairs.

"I see your bag is packed," he said, for fear of saying anything more significant.

"I was leaving here today, no matter what you might have said to the contrary."

He refused to rise to her challenge. "Have you everything you need for your trip? A water bottle? Spectacles to keep the cinders from your eyes?"

"Do you wish to inspect my bag, sir? Or take an inventory?"

She stood in the doorway, holding open the handles of her new portmanteau, her stalwart bonnet failing to subdue her bountiful hair, and dreams of adventure pinking her cheeks. No doubt already celebrating her independence from him.

"You needn't look at me like that, Mr. Claybourne. I can assure you that I'm taking nothing more than you've given me."

"I didn't think you had, Miss Mayfield."

Yes, he would find his jealously-guarded peace again when she was gone. And the solitary stillness of a tomb.

"Good-bye, Mr. Claybourne."

It was only then, with her footsteps receding down the hallway far away from him, that he realized she wore no wedding band. Nothing to mark her as married. No outward indication that she belonged to him.

This would not do.

Felicity suspected Claybourne's motives immediately. He'd been too reasonable and accepting of her travel plans. He'd even sent her to the train station in his brougham. She half-expected him to stop her, to ambush her on the way, but she had arrived at the station in plenty of time to board.

Branson hadn't looked too pleased as he watched her take a seat in a crowded, third-class, nearly open-roofed car. The wind had come up and flapped at the canvas above her head.

"You're riding in this thing?" he said, hiking himself onto the running board and peering over the side walls into the car. "All the way to Northumberland? If it rains you'll be drenched."

"It's all I can afford." A big-boned woman sat down beside Felicity and rammed her against the wall to make room for three other passengers. Felicity usually traveled second-class, more comfortable and not nearly as crowded, but it wouldn't be the first time she'd pinched her pennies. She would return as much of her travel advance to Claybourne as she possibly could. The last thing she wanted to do was to get used to his obscene fortune.

"You're married to a very wealthy man, Mrs. Claybourne. The master can well afford to buy a railcar of his own. You needn't ride in the open with a canvas over your head, packed in with all these . . ." He rolled his eyes and spoke in a hush that everyone could hear. "All these *people.*"

She held his hand. "I'll be all right, Branson. This is my trip, not Mr. Claybourne's. Besides, I'm used to this." The sky looked a bit threatening, but Felicity chose to ignore it. She had managed to hold most of the storms in her life at bay, but there wasn't anything she could do about just plain rain.

The train gave a whistle and with a great breath of steam, the car lurched forward. "I'll miss you, Branson!"

He followed along, anxiously clutching the sides of the car as he stood on the running board. "Take care of yourself, Mrs. Claybourne."

He let go and waved his hat at her. Felicity waved back. He was a sweet man. They were all sweet at Claybourne Manor, except for Claybourne himself. He was . . . well, like no other man she'd ever met.

At Hertford she took tea with the station master, an old friend of her father's; at Biggleswaite another third-class car was added, leaving her time to visit with the postal master, another friend of the family.

But she still had three hours or more to Peterborough, so she climbed aboard the new car, settled herself into a corner seat, then closed her eyes for a nap.

"That's an awful pretty bonnet, miss."

Felicity looked up into a tiny face and pair of soft brown eyes that she would expect to find on a milk cow. The little girl sat directly across from her, clutching a ragged, redheaded doll and a bulging flour sack.

Felicity smiled. "Why, thank you."

"What's your name?"

"Felicity. What's yours?"

The little face lit up. "Mine is Kerrie Slade." **Kerrie**

looked into the face of her doll and sighed. "I don't know the name of my dolly. She was just given to me."

Kerrie laid the doll on her lap, revealing a piece of paper pinned to her shawl.

"Are you traveling alone?" Felicity asked, hoping the girl wasn't, because Kerrie was a good five years younger than Giles.

Kerrie nodded. "By myself."

"Where are your parents?" Felicity leaned forward to read the note, and her spirits plummeted.

Workhouse—Waincross.

"My mama went up to heaven last week. But I'm six now, and I'm going to school to learn to sew like my mama did."

Felicity wanted to cry. Kerrie was going to a workhouse!

The brave little girl scooted forward in the seat and touched her toes to the floor. "I'm going to Waincross, Miss Felicity. Where are you going?"

Felicity had hoped to make Peterborough tonight, but it looked like she'd be stopping sooner. "Well, fancy a thing like that, Miss Kerrie Slade. I'm going to Waincross, too."

When the rains came and drove sideways into the car from under the canvas roof, Felicity tucked Kerrie under her new woolen shawl and took the brunt of the cold herself. Night fell and Kerrie slept, leaving Felicity to hold her. She'd heard about these workhouses, and thanked God that Giles had been sent to an apprentice school instead. Giles would learn reading and a trade; the children in a workhouse were bonded out to heartless, greedy men who paid them nothing, stealing their skills along with their childhood.

Kerrie shifted in Felicity's arms, scrubbed at her nose, then settled in deeper. She had certainly collected her share of lost puppies since she married Claybourne. Now, what to do with this one?

The train was on time at Waincross, but no one was waiting for Kerrie. Felicity wasn't about to drag her through the downpour looking for the workhouse. She took a room in an inn that was owned by a longtime friend, Mrs. Pagett, and then treated Kerrie to what must have been the most wonderful meal of the little girl's life. Kerrie slept through the night and awakened like a robin in springtime, ready to frolic among the flowers at the rear of the inn.

Felicity left Kerrie with Mrs. Pagett, and went alone to stand outside the workhouse. It was a dreary, ill-kept enterprise that looked like a prison—just as she suspected it would. She returned to Mrs. Pagett's inn without ever having set foot inside.

"I can't leave her in that dreadful place, Mrs. Pagett!" Felicity sat in the morning room, her head hanging heavily in her hands, and watched Kerrie through the kitchen door. The little girl was scrubbing happily and efficiently at that morning's dishes, singing brightly about a duck on a spillway. "And I surely can't take her with me to Northumberland."

"Such a bloody shame!" Mrs. Pagett said, plucking at a flower embroidered into the tablecloth. "That workhouse is a disgrace. The vicar and I've been trying to shut down it for years. Not a bit of luck at all. The parish governors don't seem to have a human bone in their bodies."

Felicity couldn't help thinking of Claybourne and his hostile, undisguised prejudice toward the poor. He was enormously wealthy, owned stock in railways and factories, and who knew what else. Now she'd begun to wonder if he ever gave a thought to those whose labors made his wealth possible. Was he the kind of man who would allow innocent children to work under such horrible conditions—all in the name of profits?

Mrs. Pagett got up from the table and stood at the kitchen door. "Such a sweet-natured little thing. They'll beat it out of her at the workhouse. Oh, Felicity, girl. Tell me if you think I'm overstepping myself, but . . . do you think that I might arrange to keep her here with me?''

"Here?"

"I could use the help, and Kerrie could surely use the home."

The answer was almost too simple. Felicity thought of Jonathan and Floree and all the other children who needed such care, and she nearly cried. "Oh, yes, Mrs. Pagett. I think that's a grand idea!''

"I'll check with the vicar; he'll know what to do." Mrs. Pagett took Felicity's hands. "You're an angel, Felicity Mayfield.''

"No, you're the angel, Mrs. Pagett." Felicity didn't have the heart to tell her that she was now Felicity Claybourne, the much-indebted wife of a man who quite possibly would allow little Kerrie to starve— given a ha'penny's profit.

Felicity left Waincross as the day clouded over again, and it grew ever colder and wetter the farther north she traveled. She was glad she had worn her new dark-blue wool suit; glad, too, that she had decided to take her chances without stays. Travel was hellish with whalebone cutting into her hips for hours at a time. An hour north of York, just before dark, she disembarked to change trains for Blenwick and Giles's apprentice school.

She had missed the infamous cheese race in Brimsleigh, so she might as well start her plans anew. There was a turf maze near the parish church, and the Boar's Noggin Tavern boasted of a connection to Richard the Third. Perhaps tomorrow she could treat Giles to an outing and a lunch—

"Felicity Claybourne?"

Felicity had been about to climb the steps to the third-class car but stopped and turned to find a conductor peering at her in a way that reminded her far too much of Mr. Cobson.

"Who did you want?" she asked, deciding not to offer any more information than she absolutely had to.

"Please come with me, ma'am. There's been a change in your ticket."

"What kind of change?"

"This way, if you please." He snatched her ticket out of her hand and started toward the rear of the train.

"But there's nothing wrong with my ticket, sir!" Indeed the new car was still third-class, but it was protected by a solid metal roof and rain-stopping leather curtains along the roofline.

Felicity ran to catch up, but the conductor had stopped at the last passenger car.

First class. This was Claybourne's doing.

"I want my ticket back." Felicity made a grab for the one the conductor had stolen. She missed.

"Your ticket's no good, Mrs. Claybourne. It's this car or none at all." He opened the door and motioned her inside.

A paraffin lamp glowed from a double sconce, and a new boiled-water heater warmed the compartment like a cozy parlor, wrapping her in its welcome as it poured heat out into the night air. She had always envied the people who traveled in these private coaches, a third of a railcar in size and large enough to permanently house three families from Bethnal Green.

"We're in station for only a few minutes more, miss. Please climb aboard."

"No, thank you, sir." If Claybourne thought he could control her all the way from London, he would soon learn otherwise. "And if you won't give me back my ticket, I'll go purchase another, and wait for the next train."

The conductor's worried eyes darted up over the top of her head and fixed there with an anxious frown. "Sorry, miss, there's not another train to Blenwick until tomorrow."

"Very well; I'll just stay the night on a bench in the station." Felicity turned from the conductor and would have stalked off, but there was a very tall and very familiar obstacle in her way.

"You're not going anywhere, wife. You'll be staying with me."

Chapter 11

"I'm not riding in the same train with you, Mr. Claybourne. This is my trip—"

Not wanting the woman to make any more of a scene, Hunter scooped her into his arms and stepped up into his private compartment.

"I'll not have my wife riding like a guernsey in an open car."

"And I won't ride with an ass!"

Hunter slammed the door behind him. He'd found her. It had taken him all day. And he was so damned relieved, he couldn't speak.

"You've imprisoned me again, Mr. Claybourne. Don't you ever tire of this game?"

She looked like something dredged up from a drowning. Her bonnet was missing; her hair was wet to the scalp. Her eyes were as big and bright as the moon, and blazing with anger.

"Where have you been, Miss Mayfield?" he finally managed.

"I haven't been anywhere yet, Mr. Claybourne, though God knows I've tried. Now, step aside and let me out of here!"

The train shuddered forward, and Hunter caught

hold of the luggage rack to keep from pitching to the floor.

"You have remarkable timing, Mr. Claybourne." She threw her portmanteau onto the seat.

His scowling wife seemed entirely unaffected by the jerking movement of the train, as untroubled as a sailor riding out a violent storm on his sea legs.

"Tell me where you have been!" he demanded.

She lifted her chin. "Are you following me?"

Hunter would have fired Tilson for such insubordination. He tossed his hat into the rack. "You were to telegraph me, Miss Mayfield."

"I've only been away one night. You knew where I would be." She settled herself into the seat and seemed to be sizing him up for a coffin.

"You were to stop in Peterborough last night. You didn't."

"I . . ." She dropped her gaze, then unwound herself from her soggy cocoon and stretched her hands out toward the heater. "I was detained along the way."

"Detained how?" He remembered the delight in her eyes when that reporter had embraced her. He hadn't slept well last night for the memory of it, and for wondering who she would meet in her travels, who might be waiting to enfold her in his arms. He'd wondered most of all why the thought of her meeting another man set his blood to boiling.

"I stopped to see a friend," she said, picking hairpins from her hair.

"A friend?" Hunter asked, taking his usual place in the center of the seat, chiding himself for sounding too much like a jealous husband. He was jealous of his name, and his time, nothing more. He had purchased a wedding band to simplify their relationship. But now the damn thing had begun to burn a hole in his vest pocket.

"I visited with a woman I've known since I was a child. She lives in Waincross, runs an inn there." She seemed too easy with her explanation, fluffing her hair and speaking offhandedly in that smoke-wrapped voice that warmed the air around him.

"You should have telegraphed your changed itinerary."

"I didn't have time to send a telegraph, Mr. Claybourne."

"You should have made time." Hunter waited for her response, but she only blinked twice, sighed her dismissal of the subject, and began unlacing her shoes.

"I'm wildly curious, Mr. Claybourne: how did you find me?"

The woman must have thought she was invisible. She was an uncommon passenger. "It seems you have more than a few friends along the Great Northern, Miss Mayfield. And the telegraph is a powerful tool for reaching ahead."

"That doesn't explain what brings you here. This railway line ends at Blenwick, Mr. Claybourne. You are following me."

Hunter snorted and unfolded the *Times*. "I've come on business."

"So have I." She glared at him as she hung her shawl on a hook. "I hope you don't expect me to return to Claybourne Manor with you."

"Go wherever you like." Hunter forced his attention away from the cynical shake of her head and went back to the news of the day. But his gaze was drawn to her movements. She leaned back against the side wall of the compartment and stuck her legs out in front of her on the seat. So comfortable, so settled. She was like a stream that always found its way down the mountain, no matter the obstacle in its path.

He still wanted to know where she'd been the night before. He'd wandered the shadowed halls of Claybourne Manor, dodging sticks of furniture he'd never seen before, following fragrant trails that lead to clouds of cut flowers. Twice he'd started toward her chamber, only to remember that she was gone.

"This woman in Waincross," he said, lowering the newspaper to study her more closely. "How do you know her?"

"Is this an investigation, or are you bored, Mr. Claybourne?"

It had taken Hunter years to train his staff not to answer his questions with other questions. *She* did it constantly. He'd been allotted only a single year with his wife—the chances were slim that she would change in so short a time. He decided to look bored.

He gave a half-shrug. "Just idly curious, Miss Mayfield."

She studied him, her gaze touching his eyes, then riding leisurely across his mouth until a quickening rose up in his chest. She offered him a grudging smile.

"Fair enough. Mrs. Pagett and her husband were friends of my father's." She gathered her stockinged feet up under her skirt and covered her legs with a blanket. "We knew everyone along the railway. Mother died when I was six. From then on, I traveled with Father. I lived where he lived; learned geology, surveying, drafting, geometry—"

"Geometry?" Hunter greatly doubted this knowledge of hers; the woman had a mind that ran three miles ahead of itself. He couldn't imagine her fastened to a chair for hours on end, writing out mathematical problems.

"Don't look so skeptical, Mr. Claybourne. I learned from Father's engineering crews, and from him, of course. I actually helped survey now and again when a team was short a member."

"You surveyed for your father?" A female surveyor? It wasn't possible. Yet she seemed unconcerned with his disbelief, wasn't even paying attention to him as she tucked herself deeper beneath the blanket.

"And I did some drafting. I think that was my favorite thing. In any case, it's left me a very good judge of railways."

"You think so?" Now he was certain she was taking

him down a spur line only to dump him off a cliff. Let her play out her little game. It was actually beginning to amuse him. "Then what of this railway? The Blenwick Line?"

She clicked her tongue. "The grade is too steep for the size of the locomotive, and the curves are too tight." She turned and shook her head. "Frankly, Mr. Claybourne, it's a bit dangerous—"

"Dangerous? Explain yourself." Hunter sat forward, his elbows on his knees, ready to watch her bragging come to a sputtering halt. Instead, she sat up and squinted out the window into the darkening evening and seemed to be making a calculation of some sort.

"The track along here should have been cut through a tunnel, or should have been half again as long to accommodate the steepness of the grade. A one foot rise for every one hundred feet of distance would have been perfect; one-in-sixty is too much for the curves. But of course, a tunnel is much more expensive—"

"And you're so sure this is a one-in-sixty?"

Her nod was emphatic and troubled. "Father would never have allowed the track to be laid."

"And yet still you ride on the Blenwick?" Hunter didn't want to make much of her speculation, but she seemed so sure of herself, and still not at all concerned whether he believed her.

"I plan to make certain that my readers know the dangers to be avoided, along with the sights to be seen. I'll recommend the post road that runs through the valley."

"I see. So, your father told you the shortcomings of the Blenwick Line?"

"No. I can tell by the pull and the speed—and that occasional shudder."

"Which?"

She held her hand up and listened for a moment to the steady clatter of the rails. "There, did you feel that?"

He had, and was amazed.

"Thank you," he said, pulling a notepad from his coat pocket. The problem was at least worth investigating.

"Thank you? What for, Mr. Claybourne?"

Hunter jotted down a reminder to himself, then looked up at his inquisitive wife. "Because I have been offered a quarter interest in the Blenwick Line and I hadn't decided if I should invest or not."

She looked horrified. "I wouldn't."

"I won't." Hunter allowed himself to smile at her earnestness, oddly pleased that she would care to advise him against ruin. When she smiled back, his heart took a capricious leap.

"Well, that's a relief, Mr. Claybourne. You see, Blenwick is one of Hudson's lines."

"Yes, I know. And at the moment, some of his railways can be bought for a song."

"Far less expensive than a marriage, Mr. Claybourne."

Hunter caught himself smiling again. "Touché, madam."

"So you were here on business after all?"

His wife seemed charmingly humble all of a sudden. She buffed her toes back and forth against the leather upholstery, putting him in mind of a cat having found the most comfortable place in the house and claiming it for herself.

He would make the most of this windfall peace. Better to keep the cat's claws retracted. He settled back against the seat, trying to maneuver the conversation around to the gold band in his pocket, and the meaning it might convey between them: business only, yet a symbol to others.

"I'll admit, Miss Mayfield, that my timing is somewhat tied to your venture. Your mention of Northumberland reminded me of the Blenwick prospectus, and—"

"And so you had found yourself a ready excuse to follow me, and see that I was staying out of trouble?"

He'd landed right in her trap, and yet found it surprisingly comfortable. He could escape at any time, and he decided to relax into it. "In truth, Miss Mayfield, when you declared that you were bound for two weeks of rail travel, I thought you a novice at this sort of thing."

"Me, a novice?" Her laughter warmed the whole of the car. "I'd hate to calculate the miles I've traveled on the rails. I sleep best on a rocking train. Though I must admit I've never, ever traveled in this kind luxury—a whole bench seat to myself, paraffin lamps. Second-class is the best I can afford. When I'm tired, I usually lean forward and fall asleep with my head against the back of the seat in front of me."

Hunter frowned at the idea.

"Makes a terrible dent in my forehead."

She made a face and laughed again, and Hunter found himself laughing along with her, a disquietingly comfortable feeling that shed the tension from his shoulders, yet stung the corners of his eyes.

He envied her ease, her ability to bend to the pressure of the moment. Train travel always meant more time for him to work without interruptions. He sat as he always did, in the center of the seat—usually surrounded with charts and graphs and proposals, but enveloped now in the scent of vanilla, and the lure of her voice. And he hadn't given a thought to a single investment.

The car had become exceedingly warm, the ring seeming to produce a strange heat of its own. Hunter stood and shrugged out of his coat, leaving himself in his waistcoat and shirtsleeves. He loosened his stock, then sat down and leaned against the same wall his wife had claimed.

"When I was fifteen," she said, pulling a magazine out of her portmanteau, "I made a list of all the places I had lived. There were forty-three. But that was nearly five years ago. I'm afraid to add the rest to the figure." She rolled her head to smile at him as he stuck his legs out across the bench opposite. They could have been sharing some strange, upright bed.

She drew in a deep breath and pulled the blanket around her legs. "I confess that I love the look of trains, and the sound of trains, and the smell of trains."

"I find them convenient."

"Is your mother still alive, Mr. Claybourne?"

The question hit him like a blow to the stomach. He felt her steady gaze on him, but could only look at the back of his hands, past the scars on his knuckles.

"No, she's not."

"I'm truly sorry, Mr. Claybourne. Did she pass on recently?"

He had recovered enough from the first blow to shake his head and return her steady gaze. "No."

"Then she died when you were young?"

These were innocently asked questions, and an innocent moment; he would make no more of them than that. "By coincidence, Miss Mayfield, I, too, was six when I lost my mother."

Felicity felt an unexpected bond of sympathy with this keen-edged husband of hers. A softness moved across his mouth, and at the fine lines at the corners of his eyes. She had expected to spend the trip to Blenwick boiling with anger, pressed under the thumb of Claybourne's rude threats. But he'd been almost pleasant, and here he was offering answers that hadn't a thing to do with his financial empire. She decided to press on while he was open to her questions.

"Did your father ever remarry?"

"No," he said, his profile carved once again in granite.

"Is your father still alive? And is he very much like you?"

"My father is gone, too."

Claybourne lifted his newspaper abruptly, and Felicity thought it best to quit before his mood darkened.

"I'm sorry, Mr. Claybourne. I'm afraid I carry around a bucket of questions, and I sometimes forget that people would rather I not toss it over their heads."

The train shuddered and the brakes squealed.

"Damnation!" Her husband jumped to his feet and threw open the door to the night air before the train came to a stop.

"Take care, Mr. Claybourne." Felicity made a grab for him, and caught a handful of wool at the seat of his trousers.

He looked over his shoulder at her. His eyes blazed. "Not now, wife!"

Felicity uncrumpled the fabric as if it were afire. Not now? What the devil did he mean by that? She tried to ignore the shape that seemed to have branded itself into her hand: slopes and vales, hard muscle and heated flesh. The blasted train had ground to a halt in the middle of its route, yet here she was staring at her palm, memorizing the contours of her husband's backside.

"Traction problems?" she asked, rubbing her hands together to erase the image.

He popped back inside and closed the door. "Too dark to see ahead."

"I'm sorry," Felicity said, shoving her hands beneath the blanket to hide the phantom imprint.

"You're sorry?" he asked, his wind-whipped hair flopped across his brow. "It's hardly your fault—"

"No, Mr. Claybourne, I'm sorry that I grabbed your . . ." She made a lame gesture toward his backside. "Your trousers. I didn't mean . . . Oh, just drop it."

An artful smile perched at the corner of his mouth, ready to pounce upon her discomfort. "Drop my trousers, Miss Mayfield?"

"That's not what I—Mr. Claybourne!"

The miserable cad laughed outright, and Felicity was left with a too-intriguing image of her husband without his trousers. She had never seen any man in such a state of undress, so the best she could manage was bare legs and shirttails. And that was quite enough to imagine. Enough to singe her ears!

Felicity threw off the blanket and popped up from her seat to retrieve the basket. "Well, at least we won't starve, Mr. Claybourne. You've brought enough food for a banquet."

"Mrs. Sweeney's doing," he said, unsnagging the basket from the rack and setting it on the seat in front of her. "She wanted you to try her new currant cakes."

Claybourne was throwing off a scorching heat, his head bent near to accommodate the low ceiling and to peer into the basket. He smelled wonderful, of lime and the cool night air that still clung to his hair.

His breathing riffled her sleeve, heating through the weave to her skin. Felicity willed her fingers to stop shaking, willed herself to think of something besides his mouth and the calling curve of his upper lip. This was the same contemptuous man who vilified the wretched, who had threatened to keep her in prison, and who seemed compelled to repeat both themes on a daily basis.

Felicity righted her thoughts. "Mrs. Sweeney has made something other than bread and stew? I'm astounded."

He planted a boot on the seat and seemed exceedingly interested in her expedition through the cups and containers. He must have been interested, or he wouldn't be standing so very close. Perhaps he was hungry.

"She said the recipe is from a cookbook you gave to her."

"The menu at Claybourne Manor needed variety." She could feel him looking at her, frowning, she was sure, and near enough to kiss. To kiss?

Dear God, whatever made her think a thing like

that? Oh, but the idea had been in her head since he'd thrown her into the coach. She hated to admit it, but she'd actually been thinking of her husband's kiss ever since Mr. Denning had registered their marriage in his book. Unfinished business, she supposed; a misplaced hope for something better to come of their union. Now there was a fool notion! Yet Claybourne was her husband, after all, and he was patently attractive.

And right now his breath was lifting the hair at her temple . . .

Completely unstrung, Felicity popped open a crock of strawberry-sharp preserves and dipped her finger into its coolness. It was a tangy distraction on her tongue, but couldn't overtake the rising heat caused by Claybourne's close study of her face.

He seemed very interested in watching her draw her finger from her mouth, even sent his tongue to dampen his lower lip as if he were tasting the strawberries, too.

"Mrs. Sweeney doesn't read," he said, lifting his dark gaze to hers.

"Then how, Mr. Claybourne, did she know what to put into the recipe?" Felicity knew that her cheeks had gone stark pink and the rest of her face pale.

He had such fine lips.

"Branson probably helped her."

She giggled like a schoolgirl and tried to recap the jar. "I didn't think they liked each other very much."

"Perfect enemies."

She found her gaze wandering freely to the crook of his knee, so near her hip, and to the inciting fit of his trousers. That only served to remind her of the shape of his backside against the flat of her hand, the very hand which was cupped at the moment around the smoothly rounded underside of a crock of strawberry preserves, whose lid refused to cooperate—

"Here!" Felicity handed the crock to Claybourne and fixed her attention on the rest of the basket. She opened the tin of cakes and took an impatient bite of one, determined to admire them no matter the taste. "Mmmm. Not bad at all," she mumbled past the crumbs. "Care to try for yourself, Mr. Claybourne?"

She lifted the cake to his mouth, but the train jolted forward and Claybourne was launched backward like a rocket into the seat behind them.

"Damnation!" he bellowed.

Felicity had easily kept her feet. But her husband now slumped low in the seat, knocked flat by an invisible pugilist; his knees were jammed against the opposite seat. Globs of strawberries speckled his waistcoat and shirtfront from the crock that he still held valiantly in his hand.

"How did you do that, Miss Mayfield?" Claybourne righted himself, but didn't stand.

"Do what?"

He looked altogether bewildered and pointed to her feet. "The train tossed me like a pebble and yet you never moved."

Felicity found a spoon and sat down beside him, unsure exactly what she planned to do next. "I don't know, Mr. Claybourne. I guess I can read the rails like a fortune teller can read the future."

She moved toward him with the spoon, and he flinched. "What are you doing, Miss Mayfield?"

"You're covered in preserves, Mr. Claybourne. Hold still." Felicity held off a sudden fit of giggling. Hunter Claybourne, the scone.

The man glanced down at his shirtfront and scowled, then watched dutifully as she ladled the globs of strawberries into a napkin.

Felicity kept her eyes downcast and businesslike, hoping he wouldn't feel the pounding of her heart, hoping he couldn't guess that she was thinking about what it would be like to unbutton his waistcoat and shirt, and lick the strawberries from his chest. Heavens above! Marriage had begun to cloud her judgment.

Hunter hoped his wife didn't know that he was wondering how her tongue-glistened mouth would feel gliding across his naked chest in a lingering quest for strawberries. Her gaze was fleeting, but frequent and warm, her breathing as unsteady as his own.

"Did Mrs. Sweeney make these preserves, Mr. Claybourne?"

"How the hell would I know?" Good God, he didn't know how much more of this he could take. Every scrape of the spoon was a scrape across his nerves. Then she scraped past the pocket that held the wedding band, and paused there to wipe across the opening with her finger.

Good God, he should have left her in the third-class car. Hell, he should have ridden in there himself, where the wind and rain might whip some sense into his head.

But now she was bent over him, scraping the spoon across his collar bone, her ear exposed and lovely, his breath riffling the unsprung curls at her temple. He was vividly aware of the pressure of her thigh against his, and the brush of her skirts against the woollen fabric that shielded his lust from her tender sensibilities. He hoped to hell she wasn't as aware as he. She would think him a passion-bound fiend, and throw herself from the car if she knew.

"There." She stood up and turned away from him.

Hunter sat up quickly and draped his arm across his lap as she stuffed the recapped crock and the strawberry-stained napkin into the basket.

The heat in the car had risen considerably, and made him realize that there were many sensitive matters which ought to be discussed between them if they were to remain married for an entire year. Passion and "miscalculations . . ."

And a ring. He didn't understand why the subject seemed so unbroachable for him. He prided himself on his forthrightness.

Madam, you are to wear this ring—

"I very rarely think of myself as Mrs. Claybourne."

Hunter nearly swallowed his tongue. He prayed she couldn't read his mind as well as she seemed to read the rhythm of the rails. He had no idea where she was going with this statement, or even if it had been preceded by a transition from another subject. He hadn't been listening. He'd been day-dreaming, measuring the fit of his hand against the underswell of her breast.

"Nevertheless, you are my wife, Miss Mayfield." Now the subject was at hand. If his own would only stop shaking, he could lift the ring from his pocket—

"Yes. But, there, you see? You have the same problem as I, Mr. Claybourne: you keep calling me Miss Mayfield. I doubt you even know my given name."

"I do."

"You've never used it."

"It's Felicity. Felicity . . . Claybourne."

She sniffed, obviously unconvinced, then picked up the basket and hoisted it to her shoulder. "It's no wonder I sometimes act as if I were not married—it's so hard to believe that I am."

Nervous beyond reason, Hunter stood up as she struggled to replace the basket in the rack, and secured it for her.

"Thank you," she said.

"You're welcome, Miss . . . Mrs. Claybourne, but I remind you that we *are* married." And they were standing very close again. The slope of the roof brought his head bare inches from hers, his mouth poised at her ear again because she didn't seem to want to look at him.

"But do you suppose our marriage is truly legal?" She sat down abruptly, flicking her eyes to him twice before she settled her gaze on her hands, clasped tightly in her lap.

"What makes you think it might not be legal?" He sat down across from her. He couldn't wait to hear her excuse.

"Well . . ." She finally fixed him with a precipitous sea-green stare. "We never kissed after we were married, Mr. Claybourne. Did you notice that?"

Hunter had noticed.

Felicity felt that odd flush rise out of her bodice to engulf her face. It always began with a fluttering just above her heart, but spread deeper, especially when he was looking at her with those half-lidded eyes. A kiss! Why the devil had she brought that up?

"A kiss, Mrs. Claybourne?" His long legs were bent and spread, his knees on either side of hers.

She had no trouble at all imagining his mouth pressed against her own, especially now with her knees trapped lightly between his, and his dark gaze feathering her cheek.

"Well, I just meant that—"

"Madam, a kiss is the least of the seals we have not set upon this marriage." His voice was a dark melody that rose above the unrelenting percussion of the wheels.

He took a small bright object from the pocket of his waistcoat. She saw it flash gold just before he caught her hand in his.

And then he was slipping a ring onto her finger. It was very warm and a little too large.

"There," he said, encasing her hand completely in his. "Now there will be no question of it, Mrs. Claybourne."

Felicity suddenly felt astonishingly married. "No question?" Her heart had taken flight.

"No question that you are married to me."

Married!

She looked down to see the ring, but his hand still held hers trapped inside his. She didn't know what to say, didn't quite know what to think.

Only that he was very close, his wonderful mouth just inches from hers.

"And should I kiss you, Mrs. Claybourne?"

That might have been a kiss; the rush of his sweet,

spicy breath past her lips. But he hadn't moved, save for the gentle, insistent rocking of the train.

"I think you should, Mr. Claybourne. In case anyone asks about . . . you know."

He smiled then, this husband of hers, amused in some way by her concern, and still smelling of strawberries.

"My dear, they wouldn't dare ask." He brushed his splendid fingers lightly, too gently through the curls at her temple, lifting the disarray over her shoulder, straying to her nape, sliding under her collar.

"Wouldn't dare, Mr. Claybourne?" She could hardly breathe for the sweetness of his touch.

"Can you imagine such a question?" He'd laid his soft words against her ear: the barest brush of his mouth, unspoken images of fire and promise, the slight gruffness of his evening bristles scrubbing past her cheek.

Felicity heard herself take in a noisy breath, then expel it with an indelicate sigh. He wasn't quite making sense anymore. "What sort of question would that be, Mr. Claybourne?"

"An irrational one, certainly." Now his gaze smoldered and strayed back to her mouth, as palpable as his whisper had been. "What kind of fool would ever doubt that I had kissed my beautiful wife?"

Beautiful? But he'd hardly ever looked at her, and when he had, he was so often scowling. But he wasn't now. A half-smile lifted the corner of his mouth. His touch was feather-light and breathtaking. He followed the course of her jaw, drawing his fingers to her chin and tilting it up to him.

"But if they did ask, Mr. Claybourne, you'd have to tell a lie."

His hand trembled, or she did, or maybe it was simply the train's steady progress along the track.

"No, I won't, Mrs. Claybourne."

"No?" There was a moment when his exquisitely shaped mouth was poised above hers, when he smiled crookedly, when she wondered if he'd been teasing her. And in the next moment there was nothing else in the world but the bliss of his wonderful mouth on hers.

She'd have guessed that a man with a soul of granite would have cold, unyielding lips. But his were supple and caressing and welcomed her own with a passion that warmed her from the tips of her fingers to the soles of her feet, and carried a fever to every place else inbetween.

His eyes where half-closed and his brow furrowed, and she wondered if he felt the same heat and heard the same song. So different than she had expected, his mouth soft and yet firmly seeking. He was making growling noises in his throat, and holding her face steady with both hands, planting his lingering kisses everywhere. Now, if he'd only put his arms around her!

Hunter endured the gut-knotting intoxication like a man about to be dragged out of paradise. She was honey and steam and vanilla, and this kiss would leave him suffering for her when it ended. She pulled away slightly, staggering him when she put her fingers to his mouth, as if she were deaf and mute and searching for some kind of knowledge of him. His ring glistened there, looking solid and bright.

"You taste very good, Mr. Claybourne." Then his enchanting wife smiled and kissed him hard, wrapping her fingers in his hair and pulling him even closer.

Dear God, he wanted her, in all the possible measures of the word. To stand naked with her in a stream, to sup at her breast, to explore this wave of desire to its fullest. She was his wife, bound by his ring and by a contract, yet she wouldn't be for long. And so he let the muscles seize up in his arms, left them aching when he bridled the yearning to embrace her.

"Enough," he whispered against her mouth, and then against her ear, where his words drew a sweet sound from her that only made him want to taste more of her, to lay with her on the seat and make her his wife in truth, while the train rattled on into Blenwick.

"Is this one long kiss, Mr. Claybourne? Or would this be considered many kisses piled one atop the other?"

He was about to answer her with another dozen kisses when he felt the sultry drift of her hand hovering above his knee. If it should touch down— "Stop!"

"What's the matter, Mr. Claybourne?" She sat upright in the seat, her eyes wide and wounded. "Did I hurt you?"

"No, you didn't hurt me, damn it."

Hunter abruptly stood up and opened the window, framed it with his forearms, and drew in deep draughts of cinder-tainted air as the dark landscape slid by. Discomfort was his aim. Anything to erase the memory of his wife's mouth parting to accept more than a simple kiss. The kiss was a mistake.

"Well, that's done," she said, as if she'd just stuck a pie to cooling on the sill.

"Done?"

"A ring and the kiss."

He glanced back at her and found her staring down at the ring, turning it on her finger. The band was plain and wider than it might have been, but it said clearly what he had intended it to say. She was his wife— however briefly. And now she was straightening her bodice as if he'd caressed her there at the rise and fall of her breasts.

"The ring was a detail that had escaped me. Traveling as you do, unescorted, you will be better protected from discourteous men, Miss Mayfield. As for the other . . . the kiss—"

"Yes, Mr. Claybourne?"

"A simple one would have sufficed. I . . . overstepped my intentions."

"Yes, I suppose we both did." She shrugged and

repaired the drape of her skirts over her knees. "I don't usually kiss men that I don't like. So, I don't know why I kissed you."

Hunter slammed the window so fiercely it rattled. "Whether you like a man or not, Miss Mayfield, you'll kiss no one but me while you and I are married."

She heaved a dramatic sigh. "I see that I'm back to being *Miss Mayfield*."

"Habit." He watched her sweep her riled hair into a loose knot at the back of her head. His timing had been inopportune. The blame was his; he was the stronger of the pair. But at least he'd managed to deliver the ring to its proper place.

"Whatever pleases you, Mr. Claybourne. We'll be divorced in eleven months, two weeks, and two days. Why bother learning a different name?"

"You'll always be Mrs. Claybourne."

"Not after we're divorced."

"A divorced woman keeps her ex-husband's name unless and until she marries again."

"I won't be keeping yours, Mr. Claybourne. The last thing I need is a—" She shot to her feet, a fox about to flee a pack of hounds. "God, no! Do you feel it, Mr. Claybourne?"

"Feel what?" Hunter asked, standing as she was, trying to sense what she was feeling.

"The train—"

Hunter heard it then, the horrible squealing of brakes and the shriek of metal against metal. "What the bloody hell?"

"Please, God, no!"

The car suffered a sharp jolt, then rocked to the side, sending the basket and his travel case flying.

"Christ, Felicity!" Hunter shoved her down between the seats and covered her with his body. "Hang on, sweet!"

Their car plowed forward, its momentum still caught up in the track, surviving the waves of collisions ahead, one car hitting another, and another, and another.

Hunter held fast to his wife, hugged her against his chest, every moment ripping past him and lagging like an eternity. It couldn't end this way! Not now. Not just when . . .

Their car shot sideways off the rail, shattering the window glass and dousing the lamps. Hunter felt himself being yanked away from her and sent airborne as the car dropped sharply onto its side and started to skid downward in the darkness.

He'd lost her. "Felicity!"

He heard her cry out, but was thrown against the baggage rack. The car kept sliding downward on its side, off an embankment, or off a bridge, not yet rolling. He prayed it wouldn't, but the world had gone mad and he couldn't tell up from down—only that he kept calling her name, kept hearing her cry from somewhere above him.

The car came to rest abruptly, almost peacefully.

"Felicity!" He panicked for the sound of her in the darkness. "Speak to me!"

Somewhere distant, the downed locomotive shrieked like a dying beast. Hunter reached out across the glass shards and felt no trace of his wife; only the rubble of their belongings thrown around him in a corner of the broken-out ceiling.

"Please, Felicity—"

"I'm here, Mr. Claybourne." Her voice was small and winded, but she grabbed hold of his ankle and was suddenly kneeling in the circle of his arms.

Chapter 12

"**H**unter!" Felicity had kept her wits because he'd kept calling her name, the light of hope in the terrible darkness.

"Thank God, you're alive, Felicity!" He kissed her cheek and ran his hands quickly down her arms. "Are you all right?"

"Are you?" Felicity wanted to see his face, but she settled for touching it, landing a kiss on his forehead.

"Ouch!"

"Good," she said, finally able to see a glint from his eyes. "It's just your head."

"Thank you, madam." His laughter calmed her, and his gentleness soothed like balm as he brushed her hair out of her face. His hands shook. "I see that your wit survived intact."

"Dear God . . ." A faraway glow of orange-red lit the hard planes of his face. "Fire, Mr. Claybourne! Up ahead—the engine, and the coal car. The very worst thing that could happen—"

"Damnation." Claybourne struggled to his feet and pulled her along with him toward the doorway, now a gaping hole above them. "Out you go, wife."

Then he was suddenly shoving her up through the hole to the outside of the railcar. He followed her in the next instant and knelt on the canted siding, his hair lifting in the rising night wind, his strong, bare hand clamped around her calf as she clung to the door frame.

"The fire is up ahead on the track," he said. "I can't see a thing beyond our car."

They were nose-down in an embankment, and Felicity feared for his footing. But he seemed remarkably stable-legged as he slid down its face and landed on his feet below her.

"Do you hear it, Mr. Claybourne?"

A great shouting and wailing had begun, the human sound mixed with the steady shriek of the whistle and the thundering thrum of the drivers spinning freely.

"Come," he said, as he handed her to the ground. "You are to stay out of the way, where it's safe . . ."

But Felicity was already on her way through the bracken to the opposite side of the ditch, toward a crooked-limbed man who had been thrown free of a first-class compartment.

"Quick, Mr. Claybourne, he's hurt!"

She heard her husband move up behind her. He had found and lit a lamp and now held it aloft.

"You'll need this," he said, kneeling beside her.

"Thank you, Mr. Claybourne. But I'm afraid the poor man is gone. His neck seems broken."

Felicity righted the dead man's clothes, and settled his hands across his chest, taking great comfort in it. She'd done the same for her father when he died, had tucked the collar of his nightshirt neatly against the lapel of his robe. A detail of death.

She feared there would be many others before the night was through.

Hunter searched the two other sections of their railcar, but found no sign of anyone. His wife had already scaled the incline to the tracks in search of wounded passengers. There was no use in trying to change her mind. When he reached her, she had made a hospital between the wheels of a fallen freight car. She offered bandages and words of comfort to a white-faced woman whose arm trailed too loosely across her lap. A man and a child staggered toward her out of the clouds of smoke and steam. She gathered them in and settled their fears as easily as if they had come to tea.

As for himself, hell beckoned from farther down the tracks, where blinding flames and utter darkness danced wickedly together.

He ran toward the locomotive and the fire, past railcars that lay scattered like toys tossed in a tantrum around a playroom. He sent the injured toward his wife, and urged the able-bodied forward to the worst of the nightmare.

The shrieking of the whistle had subsided, and the useless spinning of the drivers had stilled. But the sounds of human anguish had increased.

Hunter swore as he reached the embankment. One of the rails had snapped free of its stone block ties and the locomotive had spilled off the track into a ravine, taking the tender, two freight cars, and the third-class car with it. Flames that fed off the oil and the engine fire leaped up the heavily wooded embankment toward the coach. Another thirty feet and the fire would be licking at the coach, heating the metal siding until it roasted the passengers alive.

Hunter gathered a group of men and boys and set some to work battling the flames, then climbed on top of the car itself. The coach lay on its side, the single door stuck shut. The inadequate metal roof had collapsed onto the body like the lid shut down on a tin of biscuits.

"Find me a crowbar!" Hunter shouted, stripping off his waistcoat, while behind him the flames of hell tried to peel the shirt from his back.

He hoped his wife would stay out of trouble.

*   *   *

"She's bad off, miss."

Felicity knelt down beside a little girl who was holding the hand of an elderly woman. A younger boy was with them, sitting on his heels and crooning a bedtime song.

"Is this your grandmother?" Felicity asked. The woman's translucent skin had been torn off her brow like paper, but she was conscious and moaning.

"Oh, no, miss, we ain't got no gran, do we, Arleigh?"

"No, miss," the boy said, wiping his nose down the length of his sleeve. "Betts and I don't have a gran."

"Well, then, you're being very kind to someone else's grandmother, and I'm sure they'd be very happy to know it."

Felicity covered the woman with a man's coat to keep her warm. She wrapped a flannel bandage around the woman's forehead and comforted her.

When she moved on to the next patient, Betts and her little brother followed on her heels. She soon had them expertly tearing bandages for her out of the clothes that had scattered when the luggage burst open.

"Your mother and father, Betts, were they on the train with you?"

"No." Betts lifted her bony shoulders in a shrug. "We're alone, miss."

"Well, your parents will be proud of you for being a great help. Will you stay here and make more bandages for me?"

Arleigh nodded gravely. " 'Pon our word, miss."

Felicity left them to work among the shocked and the injured, and walked the track looking for stragglers. Her throat and nostrils seemed coated with the metallic taste of blood, her lungs filled with sickmaking plumes of burning oil.

The sight of blood usually made her sway on her feet, but she found strength to approach the bloodied victims without flinching. It wasn't the gore that coiled her stomach into her throat, it was the suffering: the weeping children and their terrified parents, the sight of a courageous young woman cradling an elderly stranger.

She had begun to hear stories of a man who had taken command of the horror. She hoped that her hardheaded husband would help this brave hero who had sent her a half-dozen women to sort out the severely injured from those who were merely dazed and scraped.

Felicity saw her husband as she came to the edge of the embankment, a giant silhouette against the roiling fire. He was standing on top of the tilted side of the third-class car, the very same car she would have been traveling in had he not insisted she ride with him. She wondered where the passengers had gone, how they had escaped such a twisted wreckage.

Then she heard the keening coming from within. Dear God, there were people trapped inside!

"Mr. Claybourne!" She ran to the car and stepped up onto its wheel, about to insist that he hurry. But as the words formed, she noticed the huge hammer and the thick rail spike in his hands. He could have been one of her father's railway construction workers. She was struck dumb by the sight.

"Hey, Claybourne!" A man scrambled toward him on his hands and knees along the side of the listing car. "Over here! We've found a breach. We saw a finger poke through. Looked to be a child's."

Her husband shouted orders, and the other men scrambled into position as if he were a general and they his regiment of battle-hardened soldiers.

Hunter Claybourne—taking charge of the rescue effort? Was he the man that everyone had been praising? Not possible. What was in this for him? Perhaps he'd discovered a way to salvage something from the disaster. George Hudson's railway line would certainly be a better bargain now.

But Claybourne was moving like a man possessed.

Flames crept up the embankment, engulfing the brush and scrub alders, gaining ground even as the straggling crew tried to put out the blaze.

Felicity felt utterly helpless, but could only wait for the injured.

She watched him shove a makeshift crowbar between two pieces of siding. He bore down on it repeatedly with all his weight, exhaling great grunts of air each time.

"Add the other," he shouted. Another man wedged an iron brace into the gap Claybourne had created. Still another length of bracing was added, and more pressure applied by the other men until a rivet popped and the siding came loose from the beam.

Felicity held her breath as her husband and his crew bent the metal siding backward to give access to the inside.

Claybourne knelt over the gap. "Christ! The hole isn't big enough!"

Felicity had climbed onto the side of the car and was already peering into the hole. "Let me go down, Mr. Claybourne," she said.

"Absolutely not." He tried to brush her away, but she clung to the bent metal.

"If they're injured in there, I might be able to help."

"No! You'll be roasted alive."

"Blast it, Mr. Claybourne! Look around. I'm the only one who'll fit."

His face glistened a red and black amalgam of sweat and soot and dancing flames. He suddenly laced his fingers through her hair and cradled her head between his hands, said something she didn't catch, then planted a rough kiss on her mouth. He tasted of oil and gritty cinders. His eyes were bright as he studied her for the briefest span of time.

"You'll come up from there when I command it, Mrs. Claybourne."

Felicity nodded. "I promise."

He gathered her hands in his and lowered her into

the darkness. A hand caught her from below, tugged on her skirt.

"Help us, miss!"

"Clear the way, please," Felicity said, wriggling her feet but never doubting that her husband would hold her until she was safely landed. "I can't help anyone until I'm all the way down."

"Be careful, wife," Claybourne shouted as she touched down. He was only a pale orange glow from above, and then he disappeared and the hammering and straining began again above her.

"My mother . . ." came a feeble voice in the darkness, "she's bleeding awful bad."

Someone took Felicity's wrist and whimpered, "Please . . . I can't see."

"I think my arm's broke," wailed another.

"We'll get to everyone," Felicity said, trying not to think of the flames that threatened just outside their metal prison. The children would fit through the hole as it was. The injured would have to be hoisted out. She gathered the children together and called out to her husband over the ringing sounds of the tearing metal.

"Mr. Claybourne!" His head appeared and she lifted one of the children. "Take him! Please!"

"How many?" he shouted as he grabbed the boy's scrawny arm and hauled him up.

"Two more children. Maybe a dozen others!" She handed up the children one at a time, straining under their weight. Claybourne's growling gave her hope, even as the temperature rose inside the iron box. At least there was no smoke.

"Come out now, woman!" he hissed. "We're losing to the fire! And we can't make the hole any larger."

"No, Mr. Claybourne. They need help in here. I can't leave them."

"I said come!" His voice had become a fearsome roar that reverberated inside the car. He made a swipe toward her with his powerful arm, but Felicity was far out of his reach and thankful that he couldn't fit his shoulders through.

"We both have work to do, Mr. Claybourne. Make a sling. You'll have to drag the rest out." Felicity left him to his blazing anger and crawled among the injured. Most looked as broken as the benches and the sprung baggage.

She bandaged a young man's eyes, and stabilized a woman's broken arm against her chest. The inside of the car was growing hotter. Sweat ran in rivulets off her brow and down her back. She knew she ought to be frightened out of her mind, but Mr. Claybourne was up there with his crowbars and his hammering, and she was positive that he wouldn't let her or anyone else die.

"Mrs. Claybourne!" Her husband was looking down on her, fiend-featured in the red-tinged shadows. "Damn your eyes, woman! Here's your sling; now put yourself into it. I've lost three men to the heat."

But Felicity was already fitting an injured woman into the blanket hoist. "We don't need a panic down here, Mr. Claybourne. Now, hoist away."

He did as she'd asked, dragging the frightened woman to the hole in a single movement.

Her husband had taken on the guise of an avenging angel, a contrast completely at odds with the craven fiend of a few weeks ago. He dropped the sling at her feet and she loaded another passenger.

"This was to be your car, Mrs. Claybourne," he said through his teeth, as he hauled the man out of the stifling car. "You would have been one of the bruised and battered."

Felicity helped another man across the rubble. "Are you saying, Mr. Claybourne, that you saved my life by bullying me into riding with you?"

"Whatever my methods, they worked. Now, hurry!"

"And if I had refused your invitation?"

He snorted. "Then I'd have torn my way into this car with my bare hands, Mrs. Claybourne."

Felicity touched her thumb to the back of her wedding band, a new and surprisingly weighty presence in her life. She felt suddenly lighthearted, and very much in awe as she looked up into his frowning face. "I think you did already."

Claybourne growled at her each time he lifted another victim from the railcar, but the system was working and only a few remained.

"Hurry, Claybourne!" The panicked shout had come from somewhere outside, beyond her husband. "Another oil tank has split. We can't hold back the flames."

"Out, wife!" Claybourne bellowed. "Get into the sling! Now!"

"There are two more before me, Mr. Claybourne." Felicity steered a young man along the bank of upright benches, hoping that he hadn't lost his sight for good. Claybourne yanked the young man skyward, and nearly unseated the last young woman in his hurry.

"Sit down now, Mrs. Claybourne!"

"Yes, I'm coming, Mr. Claybourne." The heat had grown tremendous, and she was light-headed enough to think she saw flames eating through the rear of the car.

"Bloody hell, woman! Into the sling."

"Yes sir." As she was about to sit down, a mound of clothing moved in the corner—and then it moaned. She'd missed someone.

"Wait, Mr. Claybourne!" Felicity stumbled away from the sling and heard her husband's voice roar. She coughed into the hem of her skirt as she helped the woman from the pile of debris into the safety of the sling.

Her eyes stung and her ears, too, as the car filled with smoke and Mr. Claybourne's bellowing. She coughed and tried to see through the coming darkness, but the world had become much too hot and much too close. And it sounded of wrenching metal and seemed to be hammering on her skull.

"Felicity!"

As she heard her name called from some brighter place, she wondered where the enormous, dark angel had come from, and how he'd managed to find his way through the flames and the smoke.

Hunter's heart had crammed itself into his throat while he'd torn away the last of the metal sheeting with a strength he hadn't known he possessed. He had leaped into the smoke-filled railcar, and found her where he'd seen her fall.

"Fool woman!" He lifted her into his arms, wanting to embrace her, but knowing there was little time left before he succumbed as well.

"I'm all right, Mr. Claybourne!" She started coughing and struggled with him.

"Be still, wife!" But Hunter kissed her forehead even as he put her into the sling. He didn't want to think about how glad he'd been to hear her impatient little voice, squawking at him through the smoke.

Hunter watched her rise up, damning the smoke that stung his lungs, and cursing his wife for being bull-headed. When he was brought out of the hole, he found her bent over on her hands and knees in the bushes, retching and coughing.

Hiding his immeasurable fear in righteous anger, Hunter left her to her misery, wiping the sting of smoke from his eyes, and dismissing the tidal wave of relief that blocked off his breathing.

The little fool would live. And he couldn't remember ever being so exceedingly happy in all his life.

Hunter heard the sweet-sounding train whistle in the distance, but didn't have the strength to join in the cheer that went up as the others ran toward the rescue train steaming in from Blenwick. The engine and a passenger car chugged to a stop a hundred yards from the wreckage. An old locomotive and a rattle-trap railcar, but they would do the job.

"Thank God," Hunter whispered, his throat scraped

raw with the smoke and his shouting. He'd barked enough orders in the last few hours to last him a lifetime. They had only listened to him because they thought he knew what he was doing. He had discovered early that people were sheep, constantly searching for a shepherd, too timid or uncertain to claim the title for themselves.

Hunter was grateful for his wife's command over the injured, for the way she had rallied after her foolhardy rescue. She had a flair for ordering people around, and not even the bystanders had been left without a task.

God, he was tired.

The somber-faced station master wheezed as he approached, wheeling his arms to stay upright amid the debris. "There you are, sir. A team of inspectors from the Railway Department has come by the post road from York."

"Already?"

"I wired them as soon as I could. When I mentioned your name, sir, they said they wanted to talk with you about the accident."

The Railway Department would be vastly interested in anything associated with George Hudson, especially an accident. Another brush with the Board of Trade could only enhance his own position. Lord Meath would be impressed to learn of his involvement.

Hunter glanced around for his wife, a reaction that had become quite automatic and inordinately pleasing in the last few hours—despite the fact that she looked, from head to toe, like a sooted-up chimney sweep. She was absorbed in herding a group of children toward the railcar. She paused at the door, and raised her hand to shield her eyes against the first gilding rays of the sun. He was overly delighted that his ring had made it through the long night, and still encircled her finger. She smiled at him, and his quixotic heart took a mad tumble against his chest.

"Damned woman," he muttered.

"What's that, sir?"

"Never mind. Show me to the inspectors."

Felicity made sure Arleigh and Betts were safely on the train, tucked together in the same seat, their skinny limbs covered with her battered shawl.

"Thank you, miss!" Arleigh said, as he stretched up to hug her. "You've been ever so kind. Hasn't she, Betts?"

"An angel, surely," Betts said through sleep-heavy eyes.

"And you have been ever so helpful!" Felicity kissed both of the smudged foreheads. "And don't forget to tell your parents how brave you both were."

Betts dipped her head at the compliment, and shared a solemn countenance with her brother. "We won't forget to tell nobody about you, miss."

The whistle blew, and Felicity felt suddenly guilty for leaving them. But their parents were no doubt waiting at the station in Blenwick, terrified and relieved that neither had received more than a scratch in the accident. And she had promised the injured passengers that she would help collect their belongings and have them waiting at Blenwick Station.

The train lurched forward in warning.

"Take care of each other," Felicity whispered, hurriedly kissing them again before stepping out of the car onto the landing. A belch of smoke rolled into her face.

"Jump, for God's sake!"

Felicity looked down through the gritty cloud to find her husband striding along the embankment, steaming like a locomotive and keeping pace with the train, his arms extended as if he were one of those Italian circus performers, waiting to catch her as she flew through the air.

"Jump, damn it!"

Felicity would have stepped off the barely moving train in her usual manner, but he caught her around the waist, whirled her out of the way of the car, and slung her under his arm like a sack of potatoes—all in a single, fluid motion.

"Put me down, Mr. Claybourne. I can walk." Felicity kicked her legs and tried to meet the ground with her foot. He merely held her tighter and kept walking.

"What the hell do you think you were doing?" he asked, his chin squared off, focused on the wreckage ahead of them.

"I was bidding farewell to the injured," she said.

"You were trying to kill yourself."

"Poppycock, Mr. Claybourne."

He finally set her on her feet, but leveled a soot-blackened finger at her. "The train was in motion, Mrs. Claybourne. Or hadn't you noticed?"

Felicity smiled, because he was hovering like a storm and thundering at her. "It was hardly moving at all. I used to jump from trains all the time when I worked with Father."

"You did what?"

"Jump, tuck, and roll—that's the trick. Oh, and it helps to be relaxed, and not to land in a briar patch. I did that once. I was plucking thorns from my . . . well, from everywhere for months."

"Your father let you jump from moving trains?"

"He taught me how."

"The damn fool!"

"It was part of the job, Mr. Claybourne; part of engineering a well-laid track, part of evaluating the final product."

"Don't let me catch you leaping from a moving train again." With his sinewy, sooty arm extended above his shoulder in a gesture worthy of a member of parliament, he looked like an orator.

She had to smile. "You won't catch me, Mr. Claybourne. I assure you."

Felicity left him to his scowling and began the weary task of gathering up scattered belongings and piling them at the railhead. She sent a would-be scavenger scurrying with a well-aimed rock to his backside.

"Thief!" she shouted after him, and doubled her search for lost items.

She had been watching Claybourne and the investigators as she collected the baggage. They were terribly uncoordinated in their efforts. She stood at a spot below the grade of the railroad bed and decided to point out a few things, just in case.

"You missed this!" she shouted.

Her husband was the first to look up out of the knot of men. A frown of incomprehension made him appear fierce and very unlike the man who had kissed her so nicely in the train.

"Never mind, Mrs. Claybourne," he shouted.

He returned his attention to the stout man beside him. But his bellowing had caused a half-dozen pair of eyes to focus on her, and then back onto him.

"I thought you ought to see this," she shouted.

Claybourne left the group and came toward her, striding down the slight incline like an avalanche. "We're conducting an official investigation here—"

"I would hope so." Felicity ignored his displeasure and pointed to the slightly misaligned railroad blocks. "You can see the problem there, Mr. Claybourne: this part of the curve takes too much of the kinetic force. The blocks beneath have twisted out of place over the years. The embankment should have been strengthened when the bigger engines—"

He hauled her backward, fitting her against his chest, and spoke behind her ear in that very low tone. "Stay out of this, Mrs. Claybourne. These men are from the Railway Department of the Board of Trade. They know what they are doing."

Two of the investigators arrived in a hail of sliding gravel. "Is this your wife, Mr. Claybourne?" the stouter one asked.

"She is that, Mr. Sawyer. And fancies herself a railway inspector, I'm afraid."

"I was just showing Mr. Claybourne the maladjusted track."

"Yes, of course." Sawyer nudged the other man and looked at Felicity with grave suspicion.

Felicity walked out of her husband's arms and prodded her foot along the section of rail that had sprung loose from its moorings, and now stuck out perpendicular to the track. "And this rail is only forty-two pounds to the yard, far too light for the weight of the rolling stock."

Sawyer lifted his spectacles to his forehead and looked at her with an intensity matched only by the glare she was certain that her husband had fixed on the back of her head. "How is it you know this, madam?"

"My father was a railway engineer: Philip Mayfield. You may have heard his name."

Sawyer rocked back on his heels. "A fine fellow, a fine engineer, indeed." He beamed suddenly. "Then you must be little Felicity! By gravy, you are! I haven't seen you since you were a kitten, and I was your father's draftsman. Ah, but since then, you've become a beauty, and I've lost most of my hair."

"John Sawyer! I do remember you." Felicity recalled a much leaner man, with a full head of curly red hair, and a fine tenor voice. As she offered her hand, she saw Claybourne scowl.

Sawyer graciously took her hand in his and turned her toward the others. "All of you must remember Philip Mayfield. This is his daughter, Felicity Mayfield."

Her husband's eyes hardened. "Felicity Claybourne," he muttered.

Good God, his wife had taken over the investigation! These very distinguished inspectors were nodding and preening as if they'd been gifted by a visit from the queen.

"And you were with your husband in the first-class car when the accident occurred? You must have seen it all."

"I knew it was going to happen—"

"Did you now . . . ?"

Hunter listened as his wife explained her impossible-to-credit gift for gauging the condition of the tracks by the sensations she felt in her feet, and he wondered how grown men could stand there gaping at her as if they believed every word. It was the pink of her cheeks, not her experience, they were watching as she gamboled along the twisted track like a bit of eiderdown, pointing out her observations and pronouncing her suspicions, which ran the gamut from the effects of mud and humidity on iron rails to the load on the locomotive to George Hudson's bunions.

Sawyer scribbled earnestly on his notepad, and stroked his chin; he nodded his approval to the others, and occasionally to Hunter himself, including him in the conversation without actually having to consult with him.

Hunter was finally dragged away from his wife's performance to reconstruct the rescue effort. He hoisted rails and yanked aside sheets of iron, every movement a labor to evict his wife from his thoughts.

She stayed anyway.

It was nearly eight o'clock in the morning, with the sun washing over the countryside, when Hunter was finally able to load Felicity into the returned passenger car and travel on toward Blenwick.

She sat beside him in the seat, her posture upright, but her eyelids drooping.

"Where are we going, Mr. Claybourne? I think I ought to see to the injured in the little hospital." She crossed her arms over her chest. Her suit jacket was missing, along with her petticoats, and her white bodice had long ago been blackened and bloodied. She had the courage and tenacity of a lioness, but she looked like one of those American raccoons he'd seen at the London zoo, her eyes scrubbed clean and the rest of her face streaked with soot and mud.

"You've done enough for one disaster, Mrs. Claybourne. The injured are in good hands at Blenwick Hospital. You need sleep. The station master recommended a place called the Brightwater Arms, one of your damnable country inns. With any kind of luck, we can sleep until sometime tomorrow. I hope that meets with your approval."

When she didn't answer, or offer an argument, Hunter lifted her curtain of hair from the side of her face.

She was fast asleep and listing away from him in rhythm with the rocking train.

He settled her against him and wondered how she would rate the Brightwater Arms for her travel gazette.

Hell, he wondered how she would rate him.

Felicity fell asleep again in the common room of the Brightwater, and Hunter carried her up to their room, then settled her onto the bed—his bed.

"No choice in the matter, my dear," he told his sleeping wife as he unlaced her shoes and dropped them on the floor. "It was the only room left."

He shucked off his shirt and would have done the same for his trousers and his drawers, but he thought it best not to shock the woman when she awoke. She slept on like a brick, even as he covered her with a blanket and dragged himself under it with an involuntary groan. He should have removed her soot-streaked, blood-stained clothes, but he wasn't sure he'd be the first to awaken, and he didn't want her to strangle him in his sleep.

"Good night, Felicity," he whispered. Or maybe he just thought it.

And maybe he just thought he heard a sleepy, "Good night, Hunter."

Chapter 13

⁓◦⦿◦⁓

Felicity dreamed of hard-edged light and utter darkness, of a place where people were shadows and only fire had substance. It was cold there and lonely, except in those shadows, which were more like warm, inviting clouds, which were more like an embrace, or a kiss, more like Hunter.

"Hunter?" She sat up on her elbows and the shadows cleared.

He was sleeping peacefully beside her, the counterpane pulled to his chin. The room was very plain, with a low ceiling and a window that spilled warm, late-afternoon sunlight across the bed like a blanket.

The last thing she remembered was thinking how wonderfully comfortable the chair had been. How the devil did she get here, on the pillow beside Claybourne? She lifted the cover, blushing in advance, in case her husband had undressed her. Thankfully he'd only taken off her shoes.

Still weary to the bone, she settled back against the pillows. Claybourne stirred. A bruise had taken root on his forehead, and his face was so smeared with soot and grime he might well have been a chimney sweep, or one of the street urchins he despised so much.

She wanted to dislike him for the hundred different reasons she'd discovered already. And yet she'd seen startling moments of virtue in him. He'd taken command of the accident, and hadn't let go. He'd been gentle and generous with the injured, giving up his cloak and then his coat to warm a family who had suffered a great loss.

But how could she forgive him the callous intolerance he felt for the poor? He had treated Giles as if the boy was nothing more than leavings swept from the street. He had become a wild-eyed madman when he had found her near the slums; and had nearly drowned her until he had scrubbed the muck off her skirts.

Where did he come by such prejudice? His father, perhaps? A brutal father could as easily teach a son to loathe as well as he could to fish; could beat a son and abuse his heart until that son learned to raise himself up and fight back the only way he knew how.

She thought of Claybourne Manor and its windows, sealed up against the light, as gray as a tomb, and silent—a peculiar refuge against the encroaching wildness of the heath. At first she thought her husband miserly, his pride propped up by the imperious trappings of his wealth and position. But when she had dressed her chamber like that of a princess, he'd only asked after her comfort. When she opened the windows to the sunlight, he had shied from the brightness, but he hadn't complained. He'd been conspicuously generous to her with his money and with his servants. He had grumbled about the cost of her wardrobe, but rightly so. Seven hundred pounds was a workingman's lifetime fortune. But he'd paid it, then never begrudged her a stitch of it, never mentioned the cost again, even when the lot was delivered just before she left.

She would have predicted that traveling in the rail carriage with him would have been ghastly: an icebound silence, a cloud of ill-humor, and unvoiced accusations. But once he had settled into the rhythm, he'd been almost gracious and nearly conversational.

And then he'd given her a wedding band.

She hadn't expected one, hadn't even thought about it until he had slipped it onto her finger. But something had changed in that moment, something inside herself—a commitment she hadn't meant to make. And now her heart had gotten involved, had become encircled by the band.

She shouldn't have kissed him back so eagerly, but she hadn't been able to help herself. It had been a yearning she'd harbored for the past week. How was the man to be expected to restrain his urges if she encouraged him?

Urges. She'd heard about such things and had felt them in herself when he kissed her, felt them rising even now, made even stronger by the encircling gold on her finger.

Spending too much time in study of his mouth seemed to make her pulse rise and her breathing go ragged, but she was studying him anyway, and decided that a kiss on his temple wouldn't hurt.

His skin was cool and dry and tasted of salt and oily soot, and made her heart ache for him—the man who had lifted a broken old woman to safety from the belly of a dark hole. He brushed the back of his hand across the place she'd just kissed.

Better to let him sleep. Every bone in her body felt pummeled and bruised, and she'd twisted her ankle in the midst of the rescue, but what she really needed was a bath. A long, steaming hot bath.

She found one in the bath closet down the hall, and lounged for half an hour before drying off and dressing in her clean brown traveling suit and returning to the room.

Her husband was still sleeping. So Felicity took her portmanteau with her folios and went downstairs to have dinner in the common room.

* * *

A full two hours later, Felicity heard a thump and a thunderous voice above the stairs, and looked up from her writing. The three women who sat nearby had heard it, too, and stared at her as if she could explain the sounds.

She had her suspicions.

Footsteps raged down the narrow stairwell, and an instant later Hunter Claybourne stumbled into the doorway, his chest bare and heaving, his hair rumpled, his face still smudged, and his eyes blazing.

"Where do you think you're going, wife?" he bellowed, coming to a staggering halt on the last step, holding fast to either side of the opening. He looked very large.

Felicity hadn't known he could move so quickly.

"I'm not going anywhere, Mr. Claybourne, and neither should you. Especially without your shirt." Felicity tried to hide her smile from him. The other women now stared openly at the scandalously deranged man who had just swooped down on the common room. "This isn't your house, you know."

Felicity wondered if he felt as ridiculous as he looked. He looked toward the sheltered giggles from the other side of the room, then turned and disappeared abovestairs.

When her scowling husband was out of earshot, Felicity winked at the three women. "As handsome as he is mad, isn't he?"

They must have agreed, because the giggling continued amid talk of the train wreck and the mysterious man who had exhibited superhuman powers in his single-handed rescue.

Her husband seemed more opaque and confusing to her now than he had a week ago. He'd been very easy to loathe then, and easier still to dismiss. But the more she learned about him, the more she wanted to know. At the moment, the only thought she allowed to linger was the image of the breadth of Mr. Claybourne's naked, glistening chest, with its fascinating ridges and cords.

When he finally descended the stairs, he looked as he always did, scrubbed and tailored and confident, except for the wary gaze he swept across the room.

"The ladies are gone, Mr. Claybourne," Felicity said, strangely pleased to be alone with him. Her heart fluttered when his gaze landed on her.

"And the inspectors?" He tugged stiffly on each cuff, gave his neckcloth a tug, and came toward her with a slight hitch in his step.

"Gone to a tavern, it seems. Mr. Sawyer said there'd be a photographer here tomorrow morning."

"Good." He exhaled a short, stiff grunt as he sat down opposite her at the table.

She wanted to inspect the bruise that hid among the loosened curls at his hairline, but decided against drawing his temper. "You seem not much the worse for last night's wear."

"I'm older by a decade, at least."

"That would make you how old, Mr. Claybourne? About forty?"

"Well into my eighties."

"Then you've aged nicely, sir." Her husband looked quite miserable in his stiff collar. "But truthfully speaking, husband, I really ought to know how old you are. In case anyone asks. You know, like when they ask if you've kissed me."

He leaned toward her with such imposing determination, she thought he would kiss her again right there in the common room. But he stopped short of such a display and said in a very low, very pointed tone, "Tell them to mind their own business."

"Very well." Felicity felt greatly disappointed when he settled back against the chair.

"Have you eaten?" he asked, eyeing the cook as she came toward them with a plate.

"Twice," she said. "I told the cook you'd be hungry

as soon as you came down. I also thought you'd like this." She handed him a copy of the *Times*.

He looked surprised and cleared his throat. "Thank you."

Felicity forgave him his brusqueness, and moved her writing out of the way as the woman sat a heaping plate of sliced beef and roasted potatoes in front of Claybourne. "And I ordered your favorite wine."

"And how would you know what kind of wine I prefer?"

"You have crates of it in your cellar."

Hunter felt suddenly catered to, and altogether suspicious of her motives. "Ah, yes, my cellar. I might have thought you'd have found your way down there."

He decided that his wife was entirely too observant, and entirely too lovely this evening. Her hair hung down her back, tied away from her face by a ribbon of the same lush green as her eyes. She was dressed again in her travel-brown, poised, it seemed, to leave him at a moment's notice. And yet she was gazing at him over the top of her tea cup, and he wondered what devilment she was designing and what part she had planned for him.

"By the way, Mr. Claybourne, I took the liberty of hiring a vintner to sort your stock of wines for you, and to store it correctly."

Hunter set the glass down. "You did what?"

"Wine goes bad if it isn't cared for properly. And that would be a sad waste of good money, wouldn't it?"

"That doesn't give you leave to hire people without my permission."

"It's for your own good. Mr. Claybourne, your house is not a home. It's a huge, cold-storage building."

"I'm a very busy man. I can't worry about which lamp goes where—"

"That's a wife's job."

"So is warming a husband's bed." He didn't know why he'd brought that up, especially when it was the very last thing he should have said—given their cozy isolation, and the fact that she had been tangled in his bedclothes so very recently, and she now wore a gold band on her finger that seemed to be the only thing he could see anymore. A vexing warmth slid up his neck from his chest.

She fiddled with her pen and looked out at him through her feathery lashes. "You confuse me, Mr. Claybourne."

"Please ignore my outburst." He was beginning to sweat.

"With pleasure. Your living conditions are deplorable. I have been attempting to make your house more homelike, but if you're going to fight me, or forbid me, say so now and I'll stop trying. I'll keep to my chamber and tend a small corner of the garden, and I'll try to spend more time on my travels."

More time away? He hadn't liked the silence she'd left behind. And he'd come to expect the scent of wildflowers she'd brought into the house, and the perfumed breezes skipping through the open windows, and all the sunlight. "You have my permission to do whatever you think needs doing around the house."

She smiled broadly and clapped her hands together. "Outside and in?"

"Within reason."

He wondered what rare vistas she saw when her eyes grew so bright. Was she painting the foyer staircase a brilliant canary yellow, or burning the drapes in a courtyard bonfire? It didn't matter to him. What damage could she do? There wasn't a stick of furniture or brass bowl he couldn't do without. And if redecorating kept his wife at home and occupied, and out of trouble, then he wouldn't complain.

"By the way, your name is in the *Times*, Mr. Claybourne."

Hunter had been in the middle of skimming a story

about the cotton crop in New Delhi, but snapped the paper down to stare at his wife. "My name is where?"

Felicity finished writing a word and looked up at him. "I'm surprised you didn't see it there on the front page."

"*My* name? On the front page?"

. "I had nothing at all to do with it, sir. It was the accident."

Hunter heard himself mumbling as he sped through the narrow columns on the front page, unable to see his name for the black spot of fear that blotted his vision.

"It's right here." His wife came around the table and tapped her finger on his name. "Someone reported the accident by telegraph last night. The article explains how you took command of the rescue. . . ." She cleared her throat before reading, "'With the same efficiency and success with which he commands the peerless Claybourne Exchange.'"

Hunter stared at his name, relieved, but on edge. What would his clients think of the publicity? They might be concerned over his health, wondering how long an injured man could remain a shrewd investment director. "I didn't take command. And I don't like having my name in the paper."

"That's the lot of a hero, Mr. Claybourne. And you were very heroic last night."

"We were lucky to be alive." Hunter read ahead to see if his name appeared among the injured. It didn't.

"If you look closely, you'll find my name there, too. And don't bother to look for *Mayfield*, Mr. Claybourne."

Hunter felt his wife's soft breath at his neck as she leaned over his shoulder to read, "'Claybourne and his wife were miraculously unharmed.' See, there I am: 'his wife.'"

His wife.

Now Lord Vincent and the Chancellor and all the rest would know that he had married. He could see the sly winks and the knowing nods, as they assumed his marriage to be of the usual sort. It was not usual in any way. How could they know he had married a restless zephyr, a woman who would only graze his life, then pass him by like a dandelion seed in search of a more agreeable meadow?

She was still pressed up against his shoulder, her breasts a sublime impression against his arm, a sensation that diminished the importance of the Claybourne Exchange to nothing. Her hair caressed his cheek with its soft scent of vanilla, a fragrance that filled his lungs and coursed like fine Scotch through his belly.

"The Blenwick Line is one of Hudson's older enterprises," she said.

"Hudson?" Hunter wasn't sure what she was talking about and turned his head, only to find her green eyes focused boldly on his mouth. "What's this about Hudson?" he asked lamely.

He ought to listen more carefully, but he could hardly remember his own name at the moment. She lifted her gaze and it skimmed his cheek and his nose; and then she brushed her cool, damp mouth against his temple where the throbbing bruise had suddenly become pain-free, his swiftly coursing fluids diverted now to other regions.

"You weren't listening," she whispered, as if she knew his thoughts.

But she couldn't know; she couldn't. She had proclaimed her chastity quite boldly in their negotiations, had proclaimed her intention of gifting her "real" husband with her virtue.

Damnation, but that was the predicament as he sat here in this quaint inn, awash in her scent, sharing a meal with his legal wife: he'd begun to feel altogether . . . married.

He would have stood up and taken himself outside for a bellyful of cool air, but he was roundly aroused and he'd have embarrassed himself and her, and anyone else who happened by if he had tried.

"I was saying, Mr. Claybourne, that George Hudson has owned the Blenwick Line since its beginnings. As it says there in the *Times*."

It was a bit easier to center his thoughts now that she was walking back to her chair, though her hips played enticingly against the sway of her skirt.

"I'll have to read the full article," he said, his jaw aching with the grinding of his teeth.

She yawned and gathered her papers and pencils. "I know it's barely eight o'clock, but I can't hold my eyes open any longer. Good night, Mr. Claybourne."

Hunter waited downstairs, wanting to be certain that his wife would be deeply asleep when he entered their chamber. The inspectors joined him after their night at the tavern. They stayed for a while, exchanging ghoulish stories about other horrific accidents they'd investigated, managing to find a great deal of humor in their gruesome work. The distraction didn't last. His thoughts drifted up the stairs.

Sitting across from her and her unorthodox opinions on the train had been a seductive torture; kissing her had sent him reeling; watching her stubborn courage in the face of the tragedy had been breathtaking. And his ring had fit her so rightly.

Now she was upstairs in bed—in his bed.

He entered the room quietly, undressed himself down to his shirtsleeves and trousers, flipped off his shoes, and settled for the night into the small, lumpy chair near the window.

He found wire springs where there ought to be padding, and the chair arms creaked and sagged under his leaning, but he adjusted his position a few times and finally drifted into a twilight sleep.

"What are you doing here, Mr. Claybourne?"

He thought she had kissed him, but it was her voice breaking close against his ear.

"Wake up, Mr. Claybourne." She was kneeling beside him in her serviceable nightgown.

Hunter shifted away from her inquest and sagged against the broken chair arm. He wondered why she'd become so interested in him all of a sudden. "Go back to sleep, Miss Mayfield."

"Mrs. *Claybourne*, remember?"

He remembered.

"You can't sleep the night in this chair, Mr. Claybourne."

"I can."

"You'll have a sprained neck in the morning, and you'll be crabby and miserable to live with tomorrow." She stood up and tugged at his hand. "Come sleep in the bed."

"No. Leave me alone. I need sleep."

Her gentle laughter fell on him like warm rain across a desert. She knelt down, using his bent knees as armrests. He sat upright. There was a layer of wool gabardine between her palms and his skin, but it might as well have been nothing at all. Her fire leapt along his thighs like a fever.

"Then you take the bed, Mr. Claybourne, and I'll sleep in the chair. I'm smaller than you." When she patted his knees, he pinned her hands down with his own to stop their movement.

"I'm the man, Mrs. Claybourne."

"Oh? And what does that mean?"

"*I* make the sacrifices."

She laughed and sat back on her heels. "That'll be the day: when a man out-sacrifices a woman. And why don't you want to share the bed? We're married, as you pointed out so well on our wedding night."

He released her hands and settled back against the chair to keep an eye on her. "I'll stay here in the chair." Now she was fiddling with his foot. "What are you doing?"

But she had his sock off by the time he'd finished the question. "I'm making you comfortable, Mr. Claybourne."

"I don't want to be comfortable."

"And I don't want to suffer your crabbiness tomorrow."

When she lifted his foot into her lap and dug her thumbs into his arch, Hunter grabbed the arms of the chair and let go an ungainly groan. "What are you doing, woman?"

"Just relax. I'm not going to hurt you."

He heard himself making other, more protracted sounds, low in his throat, suffering bearable pain and ecstasy as she twisted his toes and ground her knuckles against the ball of his foot.

"Mr. Claybourne?"

"Yes?" It was difficult to say more.

"You have a terrible scar here on your foot."

God, he'd forgotten. He yanked his foot away. Old scars given new meaning, and abounding in new threats. She would find more than one if he let her stay. "An accident in childhood. Playing where I shouldn't have been."

"Looking for profits even then?"

He froze, and she left him. Relieved, he closed his eyes to find his focus. But her thumbs found the knotted muscles in his shoulders, and he moaned and lurched upward into her hands.

"Come to the bed, Mr. Claybourne. You'll feel much better."

"God help me," he said as he stood up and took her hand.

She had bewitched him, laced his wine or the air with her enchantment. Hunter let her lead him witlessly to the bed, and suffered her provoking massage and her gentle humming as he would a visit from an angel bent on killing him with inconceivable kindness. He moaned and wheezed like a shameless old accordion, aching from her touch, and aching for it. And he drifted across the sea, lifted by the sun-warmed waves to a beach with diamond sands. . . .

Hunter awoke sometime later, unconvinced that he

had actually fallen asleep. But the sky was pinkening, and his wife was beside him, tangled in his pillow.

Christ, she was beautiful. And she would be his for the coming year—for less than a year, as she kept reminding him. What kind of madness had he brought upon them? He wasn't the husbandly type, and she certainly wasn't the wifely type. When, and if, he ever decided to search out a wife, he would scrutinize carefully for docility and reverent obedience to his word. He'd never willingly take a wife like this one, who had stolen from him, upset his household, embroiled him in a railway disaster, and now claimed more than her share of his bed.

And yet, he couldn't imagine a different kind of wife than Felicity. He brushed her tumbled hair away from her cheek and she followed the course of his fingers, seeking his touch, frowning when he lifted his hand away, and dampening her lips in a sleepy pout. She'd stolen the blanket and had wrapped herself in it completely, all except one of her legs, which dangled over the farside, bare and enticing from knee to sole.

And all this disarming magic so very few inches from him, rousing him in an instant, quickening his heart as well as his flesh. That was the real danger: beyond the blatant lust she roused in him, the woman had drawn him out of London. He had convinced himself their separate travels were a coincidence, but he knew better, and would admit it to himself now.

He'd come to bring her a wedding ring—his ring. But she didn't need to know that he harbored such a simple weakness.

Like the weakness he had for her kiss.

Chapter 14

❧

Felicity awoke to the sweetest pressure against her mouth and a splendid tightness low in her belly. She thought her husband was touching her in her secret place, but when she groaned and opened her eyes, he was standing near the bed table, working furiously to button the front of his shirt.

"Good morning, wife," he said briskly, looking very businesslike, and sounding even more so.

Felicity decided she must have been shamelessly dreaming of his kiss. Yet her lips felt damp and tasted of him. She certainly felt kissed. She sat up and gathered the blankets around her feet.

"Are you dressing for the day, Mr. Claybourne?"

"Yes."

"But it's not yet seven."

"I meet with the investigators at nine." He fought with his stock and the clip at the back of his neck.

"Allow me." She stood up in the bed, took the neckcloth, and motioned him to turn around. He seemed transfixed for a moment on the front of her gown, then on her mouth, but he finally caught his lip with his teeth and turned away.

"Your meeting is fully two hours from now, Mr. Claybourne. What will you do till then?"

Hunter nearly jumped as she brushed his hair away from his collar. The graze of her finger against his nape made him tilt his head toward her hand. Yet her simple touch was the very thing he ought to deny: that subtlety of the morning, the sheltered intimacy of dressing. Domesticity.

"I plan to dine downstairs, Mrs. Claybourne; do a little of the work I brought with me; visit the site of the accident . . ."

"Did you sleep well?" she asked. "I mean, afterward." She lifted herself closer to her work, and Hunter held his breath as the tips of her breasts scripted her movements across his back. He shuddered in the wake of the warm tracings, fancifully certain that she had written her name or some other testament that would someday prove his downfall.

"I did sleep well," he said when he'd caught his breath again. He reassembled his scattered efforts at threading his rebellious cufflink through his shirt and tried again. "Yes, yes. I slept very well."

"Good. I did too—after you came to bed."

The memory of her intoxicating massage struck him down again, gave challenge to his dexterity. He excused his desire to bed her; what man wouldn't be stirred to insanity by her beauty, by the luscious curves that broke against her skirts and the boldness in her stare? Damnation, she was his wife, and she'd slept in the bed beside him all night.

When she had fastened the stock, she leaned over his shoulder to whisper at the back of his ear. "Excuse me for asking, Mr. Claybourne, but were you kissing me just now?"

Hunter stopped the futile work on his cuff and felt his face and ears go crimson. He'd been caught.

"Just now?" he asked, turning calmly in place to find her still standing on the bed.

Her nightgown was the plainest imaginable, nothing more than a scaled-down version of the one that

Earnest had loaned her. Yet that independent plainness suited her, made her all the more intriguing.

She's your wife.

"When I woke, Mr. Claybourne, I thought I was being kissed, and since you were the only man in the room, I assumed—"

"Yes, I kissed you," he snapped. "Yes." And if he didn't keep close tabs on his desire, he'd do it again. He'd do more than that.

She stuck her fists into her hips, drawing the linen across her breasts, thrusting the unguarded peaks against the fabric. If she were really his wife, he would lift aside the linen and take her into his mouth.

"That's four kisses, Mr. Claybourne."

"What?" He flushed again at the direction of his thoughts, then frowned down at his cuff. "You're counting?" He tried once more to push the link through, but gave up with a curse.

"Let me." She led him to the window, where the light was better. "You seem to be all thumbs this morning."

He refused to comment.

As she lifted his wrist, her hair whisked across his fingers and his palm, feathery and welcome.

"You also kissed me immediately after the train came to rest. Do you remember?"

Was it possible to forget? Hunter fit his finger through a coil of silken hair and brought it to his lips, tamped her scent into his memory.

"I kissed you then, Mrs. Claybourne, because I was very glad you weren't hurt."

"Were you?" She looked up and her eyes offered him a glimpse of green meadows and springtime. Her gaze was as bold as midsummer, but he so feared the frost. He warned himself to walk away, but he couldn't keep his fingers from playing along the soft ridge of her ear and the valley below, and she leaned into his caress.

"And then you kissed me again just before you lowered me into the railcar—"

"That time was for luck."

"My luck or yours, Mr. Claybourne?"

"Ours, to be sure."

"And what was this last kiss for, Mr. Claybourne?"

Calling himself every kind of a fool, Hunter laced his fingers through her hair, cradled the back of her head.

"I wanted to wish you a good morning, Mrs. Claybourne," he said, indulging himself in her nearness, in the perfume of her sunrise. "I understand it's a practice among some married couples."

"I've heard that, too."

But Felicity hadn't felt completely married until that moment, when her husband settled his heavenly mouth on hers. A morning kiss, a kiss hello, a sweet beginning that would only mean a more bitter-tasting farewell if she kept up her fancies. But that was sometime distant from now; for the moment, she surrendered to this bewildering, cold-hearted man, who made her feel so wonderfully alive.

His eyes glittered darkly as he brought his fingers beside her mouth and ran his scarred thumb across the parting, drawing moisture from her lips. When she stopped his hand to tease the tip of his fingers with her tongue, he took in a half-voiced breath.

"You shouldn't do that, my dear."

Felicity was in the midst of asking why, when he slanted his mouth across hers again, fiercely and randomly.

He hadn't yet touched her, except to caress her face, but now he tipped her chin and slid his searing mouth along the line of her jaw, and down her neck, sliding her nightgown part way off her shoulder as he followed the swell of her breast. His odyssey caused a storm to rumble through every part of her, and made her press her hips against him in a shameless, unthinkable way.

"Oh, my dear Mr. Claybourne! Next time make sure I'm awake before you kiss me."

Hunter groaned and shuddered. He'd meant only to taste her again, but her skin was the air he breathed and her pulse was his, and her fingers were locked insistently in his hair.

He pulled her into his arms, fitting her against the length of him, memorizing the slope of her waist as it met her hip. There wouldn't be another kiss like this. There couldn't be. He would let her go on her damnable travels to Northumberland, or to the Arctic, if it pleased her; hell, he'd finance a safari if she cared to go. Anything to put a great distance between them, to quell this terrifying feeling of contentment.

She's your wife.

The voice came from some irresponsible part of him, one he thought he'd evicted long years ago. She was nothing more than shifting sand that dazzled him even as it fell through his fingers. *Let her go.*

"Do you always sleep in your clothes, Mr. Claybourne?"

"No."

"Then do you sleep in a nightshirt?"

"Why?"

"I think I should know such things when I'm supervising the laundry, on such occasions that I'm at home."

"Ah. Well . . ." he said, drawing his fingers lightly from her brow, down the bridge of her nose, to settle in the vale between her lips. "You won't find my nightshirts in the laundry, or anywhere, madam."

"Then you . . ."

Hunter lifted his eyebrow, waiting for the question she would not finish.

"Oh, my." Felicity felt her cheeks grow warm, not out of embarrassment over his sleeping in the nude, but because some facts had just been added to her imagination. She could quite easily imagine her husband standing naked without his shirttails. There was still a blurring about his midsection, but she had seen and felt enough of his chest to know that an arrow of sleek dark hair purposely directed her attention downward toward some point of intense interest.

And she was pretty sure what she'd find there. The British Museum abounded in statues of well-formed Greek gods and warriors, and paintings of men wearing nothing but . . . paint. She just couldn't quite imagine such a thing made flesh. And the very thought of her husband having that sort of . . . apparatus down there, well . . . No wonder she could hardly breathe for the pounding of her heart.

"Mr. Claybourne?" She touched her palm to his chest, a feverish place that drew a sound from between her husband's teeth.

"Yes, Mrs. Claybourne?" He lifted her hand to kiss it, but stopped to stare at his gaping shirtfront.

"You've unbuttoned me, woman!"

Felicity hadn't remembered any shirt buttons, only the softly curling hair against her fingertips and the warmth of his chest.

"Sorry, Mr. Claybourne. I . . ." She'd been thinking about the strawberries from the day before. But she couldn't very well confess a thing like that. Her behavior might be wanton, and might encourage him, but the man was her husband, after all. And she was beginning to suffer the idea with some gladness. He wasn't at all the sort of husband she'd have chosen for herself. Just like his house, the man needed uncrating. He was still a hopeless mystery to her, but he was becoming a joy.

Her husband fumbled with the buttons at the front of his shirt, but she brushed aside his floundering fingers and went to work on them herself, then broke away from him and handed him his waistcoat.

Felicity had always wondered what it would be like to take lodgings with a husband in one of the country inns she'd so often written about.

There was much to recommend.

"I didn't mean to pry into your clothes, Mr. Clay-bourne." She stopped and adjusted the image in her head. "I mean, I just thought that I ought to know more about you and your habits, your life."

"You know enough."

"I know that you're a man of vast wealth; your parents are no longer living; and that you and I are married to each other at the moment. But that's all I know. You didn't even tell me your age when I asked. Do tell me about yourself, Mr. Claybourne."

He went still for a moment, then righted his neck-cloth with a yank. "I'm nearly thirty."

"I thought so. And your birthday?"

Hunter steeled himself against the dread, fought to hold it at bay. His wife perched herself impudently on the edge of the bed as if this were a game of questions and his role was to answer her. "I was born in 1820. It was the ninth of October."

"Did you grow up in London?" she asked.

He looked out the window and frowned through the shimmering images of his childhood, wondering which London she meant.

"Yes," he said finally, hearing the word drop flatly between them. Perhaps she wouldn't notice. She must not have; her smile never flickered.

"Which part of London, Mr. Claybourne?"

His fists were clenched at his side, distant from him, a foreign and convicting memory of a time he'd sought to forget. He had to unlock his jaw to answer.

"I lived in a number of places."

"How exciting! And did your family also have a house in the country?"

"No." He spat the answer and she flinched. He'd frightened her. Good. Fear would restore the bound-aries, would remind her of the basis for this sham of a marriage. No more questions.

"Did you attend Eton or Harrow?"

"Good God, woman!"

Felicity scrambled away from the malevolent strang-

er who had threatened her at the Cobsons. His warm
and supple mouth had become a rigid line. His gaze
had hardened; the light that seemed to have brightened with every passing day had shuttered itself.

"I attended neither school, Mrs. Claybourne, and let
that be the end of it." He reached the door but didn't
turn. "I don't know when I'll be back."

"It doesn't matter, Mr. Claybourne. I may be gone
by then."

"Go wherever the hell you want." He threw a fistful
of coins onto the dressing table and slammed the door
behind him.

The man had all the charm and manners of a rock
slide. Answering a few questions about his past
wouldn't hurt him. They were the very same kind of
questions she often asked of perfect strangers sitting
beside her on the train.

But he wasn't a stranger, he was her husband. And a
puzzle. And she wanted to know his heart.

Refusing to take the blame for Claybourne's groundless anger, Felicity bathed and took her time dressing,
then sauntered into the common room for her breakfast. Claybourne wasn't there.

Trying to get her bearings, she read over the notes
she'd taken in the last few days, and found little to
recommend to her readers. The description of a workhouse and a forsaken child wouldn't work well in a
book whose aim was to encourage travel. She could
recommend the Brightwater Arms for its reasonable
food and lodging, but would have to warn her readers
against taking a room with a madman. Even if she had
married him.

Nearly four days on the road and nothing to show
for it. Mr. Dolan would be mightily disappointed. She
would visit with Giles this morning and then leave
Blenwick today by post road to rejoin her original
trip—without her husband, and without the pile of
coins he'd left her. She would have to sort out this
marriage of hers when she got back to London.

Felicity made her way into the kitchen.

"Ah, Mrs. Claybourne. A bit more bacon?" The Brightwater cook was an artist compared to Mrs. Sweeney, and Felicity had lavished the woman with praise.

"No, thank you," Felicity said. "But if you could point me toward the Blenwick School—"

The cook's face screwed into a grimace. "What do you want with that horrible place?"

Apprehension wriggled against Felicity's heart. "Horrible? It's an apprentice school."

The cook's mouth soured. "Call it what you like, but it's a workhouse—for children."

Felicity went cold. No, she couldn't have heard right.

"It's a foul place—governed by a man named Rundull."

Giles in a workhouse? The very punishment he had dreaded most of all! And here she'd been lounging about like a sightseer.

Felicity cursed herself for being a naive fool. She should have known the police wouldn't give a boy like Giles the chance to make something honest of himself.

"What's the matter, dear?" the cook asked, coming around the table to place her age-softened hand on Felicity's forehead. "You've gone pale, my dear. Would you like to sit down?"

Felicity shook her head and backed away. "No, no, I'm fine. Where is the school? Is it nearby?"

"South of town. But you don't want to go there, Mrs. Claybourne. There isn't anything you can do."

Felicity left the kitchen in a fury, packed her portmanteau, and left the Brightwater Arms.

She didn't have a plan, but she would rescue Giles— even if she had to burn the place to the ground.

Felicity stood outside the Blenwick School for Apprentices, clutching the cold iron bars of the towering gates. She wondered if Giles had been as frightened as she was of the forbidding redbrick walls and the pinprick windows that reflected darkly, even in the midst of the morning.

The grounds were pinched and enclosed by an impregnable stone and iron fence, and soiled in coal smut and mud. The Queen's Bench Prison and Newgate all rolled into one dismal complex, and guarded by a man who appeared to be asleep, but whose eye had opened a slit as she arrived.

She had exactly six pounds in her purse. How the devil was she going to get Giles out of there?

She glanced toward the guardhouse and the shuffling sound on the other side of the gate.

"Yer here fer the job?" The voice blared like a steam horn that warns ships off the rocks. His foul breath could have melted the iron bars as it clouded past them and broke against her face.

Felicity stepped backward, well out of his reach. She could bless him for only one thing: the seed of her plan.

"The job, yes. Could you tell me about it, please."

He scowled with only one of his eyes. "Tell you about a cook's job? Hell, you'll be cookin'."

"Yes, of course, it seems a basic sort of position; but I was wondering about . . . the facilities, the number of meals per day, the menu . . ."

She stopped because he was laughing—a rather good-natured kind of laugh, one more suited for a public house than this juvenile prison that reeked of vinegar, and rotting leather, and other smells that she could not identify.

"Menu? Lady, this here's a school for apprentices, not Windsor Castle."

"And where do I apply for this job?"

He turned his laughter off like a spigot and peered at her. "Suit yerself, lady. Come on with me."

Metal scraped against stone as the gate parted just far enough to allow her inside. The guard passed behind her, then bolted the gate again. Now she was a prisoner in truth.

He allowed her to follow a pace behind him at his elbow and led her toward a low-slung building, an annex to the larger, darker one.

The yard was pitted with puddles and littered with unsalvageable trash. A school yard should be grassy and clean. There should be courts for playing ball and jumping rope. The Blenwick School for Apprentices was an outrage.

"Who am I to see, sir?" Felicity forced the civility back into her voice. This man seemed to harbor a modicum of caring beneath his frightening exterior.

"Mr. Rundull."

"Is he a fair employer? A trustworthy man? I mean . . . if I'm to work for him . . ."

The guard stopped to look at her quite earnestly. "Let me just say that I'll be prayin', miss, that you don't get the job."

"Have you worked for Mr. Rundull for very long, Mister . . . ?"

"Everyone calls me Arthur. I was eight when I come here. Twenty years, it's been."

He was only twenty-eight? The man's eyes were as old as Mr. Biddle's.

"My back don't work so good now; Rundull said that I owed him."

"Owed him?"

"For feeding me all those years. Says I have to work for him for the rest of my life."

"He can't do that, Arthur. There are laws against slavery."

"I don't know about any laws—I just know Rundull's strap."

"Take me to Mr. Rundull. He's the one needs strapping."

Arthur's eyes got very large, and she could finally see that they were the color of brick. "If you go in talkin' like that, miss, you'll never get the job."

"I'll take my chances, Arthur."

He muttered something and started off again. Felicity swallowed hard before she followed him, sobered by the fact that she was, in truth, destitute enough to be forced into such a position. Mr. Claybourne's support was temporary.

She slipped her wedding band off her finger and slid it into the pocket of her brown traveling skirt. It would only be in the way at the Blenwick School for Apprentices.

Chapter 15

~~~OO~~~

Felicity studied every door and lock as she followed Arthur through a series of twisting passages. She lingered at the grimy row of windows that looked from the connecting corridor into a huge workroom.

"Don't be standing around here," Arthur whispered, tugging at her arm. "Rundull don't like it."

Felicity shook him off and searched for Giles among the rows of children who hunkered on the floor on either side of a long center aisle. Watery light fell from the upper-story windows across a sea of small, hunched shoulders and bowed heads. Gray on gray, ashen profiles, and slate-colored uniforms. She couldn't tell one child from another.

Some worked with hammers against small anvil-like things, and others seemed to be sewing.

"What are they doing?" Felicity whispered, consumed with the horror.

"Makin' shoe tops."

"Shoe tops?"

"You know. For ladies shoes. Like the ones you got on."

Felicity looked down at her fashionable traveling shoes and felt herself blush in shame. Had her own shoes come from a place like this? She forced herself to lift her eyes to the workshop, but couldn't see past the grimy glass for the pool of tears.

"How can they sit like that all day?" Her voice shook as intensely as her hands did.

"They do it, lady, or that fellow with the birch rod gives 'em a good rap."

Felicity wiped a stream of hot tears from her cheeks. The guard was on the move toward two little girls who seemed to be sharing a brief giggle, probably over some childhood silliness. But they were too absorbed to see the man raising the rod high above his head.

Felicity was about to strike her fist against the window to stop him when a shout from the end of the corridor startled her into inaction. She saw the first blow land on the little girl's back and turned away like a coward.

A man was stalking toward Felicity in long, furious strides.

"What the hell are you doing in here, Arthur? You should be . . ." Then the face twitched into a patently false, practiced smile. "Ah, we have a visitor, I see."

"The lady's come for the job."

"The cook's job?" Rundull looked roundly confused for a moment, then shook himself from some unreadable notion and cast Arthur a seething frown as he motioned for him to leave.

Arthur's departure left Felicity feeling exposed to a choking kind of evil.

The man's sparse mustache clung like a smudged washtub ring to the ridge of his lip, and dropped in sinister wings to his jaw line. If he were an actor in a melodrama, he couldn't have made up his face with any better design for terror. His gaze stung Felicity, and would surely paralyze a child.

"Come this way, Miss . . ."

"Mayfield. Felicity Mayfield."

"Delightful," he said, leading her along the corridor

in a cloud of camphor, into an office nearly as well appointed as Claybourne's.

"Please, please, do sit down, Miss Mayfield." The voice that had barked at Arthur now took on the consistency of molasses, darkly smooth and annoyingly sticky.

"I'll stand, thank you."

"As you please," he said, motioning to the dinner steaming on a tray. "Tea?"

"Not for me, sir."

He declined the same for himself and leaned against his desk, one ankle crossing the other. He looked to be in his midfifties, well fed, and not easily sated. He nodded slightly as he scrutinized her from her shoes to the very top of her head.

"Now, tell me, Miss Mayfield, where have you cooked before?"

Felicity was so used to spinning stories of late, this one came easily. "Most recently, sir, for Claybourne Manor, in Hampstead."

He lifted his chin and looked at her over the ridge of his nose. "How long were you in service there?"

What was another lie? After all—she was about to kidnap a child. "I worked there two years, Mr. Rundull, as an undercook."

"And why did you leave?"

Felicity shook her head in pity. "The master's finances dwindled, sir." She could imagine Claybourne's look of shock and disgust if he ever heard her speak of his finances as dwindling. "Invested in an unlimited venture—railroading, it was. He lost everything."

"How inopportune." Rundull drummed his stout fingertips lightly on the back of his chair as he studied her. "You seem to know a great deal about the master's business. Were you his . . . confidant?"

Felicity blushed at the implication, at the palpable approval in Rundull's voice, and his too obvious anticipation of such favors should he deign to hire her on as cook. She widened her stance by a half-step.

"Honest gossip among the staff, sir. Our livelihoods were at stake in the matter." Felicity swallowed past a desert-dry throat.

"Yes, certainly. Well," Rundull said, indicating the door with his outstretched hand, "come this way, Miss Mayfield, and I will show you the kitchen."

It wasn't a kitchen; it was a filthy, blackened cave, leaned up against the back of the hall. Traffic channels had been worn into the blackened earth. Rotting refuse of every kind filled the corners.

"How many . . . students do you have, Mr. Rundull?"

"Seventy-three, as of yesterday's count. Twenty-eight girls and forty-five boys. And seven journeymen-teachers. So you see, you wouldn't be cooking for many."

The kitchen wasn't large enough to supply a single family, let alone a school full of children. The oven couldn't manage more than a dozen loaves a day. The stove had the remains of some grainy gruel drying against the sides of a dented cauldron. It couldn't have been left from lunch; there hadn't been a live fire in the hearth for at least a day.

"What happened to the last cook?"

"Well, I think that's my business, isn't it?" Rundull opened a small closet at the rear of the room. "Here is the larder. Well stocked, as you see."

Felicity peered inside. Well stocked with two sacks of flour, one each of oats and indian meal, and a barrel of some sort.

"Have the children eaten this evening?" Felicity asked.

Rundull touched his lips with his knuckle and lightly cleared his throat. "As you can see, we were entirely without a cook."

"All day?" Felicity couldn't mask the outrage in her

voice. "Do you mean the children haven't been fed since yesterday?"

Little spots of color blotched Rundull's face as quickly as if she'd hit him with a tomato.

"You won't succeed in my school if you take that tone with me, Miss Mayfield. The welfare of my students is paramount with me."

But she couldn't hold back the question. "Have they been fed today?"

He fixed her with glower. "Yes. Of course they have."

They both knew he was lying.

"Then I beg your pardon, Mr. Rundull, for my impertinence. Let me start dinner. If you don't approve of my cooking, you can fire me without having ever hired me. Although . . ." She turned liquid eyes on him, tears that came quite easily given the horror of the last half-hour. "I do need this job."

Her moment of groveling seemed to make up for her defiance. The man's face broke into the benevolent smile of the philanthropic victor.

"Well, then. A half-cup each of porridge is the dinner fare. Nothing more. Now, if you'll excuse me, my own dinner is getting cold." He left her.

Felicity listened to the blackguard's footsteps receding into the distance. Not a single child had eaten that day, and yet the man was concerned that his own meal might become inedible. She ought to snatch it from under his chin and distribute it among his victims.

But what to do now? She didn't want to waste precious moments cooking, but she needed time to plan. And if she stayed, seventy-two other children would go to bed without hunger gnawing at their innards. Felicity had known hunger, but it was usually caused by inconvenience or an unreasonable schedule. And she had always had friends like Mrs. Pagett who could put her up indefinitely. These children had no one but Felicity Claybourne.

She built a fire in the stove and took a quick

inventory of the kitchen. Besides the grains, she found salted herring and a good measure of pepper. She sent Arthur out with a few precious coins to find a bushel each of carrots and onions. He returned with her order just as she was putting the scrubbed-out cauldron to boil.

"He's not going to like this, Miss Mayfield."

"Don't worry; he'll never know that you aided me. Does he supervise the meals himself?"

"Not usually. The guards bring 'em to the door and they eat standing in the hall."

"I should have guessed."

That's when she would see Giles, and they could plan his rescue.

She added the carrots and onions to the water and soon had a hardy brew boiling. Sweat and tears salted her face as she worked.

She tried not to think of her husband.

An hour later, a line of children snaked past the kitchen door. They lifted up their little bowls and their weary-eyed thank-yous to her. They were supervised by a bandy-legged man whose hands were as tanned as the leather he worked, and streaked with white scars. He barked his orders, and the children obeyed in silence.

Then she found Giles. She knew him even with his head bowed. He wore workhouse gray, and his hair had been mowed nearly to his scalp, but his back was still straight.

He looked up from his bowl and Felicity heard the small cry in his throat; she saw relief in the start of his smile. Then the joy and hope in his eyes faded into a surly, red-faced anger.

She touched his hand, but he yanked it away, sloshing the soup across his wrist as he left her.

Felicity swallowed the insult, but felt a great stabbing in her heart. She'd come to help.

What if he wouldn't let her?

She was just recovering her wits when she saw Betts.

Felicity's heart nearly stopped. What a blind idiot she'd been! Betts and Arleigh were workhouse children. They'd been on their way to the Blenwick School, and Felicity had let them go!

Betts's face brightened and she opened her mouth to speak, but Felicity gave her a warning-look not to, and Betts saved her whisper for her brother's ear. Arleigh grinned as Felicity filled his bowl, and kept grinning at her even as Betts led him past the kitchen door.

Felicity had come for one, and now there were three.

More than three—there was an entire workhouse full of children who needed rescuing.

She leaned against the wall and wept.

The inspection had dragged on far longer than Hunter had expected, and it was early evening before he returned to the Brightwater. The inspectors had concluded, as his own wife had, that Hudson's contractors were at fault. What that meant for the rail line itself was anybody's guess. If the Board of Directors for the line was interested in a pennies on the pound resurrection, then he might be interested in making a purchase and financing the refurbishing, if the profits were high enough.

His wife wasn't in the common room, though it was time for dinner, and he'd hoped to smooth over some of the rough edges.

But, damnation, the woman had a mind for questions, sticking them between his ribs and twisting them. He would have to learn to answer them with more aplomb.

Perhaps she had retired early, and was sprawled out on his bed. He had ached for her all morning, watched for her, listened for her footfalls in the gravel. But she hadn't come.

And their chamber was empty.

"Mrs. Claybourne?" Stupidly, he looked around the back of the door. She wasn't there either.

A sourceless panic set in, a spooling out of his

connection to something he hadn't known he'd been lacking. His business yielded him hard, hollow comfort; an existence he'd grown use to. But his wife . . . Felicity—yes, he should think of her as Felicity. Felicity had softened the edges, filled in the hollowness, quite without his permission.

He had come to anticipate the remainder of the year. "Blasted woman!"

Hunter left the room and went straight to the kitchen. The cook looked at him in honest innocence when he demanded to know where his wife was.

"I haven't seen her since breakfast, sir. She left right after."

Hunter checked his temper. "Did she say where she was going?"

"Asked about the Blenwick School."

"The—?" Hunter hesitated. "What sort of a school is it?"

"As I told her myself, it isn't really a school—"

"What is it then?"

Hunter knew he'd bellowed the question by the way the cook stepped backward a pace.

"It's a workhouse. She seemed to get mighty agitated when I mentioned it. I thought she was going to swoon."

A workhouse! Damn her and her meddling! She'd gone after those kids who'd followed her around after the accident. They were orphans, or had been abandoned—he had known it from the moment he'd seen them with her. Even in the dimness and the disorder, he'd seen the emptiness in their eyes, had smelled the taint of the slums. He had kept it from her, because he feared the very thing she had done.

Well, let her go. Let her chase after her conscience. It would do her no good. Pull one wretch out of the sewer, and you'd find two more hanging on to his trouser legs.

She'd soon learn that a hand held out in charity was an admission of guilt, a firebrand in the gut. He refused to bear the guilt of someone else's misfortune. Allow them to set their own course; that was the guiltless thing to do. Every man, every child for himself.

Let her discover the uncharitable truth herself.

Felicity had just finished washing out the bowls when a tiny face peered around the corner.

"Betts! You shouldn't be here!"

But Arleigh ran past his sister and wound his fists into Felicity's skirts. "Oh, miss, we're so glad to see you."

Felicity bent down and held him; she might have been holding a ragged sack, packed loosely with spindle sticks.

"And I'm glad to see you, too. Why didn't you tell me you were coming here?"

"Have you come to cook for the school, then, miss?" Betts put her arm over Felicity's shoulder. "We'd be awful happy to see you every day."

Felicity tried to keep her tears at bay as she ran her fingers through Betts's chopped-off hair. "I'm not going to be the cook here. And you're not staying either. You're coming with me."

Betts dipped her chin and plucked at the front of her shirt. "Please don't fun us now, miss. Are you wroth with us?"

"I'm not angry with you, or funning you. We'll be leaving tonight, but you can't stay here in the kitchen right now. I don't want Mr. Rundull to see us together. And surely the guards will strap you."

Arleigh wasn't listening at all. He'd taken up his thumb and a hank of Felicity's skirt and seemed perfectly happy snuggled against her breast, rocking gently, his head tucked under her chin.

"Dear heart, you must go with Betts." When she stood up and lifted him away, his eyes puddled. "Don't cry, sweet. But you must hurry."

Betts seemed to understand the urgency and

grabbed her brother's hand. "Come, Arleigh. Best we do what the miss says."

Arleigh went placidly with his sister, though tears slid down his gray cheeks and his badly shod feet shuffled against the dirt. Betts turned back at the door.

"I know you're not funnin' us, miss, but if you change your mind, and you think it best to leave us— then I thank you anyway for givin' us the lovely thought."

Then the little girl was gone around the corner.

Felicity jammed her stained skirts against her eyes, anything to sop up the brittle, hot tears. Taking only three children, when she ought to take seventy? When she ought to burn down the loathsome school and the detestable Rundull with it.

"I smell onions!"

Rundull was standing in the doorway, leaning against the frame. He looked smug and well fed, a crumb of bread caught in his mustache.

"I didn't find any onions in the larder, Mr. Rundull, so I . . . obtained some from the grocer."

"Inventive, Miss Mayfield, but not in my budget." He sauntered into the room like a country squire surveying his hen house. "You'll get no money back from me."

"No, sir." Felicity busied her hands folding the flour sack she'd used for a drying cloth, hoping to distract the anger from her voice. It wouldn't do to be evicted just yet.

He drew his fingers along the scoured table and peered into the clean caldron sitting on the dying heat of the stove. "Have you given up making dinner? Where are these very expensive onions?"

"The children have been fed and returned to the evening shift." Felicity laced her hands behind her back, but loosened them when Rundull's gaze slid across the front of her bodice. The corners of his mouth lifted, and she moved away from him to close the larder door. "I've cleaned and straightened, as you can see."

"Yes, I see very well, Miss Mayfield." He rubbed his palms together. "Tell you what—I'll hire you for a week's trial. If your work appears satisfactory, you'll be paid your ten shillings, less room and board, of course. If I am not satisfied with every measure of your work, then I will let you go, and you will owe me seven shillings for your upkeep. Do you understand?" He raised an eyebrow as if he were the most honest and fairminded employer in the world.

Her neck stiffened in anger as she nodded. "Yes sir."

"Then bring your bag and I'll show you to your room."

Rundull led Felicity out the door and through the workshop.

The smell was worse than she had imagined. Vinegar and unwashed bodies, and the sharp smell of shoe blacking.

She found Giles when their eyes met across the room. He was standing over a table, shame drooping his shoulders. She found hope in that—maybe he wasn't too angry to leave with her.

But Giles shook his head and turned back to his work to lay a ringing hammer to the end of a chisel.

Betts and Arleigh were bent over a shoe-form in one of the stalls ahead of her. Betts was wisely doing her best to keep Arleigh from spotting her, but the boy was wriggling and fussing and not paying attention to his stitching. He took an angry stab at the shoe top and jammed the huge needle into his thumb. He let out a wailing howl.

Felicity winced in sympathy but continued trailing after Rundull.

Arleigh whirled away from Betts's attempts at comforting him, his injured thumb stuck like a stopper in his mouth.

"Quiet that boy," Rundull shouted, across the shop

to a guard who was already on his way toward the commotion.

Arleigh's weepy gaze found Rundull, and then Felicity. His eyes widened and his tears came even harder. He stumbled toward her, sobbing, and she could only bend and let him come into her arms before the guard could reach him.

Betts was on his heels. "Oh, miss, we're sorry for this. We are."

Felicity hushed and cuddled Arleigh, and took Betts into her arms all the while Rundull stood staring at this singular and most preposterous scene taking place in his school.

"What the holy hell is going on here, Miss Mayfield?"

The guard made a grab for both children, but Felicity was faster and scrambled out of his reach behind a pillar.

Rundull grabbed at the guard's nape. "Stand away, Flint!" He snapped the guard out of his way and came toward Felicity.

Rundull's face was rage-mottled, his neck bulged out above his collar. He pointed at her. "You are fired, Miss Mayfield."

"I was never hired, Mr. Rundull." Felicity lifted the children onto her hips and stomped away, surprised at her own strength. "Come along, Giles!"

Rundull was on her before she had made a half-dozen steps. "I'll have you in jail for this."

Felicity shoved the children behind her and planted herself in front of Rundull. "I'll gladly pay for the time they spent here and for your efforts at bringing them. And for that boy's charges as well." Giles cringed when she pointed at him.

"Pay me?" Rundull said with a sneer. "On a cook's salary?"

"I'm not a cook, Mr. Rundull. I'm a . . ." She couldn't very well say she was a travel writer—what kind of threat would that be? "I'm an investigative reporter for the *Hearth and Heath.*"

"A reporter?" Rundull unballed his fists. His shoulders dropped abruptly, and his voice mellowed as he straightened his skewed neckcloth. "Madam, you have taken us wrong. We are an apprentice school, doing our best here. I'm paid by a number of London parishes to school their cast-off children—"

"Mr. Rundull, this is no kind of school!" Felicity looked out across the room and realized that work had come to a standstill and every eye was on her.

"They learn the shoemaking trade," Rundull hissed, his attempt at hiding his anger from a reporter gone in a puff of smoke.

"And they pay for it with their crooked backs!"

Rundull growled and grabbed a double hold of her hair at the back of her head, and yanked her against him. "It's time you leave here, Miss Mayfield. But you'll be leaving with a strap laid across your back to remind you of your visit."

Felicity sent Betts and Arleigh scurrying away from her and from Rundull's wrath.

"Let go of me!" Felicity dug her fingernails into his wrist, but he shoved her forward. She tried not to panic for the sake of the children, but she had the horrible feeling that she had only made matters worse than ever. Any moment Rundull's guards would descend on them all. And what would happen to the children?

"Leave her alone, I tell you!" Giles came shouting out of nowhere, and leaped upon Rundull's back, fists flailing.

"No, Giles!" Felicity pushed at Rundull, but he threw Giles off and tightened his grip on her hair. Giles had the sense to keep Arleigh and Betts out of the way when they tried to help her.

"This way, missy." As Rundull propelled her forward, a great roaring cleaved the air, a paralyzing sound that sliced through the stone walls.

"Keep your filthy hands off my wife!"

Suddenly Felicity was looking past Rundull's shoulder into the eyes of an angel—a seething, angry-beyond-words angel.

Rundull's forward motion stopped abruptly. His fists opened so fast that Felicity stumbled forward and landed on her hands. Rundull made a gagging sound as he arched into the air, a rangy, flightless bird twisting against a sky of rafters.

Her husband stood above her, his face gone hard as marble, his eyes locked on hers.

Hunter had seen it all through a red haze, his vision narrowed tightly on his wife and the suicidal man who had seemed bent on hurting her. She was rumpled beyond recognition, her skirts floured and blackened, her hair sprung every which way. He sought details—his wife's enduring, familiar details. Gratitude in her eyes, a trembling courage on her lips, she stood up and brushed herself off.

His wife. Yes, Felicity. Her lovely details: quizzical brows, her head canted in concern, a cautious step toward him.

"Mr. Claybourne?"

Details only. He didn't dare look around; he knew what he would find: spidery, yellow-stained fingers; bent and broken limbs. The stink. The tanning pits. He had recognized the smell the moment the train had pulled into town. He had fought the effects, chided himself for his weakness. But he had come anyway, against his judgment, against every promise he had ever made to himself that he wouldn't.

He'd done it for *her*.

"Hunter?"

She touched his hand and he flinched.

Rundull stirred. "Get off my property, sir!"

Hunter straightened from his stupor. He yanked Felicity roughly behind him. "Be thankful you escaped with your life, you bastard." Hunter scooped up Felicity's fallen portmanteau and took her elbow. "Come."

But she stayed rooted to the planking, caught in

Rundull's mire. "I can't leave, Mr. Claybourne. Not without the children."

"You will come with me, wife." Hunter's hands were clammy and cold, and didn't work as they should, but he tried to pull her along with him.

"No, Mr. Claybourne!"

She slipped easily out of his hands and ran to the two children who'd been cowering between crates of finished shoe tops. She grabbed them up into her arms while her young cutpurse stood nearby. Giles. The boy from London. She had come here for him.

"I will not leave without these children, Mr. Claybourne."

Rundull puffed himself up like a toad. "You can't take them. I am paid twelve pounds a year per student. I'll not let them go for a penny less."

"I need a loan, Mr. Claybourne," Felicity said, fixing her glare on Rundull. "Thirty-six pounds."

"Per year," Rundull added, tapping his tented fingertips together. "Times ten years for the girl and the older boy, and twelve for the youngest."

"I need three-hundred eighty-four pounds, Mr. Claybourne."

Hunter couldn't move, was rooted to the sagging wooden flooring, barely able to concentrate, drenched in sweat. The corners of the room hung in boiling shadows, the twilight too weak to filter through the filthy glass. Welcome shadows that blotted his vision. Yet he didn't have to see to remember.

"Please, Mr. Claybourne."

Hunter's guts were knotted and nagging. He would surely disgrace himself if he turned.

"Mrs. Claybourne . . ." His breath escaped him in trembling, ragged torrents. "You can't rescue them all—"

"Maybe not, Mr. Claybourne, but I can rescue these three."

Hunter lifted the banknotes from his breast pocket,

then dropped them on the floor. "Tell the bastard to keep the bloody change."

Hunter waited until Felicity and her wretched foundlings had gone ahead, placing himself between his deluded wife and the workhouse. She was a cloud of freshness amidst the foulness.

And then he noticed it. Noticed the lack. His stomach reeled.

She had taken off his wedding ring.

Felicity watched her silent husband load her portmanteau into the carriage.

"You're not going with us?" she asked, hardly expecting an answer from him. He hadn't spoken more than a word to her since he'd dropped her off at the inn with the children, the night before.

"No." His eyes followed Arleigh and Betts into the carriage as if they were vermin. He didn't even look at Giles.

Felicity had spent hours cleaning up the two younger children, scrubbing years of neglect off their tender skin until they both were pink and glowing and squealing with laughter. She had burned their clothes, and they had slept in Claybourne's shirts.

Giles's mood had been as detached as Claybourne's had been. And she hadn't pressed him. There would be time for that later. He took his own bath and grudgingly wore the clothes she found for him. He'd slept in the chair that Claybourne had claimed the night before, and now sat stiffly inside the carriage. She wondered what he would do when they returned to London.

She had bought barely worn children's clothes for Arleigh and Betts, and now they looked like any other children one might see in Kensington Park.

And still Claybourne disapproved of them.

All of which drove her temper through the top of her head. "May I have a word with you, Mr. Claybourne?"

He followed her a few steps to the hitching post, but said nothing, keeping his gaze fixed on a meadow in the distance.

"Are they so far below you, sir?" she asked, keeping her voice hushed so the children wouldn't overhear. "Is that why you won't ride to London with us?"

"I have business to tend to."

"They're only children, Mr. Claybourne. If you'd only give them time—"

"Do not board them in my house." His eyes were clear when he fixed them on her, and as distant as the hills.

"In that dismal rabbit warren you call a home? They're better off on the streets of Bethnal Green."

His hands gripped the hitch rail, his knuckles white, his fingers flexing. "Then take them there, Mrs. Claybourne. Leave them. And let them forget about you."

"I will not let them forget. They will know that I care."

"How very honorable of you. And what of all the other children enrolled in the Blenwick School? Will they know you care?"

Felicity had tried to put that from her mind, but he bewildered her with his guttural questions. "They must know I care: I cooked for them—"

"Oh, yes, Mrs. Claybourne. How sweet, Mrs. Claybourne! A hearty meal and one of your charming smiles, perhaps a heart-stealing caress from your mothering hand—just enough to tantalize, just enough to send a child to bed with his hopes soaring. And when they wake to the hunger and the hope gnawing in their bellies, how will they feel when they learn you deserted them?"

"I didn't desert them."

"Would you care to go back and ask them? Rundull's little apprentices, his bony-fingered drudges stitching shoe tops for no pay at all, while Rundull himself collects three pence a pair from a partner in the London slop-trade, and calls himself a school."

"The slop-trade?"

"Those fashionable shoes you're wearing no doubt came from a place just like Rundull's. If you look closely enough inside, madam, by the instep, or down near the toe, you'll find bloodstains—"

Arthur's words had held the same accusation. "Stop it, Mr. Claybourne!"

"Blood from a pricked finger, or from a chunk of flesh torn out by a dull-bladed awl—"

"How do you know this? Are you one of these partners, Mr. Claybourne? Do you—"

His head reared back. "It doesn't matter how I know!" He recovered and bore down on her, his dark eyes hot and unrelenting. "Did you see their faces when they looked at you? Did you see precious hope twisted up in despair, Mrs. Claybourne? Did you smell it? Could you taste it? Because I did. God help me, I did."

Felicity swiped at the tears coursing down her cheeks. "But we brought out three—"

"And left how many more behind, praying for their own angel? Did you think of them?"

"We had no choice."

"Self-serving charity, Mrs. Claybourne! The kind that makes you *feel* good."

"Yes, it does, but—"

"God damn you, woman!"

"Mr. Claybourne, how dare you speak—"

But he took her by the elbow and lifted her into the carriage.

"When are you coming home, Mr. Claybourne?"

"I don't know." He ground a twenty pound note into her hand and strode away without a backward glance.

Arleigh and Betts huddled together beside her, their eyes wide in dread. They couldn't have heard or understood the sense of the argument, but they must have felt the heat.

Giles had obviously heard everything. He sat opposite, his jaw clenched and working. She knew he wanted to say something, but he kept his opinions to himself and settled his gaze out the window as the carriage jolted off.

"Well, my loves, we're on our way to London." Felicity wiped her nose on her kerchief.

Arleigh and Betts snuggled next to her, one under each arm, leaving her to stare at the empty seat where Claybourne ought to be.

He was quite mad. He had damned her for caring at all about the children, and then had damned her for not caring enough. It was one or the other, Mr. Claybourne. She couldn't be blamed for both.

But he'd made her feel callous and vain and guilty. He was the one who had blustered his way into the workhouse, who had demanded she leave without the children.

He was the heartless one.

He was the one who had stood mutely in the midst of the squalor, his face ashen, his eyes as wild as a spooked horse.

He'd known all about the shoe tops and the sharp tools . . .

"Why was the big man so very wrothful, miss?"

Felicity brushed the curls from Betts's forehead and nuzzled her sweet-smelling hair. "I don't know, Betts. I really don't know."

And then a tiny, jangling thought came to her, something that had not seemed quite right at the time, something that haunted her now. . . .

Hunter Claybourne hadn't been disgusted or enraged. He'd been terrified.

Chapter 16

Hunter returned to Claybourne Manor on a drizzly moonless night, feeling as solitary as he ever had in his life. He had consulted with his business contacts in the north, sat in on the Railway Department inquest concerning the accident, and made substantial progress in his bid for recognition by the Board of Trade. But he'd been restless to return home, and honest enough with himself to know the cause.

Felicity.

He'd said her name a hundred times a day, and cursed her with every breath. Yet he hadn't been able to shake her from his thoughts, nor could he quiet the hammering of his heart. And now she seemed to live there. Like a determined morning glory, she had entwined herself and her inclinations into his life. He damned himself for basking in her comfort.

And yet he had worried what she would think of him and his rage that final morning. Even at the time, the rational side of him knew his reaction was out of all proportion. He must have seemed a lunatic; and yet he couldn't recall a single word he had said to her. He had probably ranted and swung his wrath around like a cudgel. He had felt insane after pulling her from the workhouse, had stripped off his clothes in the moonlight and scrubbed himself clean in the stream nearby the inn.

He would try somehow to explain himself, to ward off her queries with reasonableness. And if she wanted to waste her time and money on ill-conceived charities, that was her choice. Condemning her would only make her delve deeper into his reasons, and he couldn't have that.

Claybourne Manor was dark and battened down for the night. The wild perfume of flowers lingered in the air, a foreign and familiar scent that chipped at his self-assurance. She was here somewhere, no doubt fast asleep and taking up too much of her bed.

Hunter shucked off his slicker and started across the broad expanse of the foyer. He'd only taken a dozen steps when he ran smack into something that caught him across the waist.

"Blast it!" The woman had stuck a damn table in the middle of the entry!

And something in the center of the table was teetering, wobbling, growing ever more precarious in its circling tilt. His eyes adjusted to the dark just as an extraordinarily tall vase pitched forward and smashed against his shoulder. Flowers rocketed everywhere, the vase landed on the floor with a ringing crash.

"Mr. Claybourne!"

Hunter knew the whisper. It came floating down from abovestairs, and the music of it set off his pulse. Its owner padded barefooted down the staircase, the white glow of her night-robe making her seem ghostly and untouchable.

Without sparing him a single glance or another word, she set her lantern on the table and bent to the sloppy mess on the floor, muttering, sifting through broken stems and shards of ceramic.

Her hair was more golden and wilder than his memory had made it, her scent more searching. He stood there like a simpleton, fisting his aching hands into his coat pockets to keep from harrowing his fingers through the flaxen cloud of her hair at his knees. Spots of heat singed his cheeks, blotches of bitterness to know that she would consider the distressed state of the flowers above his own.

She raised her eyes and they glistened in disappointment. Her mouth glistened, too, her lower lip caught between her teeth as she stood, having rescued a sprig of honeysuckle. The fragrance hooked around his nose and made him step closer.

"I should have left a light for you in the window." She smiled then, but hesitantly.

"It's no matter," he said, hearing soft voices and lighter footfalls receding into the darkness, into other parts of the house.

He watched as she smoothed her alabaster hand across his coat, and slipped it comfortably beneath the ridge of his lapel. Her fingers idled among the buttons; he wanted to lift them to his mouth, to touch his lips to the ring that shone there again, the ring he'd thought she had abandoned.

"I rather thought you would return during the daylight, Mr. Claybourne." She tucked the sprig of honeysuckle into his breast pocket and patted it. "I didn't mean to leave a trap so that you might rouse the entire house."

"You smell very nice," he said, instantly thinking himself a dolt for saying it aloud.

"Thank you, Mr. Claybourne." She looked shyly up at him from beneath her lashes. "But I think you smell the honeysuckle."

He'd never given a thought to the name of that particular flower, but the breathy way the word lifted off her mouth and stirred against his throat carried erotic pictures to his mind and a sheen of sweat to his brow.

"Did I wake you?" he asked.

"I wasn't sleeping. I heard a horse in the drive."

"Hired in Hampstead. He's put away now."

"And so should you be, Mr. Claybourne. It's well after midnight. Come, I'll take you to your chamber." She hooked her arm into his and led him up the stairs.

Hunter knew the way to his chamber, but he followed her anyway, his senses dilated, marking the soft skiffing of her bare footfalls and his own hard-booted ones, separating vanilla from honeysuckle, sequestering the heat of her hand that kindled its way through his coat sleeve to his arm.

He hadn't expected this sort of welcome: fragrant flowers and her feathery whispers. As he opened the door to his chamber, he knew even less what he ought to do about it.

Felicity felt her heart flitting around inside her chest like a bird demanding its freedom. He smelled of the coldest night, and trailed honeysuckle after him. His profile was resolute, but had lost its sharpness.

She had prepared herself to be annoyed at him, and unaffected by his nearness, but he'd looked so confused and contrite when she found him standing among the fallen flowers and shattered vase, as if he were a clumsy child awaiting a scolding.

She had never known a man who could confuse her as this one did. In the last four days, she had revisited everything they had said to each other in the workhouse, and everything he had done. And she was no closer to an explanation. She only knew that something was dreadfully wrong, and that she had missed him.

Missed him! She must have: she had waited every night at the window for him, turning his ring on her finger, and had made excuses for Branson to drive past the Claybourne Exchange every day on her way to the Beggar's Academy; and she had drifted in and out of bliss at the memory of his kisses—but that couldn't mean she actually missed him. Missed him? No, it was more than that. Much more. Oh, dear God—

She loved him!

And she'd known it since driving away from him in Blenwick. She loved him for all his flaws and failings, for his heroic courage, and for the goodness he hid even from himself. Loved him for all the things he didn't say, and couldn't understand. She loved him because he thought he didn't want her to.

Because he didn't know how to love in return. Felicity looked down at her wedding band, and decided that it was time he learned. To the devil with the settlement. She was married to Hunter Claybourne, and it was about time she did something about it.

But how was she going to manage? Her limbs had gone warmly liquid, and her fingers unsure as she raised a fire in the grate, under his watchful silence from the doorway.

"There," she said, finally finding her voice. "A kettle heating for your bath, clean water in the bath closet. Welcome home, Mr. Claybourne."

"My name is Hunter," he said, striding into the room and closing the door.

"Yes, I know."

"Then use it, please, when we are in private company. A year is a very long time—"

"Eleven months, six days."

Hunter despised the fact that she brought up the remaining time on her sentence every time he mentioned the length of their contract. And he wondered how to reconcile her eagerness to leave him with the fact that she had acted the role of a dutiful wife just now: fluffing his pillows, turning down his bed. "Madam, even one day is a very long time to spend with you."

She gave an incensed little sniff. "Am I that much of a nuisance?"

"That much, and more, my dear."

Yet Hunter felt more at home, more welcomed home, than he had in all his life. It pleased him a great deal to think that she might have been waiting up for him, and he'd begun to hope that she had forgiven him for his outburst in Blenwick. He pulled off his coat and tossed it into the dressing-room laundry.

"I don't mean to be a nuisance . . . Hunter. But it seems to be the nature of our affiliation."

"I suppose it is." Hunter allowed a smile and set his traveling case across the arms of the chair. Things were proceeding well. Their words were calm; she was about to pour him a glass of brandy. "The invitation from Lord and Lady Meath came to my office today—"

"To the Exchange?" She put the glass down abruptly and took two scolding steps in his direction. "You were in London today?"

Hunter frowned at her attack, at the wrathful angle of her delicate brow. "Most of the day—"

"And you sent no word?" she snapped.

He was puzzled by her sudden annoyance and decided to tread the next few steps very lightly. "I hadn't thought to. I never have before."

"You haven't been married before!"

He ventured a smile. "No, that's true. No one has ever cared to know where I am."

"Well, I do."

Her indignation warmed him to the marrow. She'd been worried. Hunter tried not to grin. "Then I should have sent word that I had returned to the City?" he asked, fortifying his voice with honest concern.

She sniffed sharply again and a strand of hair fell from its moorings at her temple. "That's the proper courtesy between a husband and wife."

"Ah." He wanted to tuck the strand behind her ear, to test the silkiness of both against his memory. "Then I shall send word to you directly should another occasion arise in the next eleven months and six days. Though, I will be far more constant in my communication than you were in your promise to telegraph me of your whereabouts."

"As I told you then, Mr . . . Hunter, I would have sent word that night from Blenwick."

"Not likely—given the circumstances." He could taste his fear again, metallic and oily, felt it licking at his heart. "You would have been in that other railcar, Felicity. I wouldn't have liked that."

"And we never would have found Giles, or Arleigh and Betts."

Hunter had purposely forgotten about the extra baggage; he looked toward the door. "Ah, yes, the children—"

"No. They are not here, Mr. Claybourne," she snapped. "They sleep in Bethnal Green beneath warm blankets in a room heated with wood from your stores. Fresh food is delivered daily and feeds fifty or more. I've given them four washtubs, a crate of soap and linens, clothing and shoes, writing slates and chalk. I have ordered new schoolbooks, which should arrive very soon. I see Arleigh and Betts every day. And Giles is learning arithmetic. I've kept a detailed list of my debts to you. You'll find it on your desk, near the ledger where you've listed my other expenses. This, too, is a loan, and I will pay back every penny when my uncle returns from the gold country—"

"Felicity—"

"Please don't start an argument, Hunter, not when you've only just arrived and there is peace between—"

"Felicity—I meant only to ask how they were."

She looked sideways at him, righteously skeptical. "They are doing very well, thank you."

"Then, I'm pleased."

Felicity didn't believe him, but she lifted his neatly folded shirts from his traveling case. They carried his scent of lime and spices, and she resisted the urge to bury her nose in the linen.

"I'm not a monster, Felicity." He pulled off his neckcloth and unbuttoned his collar. It sprang back from his throat like the wings of an angelic beetle. She fought back a highly inappropriate giggle.

"Neither am I."

"I'm quite sure of that." His voice had a habit of rolling down her spine and lodging very low in her belly. She had missed that, too.

Felicity carried the shirts to the laundry hamper in his dressing room, feeling a great deal of heat at the back of her neck. He was leaning against the doorway, unbuttoning the back of his collar, when she turned to leave the small room.

His eyes had gone very soft, and her muscles felt like plum jelly as she crossed beneath his gaze.

"I don't mean to hurt anyone, Hunter." She pulled out his folded trousers and his extra coat, and draped them across the back of the chair. "Least of all innocent children."

"I'm sure of that, too."

He was being quite understanding, and she wondered how far his goodwill would travel. "That's not what you said at Blenwick. You were not very complimentary."

He grew quiet for a moment and seemed to consider his answer carefully. "I was . . . angry. Angry at you and at the likes of Rundull."

Felicity felt the sting again, unjustly condemned. "Lumping us together? You are unfair—"

"And you are not at all like Rundull. That isn't my point at all." He lifted his hands as if the right words were out there to be grabbed. "It's just that, in my circle . . ." He glanced at her, and then away, idly lifting the cover of a book. "In my life . . . I see the competitive aspects of charity, and it has always galled me. Lady Jerganson making the rounds in the boxes at the Opera House, begging donations for distressed hatmakers; and when Lady Tuckworth gets wind of her rival's new charity, she starts one of her own for distressed, *lame* hatmakers. And neither woman has a clue what these hardworking hatmakers really need."

It seemed odd to her that he'd given this much thought to charity, when he was so very uncharitable.

"But, Hunter, wouldn't you think that the hatmaker

would rather grumble about his lot on a half-filled stomach than on a completely empty one?"

He looked up at Felicity, and she was heartened to see a calmness about his eyes. "I don't know, madam. Perhaps Lady Jerganson ought to ask the hatmakers directly. But she never will."

"Is that where I went wrong, Hunter?"

"You haven't gone wrong, exactly. It's just that I've met so many of these dewlapped, moist-eyed, philanthropic matrons and their—"

"Dewlapped!" Felicity grabbed a pillow off the bed and hurled it at Hunter. The lout ducked and it missed him. She launched a second pillow and caught him smack in the face as he turned back to her. "Moist-eyed? Is that how you see me?"

"Felicity—"

"I am no matron, Mr. Claybourne! Dewlapped or otherwise."

He grunted as he grabbed the next pillow out of the air, and then Felicity saw true mayhem in her husband's eyes. He started toward her, and she let out a scream. She swung around the bed post, and he followed in his steady stride, a self-possessed smile on his lips.

"And I'm no easy target to be buffeted by pillows, my dear." He came effortlessly around the corner of the bed and reached for her. Felicity hit him in the head with another pillow, then dove onto the mattress on her hands and knees.

"Not so fast, woman."

Felicity screeched as he caught her by the ankle and flipped her onto her back, baring her legs to his ripening gaze. He hauled her ever closer to him across the mattress.

"Mind my nightclothes, sir!" But then her thighs were bare, and then her hips, and then so was the patch of her womanhood—and he was looking!

At everything!

"Mr. Claybourne!"

"The name is *Hunter*," he said, as he knelt down on the floor and pulled her over the edge of the bed to a kneeling position between his legs. He was smiling, and his eyes were a dense and smoky gray. "If I'm to see *that* much of you, my dear wife, you'll have to call me Hunter."

"Call you *Hunter?* I'll call you a libertine!" Felicity tried to tug her hem down to cover her nakedness. But his eyes lit with brimstone as he caught her hands and pinned them back against the bedside. "Let me straighten my nightgown, sir!"

She was naked from the underside of her breasts downward, and forced against the silk of his waistcoat. Her knees were spread between his thighs and pressed into the carpet. She must be blushed crimson all the way to the soles of her feet.

"Fear not, wife," he said in a voice that had gone marvelously husky, "I can't see much from here."

"But you *did* see, sir!"

His sigh was light and roguish. "I cannot deny it."

A delicious, lime-scented heat poured off him, seeping into her skin from his clothing. "A gentleman would allow me to right my clothing."

"I am not a gentleman, as you well know." He caught her completely naked hips with his overwarm, overlarge hands, and fit her even deeper between his thighs. "But I am your husband."

"Yes, but you're not a regular kind of a husband." Felicity's anger and embarrassment were quickly deserting her efforts to regain a measure of control, even while her belly was pressed scandalously, deliciously, against his trousers.

"I may not be a regular husband. I'm not made of flint." He teased her ear, leaving traces of his breath to tickle at her neck. "But you are made of sunlight, my dear. And I want you."

"Want me?" Felicity found herself plagued by a huge curiosity. Strangely open-minded toward the way he played his mouth along her jawline, she bent her head and lent him access. He was her husband, after all, regular or not. This was entirely legal and moral. And wonderful.

"God, yes, I want to drink your sunlight."

Hunter fought to keep his voice even and his hands still. Dear God, if he had been able to explore at leisure the poetry that had sailed past his eyes, he might have drowned in bliss! Pink, pristine flesh, lean thighs, a triangle of golden curls, and a softly cleaving shadow that had begged his hand as well as his mouth. He couldn't let go of her just yet.

"My dear, you have me thinking things I oughtn't be," he whispered, as he coursed his tongue along the ridges of her ear.

"What sort of things, Hunter?"

His answer was interrupted by the sound of footsteps clattering down the hallway. A rap sounded on the door.

"Mr. Claybourne, sir! We heard a scream!"

Hunter didn't move, and took heart that his wife hadn't either.

"Sir, are you there?"

"Yes, Branson," Hunter said, feeling remarkably at peace, as if he were sitting in his chair perusing the *Times*, not squatting on his chamber floor with his wide-eyed, half-naked wife caught with her knees spread apart between his thighs. "I'm here."

"Sir, I went to Mrs. Claybourne's room, thinking she needed our assistance, and . . . she's not there."

Hunter sensed every beat of her heart as it thundered against his chest. "She's here with me, Branson."

There was a pause on the other side of the door, then a voice of deep concern. "Are you all right, Mrs. Claybourne?"

Felicity looked up into her husband's smoldering eyes and decided she was quite all right. She had missed him while he was away. And the very idea was significant, and made her want to kiss him, made her want to squirm beneath his hands. He had the manners of a mule, and ideas that needed changing, but she knew above everything that he had no intention of hurting her, and that thought sent her heart and her hopes soaring.

"Yes, Branson," Felicity said plainly and loudly. "I'm . . . in very good hands, thank you."

Her husband's eyebrows rose quite charmingly.

A throat cleared politely in the corridor. "Very well. A good night, then, to you both." Branson's footsteps receded.

Felicity hadn't taken her eyes off Hunter. He canted his head and asked, "In very good hands, madam?" He grinned and splayed his fingers across her bare bottom, laying down prints of heat like a brand. "I'm glad you think so."

"I didn't mean—"

"Oh, I think you did." He closed his eyes as he shaped his extraordinary hands over her backside as if he were inspecting a summer melon for its ripeness. "You are very cool here, wife."

Feeling altogether wanton, Felicity kissed the underside of his bristly jaw. "There's a knavish breeze whisking around on the floor, sir. Just above the carpet."

His rumbling growl blew across her lashes, and she was suddenly looking up into his eyes, and riding the rise and fall of his chest. "Lucky fellow, that breeze."

His wild words sent a surging rush of outrageous pleasure to clog her veins. He was smiling as he leaned closer, as he glided his tongue along the arc of her lips, and then between them with an agonizing leisure.

Felicity sighed and leaned against him. From the moment he had dragged her off the edge of the bed and fit her against him, she had noticed a length of hardness just below his waist, a formation which seemed even harder at the moment, and very much larger than it had been before. Her hand was eager to discover the source, but there was no room between them, so she moved her hips instead.

That drew a gasp from him, and he reared up. "Take care, Felicity!"

He looked dazed, his mouth damp and his smile crooked and flickering. But she liked the roll of his hardness against her belly, her woman's wool against the wool of his trousers.

She recalled the Greek statues in the British Museum. Hunter's apparatus seemed to be doing something completely on its own. And his face had gone enchantingly red.

"Welcome home, Hunter," Felicity said, wondering when his eyes had stopped being so darkly opaque, when they'd become bright and clear.

"Yes, home," he whispered, in the bare moment before he covered her mouth with his, before he began to tug and nibble and make delicious sounds in his throat, before his magic roared through her chest and lit the ends of her fingers and caused her to want to ride his hips with her own.

Felicity welcomed his tongue as if it were the most natural thing in the world to be kissing with her mouth open. He was a devastatingly thorough explorer, discovering her sighs and her soft moaning. She brushed her tongue hesitantly against his. He must have approved; he groaned and ground his hips against hers and met her tongue in a frenzied dance.

He came up clamoring for air, still kissing her temple. "Madam, you taste more sweet than I remembered."

Felicity loved the way his words caught against her hair, moist and textured by the insistent softness of his mouth. "I don't recall being quite so completely kissed before this."

He smiled like a rogue and studied her, his chest steaming like a locomotive. "Never? Not by anyone?" He drew a finger from her chin to the base of her throat. "What about all those other men you liked to kiss?"

Felicity remembered too late that she had professed to having kissed numerous other men, but she found no shame in being forthright with this truth. "Fictional, every one of them."

Her confession drew an arrogantly possessive smile from him. "I'm pleased to hear it."

Felicity had expected a chiding remark; instead, Hunter touched her mouth reverently with his fingers and followed with a tender, worshipful kiss that quickly deepened until she had twined her arms around his neck and buried herself in his embrace.

"Hunter . . ." Her skin was flushed with some kind of magical energy that made her want to open herself to him. His mouth had become unyieldingly hot and hard, and traveled to the limits of her nightshirt. She had climbed so deeply into his arms that he was forced back onto his heels, and now she sat brazenly astride his lap, her bare legs spread indelicately, her tender, swollen flesh at the junction of her thighs snuggled against the wool of his trousers and that simmering hardness just below—and she yearned for him to touch her there.

"You were saying, wife?"

She'd had a thought in there somewhere, something important and far-reaching. Yes, she remembered it. "Can a child come from kissing in this way?"

Hunter heard himself groan. "Not directly." He let himself be drawn into another of her consuming kisses, until he was toying dangerously with the buttons that fastened the front of her gown, and with the irrational idea of undoing them.

"Indirectly, then?"

"There comes a point of no return."

"And are we near it?"

Hunter had begun to think he'd been near it ever since he'd met her. "I don't know, Felicity."

"Would you know where that point was? I mean . . . if we got too close to it?"

"I'm sure I would know exactly." Then the straining at his groin would be freed of its prison and she would be lush and wet. She was near enough just now, and wriggling, only a few buttons between the root of him and her sleekness.

"And could we stop there?"

"I doubt I'd have the strength." He held back another groan as she slid her tongue along his upper lip and then followed the line of his jaw to his ear and to his neck; her fingers played at his collar band. He held fast to her hips, stilling his own fingers from a quest that he dare not accept.

He slid his hands upward across her silky flesh—the distance from her ever-wriggling hips to the lush curve of her waist was nothing, and everything.

And her breath came against his ear in a long, hissing draft. "Your hands are very warm, Hunter." She stretched out against his chest. Her eyes were half-closed and her mouth was turned up in a contented smile.

"They shouldn't even be there." Yet he couldn't remove them any more than he could evict her from his lap, though his knees were beginning to ache.

Her brow flickered and she opened her sea-green eyes. "But we're married, Hunter. The courts recognize it. We kissed on it. I have a ring. . . ."

"Felicity." Hunter wondered how she could remain so unruffled; most women would have swooned to find him so inflamed, would not have pressed against him for more. But Felicity wasn't just any woman: she was unbridled passion, and magnificent curiosity, and would soon have him howling at the moon if he didn't stop this. And yet he wanted to stay here, and stray, and he imagined her writhing beneath his hands.

"Oh, Hunter! Yes, that's lovely."

Dear God, he'd been sliding his hands ever upward,

skimming over her silken ribs, and he'd caught his thumbs beneath the gentle rise of her breasts. Sweet, soft mounds that begged his touch, begged his lips.

"Please, Hunter." Then she settled a kiss on his mouth.

Please? But Hunter was already drowning in her clean, cool breezes, his resistance having drifted away long ago. And she was holding his face between her honeysuckle hands, feathering her mouth across his brow and over his cheeks.

"Felicity, you can't know what you're doing to me."

"What am I doing, Hunter?"

"You're making it very difficult for me to resist you."

"Then don't." She was making contented little noises that hummed inside his chest and caused her to sway like milkweed in the wind.

"Ten minutes ago you were screaming for me to unhand you, and worried that I might see a bit of skin."

She giggled against his ear. "Ten minutes ago, I didn't know what I was missing."

He had to keep a cool head; his wife had become a lunatic—a captivating one, but a lunatic all the same.

"You'll have to show me." She slipped her hands over his and dragged them upward to cup her breasts. "Ah, yes! You see, I'm a woman, Hunter."

Her nipples pressed like compact miracles into his palms. "Yes, I know you're a woman, Felicity."

"And as a woman, I'm allowed to change my mind." Her eyes were closed again, and she had the look of the angels on her face as she swayed. "And your hands feel very good there, Hunter, as if I were standing on a cliff without a stitch to hide me from the eyes of the world; and you are the rising summer breeze that wraps me in splendor."

"Madam, you are fully clothed."

She opened her eyes. "Yes, but I think I'd rather not be."

His head had gone light from lack of air. His jaw

ached; he commanded his thumbs to be still when they would ride the honeyed peaks. He was a single breath from taking her there on the carpet.

"Hunter? Are you interested in making love with me? We're way overdue." She stood up and began to unbutton the neck of her gown.

"Overdue?" Entranced and speechless, Hunter staggered to his feet as he watched button after button fall to her fingers until nothing held her gown together across her shoulders but the weight of the linen.

"Are you interested, Hunter?"

"Interested?" he hissed, his brain boiled by a conversation that no man could ever survive. "With all your squirming and your drunk-making kisses? Madam, I want nothing more!"

"But are you willing?"

"Am I willing?" He had tried patience. He hoped anger would serve, because that was all he could muster. "You incite me to the brink of ravishing you, and you have to ask such a question?"

"Well, I do, because I don't know—"

"Of course I'm willing!" he bellowed.

"But will you?"

Hunter opened his mouth to answer and couldn't. He was damned to hell either way. Serve his passion and he would probably lose her goodwill; serve hers, and his fate would be same. He hadn't bedded or even kissed a woman in years. He'd kept himself aloof from the daughters of society and their trap-setting mothers. And he would have nothing to do with prostitutes or other women whose moral code might put the Claybourne name at risk for a scandal. He had lived without intimacy of any kind for so long, he had thought himself immune to the need.

Oh, but God, he had the need right now . . . and it was for her, for his vagabond wife. He couldn't risk a real marriage. His heart would betray him, and she would come to hate him, then she would turn on him in anger.

But now he was standing in his own chamber, wrapped in a heady cloud of her scent, quaking like a tempted vicar, his extraordinary wife begging his hand to her breast.

His wife.

She had waited up for him, turned down his bed, put away his clothes, uncrated his life, greeted him with honeysuckle . . . and had forgiven him.

Why did he want to weep?

"Hunter?" Now she was looking up into his eyes with that sympathetic inquisition of hers. "Are you all right?"

His throat worked and his mouth grew dry. Sweat wicked through his shirtsleeves. "I'm fine."

"Are you sure?" She frowned and felt his forehead. "You're sweating like a racehorse, but you have no fever."

"Like hell, I don't," he murmured.

She reached up a hand to his chest but he stepped away, a coward, and turned his back on her.

"Hunter?"

He fought the urge to turn back, to gather her into his arms and do just as she had asked. But he knew the risk, and he dare not take it. They had made a bargain; signed a settlement. He was the right-thinking one.

"This won't do, Felicity." He wiped at his brow with an unsteady hand and stared down into the flames.

"Won't do?"

Hunter could see her in his mind: her hair tousled from his over-eager fingers, her mouth still pouting from her unspent kisses. "I'm sorry, Felicity, I've let things develop between us that shouldn't have."

"Why shouldn't things have developed between us, Hunter? It's only natural."

"You know as well as I—"

"That we are temporary; yes, I know. But not so temporary that we haven't already become . . . well, friends, at the least."

He turned then, too astounded not to. She was

stunningly puritanical and practical again in her plain nightgown, now buttoned up tightly. "Friends?"

"When this is over, Hunter—our marriage, that is— I'm quite sure I shall still consider you a friend."

"A friend?" he said, not believing his ears.

"At least a friend. A very good friend. That's been an unexpected development between us."

Hunter willed his heart to keep a steady pace, but it bounced around inside his chest. Yes, she had become a companion, a friend, a quickening. Someone to come home to—and he suddenly couldn't imagine the day she would walk out of his life and not return. "Yes, things have developed unexpectedly."

And he wasn't yet sure what to do about it in order to limit the risks. It needed cold analysis, not her heated kisses.

"We were married quite inconveniently, Hunter, but I think we've made a success of it so far. Gotten over the bumps better than most. And I thought that we were developing an unexpected . . . intimacy—"

"Damn it, Felicity! Intimate or not, friend or not, I won't leave you unchaste for your 'real' husband. The one you will marry next." He looked back at the hearth and his steaming bath kettle, convincing himself that the heat that braced his neck was from the fire and not from a sudden fit of jealousy.

"I see." There was a tremble that rattled around in her sigh and made him feel guilty. "Not that it matters to you, Hunter, but I doubt that there will ever be such a man."

Hunter turned abruptly. She had retied her robe, and except for the flush on her cheeks, she looked as virginal as ever. And he ached all the more.

"What do you mean?" he asked, shamed to admit that he had selfishly hoped that when their marriage ended she would live a single life, instead of falling in love and giving children to another man. He felt a bastard for allowing the thought to remain a hope. But with every passing hour, the idea of Felicity taking up residence in another man's life seemed utterly unthinkable.

"I doubt I'll ever have the opportunity, Mr. Claybourne." She picked up one of the pillows that she had hurled at him and clutched it to her chest.

"Why not? Any man in the world would want you, Felicity."

"Oh, would they?" she said as she efficiently plumped the pillow and set it against the headboard. "Can you see yourself wedding a virginal bride who had been married once before? What kind of a recommendation would that be for a husband?"

"The explanation of the circumstances of our marriage should be sufficient to any man worthy to claim you as wife. If not, I could certify the situation myself." The words stuck on his tongue, and sounded patently false as they stumbled out. He could hardly see himself describing the intimate details of their marriage, least of all Felicity's virtue, to some disapproving, disbelieving husband-to-be.

"Thank you for the offer, Hunter, but no." She stalked past him, leaving her scent on the air and his hands aching to reach out to her. "What kind of woman is so repugnant to a man that she is incapable of tempting a passionate man like you to her bed? I'd rather not face the shame of trying. Good night, Hunter."

"Felicity—"

She had opened the door and was halfway down the hall before Hunter had realized she was leaving.

"Damnation! Come back here!"

When she didn't, Hunter followed.

Chapter 17

He crossed the hall in a dead run, and slipped on the new carpet runner. He barely caught himself, only to slam into a spindle-legged table that now waited outside her chamber door. Bric-a-brac clattered, but he remained upright as he launched himself toward her door.

He found his wife as she was turning down the lamp at her desk.

"Madam, were you truly hoping to tempt me to your bed?" he asked, raw desire scraping at his throat.

"Frankly, Hunter, I don't know what I'm hoping for. I'm very confused. I'm your wife, and yet I'm not."

"You *are* my wife." But she never even spared him a glance as she whisked past him on her way to her bed. Hunter felt like a schoolboy suffering a drubbing by his lady love.

"Hunter, I know that I said that I ought to save my chastity for a real husband, but you seem quite real to me at the moment."

"Do I?" His palms still burned with the shape of her breasts, still sweated with the memory.

"As I figure it, Hunter, if I'm to be damned for the perception, I might as well be damned for the deed."

Her eyes were clear and honest, and brutally trusting.

"So, I've ruined you already?" he asked.

"No, Hunter, I'm the only one who can ruin me." She lowered the wick on the bedside lamp to a gentle glow and turned back to him. "I just think it would take an unusually open-minded man to want me after . . . you know."

Hunter wanted her all right—wanted to touch her hair, and wrap his arms around her, but he had become more and more certain that it couldn't possibly stop there.

"I may never have another chance to have a man make love to me, Hunter. So I thought perhaps you could show me what becomes of all this wanting stuff—sometime, when you have a minute—"

"A minute!"

"Well, however long it takes." She dropped her robe off her shoulders and draped it across the end of the bed.

"Done right, Felicity, lovemaking takes hours."

She straightened the counterpane with her precise efficiency. "Hours?"

"The longer the better."

She turned from her fussing and raked her gaze, as hot as a furnace, down the length of him, lingered recklessly below his waist, and then lighted brightly on his face. "Can a body endure hours of that sort of thing?"

"It can," Hunter said, between clenched teeth. "With a great deal of concentration."

"There, you see, Hunter?" She climbed into her bed and pulled the counterpane up to her waist. "What a dolt I would seem to my next husband! 'Aren't you finished, Robert? Aunt Agatha is waiting for her tea in the parlor . . .'"

"Robert? You have this man picked out already?" Hunter would kill him.

She flung her limp arms across the pillows and sighed. " 'What's taking you so long, Philip?' "

Hunter swabbed the damp from his brow and growled. "Who is Philip?"

" 'Horrr-aace, I thought we'd be finished by now—' "

"Enough, woman!" Hunter stood over her, filled with a volcanic hatred for these imaginary husbands of hers. God knew what he would feel about a husband of flesh and bone.

"You see how very stupid I would seem."

Hunter turned away in his helpless fury. "What would you have from me, Felicity?"

"Well . . . instruction, I suppose."

"Instruction!"

"Friend to friend, if it can't be husband to wife."

"Good God." Hunter raked his fingers through his hair and dropped down on the edge of the bed. He couldn't look at her for fear of giving in to her ridiculous notion.

She sat up and leaned toward him. "I think Article Four in our marriage settlement covers this sort of thing, Hunter."

He snorted. "A miscalculation, you called it."

"It wouldn't be if we both agreed to it." She touched his elbow with the sparest of pressure, an indelible entreaty.

It would be the biggest of all miscalculations. He was insane to even consider it. A child might come of it, and what then? Children would complicate matters.

"Well, Hunter? Are you willing?"

He finally dared a glance at her—the wood nymph caught inside the unsuspecting master's house, sweet of face but determined to do her inexplicable magic where it wasn't wanted.

Oh, but he did want her. His flesh had wanted her from the start, yet his heart had been the first to betray him. He needed time and distance.

"First answer me this, Felicity." He tilted his chin upward and submitted to her nibbling kiss at the base of his throat.

"Yes?"

"When did you last bleed?"

She sat upright, frowning. "That's personal and private, and no kind of a question for a man to be asking, Mr. Claybourne."

"Maybe not, *Mrs.* Claybourne, but I'm asking." He wasn't going to risk a pregnancy. He'd read of cycles and fertility, had a book somewhere in his library, and knew there was a right time and a wrong. Too many things hung in the balance. "When was it, Felicity?"

"I'm not going to tell you."

"Very well." Hunter stood up. His presumptuous question served as he'd hoped it would, to dampen her interest and postpone the matter for another day. He could better fight the battle and determine the risks when his nerves were cooler. "Good night, my dear. Sleep well."

Felicity burned with indignation as she watched her husband leave. She couldn't imagine why he'd wanted to know when she had last had her monthly visit. He was a man . . . and a very nosy one.

Yet that very realization made her feel giddy and warm inside. So did the memory of his rough-palmed hands on her breasts, and his mouth playing havoc with her senses.

With any luck his urges would remain as strong as hers, and someday he would take her to his bed and make her his wife in truth.

She relit the lamp at her desk. Work was the only way to dispel her confusion. A good dose of editorializing about the workhouse of Blenwick would do it.

She sat down and began adding to the list of horrors she had seen, planning out her idea for a new set of articles. She would continue her travels, but she would visit workhouses and apprentice schools, instead of charming little cottages and cheese festivals. Her conscience wouldn't allow her to rest a moment until the last child was rescued.

Even so, half an hour's effort to sidetrack her thoughts of Hunter had only served to make her think about him even more.

His question hadn't been completely indecent. Perhaps he just wanted to know that it wasn't happening right now—perfectly understandable, considering. He hadn't said why he needed to know such a thing, and she'd been too startled to ask.

She hadn't been fair; and she hadn't been wise.

Felicity turned down the flame on her desk lamp and crossed the dim hallway to Hunter's room. She knocked, but he didn't answer; called his name softly, but still he didn't come to the door. She had heard him leave his room soon after he'd left hers, but he had returned not five minutes later. Maybe he'd gone out again.

Determined to settle her mind before the night got any longer, Felicity let herself into his room to wait for him.

But as she closed the door, she heard a sound across the room and turned. Her husband stepped out of the bath closet just then, swabbing a towel across his face and his newly washed hair.

And he wasn't wearing a stitch of clothing. Not a stitch. And he was glorious!

"Oh, my—Hunter!"

He stopped in his tracks—the stonecutter's art made flesh. He was every bit as magnificent as the gods and the warriors on display in the British Museum. Even more so!

His midsection would no longer be blurred when she pictured him in her mind. His apparatus hung from a dark nest, suspended below an intoxicating looking appendage. The whole area had just begun to stir when he held the towel in the way of her gazing.

"May I help you, Mrs. Claybourne?" he asked, as full of business as if she'd met him in Threadneedle Street.

"My name is *Felicity*," she informed him, pleased to see a leveling blush on Hunter's face. "And if I'm to see that much of you, my dear husband, you'll have to call me Felicity."

She couldn't help staring at the bulge beneath his towel, and felt a great deal of power: she was quite certain that she had something to do with stirring it. The thought made her grin.

"Have you come just to stare, Felicity?" He seemed irritated, and turned away, revealing a godlike back-side.

"Of course not, Hunter." She righted her thoughts, but watched him anyway, muscle converging against muscle as he stuck his arms through the sleeves of his silken robe.

"What brings you across the hall?" he asked impatiently.

Felicity felt terribly disappointed when he closed the front of his robe and tied the sash across his waist. He looked even more irritated with her as he hung the towel in the closet.

"I've been thinking that a wife ought be able to discuss anything with her husband, no matter how temporary the arrangement might be. So I've come to tell you . . ." She felt her face begin to glow from a blaze that had begun in her chest.

"Tell me what?"

"There you see, Hunter, I'm blushing just to think of confessing this to you."

He threw wood onto the fire and shoved at it with the poker. "Just what are you trying to confess?"

"Well . . ." She decided to let the words rush out, and then she would leave quickly. "My last bleeding was a week and a few days ago—whatever that means to you."

"Damn . . ." The poker clattered into the brass bucket. She said nothing as he came to stand at the foot of the bed. "Are you sure?"

"Sure?" He was so very tall, and his eyes shone so brightly . . . and she loved him so very dearly. He seemed as serious as he had that first day in his office. Their wedding day.

"Are you sure of your calculations?"

"I remember such things very well, Hunter. A woman must do so, in order to keep from staining her clothes and to avoid embarrassing accidents." Felicity felt terribly giddy, felt his gaze rest as hotly on her breasts as his hands had done earlier. "So I'm certain that it started, on schedule, two days after you threw me into the stream. In the morning."

"Ah," he whispered through a voice that had a distinct creak in it. "And it happens . . . how often?"

"You've only thrown me into the stream once . . . so far." Felicity smiled because he did, and his was quirky and laced with a humor he had turned inward upon himself. And he had shaved. Which seemed altogether odd, considering that he had been about to go to bed.

"You must tell me how often you bleed." He stood there like a seething statue, his limbs made of granite, but his chest rising and falling like a bellows. She wanted him to kiss her.

"Every four weeks, Hunter, give or take a day, maybe two."

"I see." Her answer hadn't eased his breathing, it only seemed to draw him closer. And now he stood above her, a dark scowl etched into his handsome features. It took every effort not to touch him.

"Can I ask why you care, Hunter?"

"Children," he answered, his brow now profoundly fretted.

"Whose?"

"Ours."

"Children!" Felicity had thought of children between them only in the abstract—Article Four of their settlement. A possible miscalculation. She knew better now; she'd seen too many forgotten children recently, cold and starving, left out on the streets to fend for themselves by mothers who couldn't afford to feed them. And, if she should conceive tonight, she would have an innocent, two-month-old babe to protect when her year with Hunter was up, when he set her out on her own. She couldn't afford to travel with an infant, and couldn't possibly afford *not* to travel. She would be one of those pitiful creatures who was forced by the parish governors to leave her child at the workhouse door. Never!

"Good night, Hunter," she said, brushing past him to the door.

"Good night?"

She got the door partially open before Hunter closed it again. "Wait, please."

"I've changed my mind, Mr. Claybourne," she said, as he guided her gently into the room.

"We're in the middle of a discussion."

"No. We're at the *end* of it. You were right. This isn't wise." Felicity sat down on the edge of a chair, suddenly terrified. "What if a child comes of tonight?"

"It won't."

She snorted and jammed her fists between her knees. "Are you God? Do you know this for certain?"

"As certain as God's science allows. I've been consulting this book on the human fertility cycle." Hunter pointed to a thin volume on the table beside her.

"I've never heard of such a thing." But the book was opened to a chart with ascending and descending lines and the words *barren* and *procreative* written in various places on the grid.

"I recalled that I had it in my library. And I wanted to be sure I was correct."

"So do I, Hunter. And the only way we will know for certain is if we don't do this at all." Felicity left him to his book and went to the door. "I won't bring a child into the world if I can't provide a home and blankets and enough food to keep its little tummy from aching—"

"Damn it, Felicity! No child of mine will ever starve."

"But if our marriage . . . *when* our marriage ends, the child wouldn't be yours, Hunter. It would be mine. Like the settlement said."

"Well, damn the settlement. The child would be mine."

That resolved it—the wicked man intended to steal her child right out of her arms. Felicity made a grab for the latch, but he stepped between her and the door and held her away from him.

"Felicity, what's gotten into you?"

"Your deception, sir!" She twisted away, but he followed on her heels and turned her.

"I'm speaking as truly as I can." His look of injured innocence didn't sway her.

"And you've proved that, Mr. Claybourne. You would keep my child for yourself! Even after you signed your name, even after your promise to—"

"Good God, Felicity, I wouldn't desert you. I'd never leave you or my child to starve!" Hunter heard himself say the words, felt them swirling around in his chest, and knew that he had never spoken a more certain truth.

"What does that mean, Hunter?" She planted her hands firmly on her hips. He hadn't seen that pose coupled with that particular look of defiance since the night he'd first seen her, at the Cobsons.

"Felicity, I am perfectly willing and quite capable of providing anything you and our child might possibly need, should the situation ever arise. Which it won't. But, in point of fact, I would insist upon supporting you both. Comfortable beds, warm clothing, shoes, the best schools, bountiful meals—"

"And would you visit him—or her? Regularly?"

"Visit?" Somehow the picture in Hunter's mind had included Felicity and himself and their handsome family all seated happily around the dining-room table, sharing stories of their day and contentedly planning their tomorrows. The image made his eyes sting. "I would be present for the most important events."

"And for walks in the park?"

Proudly pushing a pram, Felicity at his side; he was staggered by the idea. "Of course."

"And you would love this child?"

She waited relentlessly for his answer, with her hands clasped behind her, her bare toes flexing against the carpet. A mother bear without a cub, a steadfast heart too grand for her own good, too ready to welcome unworthy strays.

"I would hope to love my child unreservedly, madam," he said through the tightening of his throat. "How could I not?"

She didn't move, and he was afraid to spook her; huge tears welled in her exquisitely green eyes. Her earnestly straight shoulders finally slackened from a weight he must have placed there in his carelessness. Her arms hung limply at her sides, and her tears streaked like rain down the front of her nightgown.

She finally snuffled. "Well, then," she said, wiping her sleeve across her eyes. "That's decided."

Hunter couldn't help but smile, couldn't help wondering who had won, or if it mattered. He was just two paces from her, but couldn't move for the tilting of the room. He'd have thought the earth was sliding about, but for Felicity's graceful steps toward him. She took his hand and his world righted.

Hunter's skin ached; he brought her palm to his mouth, and then to his kiss. The fire from the hearth danced in her eyes; it shaded and shaped her nightgown, draped her like the finest silk, made tight, tawny shadows of her nipples.

"May I?" he asked as politely as he could manage, though he'd already slipped his fingers through her hair and now cradled her head softly, wondering if she could feel the racing of his pulse in the heels of his hands.

"You may do anything you like, Hunter." Her eyes were misted, and tracked his own like a blazing lighthouse.

"That's not a wise invitation, sweet." Hunter grazed her mouth with a drift of kisses, nothing more—not yet, though desire surged through him like the highest tide.

"Oh, but I like this, Hunter. Like kissing you, and tasting you." She caught his nape with her hand and drew him closer to chart a course down his throat with her gentle kiss.

"If I did as I liked, it would be over before it began."

"But you said it took hours. . . ." Her every breath was excruciatingly warm, spent through the silk of his robe and broadcast like a storm.

"It will. I promise you." Hunter closed his eyes and imagined peonies falling from the clouds, alighting on his chest, leaving their cool kiss in the fashion of her mouth—he imagined melodies . . . He caressed her mouth with his, then fit his palm to the warm underside of her breast, cupped the sweetness through the linen.

"Ah, yessss." It was just as he had dared to remember: a small but weighty handful, a perfect fit for his hand and no other's.

And he prayed for strength and guidance.

"Hunter!" Felicity caught a little sob in her throat as she watched him rub his thumb across the peak, an elemental sensation that bored to the center of her. It rose against the fabric, and she gasped when he bent his head and kissed the new rising.

"Sweet perfection," he whispered against her gown, leaving the impression of his kiss, and the steamy dampness.

His hands were heavenly, slow and wondrous, spreading his fingers like a meadow fire across the flimsy linen. She strained toward him, toward his mouth as it trailed the aching rise of her breasts, toward an unknown ecstasy.

He tugged with his mouth, and heated the linen with his guttural growls, and then he tugged deliciously harder, and wet her through with his febrile tongue.

And then she wanted his mouth fully against her skin. But he was taunting her other breast, twirling her nipple between his fingers, and she could hardly stand for the reeling sensations.

A tight, tugging fever was building in her secret place, and she wished that Hunter had another hand, or that his manhood was freed of his robe and—"Oh, my!"

He looked up from his delicious torture, wary and sloe-eyed. "Yes?"

"I was just . . . You are . . ." Felicity shook her head madly. "Never mind."

How could she explain what he was doing to her, that he was handsome and hers, and made her heart sing? His smile was sumptuous as he kissed her, a sweep-away-the-stars kind of kiss, which she prayed had come from somewhere near his heart.

"Let me." He knelt on the carpet, bronze and dark, his eyes glinting like diamonds. The first button of her nightgown fell to his touch, and he kissed her there, slipped his hand inside and lifted her breast slightly, gave a swipe with his tongue at the underslope.

"So lovely, warm . . ." He spoke around his kiss, making her feel lazy and light of limb.

He spread his broad hands across her stomach and around her waist and worked the next pearly button free of its fastening with his teeth and his tongue, all the while shooting fire from his fingertips, clutching her backside and lifting her so close that her hips were tucked up against his chin—and, oh, the impossible sensations *that* image summoned.

"Hunter!" Bursts of lightning and blazing bedwarmers, and thoughts of him doing amazing things to her. She felt more than a little dizzy, and held tightly to his shoulders for fear of pitching backward.

He released her and sat back on his heels. She felt roundly deserted. The last button dangled in the folds of her gown, just above the patch of curls that craved his hand and wanted to be pressed against his mouth.

And he was looking just there.

"Hunter . . ."

Hunter heard her breathy little sigh, saw the shadowy triangle, dark blond and level with his mouth, scented for him. Her gown cleaved her in two across her shoulders, exquisite skin set off by linen and the rise of her breathing. It would fall from her shoulders at the slightest tug.

But he reveled in the anticipation; wanted her to bloom and cry out his name into his ear. If he could last that long.

She shrugged, and the gown fell like a shroud dropped from a stained-glass window. She was lit by flames that could never hope to match the wild colors of her hair, nor the sleek sheen of her skin. Hunter stood up and bent his head to kiss her.

"Dear God, Felicity, you are a wonder."

"Am I now?" Her eyes were glazed emerald and fixed on him like a brand. And she was fiddling with the front of his robe.

"Felicity, what are you doing?"

She held up his sash, yanked loose from his robe and displayed like a prize for a foot race. She was a wanton, but he wasn't about to tell her that.

"Hunter, you—!" She was staring gape-mouthed at his risen flesh. "You're so different from the marble kind."

He'd married a lunatic. "The marble kind?" He suddenly feared to ask what the hell she was talking about.

"And the painted kind."

"Painted?" Just where had her travels taken her?

"And an oversized one enameled onto a Chinese vase."

Hunter took a step forward, ready to sit her down

and discuss the matter. "Where exactly did you see these, Felicity?"

"In the British Museum."

Hunter was stunned. "In the museum? I thought you went there to read. Not to look at naked men."

"I don't go to look at naked men—not specifically. But one can't help but notice them when they're fourteen feet tall and standing in a hallway."

He could see her in her skewed bonnet, a notepad in hand, and her mouth agape in curiosity. If he'd come upon her like that, he'd have probably kissed her. Any man would have dreamed of doing the same. Any man would want to keep her.

"I had always wondered what one might look like in the flesh, Hunter." Now she was grinning boldly, staring at him and leaning back against the bedpost.

"Well, you needn't wonder any longer, wife."

If Hunter hadn't been so wildly inflamed by her, the object of her interest would have shrunk away for all her questions. But that was his wife's charm, the very part of her he found irreplaceable—and he burned for her.

"But, Hunter, now I wonder—"

"Enough chatter!" He dropped his robe off his shoulders and pulled her against him, pressed himself into her belly, and covered her mouth with his own.

Hunter ached to have her, to plunge inside her. But he would take his time, let her encounter the coiling ecstasy. She sighed as he slid his palm down her belly, watched him and crooned as he spread his fingers through her curls and played there.

"Oh, Hunter, my knees . . ."

"Just your knees?" Hunter left a kiss beneath her ear, tucked another beneath her chin, and then took her mouth in a raging kiss as he skimmed his fingertips along the splendid curve of her waist and across her hips and ever downward.

Felicity could hardly stand for the dreamlike pleasure of it all. Her knees were bent and slightly parted, and she clung to the bedpost. And all the while Hunter guided his fingers closer to that throbbing knot of expectation. Her blood pulsed; her skin ached for him. He was kissing her, filling her mouth with his tongue, and her thoughts with his intentions.

And then he slipped past the curls and into the sweltering dampness that had gathered to a fever between her legs, and made her bend to his caress.

"Felicity, I've dreamed of this. Of you." His words were a prayer against her ear. His eyes found hers in the midst of a smile.

Felicity let her hopes soar. He played across her breasts with his erotic tongue, and at the joining of her legs with his fingers, until she was clutching the bed post and begging for his flame.

His mouth made a pilgrimage down her belly. He murmured sweet words against her skin, still plucking and playing his fingers through her damp curls, until he was kneeling between her knees and she was nearly swooning.

She wondered if a person could die of pleasure. He slid his hands down her thighs, spreading them further, and held fast to her bent and trembling knees. He rubbed his cheek against her wool, and her legs lost more of their underpinnings.

"Oh, my!" She ought to be hiding herself from his eyes, not unveiling her secret place for him to see and to fondle. But he was a pressure and a deeper presence than she had ever known in her life. He was fullness and he was everything.

And she loved him for this, too.

And then he kissed her there. "Oh, Hunter!"

She would have called out his name again, but her throat had stopped working. His tongue was so sweetly seductive, and now he was whispering against her.

"Sweet woman!" Tremors shook Hunter to the core. She was damp with the scent of vanilla and salt and her own beguiling fragrance that he would carry in his nostrils forever. She would never be another man's wife. Not ever! He would claim her completely.

She called his name as he lifted her into his arms; she clung to him and kissed him. "Where are you taking me, Hunter?"

He settled her back against the pillows, and knelt in the joining of her legs. "Where would you like to go?"

"Anywhere with you, Hunter. Anywhere."

He groaned and made love to her mouth. "Then I know just the place." She sighed as he dipped his fingers into her honey, and pressed herself into the heel of his hand.

Hunter thought suddenly and irrationally of Northumberland. Had it only been the night before? Lying sleepless in his lonely bed, dreading his return, worried that she might turn him out of his own house?

"You're very handsome, Hunter." Her eyes were smoky as she played untamed hands down his chest, slid her fingers across his belly, until she reached for the root of him.

"Woman, you—" But he hadn't been prepared, and hissed and rocketed to his knees as she wrapped her fingers around him.

He made some animal growlings in his throat and clenched his teeth together as she caressed him, blinding him with her random ecstasies. He fell to his hands on either side of her head, whispering for her to stop, and kissing her. "Please, Felicity. I'm too fond of this."

"Hunter, you are very large. And very warm." He took a sharp breath as she fit the tip of him against her.

There was something seductive about watching, knowing with certainty where he left off and she began. She was opened to him, a spreading flower. Then she was tilting her hips to meet with that final barrier, the one she'd offered him so boldly.

"Please come to me, Hunter."

"Yes!" He was at the end of his tether, could last no longer. "One moment's suffering," he said, hoping to draw off the pain of his entry.

"Never in your arms, Hunter."

"Oh, sweet!" He thrust firmly and the very tip of his shaft disappeared just inside her creamy tightness. A miracle of blending; his heart ached and his muscles cramped.

"Hunter!"

"Are you all right?"

She arched her back and hissed a yes, then took him deeper still. Her breasts thrust out to him, to his mouth, giving him focus against his beleaguering need to thrust. His arms quaked as he drew a straining nipple into his mouth, curling it between his teeth and tongue, until she was shuddering and calling his name again.

Her hair was damply curled at the edge of her face. And she was weeping, tears sliding out of the corner of her eyes and across her temples.

When he started to pull out of her she grabbed his hips and held him. "No, Hunter."

"Not painful?"

"A wondrous stretching." She lifted her hips an inch, an irresistible invitation.

Hunter propelled himself mindlessly the rest of the way, till he was joined with her fully. God, how he had dreaded his homecoming; yet now this rapture, this overwhelming need to lose himself in her forever! He was seething, his muscles cramped, his groin on fire. She was tightness itself, and he would have ground into her if he dared.

Hunter suspended himself above her, his mind a muddle of vanilla and sweat and sighing. His wife was staring up at him with misty sea eyes, and she was tilting her hips in a quiet, pulsing rhythm.

"The point of no return?" she asked.

"Long past, my sweet Felicity." He kissed her mouth and her eyelids, riding her hips as his heart rode her pulse. "Long past."

Felicity loved this wild, earth-fragrant dance they were pursuing, the hot pleasure that licked and spiraled upward between them, like riding the currents in a balloon. She clutched at her husband's broad-muscled back and his backside, sweat-drenched with his straining. Her breasts had ripened under Hunter's mouth, he'd turned her skin to sunlight, and implanted that driving urge to thrust her hips to meet him again and again.

Her stiff-collared husband looked the perfect savage in the hearthlight, his face no longer masked but animated in exotic elation as he reared and roared, drew himself from her and returned. He was chanting her name against her ear, ever lifting her senses toward something that he held in reserve for her, something that now made her buck and strain against him, and with him—and because of him.

"Come with me, sweet." Hunter's voice was low and thick and curled around her mouth. "Look at me, please."

She found his shining, dark eyes, and wondered where he meant her to follow.

"Hunter?" Her husband trembled violently above her, and the great, heated heaviness between her thighs spread like a wildfire through her belly and out to her limbs. A splendidly potent rippling began and built where she was joined to him, making her gasp. Unrefined, undefinable bliss pounded through her, and she was launched free of the earth to soar the skies, to tumble on the clouds and ride the sea.

His name spilled out of her in a prolonged melody that rose and fell with the waves and waves of impossible pleasure. He was the cause, and the cure.

"Dear Felicity, I—" Hunter reared up on his hands, and thrust himself into her till their bones met and she was moaning, and still she pulled at him and drove him deeper. And then he finally seemed to let himself go, surged against her like the violent sea.

Felicity thought she'd reached that last great height, but she felt him stiffen and thicken inside her, heard his sharp intake of air, and then he was pouring something of himself into her, something hot and thick, something that filled her with languor even as it boiled her skin. She slipped up and over another cloud, called out to Hunter one last time, then came floating downward, spiraling and weary, slick with his sweat and hers, her nostrils sharp with a new and heady fragrance.

He brushed her lips with his and smiled lazily. "Not hours, I'm afraid." His ragged breathing seemed to keep him from saying more. Her own breathing wasn't much easier, but she hadn't been laboring like a stallion as he had been. "Next time, my sweet, I'll try to hold back."

"Yes, next time, Hunter." She had never seen his gaze so very genuine. Felicity smiled. Next time. He would hold her like this again, another time, another day. This sweetness wouldn't be their last; perhaps he was learning. He was still buried inside her, still large and ultimately intriguing, and they were swathed in dampness.

"Oh, God." His eyes looked glazed and watery, and he kept himself above her on his elbows, on arms that quaked. "You are beautiful, Felicity Claybourne."

She couldn't remember him ever saying her name with his own attached, certainly never without his scorn. She kept it in her heart, to save and examine whenever her doubts might surface.

Whatever happened, they were married now— really and truly married.

And perhaps now she could start counting forward from the day they were married, instead of backward from a year.

Chapter 18

"I ain't about to read no books for babies, miss!"
Giles slapped the storybook onto the table
and stuffed his fists into his pockets.

"Very well, Giles." Felicity refused to coddle the boy
in his tantrums, especially with all the other children
looking on. They adored him, and she wouldn't have
them picking up the worst of his habits. "If you don't
know how to read—"

"You know damn well that I can read this baby
stuff!" His cheeks flamed like cherries when he was
angry. "I just don't want to! I got things to do."

And Felicity was pretty well sure that he meant to do
them in Threadneedle Street.

"I've only asked you to read aloud to the others.
They so like to hear you. And the job pays three pence,
for a half-hour of your precious time. Where else can
you find that kind of work—guaranteed?"

Arleigh wrapped his arm around Giles's waist.
"Read to us, Giles. Please!"

"'N' read like a pirate!" Jonathan said, cuffing Giles
in the arm. "Growl up your voice like ya do!"

Felicity smiled at Giles across the heads of his
admirers. He narrowed his eyes and frowned.

"All right, miss. But I want my pay in advance." He

stuck out his grimy hand and she wondered if she would ever get him into a bath again. He'd looked so clean when they left Blenwick. But Giles had become a regular here, and it made her proud.

"I pay when the job is done, Mr. Pepperpot."

The children cheered and he was still frowning as they drew him away to the front of the schoolroom.

Their clothes were cleaner now, their faces shining and filling out. She'd had the walls whitewashed and chinked, had provided adequate food, and assisted Gran McGilly in a more rigid program of learning. But every week, twenty or more new children asked for help and had to be turned away for lack of space. Short of a miracle, all she could do was care for the lucky ones who fit inside the small building.

Hunter had been wrong about her: if her charity was truly self-serving, she'd have felt better at the end of each day, instead of worse. As it was, she now worked longer hours than ever, sometimes returning home after Hunter, and she had learned to beg castoffs from merchants in the name of the Beggar's Academy.

Hunter. The thought of him always made her heart gallop. She hadn't slept in her own bed since the night he'd returned from his travels. And she awoke each morning, wrapped in his embrace, and ever more certain that his heart was changing—that after their first year together ended, another would begin. And that there would be unending years to follow.

Their peace had lasted nearly three weeks. The subject of the slums remained untouched between them; he allowed her the time and a generous amount of money, and she never took home the misery or the stench that he hated so much.

"What have we here, Mrs. Claybourne?" Gran lifted her new spectacles and peered into one of the filthy wooden barrels Felicity had uncovered during the whitewashing. The woman lifted out an old book. *"Millstone's Reader."*

Felicity laughed and reached in for more. "You must not have opened those barrels in a long time."

"And why would I? I've been here seventeen years, and the pair were holding up our table even way back then. Could have been hiding the crown jewels and I'd not have had a notion."

"More like a feast for the bookworms! What a sad waste." Felicity blew a nest of mildewy paper-shavings off the bindings.

Gran snorted and fanned the air. "Can hardly read the title through the green. There's not much to save here."

"But you never know, Gran. I'm sure there must be pictures to salvage, and . . ." Felicity got her hand patted.

"I'll leave you to your quest, dear. It's time I see to heating up our lunch."

Felicity sat at the table and leafed through the brittle readers, feeling a bit melancholy as the edges of the pages broke off in her fingers and crumbled to the floor.

The students had written their names and the dates on the inside covers, just below where BEGGAR'S ACADEMY had been stamped in watery black ink. Most of the books had at least five names, and the dates went back as far as twenty-five years.

She wondered where these grown-up children were right now—which ones had learned their reading and arithmetic, and escaped the squalor of Bethnal Green. And she wondered which of them still lived in these same twisted lanes; which of them had died too young of the cholera or the whooping cough.

So far, she had found little to save. Refusing to give up, she flipped open another book.

And then her world went a little topsy-turvy.

The inside cover was like all the others, yellowed and faded, the edges worn to a roundness. Five different untutored hands had scrawled signatures across the page—yet one name stood out among the others, proud and defiant, the letters every bit as bold as they were today.

HUNTER CLAYBOURNE, OCTOBER 1831.

"Hunter?" Tears blurred his signature, as if conspiring to hide the familiar hand from her.

But this couldn't be right!

Eighteen thirty-one: Hunter would have been about eleven, a young man sent off to boarding school, like all the other sons of his social class. He'd said he hadn't attended Eton or Harrow, but surely he had been schooled at one of the other fine English schools; his father would have insisted on it.

This Hunter Claybourne couldn't be hers.

But this one indisputable truth, this mildewed, pauper-schoolbook, with its telling signature, suddenly made everything she knew about her husband fall into place: his illogical intolerance for the wretched, the scars she had felt on his feet, his paralyzing panic at the workhouse, his disgust at the smell she had brought home on her clothing . . .

Hunter had grown up in Bethnal Green. Dear God, he'd been a child of poverty, not privilege!

The room around her had begun to reel.

"Are you all right, Felicity?" Gran was at her elbow.

Felicity snapped the book shut, raising a cloud of musty mildew, and stood up. "I'm fine, Gran."

"You're as pale as these walls."

Felicity turned the fragile book in her hands. Hunter's book. He'd had no tutors in Latin, no frowning headmaster. Yet he had succeeded beyond all expectations. How proud he must be!

"You've done too much today, Felicity, my dear." Gran was patting her hand again. "You haven't rested for a minute. Perhaps you should go home."

"Yes. I think I will. My husband and I have a dinner party tonight, at Lord and Lady Meath's. I needed to leave early anyway . . ." Felicity faltered and leaned against the table.

Gran reached toward the book. "Here, then, let me take this from you—"

"No! Please." Felicity hid the book behind her, unwilling to share her secret with anyone. "I'm sorry. I didn't mean to bark. I just thought I'd keep a copy of one of the old readers—just for reference."

"Very well, dear."

Giles met her at the door, a frown of worry on his forehead. "Are you sick, Mrs. Claybourne?"

Felicity wanted to hug him for asking, but only smiled and slipped the book into the pocket of her shawl. "Just a bit under the weather, Giles. I'll be fine in the morning. You help out Gran McGilly today in my place, won't you?"

Giles nodded very seriously. " 'Pon my word, miss."

Felicity accepted hugs from all the children, and finally ran out into the noisome riot that pulsed just outside the peace of Beggar's Academy. Even in the brightness of day, and in all the commotion, everything was dampened in shades of gray and the fetid color of hopelessness.

Instead of closing off her nose to the stench, and veiling her vision from the implacable indignities of such poverty, Felicity walked slowly and purposefully through the byways of Bethnal Green, imagining the boy that Hunter had been, trying to see the world as he had lived it.

A clever boy with large dreams would have loathed the tumbled-down houses, the shuttered-up windows, and the rooms that darkened like rat holes off the doorways. Idleness was a corruption to him, and he had met it here on the street corners, in the gin-soddened eyes of bricklayers and bonemen. Wicked commerce in the byways, selling flesh and stolen silver. Half-naked children squalling at their mother's milkless breasts. Had he slept cold in alleyways; had his lips cracked with the untended fevers of childhood? Had his heart broken?

If Hunter had been the boy whose name was

scrawled in the schoolbook, he must have felt his life always and forever falling in on itself.

And yet Hunter had raised himself out of it, and walked away.

No wonder he'd never wanted to return.

"Ah, a good day to you, Mrs. Claybourne!" Tilson brightened when she opened the door to Hunter's outer office.

Everything seemed so normal here, the mighty hub of the Claybourne Exchange: enduring, efficient, making her wonder why she had come. The name in the book couldn't be the same Hunter Claybourne who gave his counsel to the Bank of England, who had skillfully maneuvered her into marrying him to gain another railway, and who now was poised to take a lofty position on the Board of Trade.

The Hunter Claybourne she had married was born to this kind of financial intrigue. He was nurtured and groomed for it. How else could he have learned his business with such proficiency?

"You're looking very well, Mrs. Claybourne."

"Thank you, Tilson. And how is your wife?"

Tilson smiled fondly. "Oh, very happy. She thanks you most kindly for the raisins and dried figs. A most unexpected anniversary gift."

"The gift is from both my husband and me—"

"Yes, of course, of course. And you must be here to see him. He's inside, meeting with a panel of investors. Very, very important. I don't know how long he'll be, or I'd—"

But the door to the office clicked open and Hunter was standing in the doorway, handsome and roguish, and very sure of himself. His half-smile harbored an intimacy that was so abundantly apparent to Felicity that she could imagine him nuzzling her breast.

"Good afternoon, Mrs. Claybourne."

Her heart fluttered as if she were a schoolgirl with a

mad crush on a handsome Haymarket actor. "Good afternoon, Mr. Claybourne."

He stepped forward and stretched out his hand to her; he was financier and husband, the foundations of the earth. She had been foolish to come here seeking her answers. It didn't matter where he'd come from.

"What an unexpected pleasure, madam. I am delighted."

He jerked his head at Tilson, and the man scooted out into the mezzanine and closed the door, leaving them alone in the outer office. Voices murmured from deep within his office.

"I hope I'm not disturbing your work, Hunter."

"Madam, you can be one hundred miles from me or across the sea and still disturb my work." He lifted a curl and unwound it across her mouth.

"How do I disturb you, Hunter?" He was standing near enough to ruffle her brow with his breathing. He'd become a different man in the past three weeks, less fettered by convention, and home in time to share and suffer Mrs. Sweeney's experimental dinners.

"You keep me thinking of your mouth." He toyed with the bow beneath her chin. "In fact, just before you came in—"

"You spend time thinking of my mouth?"

"Among other things."

"You have thoughts like that right here in your office?"

"Location seems to have no bearing." Hunter yearned to remove her bonnet and kiss the daylights out of her. He hated that particular brown suit of hers, her traveling suit. It made him think of her leaving him, and he couldn't risk such thoughts just now. Not yet. But her eyes were damp around the edges, wide and stormy with a disturbingly unrecognizable emotion that made him wonder what had brought her. In nearly two months of marriage, she had never come to his office. And now she had arrived in the middle of the day.

"What brings you here, sweet? Have you come for another loan?"

She must have known he had been teasing, but her eyes shifted away for a moment, then grew damper as she shook her head. "No, Hunter. I came because . . ."

"Tell me you came for my kiss, and I will desert this meeting and take you home with me." Unwilling to wait for her answer, Hunter cradled her head between his hands and covered her sweet mouth with his, a balm to the chaffing of the morning. It seemed the most natural thing to slip his arm around her shoulders and fit her against him. There was a reckless intimacy in making love to his wife's mouth right here in his outer office, when an earl, a member of the royal family, Lord Meath, and three other peers were sitting at his conference table just beyond the door. The temple of his unyielding world invaded by a sumptuous pagan rite.

Her gaze warmed him as she licked and sampled his lips from one corner to another. "You taste of far away places, Hunter."

"East Indian nutmeg. I've been to a meeting in the spice exchange. They put the stuff into their coffee, if you can imagine."

"I can imagine most anything, Hunter. And I'm afraid if I disturb you any further, Tilson will find us on the floor behind his desk."

Her boldness made his heart race. He wanted to kiss her again, to slip the bonnet from her hair and bury his face in her vanilla sweetness. But his meeting required his attention: rumors were rife that Pittman would soon be stepping down from the Railway Department, due to his involvement in Hudson's fiasco. Nothing could keep him from an appointment to an office of the Board of Trade if it came within his reach. And it seemed the moment was quickening.

"Then, my dear, I suggest we postpone our own meeting until after Meath's party tonight. But if I can have another moment of your time . . ." Feeling unashamedly proud of his wife, Hunter put his hand to her back and guided her into his office.

"Gentlemen, may I present my wife, Mrs. Claybourne."

Hunter was gratified to see the half-dozen men rocket to their feet in a chorus of scraping of chairs and rambling greetings. Felicity was charm itself as she smiled at each man as he introduced them.

"Good God, Hunter, I shall consult you the next time I need a wife!"

Hunter joined the others in their laughter, but his hand tightened around his wife's waist. The men did their best to beguile her, employing humor and hyperbole, and Hunter looked on with pride as she enchanted them without even trying.

Lord Meath seemed especially infatuated. "Madam, I look forward to seeing you again this evening."

"Thank you, your lordship."

She cast an amused glance at Hunter when Meath bowed over her hand and said broadly, "Oh, and you can bring along that lout of a husband, if you have a mind to."

"That goes without saying, your lordship," she said, taking Hunter's hand. "I never travel anywhere without my financial advisor."

The room erupted in laughter and Hunter thought the buttons would pop from his waistcoat. He saw her to his carriage, stepped inside the cab for a simple kiss, but ended up staying long enough to loosen her bonnet and steam his neckcloth.

Then Hunter returned to his meeting, and to the envious jibes of these fate-impoverished men who didn't have Felicity Claybourne to come home to.

Felicity stepped out of the bath and dried off. A hot soaking hadn't sorted out her dilemma.

If the book was indeed Hunter's, and if she showed it to him, she knew without a doubt that he would be angry that she had uncovered his secret. He'd gone to great lengths to conceal his past from everyone. Where he ought to be proud of his success, he seemed ashamed and haunted by it.

Still, this wasn't the kind of secret to keep between husband and wife. But a man's pride was fragile, especially Hunter's. If she was to broach the subject it would take careful planning.

If the book truly belonged to him. . . .

She slipped into her drawers and camisole, and was just hooking the front of her unwieldy stays when she noticed Hunter leaning against the closed door in his rolled up shirtsleeves.

"Astoundingly lovely, even in your drawers," he said.

"Where did you come from?" Felicity flushed at the unforeseen import of the question, and felt overly impatient at his intrusion—what if she'd been looking at his book? She glanced toward her shawl, where the book remained safely hidden in a pocket. "You didn't knock."

"An abominable habit, but I have found such reward in it." He left the door and sauntered across the room to stand beside her at the cheval mirror. "I missed everything before you removed that towel. Care to repeat some of it for me—particularly the bathing part?"

The blackguard stepped in front of the mirror, hooked a finger into the neckline of her camisole, and slid the fabric off her shoulder.

"I'd love to accommodate you, husband, but I'm afraid we'll have to wait until later."

"*Later* will be at the Meath's dinner party." He was using his practiced tongue to flick a fiery trail just inside the flowered border of her bodice, over the sensitive swell of her breasts and into the cleavage between them.

"Now, there would be a scandal." Felicity tilted her head back and gladly yielded Hunter his progress. He smelled of his ledgers and lime, and wine-dark pipe smoke, Lord Meath's perhaps. "I'm sorry to have interrupted your meeting."

"I insist that you make a habit of it, sweet. You put them all in a much more receptive mood. God knows, *I* was ready to receive you." He was at her ear and behind her, and plucking the combs from her hair— her husband of great talents. "Which reminds me, I've brought you something."

"Hmmm." Felicity's eyes were closed, and her head resting back against his shoulder. To move would be to disturb his mouth from her neck, and she really didn't want to do that.

He slipped his hands around her waist from behind her. "You'll have to open your eyes, Felicity."

She finally glanced down. He was holding a rectangular box. "What is it, Hunter?"

"Open it and see."

She took the box from his hands and lifted the lid. "Dear me, Hunter . . ."

A string of pearls lay among the folds of velvet. She stood in the circle of his arms, holding the box as he lifted the strand and clasped it behind her. He led her closer to the mirror and stood behind her.

"Quite a complement to your drawers, my dear."

Felicity touched the necklace. "You shouldn't give me such things, Hunter." This was no bit of jewelry. It was probably worth half the price of the railway shares she still owed to him.

"They are yours, Felicity." His eyes found hers in the mirror, and held her gaze as tenderly as the sweep of his hand across her shoulder. "Whatever happens."

Her stomach wrenched at the unsubtle reminder of their contract and the miles she had yet to travel to find the real Hunter Claybourne. She wanted to cry, but instead she turned in his arms, rose up onto her toes, and kissed him on the forehead.

"Thank you, Hunter. They're beautiful."

"And you are stunning."

He tried to kiss her, but Felicity slipped out of his embrace and smiled with all her heart.

"How did the rest of your meeting go?" she asked, feeling like a sneak thief as her gaze touched upon the shawl.

"Remarkably well," he said. "The rumors are true: Pittman is resigning at the end of the week."

"Is he? And are you in the running for successor?"

He looked so vulnerable in his shirtsleeves, fumbling his fingers through the strand of unruly hair that probably had driven him mad as a young man trying to look his best in an exacting and unforgiving world.

"To a man, they declared they would nominate me, and then vote for me, including Lord Meath himself." A little boy's excitement glinted in his eyes.

She was proud of him. How could he not be proud of himself? "Did you ever doubt it, Hunter?"

Hunter doubted a great many things, but caught his breath as his wife slipped her arms around him, then settled her cheek against his chest. Of all the abundance she'd brought him, the gift of her embrace had been the most unexpected, an aching treasure so precious he dare not speak of it, dare not dwell on its transitory nature—because she was no more his than was her embrace, and he, too, had begun to count down the days as she did—yet for another reason. She counted her way toward freedom from their burdensome marriage, while he plodded his way toward a bleak existence without her. What would she think if she knew of his past? And who would she tell?

"I admire your success, Hunter."

Hunter wondered if she could hear his heart hammering inside his chest. He needed no one's approval of his business acumen, but this simple compliment from his wife made him want to crow like a young boy who'd just won his first kiss.

"I do my best," he said, as mildly as he could, trying to kiss away the crease that had formed on her forehead.

"You have every reason to be proud of yourself, Hunter. Every reason in the world."

Her voice had changed without warning, had taken on a kindness that raised the hackles on the back of his neck. A wariness crept over him. "I was . . . lucky in my investments."

"Lucky?" Her eyes had softened and her brows slanted as they did whenever she slipped and spoke of the children at her school. "I think it was more than that, Hunter. Much more than luck."

Yes, something had changed in her, and he knew he hated it even before he could ferret out its source. "Do you?"

"You've never said much about yourself, Hunter—what your father did; what business he was in. Did you inherit the Claybourne Exchange from him?"

"No, I didn't." He gave her his answer in measured beats, which sounded distant even to him. Where the devil was she going with her blasted questions? "The exchange is my own creation."

"That's remarkable, Hunter. But surely you had seed money from somewhere?" Her smile seemed to grow overly genuine. She even dropped her arms from his waist and stepped away from him to her cluttered desk.

"Tell me, Felicity, have you given up your charity work and travel gazettes to become a reporter?"

"Don't be absurd, Hunter."

"Then why the inquisition, madam?"

Her laughter rang falsely in his chest, made his heart race.

"I was merely asking how you started your business. What catapulted you to such a phenomenal success in such a short time?"

"Why?"

"Because you are amazing to me, Hunter." Now she was fiddling with her magazines, shifting them, then restacking them.

"Am I?" Still she confounded him. From that first moment in Cobson's parlor, she had set his world teetering on its edge and kept it there, spinning; asking questions that he dare not answer; confusing him by her persistent concern; making him want to believe the admiration he saw in her eyes, as she stood in front of him in her drawers and camisole.

"Hunter, anyone would be impressed. You're courted by kings and prime ministers; you're the financial advisor to the Bank of England—"

"I earned my success, Felicity. Every ha'penny of it."

She righted another of her magazines, then pushed away from the desk and turned to him. "Yes, Hunter, I know."

She offered her hand to him, but something deep and stinking oozed up out of a long-locked vault inside him. Her mood reeked of unspilled secrets. He turned away from her.

"Why did you come to the office today, Felicity?"

"Why?"

"Why come in the middle of the day?"

"Because I wanted to see you."

"Why today, when you knew I was meeting with Meath? When I heard your voice in the front office, I thought I was imagining it. I guess I'd stupidly hoped that you had come to see me out of some wifely interest. That you had made time for me in the midst of your charity work—"

"I am interested in you, Hunter. In your hopes and dreams, in—"

"In digging where you shouldn't!"

"If I must dig, Hunter, it's because you've buried yourself so that no one can find you! And yes, I was digging today, as I do everyday. Looking for you."

That frightened the hell out of him. "I am not missing, madam, so you can quit your—"

"I had been at the school . . ."

Hunter had heard enough, and stalked toward the door. "I don't want to hear another word about you and your Beggar's Academy—"

"Hunter, I discovered something while I was there today."

Hunter stopped and turned back to her. "Something?" A coal fire flared in the pit of his stomach, lining his lungs with a billowing stench.

"It was just . . ." She looked like a rabbit caught in a rifle site.

"Damn it woman, what did you find?" He heard the fury in his voice and hoped it scared the hell out of her.

"I found, Hunter, that—that . . ." She stammered and swallowed, and glanced out the window. When she looked back at him again, she had taken a breath, had straightened her shoulders. "I was roundly grateful for all the help you've given the school . . . against your better judgment, I know."

"You dug around and found your gratitude today? How charming."

"That's not what I mean, Hunter. I looked around and saw the effects of the money and the food, and the leavings from the house—your generosity. And so, I came to your office today to thank you for it. So you can curse me all you want, Hunter, but it won't stop me from admiring you or the success you've made."

God, how he wanted to believe her. But she was lying again, and he couldn't fathom the reason. If she knew something of his past, she would have thrown it at him in an instant and slipped herself out of their marriage with a simple bit of blackmail. But she stood there, bare to her underclothes, looking guilty of a crime he couldn't describe but which ate away at the core of him.

"I don't need your admiration, Felicity."

"I think you do."

Stubborn little chit. "Nor do I require your interest, or your gratitude, or any other petty emotion you wish to bestow upon me."

"Petty emotion?" She caught her breath and her cheeks flushed crimson. "I'll have you know, Hunter Claybourne, that none of my emotions are petty. And right now, I'm suffering through an acute bout of monumental anger."

Good. Perhaps she would keep her distance tonight, and forever afterward. He'd gone soft, and he was paying for it. As he turned his back on her, one of her workboots hit the door with a hollow thunk just above his head, and landed at his feet.

"You're a coldhearted charlatan, Mr. Claybourne!"

"Be ready in fifteen minutes, wife. I'll be waiting in the carriage."

Their carriage rocked sideways and slammed Felicity against the granite cliffside that was her husband. Neither had spoken more than a word since the ride toward the Meaths' began. In that time, she had decided that Hunter Claybourne was stubborn, arrogant, and fiercely prideful, and there wasn't much she could do to change him. He was probably born that way—slum or no slum. Let him have his past. The secret belonged to him, not to her. It was a matter of trust. And she would earn his, even if it meant they went to their graves long years from now having never shared this single secret. It didn't matter; not to her.

The carriage was close and warm. Hunter threw off heat like a forge. When she lifted her wool shawl off her shoulders and laid it on the seat beside her, her hand met the familiar rectangle in her pocket and her heart sank.

The book! She had forgotten it was there in the pocket. It would have been safer in her chamber. She would take it home tonight and burn it. That would be the end of the questions, and Hunter would never have to know.

Hunter was another matter. She didn't need a sullen husband as an escort, and he wouldn't be helping himself any if she left him in this state.

"Who will I be meeting tonight, Hunter?"

He grunted and shifted in his seat, then went still again.

"If I know a little about your associates, I can make a better impression. Will there be other wives in attendance besides Lady Meath?"

"No doubt."

"Anything I should know about any of them? Quirks, quarrels, quandaries?" Felicity tried to sound breezy, but the man's mood might require extraordinary means.

"Lady Spurling drinks."

"Hmmm. To excess?"

"At times."

"And how will I know if she is drunk? Does she get loud, or sleepy, or overly friendly with the men?"

"That's been known to happen."

"Well, if she gets overly friendly with you, Hunter Claybourne, I shall pop her one on the nose."

He gave a grudgingly small morsel of laughter. "Please don't."

Felicity turned to him and frowned grandly. "Then, you prefer her kisses to mine."

He shrugged. "I've never kissed the woman."

"I suggest you keep it that way." Felicity felt exceedingly bold, and suddenly very possessive of her husband. She stood up and faced Hunter, hiked her elegant, green velvet skirt and all her petticoats to her thighs, then climbed onto his lap to straddle his hips with her knees.

He looked startled. "What are you doing, Felicity?"

She scooted forward and wrapped her hands around his neck. "I'm staking my claim—if I might employ one of my scheming uncle's favorite phrases."

"Dear God." Hunter should have cared that she was crinkling his shirtfront, but he was just roundly relieved that she was still speaking to him, and burning with pleasure. His blustering hadn't scared her away, and now she seemed to be making a claim on his attention for the evening. He laughed out loud.

"What's so funny, husband?"

"You." But he caught his breath between his teeth as

she tightened her knees around his hips. He thought of those drawers of hers, trimmed in delicate ribbon, primly opaque, and yet split right up the center, where his hand could find her dampness if he dared, where she squirmed naked against the lustfully rising wool of his trousers.

"You taste very good tonight, Hunter. Lime pudding."

Her kiss seemed too worldly and sent a shudder through him as he imagined her hot mouth on him. "God, woman!"

And was it any wonder where his thoughts had strayed? She had unbuttoned the front of his trousers and was fondling him through his drawers and squirming against him.

"Hunter?"

"Yes, love." He groaned as her fingers came around him.

"I have a very strange urge to kiss you here—as you've so often kissed me."

She tightened her hold, and he went still for fear of spilling himself between her fingers. "Not now, Felicity," he hissed. He grabbed her hand and stilled it when she began to move it again. "Please."

She sat up, looking prim and seductively innocent. "You mean it's a reasonable thought, Hunter? To take you into my mouth, right here in the brougham, with Branson sitting on the driver's bench?"

"Dear woman, it's such a reasonable thought that I will be thinking it unceasingly as I watch you sip your turtle soup."

"Truly?" She looked far too eager.

"God help us if Lady Meath seats me beside you."

She smiled and drew a finger across the ridge of his upper lip. "If she doesn't, then we shall just have to meet under the table, won't we?"

Chapter 19

Hunter watched his wife from across the ostentatious expanse of china and crystal and linen. Her face was gilded by the light from two candelabra. Her smile was radiant, taunting the stars in the heavens, and taunting him when she cast it in his direction. The gown's velvet was the green of her eyes, and draped across her breasts as boldly as it fit her to the waist. Her shoulders were bare and honey-pale, and his need for her had become a solid throbbing.

He had been so sure it was all over, that she had found him out and was about to expose his fraudulent past. Pauper turned pirate turned prophet of finance. But he must have been imagining things. He would learn to keep his temper in check, and redirect her thoughts to more pleasurable pursuits. She had certainly redirected his during the ride over. Another few minutes alone in the carriage and they would have been beyond hope, and arrived at the Meaths' drive-up in the fragrant flush of passion fulfilled.

Now his wife was sitting across from him, flanked by Lord Oswin, a most influential member of the Board of Trade, and by the Comte de Auriville, one of Hunter's most grateful and high-placed investors. He heard snippets of conversation and stored them away to digest later. His concentration was on his wife, and he was jealous of the time she spent without him. He spoke with Oswin's wife and Lord Spurling's widowed daughter, but found them pale and uninteresting in the presence of Felicity, who seemed to hold every male eye at the table. She had even managed to charm the ladies with her genuine interest in the antics of their children.

Children. He'd purposely let the matter of fertility cycles drop, had put the book back in his library the morning after he'd made Felicity his wife in truth. He couldn't have kept himself from her, couldn't have checked his passion and still shared the house with her. He was falling like a fool. And he had stopped fighting it.

And now he had discovered a swaggering pride in the fact that she would be leaving with him tonight, hopefully assaulting him in their carriage, and sharing his bed and his breakfast. She had made a game of touring him through each newly turned room in his once-dark house. She would lock the door behind them, show him leggy sofas and brass pots, and then she would seduce him there on the floor, or in a chair, until he could stand it no longer and he would lose himself in her exquisite passion. Not even the new herb garden, with its heady scent of thyme and rosemary, had escaped her attention.

She slipped a teasing smile to him across the linen and over the cutlery, a smile that reminded him of her wish to meet him under the table. It was a ridiculous notion, but one that made him burn to the roots of his hair, and roused him when he should be most in check.

"Dear ladies," Lady Meath said, as she rose and clapped her hands together, "let us leave the gentlemen to their pipes and port, while all of you follow me outside to the glasshouse to see my new stand of bamboo. It's come straight from Tahiti. There's nothing quite like an excursion to the garden after dinner."

Hunter rose with the other men, but excused himself to tend his wife. He had an insatiable need to kiss her, and thought he could manage a moment as the other women donned their cloaks.

Felicity was the last into the butler's cloakroom. Her shawl had fallen to the floor and was now a jumble of folds. Hunter took it from the housemaid and turned toward his wife, tumbling the shawl in his hands to find the hood.

"Did you enjoy your meal, Hunter?"

She was smiling at him, a palpable and provocative greeting that made him decide to have Branson take the long way back to Claybourne Manor.

"The company was lacking, my dear, but I did enjoy the view." Hunter covered her lush mouth with his own and stayed overlong, till her breath and his were heated. The others had left the cloakroom, and the chambermaid had tactfully padded away.

They were quite alone in this house full of people.

He felt her hand in the middle of his chest; her fingers slipped through the buttons of his waistcoat and through his shirt. Her eyes glinted in the sultry light spilling in from the hallway.

"Now, how am I to leave you here, Hunter?"

"Perhaps we'll just close this door . . ."

Instead, she pulled him down to her by his buttons and browsed his mouth with her lips and with her vanilla-scented fingers, until he was sucking them and she was melting hard against his arousal.

"Hmm. And how will you leave now, Hunter? They'll certainly know what we've been doing in here."

Hunter kissed her palm and then turned her away from him. "If you'll stand here and protect my reputation, and . . . Mrs. Claybourne, mind your manners." He lifted her hand from the front of his trousers, when he would have rather moved against it.

"I missed you, Hunter. And dinner was tedious. As will be Lady Meath's stand of Tahitian bamboo."

"But we must both do our duties to our hosts. Your shawl, madam." As Hunter reached up to drape it over her shoulders, a small book fell out of the folds, and her gaze raced to the floor after it.

Hunter stooped to retrieve the book, but she was there before him, blocking his way with her palm laid across it. He put his hand over hers, trapping it against the back of the musty-scented volume. Her smile had fled, replaced by a flush of panic.

"I'll get it, Hunter."

His stomach reeled. A lover's message locked between the pages? A tryst in the planning? Nothing less could have caused her sudden pallor.

"Allow me," he said through his teeth—through a flash of impotent, baseless anger.

"It's nothing, Hunter," she whispered, her eyes downcast and ashamed as they never were when she spoke to him. "Just an old book."

She was lying. And like a madman driven toward the brink of a cliff, he yanked her precious book from under her hand and stood up, raising a dank, mildewed darkness between them. She rose more slowly, but took a step deeper into the cloakroom, away from him.

He couldn't still his fingers, or catch enough air.

Not a lover. God, Felicity, anything but that.

He rode a chill as he turned the book over in his hands.

"I found it today, Hunter, at the school."

Her whisper boiled like the demon sea, and the years washed over him, dark and fetid and stifling. He was a child, crammed into a sweltering room with fifty other wretched children; and he was struggling again to make sense of the letters, trying all over again to incant the spell that would transport him out of that hell.

He knew the book's faded red cover as he knew the map of scars across the breadth of his hands. The stilted vine, deeply embossed and trailing down the spine and across the face of it; the smudged, pencil-drawn train wheels in each of the corners.

"Your name is written inside, Hunter."

But he already knew it would be. His hands shook like a drunk's as he opened the cover.

There it was. The indictment. The evidence of his fraud, and the instrument of his demise.

Hunter Claybourne.

The stink filled his nostrils, came rolling out of his gut.

"No one else knows about it, Hunter. No one but me."

She touched his hand, and the pain shattered him.

"Damn you!" He jerked his arm away and turned from her, but she came to him like a shadow; stood behind him, ready to slip her accusations between his ribs—so ready with her incisive inquisition.

"Hunter, please." Her voice was caressing—the soft-spoken Judas.

He couldn't look at her. She knew all about him, knew what he was and what he had been.

"Hunter, it's nothing but a book."

"Just a book, Miss Mayfield? Then why bring it here among my enemies?"

"Your enemies, Hunter?"

The book was still in his hands, fused there, new fingerprints meeting old, fiercely cold and piercing him. "Did you plan to brandish it in front of them?"

"How dare you think that! I wouldn't do such a thing!"

"You wouldn't threaten me with exposure?" He turned toward her, dread solidifying to certainty as ice poured through his veins, as he pressed her backward against the unsteady wall of coats and camphor. "Not even to regain your father's railway—"

"Oh, damn the railway! I don't care about your silly book. Or about anything that's inside it."

"Oh, but this is gold, Miss Mayfield. Unmined, but the mother lode—in the right hands. Were you waiting to keep it for your uncle? Or were you about to advertise for the highest bidder?"

"Hunter Claybourne, I ought to slap you for that!"

She tried to shove past him then, but he took hold of her arm. He wouldn't be toyed with. She wanted something, but her plan had gone awry.

"If it isn't the railway, then what is it, Miss Mayfield?"

Her eyes had grown large and as innocent as a false April morn, the kind that coaxed tender buds, only to kill with the next frost.

"I want you to stop calling me 'Miss Mayfield.' I'm your wife. Felicity Claybourne."

And then he finally understood. The thing she had hated him for from the beginning—their marriage. The one he'd forced upon her. Well, then, she could have it. He slid his hand down the column of her slender throat, then wrapped his fingers in the strand of pristine pearls and pulled her close.

"Will it be a divorce, Miss Mayfield, or a quick annulment? The choice, it seems, is yours."

She obliged him with an impatient-looking scowl. "I don't want either, Hunter. I want to see Lady Meath's glasshouse."

"You don't want that damned railway, nor do you want a divorce. What is it, then, Mrs. Claybourne? Do you want your share of my staggering wealth, perhaps? Well, if that's the case, you'll have to play along for a while. One word of my ignoble past, and these scions of Britain will desert me quicker than rats off a blazing ship. You wouldn't want that, would you?"

"I don't want your money, Hunter! I would never say anything to anyone. You must trust me."

"Trust you? My wife, the unconvicted felon?"

He dropped his hand; it had begun to shake again. He couldn't seem to get enough of her eyes, that sea-storm green he'd come to crave. He wanted to believe her; he wanted that more than anything he'd ever wanted in his life.

"You have no choice at the moment, Hunter. And we'll soon be missed if you don't let me out of here. I'm quite sure I look mauled—"

"Claybourne! Here he is, Meath." It was Lord Oswin, laughing gaily. "Ah ha! Enjoying a private moment with your lovely bride, I see."

Hunter froze. Shame and guilt and blood-scorching anger melted muscle to bone.

"Who can blame the man?" Lord Meath's voice seemed to come from some great distance.

Hunter turned slowly, feeling exposed and groveling. "Your pardon, your lordship—"

"No need, Claybourne. Heedless love. Suffered it once or twice myself. I envy your youth, and again I applaud your choice in wives." Meath winked as if he understood this woman and the measureless power she had over him.

"I'm afraid I've kept my husband from his brandy, your lordships." She patted Hunter's elbow as if he were her gouty grandfather, then sauntered past him out of the cloakroom. "Please forgive me. The catch on my shawl has stuck, and Hunter was about to fix it for me. Perhaps you could help me, Lord Oswin. Over here in the light."

There she was, preparing him for his death scene. The book had grown heavy in his hand, its moldering breath roiling up his arm in gray tendrils. She had left him to dispose of it, hadn't taken it back. But she didn't need to. A whisper into the proper ear, to her publisher, or to one of her reporter friends—or to Lord Meath—and the truth of his birth, his coming of age in the squalor of Bethnal Green, would make the front page of the *Times*.

He felt a peculiar recklessness in watching her flirt with Meath and Oswin. It hadn't happened yet, but it would, and she would be the agent. The book wouldn't fit into his jacket pocket, and he'd brought no coat of his own. Carrying it on him was no longer an option, if he meant to keep his mind on the evening's events. He would give her back the means; it seemed the only way.

"Allow me, gentlemen," he said, stepping between the men.

Felicity seemed confused when he slid the book back into the pocket of her shawl. Let her wonder at his motives; let her wonder how this evening would end. He closed the catch at her neck and led her to the garden door.

"Do what you will, my dear wife," he whispered into the rumpled hair at her temple. He even set a kiss against her cool skin. "But be prepared for the consequences."

"I'd very much like to kick you, Hunter. But I'm afraid of breaking my toe." She fixed an angry scowl on him, then hurried after the other ladies.

"Come man, we've important business to discuss." Meath stood at the hallway and raised a beckoning hand.

And Hunter passed through the parlor door, a fake and a fraud.

"Brandy, sir?"

The footman's servile bow denounced Hunter, made a mockery of his deceitfully high station. Come the morning, they would all know. His wife would stumble somehow, would use his weakness against him. She had every reason to: he had stolen her railway, had paid a pittance for it, which was the reason he had accepted a promissory note instead of the share certificate; he had forced her into a sham of a marriage, this woman of high passion and unashamed needs; he hated her causes, and had restricted her movements. And all this to control her assaults upon his name. God, the irony would surely kill him.

He couldn't let his thoughts wander from the moment. Ruin might be close at hand, but much was riding on this night, spent in the company of these ranking officials of the Board of Trade.

He took the brandy from the footman and scanned

the room. Focus had been an integral part of his survival—that ability to set aside the periphery and concentrate on the essence of a problem. As he had done as a young boy, sitting in the corner of a coffeehouse, learning shipping news and investing his hard-earned cash in ship's cargo, and investing it again, living on what he could steal. He had learned the essence of risk at the elbows of master risk-takers.

And now all of his risk had come down to Felicity. She had unfocused him. She had sent him careening off track, set him up for mindless, unexpected contentment, and then yanked him backward to the time of his greatest shame.

"Pittman's resignation becomes effective at the end of the month." Meath clanged the bowl of his pipe against the back of the fireplace screen.

Focus, he needed focus. Meath looked gregarious tonight.

"And I was much impressed, Claybourne, with your presence of mind at the accident. A glowing report from the inspectors."

"I am an ordinary man. I did only what anyone would have done in the situation."

Oswin laughed and took another port off the butler's tray. "You are hardly what I would call an ordinary man, Claybourne, given your extraordinary luck in business."

"Thank you, sir." Hunter willed his face to remain immobile when he would have snarled at the man. Luck. Luck was for amateurs, for dabblers. He had survived and grown because he had planned every step of the way.

Meath chuckled. "Well, let's get on with it gentlemen. What we're asking, Claybourne, is if you're amenable to accepting a nomination to the position of secretary to the new Railway Trade committee."

Hunter granted Lord Meath a steady smile, though his gut twisted and his lungs lacked air. "It would be a pleasure, Lord Meath. I am honored to be on your list of nominees."

Lord Oswin clapped Hunter on the back. "On the top of the list, eh, Meath?"

Lord Meath slipped an imaginary piece of paper from his breast pocket, scrutinized it with exaggerated drama, and then looked up at Hunter. "By God, it's seems that Claybourne's is the only name on my list."

Everyone laughed, and Lord Spurling lifted his glass of blood-red port, then gave Hunter a nod. "To Hunter Claybourne!"

Hunter raised his own glass and swept his hollow gratitude around the room. He had no delusions that any of the five gentlemen would continue their support if they knew they were toasting a man who had begun his trade plucking spilled coal and bits of wood from the foul mudflats of the Thames.

The talk turned to Hudson, and to speculation on whether the man ought to be jailed for fraud and misuse of funds. Hunter had distanced himself from the Railway King, had looked on the man and his investors as fools, as standard-bearers for calamity. Oh, how the mighty have fallen.

"What more could we have expected from a man like George Hudson?" Lord Meath stuffed his pipe from the humidor. "That's what comes of putting one's trust in the likes of a linen draper."

"A linen draper!" The Compte de Auriville snorted. "The man's of common stock, to be sure. A lucky sod with a bit too much cash in his shallow pockets. It was bound to happen."

A tradesman? How much greater would their disgust be when they learned that fifteen years ago, Hunter Claybourne had been picking their fat pockets on Threadneedle Street?

Hunter had always alluded to a Canadian father and a beautiful English mother, tutors, travel, breaking from his father's export business when the man died. It had served as a vague but believable cover for his private fortune. And no one had ever questioned it. But now he would forever listen for the murmur as he entered a room, fearing that the next rumor of outrage and insolvency would be about him.

His life had become a waiting game.

Lady Meath's glasshouse was humid and close, and prickly with idle chatter about bamboo and orchids. Felicity didn't want to be there. She wanted to grab Hunter by the ear and drag him home with her.

Blast that book for falling out of her shawl!

She tried to keep up her end of the conversation, which only seemed to make her the center of attention among the women. They were all ladies with proper lineage, and it didn't seem to matter that she wasn't. Hunter could certainly learn something from them.

Lady Meath finally led them back into the parlor with the men, and Felicity gave up her shawl again, along with the evidence against Hunter. Lady Meath preened over the chorus of praise from the other women and stood beside Felicity as if they were fast friends.

Felicity chanced a look at Hunter. He made a solitary and sullen figure at the hearth. His profile was rugged and unchanged, but she longed for the warmth of his gaze and was afraid of the cold disgust she would find there. It made her heart ache that he didn't trust her. They had come so far—

"Mrs. Claybourne was telling us about some of the unique gardens she has seen in her travels. Come sit here, dear."

Lady Meath led Felicity to the chair nearest Hunter. She could feel his gaze on her as she sat down.

"Cottage gardens mostly," Felicity replied, trying her best to look casual. "And castle grounds and the occasional private estate. My father was a railway engineer."

Lord Meath perked up. "I say!"

Then Felicity had to tell them of her father's career,

all the while watching her husband out of the corner of her eye. The hand that raised his glass of port was steady as stone, unless she looked closely. His movements were deliberate and pained. She wished they could leave.

"Mrs. Claybourne writes those travel stories in *Hearth and Heath*." The other women nodded to each other as if they were in wholehearted support of Felicity's activities.

Lady Meath put her hand on her husband's shoulder. "I think I might go with her on one of her treks. What would you think of that, Randolph?"

Lord Meath knotted his brows, then nodded. "I don't see why not. A delightful notion, Elizabeth. You'll take a proper staff with you, of course."

"Of course!"

Felicity smiled and shook her head gently, trying to do what was best for Hunter. "I don't think I shall be traveling any time soon, Lady Meath, at least not to see gardens and the like. But the very next time I do, I would be delighted to have you along. You and your staff."

"Well, of course, marriage to a man like Mr. Claybourne must keep you very busy. And how very proud he must be of your charity work."

Felicity looked right at Hunter, but his eyes were cast down to his shoes. "He is patient with my whims, and very generous."

Lord Meath grunted and stood up. "The Meath family has always contributed regularly to the Hermitage Tract Society."

"Oh, but Mrs. Claybourne doesn't just collect cast-off clothing, dear," Lady Meath said. "She actually visits the slums, teaches at a school for beggars."

Felicity blushed for Hunter, who still hadn't said a word or met her eye.

Lady Oswin seemed especially taken with her charity work. "How brave you are, my dear, to stay there for more than a minute among those wretched people."

"They're not wretched, Lady Oswin; they're just poor. And frankly, it takes far more courage to leave the school at the end of the day than it would for me to stay."

"How is that?" Lady Meath asked.

Felicity felt her blood begin to boil at this idle, parlor-game curiosity. "Imagine a room filled with children—and this room is dark and damp, and it stinks of the sewer that flows beneath it."

"Dear me . . ." Lady Meath put a hand to her mouth and looked around to the other women.

Felicity saw Hunter shift his stance, centering himself on his heels as if ready to run. Perhaps she was going too far, but an urge had come on her to set these people straight—these scions of Britain, as Hunter had called them.

"And the children aren't plump and pretty, but bone-thin, and their clothes are ragged. Their cheeks aren't pink, but hollow and gray; and their eyes don't sparkle, and they speak in tiny voices."

"Poor little things." Lady Oswin's eyes had grown large.

"And they hold your hand and cling to your neck, and listen to stories of places where happy children romp through play yards and the air is fresh. And then it's time to leave the school, to shake off their hands and the sorrowful looks—to set them all aside. And then you return to your enormous home which has rooms that will never be slept in; you eat a huge supper of pork and pudding and then slip under a clean sheet and a warm counterpane. But you can't quite go to sleep because you wonder if little Amy has gone to bed hungry again, and if she's cold. . . ."

Felicity had seen the growing looks of horror on the faces of her hosts and their guests, but couldn't seem to stop talking. Tears were coursing down her cheeks. And Lady Meath was weeping into her hankie. She was terrified of even glancing Hunter's way.

"How simply awful!" Lady Meath uttered.

"So you see, Lady Meath, that's why leaving the school every day is far more difficult than staying."

"Those poor children," Lady Meath said, touching the kerchief to the corner of her eyes. "Imagine growing up under such circumstances!"

"Poppycock!" Lord Meath blustered. "A useless lot!"

Lord Spurling laughed. "I agree, Meath. The only thing they seem to be good at producing is more of their own kind."

Felicity was fuming. But Hunter stood like a statue, still holding his brandy in both hands, staring into some far distance—not lost in thought, only waiting. He was waiting for her to betray him.

Well, you'll wait out your whole lifetime, Mr. Claybourne, before that will happen.

"Excuse me, Lord Meath," Felicity said firmly. "Some people escape their ill-fortune. If we teach them the methods, and supply the means, most will escape to a better life. And that's why I spend my time at the Beggar's Academy."

Lord Meath dismissed her with a wave of his hand and a tolerant look at Hunter.

Lady Oswin sniffled loudly. "Do you, by any chance, need another hand, Mrs. Claybourne? I would like very much to feel that I've done my part."

"And me!" Lady Meath said.

Felicity looked at Lady Meath and tried to picture the woman picking her way through the muck in the streets of Bethnal Green, her pink face pinched and her arm clutched against her chest for fear of contamination.

"Please don't misunderstand me, your ladyships, but I'll say what a wise man once told me: charity is self-serving if it's done to make you feel good."

"Oh." Lady Meath looked thoughtful for a moment, but Lady Oswin nodded eagerly.

Lord Meath grunted. "Damn foolish sentiment!"

Felicity could feel Hunter's gaze on her, but now was not the time to meet it.

"Don't be a such a prig, Randolph!" Lady Meath took Felicity's hand. "Perhaps I could give the school a try, then?"

Felicity smiled and felt triumphant. "Very well."

The room exploded in conversation about the Poor Laws and the recent potato famine. Hunter kept himself purposely out of the discussion, not trusting his views any more than the steadfastness of his temper.

Soon the guests were playing word games and Lady Oswin was singing to Lady Spurling's pianoforte, and the evening wore on until he felt he would burst with the waiting.

But his wife was oddly peaceful in her dealings with him, a hand to his elbow, a shuttered gaze. He wondered what she was thinking, what she had whispered to the other women to draw them into her scheme of righting the wrongs of Bethnal Green.

Meath shook Hunter's hand as the evening ended. "I'll be out of town for a few weeks, Claybourne, but you and I will get together before the final selection. There are others on the Board who have additional names to submit, but we will sway their numbers, and you will be the secretary of the new Railway Trade Committee."

"I am honored, sir."

"My pleasure, son, and a good night to you, Mrs. Claybourne. Your views on the poor are positively erroneous, but you were the delight of the evening."

Hunter watched Felicity's face grow crimson as she murmured her farewells. He helped her into the carriage, but didn't enter himself.

"I'll find my own way home," he said.

"You worried for nothing, Hunter. I said nothing. I will say nothing—"

"Good night, wife."

Hunter watched the carriage fade into the dark

street, and started walking blindly along the crescented perimeter of Regent's Park. He wasn't sure where he was going, but he was certain that any road he took—from this moment onward—would lead him inexorably back to Bethnal Green.

Chapter 20

❧❧

Felicity couldn't sleep, knowing that Hunter was out there somewhere, stumbling around in his dark mood. She had upbraided herself so often since seeing the book fall from her shawl that she was now weary of it. The whole exercise of "curse and what-if" was useless anyway.

Hunter was a grown man, no matter where he'd sprung from. He should know better than to brood— but she loved the rogue, and now she would have to patch it up for him, and convince him that she was no threat to his name or to his fortune. How like a man to be so much a little boy!

She had changed from her evening gown to her nightgown, and then had felt restless and had changed into the button-fronted shirt and tieback skirt that she wore when she was working around the house. Hunter's book was now in her skirt pocket, where it would be safe until she could get rid of it while he was watching, so that he had no doubt it was gone from his life.

She found herself in one of the downstairs parlors, sorting through folds of fabric she had been collecting for her newest project. She had recently uncrated three of the newfangled sewing machines and was deter-

mined to start a small factory, where mothers of the
slum children could make clothes for their families and
then sell the rest to aid the family income.

The clatter of hooves and gravel in the drive sent
Felicity to the window, and her heart into her throat. It
was Hunter, riding beyond the house toward the
stable.

He was home and safe. She listened for his footsteps, but they never came. After fifteen minutes, she
slipped her cloak over her shoulders, lit a lamp, and
headed for the stables.

It was quiet inside, and the horse that Hunter had
ridden was curried and put up for the night. She could
hear the snores of the stable lads from the loft above
her head. But where the devil was Hunter?

In the distance, echoing softly across the vale, she
heard a ringing thump, and then another, and then
nothing for a time until the sounds repeated themselves.

She followed the thumps into the woods until the
sound turned to thwacks, and at last resolved to the
solid stroke of an ax blade against wood.

A lamp burned in a small clearing, just beyond the
stream where Hunter had rinsed her skirts of the stink
of Bethnal Green. Tonight the air was clear and sweet
and starry, and Felicity doused her light, feeling bold
enough and enchanted enough to steal the moment
and spy on her husband.

So this was what he did at night, when he would
stalk off into the woods and return coatless and
sweating. He was standing in profile to her, his shirt
and coat hanging in the crook of a tree, an ax resting
across his naked, sweat-slick shoulder. He was intent
on his work—frowning, probably cursing her under
his breath, but he was magnificent, and she felt a rush
of love and admiration that made tears swim in her
eyes.

She brushed them aside as he stood a wedge of oak

upright on a large tree stump. He swung the long-handled ax over his head, gave a mighty grunt, and drove the blade downward. One piece of oak magically became two. Then he picked up another wedge.

The ax came down with another of his grunts, and then Felicity had had quite enough of rippling muscle and glistening sinew.

"Good evening, Hunter."

He started, then looked up toward her voice, blinded by his own lamp hanging on the branch between them.

"Damn it, woman. What do you want?"

He sounded utterly disgusted. She would have to change his mood. "Just a little of your time, Hunter."

"Go away." He set another wedge on the stump.

"It's after two in the morning. I've been waiting up for you. We need to talk."

"I'm finished talking. Leave me."

Every finely fashioned muscle above his waist flexed and glistened as he took the next swing. The wood split cleanly.

"You may be finished talking, Hunter, but I'm not." Felicity threw off her cloak and entered the circle of light, aware of his anger and his impatience, and entirely taken by the tethered power in his arms as he leaned one hand against the ax handle.

"Go back to the house, Felicity. It's dangerous here. One never knows where the chips will fly."

Hunter watched and fumed as the irritatingly distracting wood nymph who haunted his thoughts ignored his threat as she knelt near his lamp, gathering twigs and sticks and putting them in a pile. "What are you doing?"

"I'm here to convince you that your secret is safe with me."

"You can't possibly." Her hair was alive in the light breeze, wispy tendrils that tempted his fingers and reached out for him. But he needed to keep his distance while he calculated the damage she had caused with her meddling.

"I haven't been plotting your downfall, Hunter."

"Not plotting? It seems that sort of thing comes naturally to you. Leave me, Miss Mayfield. We have nothing more to say to each other."

"Did I ever tell you that my great-grandfather was a lord?" She stuck a twig into the lamp's flame and held it there until the end of it flared.

"I don't care if your great-grandfather was George the Third."

"He had estates in two counties." She knelt down beside her heap of twigs and nursed the flame until a small fire rose from the center. "Unfortunately, bad business sense seems to run in my family. His ships sank, and his crops failed, and his mills burned to the ground, and finally his son's gambling drove the family from a rundown manor house into a little cottage in Cheshire, where my father grew up. He, himself, never even owned a house, and now I live in train stations."

"You live with me. You and your accursed questions."

"And that's the lamentable Mayfield story. I have only a wife's interest in your past, Hunter, nothing more." She sniffed at him and started collecting woodchips from around the stump, intent on some distracting mischief.

"You were snooping where you shouldn't have been."

"I was minding my own business and found the book among a barrelful of others at the school. And there was your name, as big as life, and it startled me. That's why I stopped in to see you today."

Sweat suddenly chilled across Hunter's back. "You had the book with you then? You took the damned thing to the exchange? What the hell were you going to do with it? Show it to my doorman?"

"Frankly, I didn't know what to do, Hunter."

Hunter thunked the ax into a log at the edge of the clearing. "So now you've come here to bargain with the devil, Miss Mayfield?"

"My name is Mrs. Claybourne. I'm your wife. And you are not the devil, Hunter."

The flames licked at the night air, tasting it the way Hunter wanted to taste the woman who kept adding fuel to the blaze. "What do you want, Mrs. Claybourne?"

"I don't want anything. I told you that."

"Then go back into the house and leave me alone."

But she calmly and tenaciously fed her eccentric blaze until the flames were as high as her waist. Baffled by the woman, Hunter left her to her ritual and began stacking the split wood into a cart. He usually enjoyed the task, one of the few labors left in his life. Tonight he had hoped to split her out of his soul.

But she was standing by the fire when he returned for another load of wood. And she was holding the book toward him.

"Here, Hunter. Burn it."

The woman still didn't understand. "It's too late."

"Burn the evidence. Then it's your word against mine. And since you are the great Hunter Claybourne, whose word is never doubted, and since I would rather be boiled in oil than reveal what I know, your secret will be forever safe."

"You're a lunatic."

"I probably am, but, Hunter, you must do this. Destroy the book and that will be the end of it. I promise never to ask another question. I'll wait patiently for you to tell me your secrets."

"No." He watched as she audaciously stole two pieces of wood from his pile and took them back to her own fire.

"You trusted me tonight," she said.

"I had no choice." She would always be a thief.

"And did I fail you? Did I parade around the parlor holding aloft Hunter Claybourne's mildewed reading book from his days as a student at the Beggar's Academy? Did I whisper to Lord Meath that you were raised up in a slum? Did I blackmail you for money, or power, or for an end to our marriage?"

When he refused to say anything, she glared that insolent glare of hers and then answered for him.

"No. No. No. And no. I did none of those things. Nor was I even tempted. I don't want to see you fail; I don't want your money, or power; I want . . . I'm sorry, Hunter."

"Sorry for what, exactly? Sorry that you didn't find my journal, too? Well, don't go looking for it, madam. I never kept one. Too dangerous." Hunter tossed another chunk of wood into the cart, careless of his aim. "Wouldn't want anyone to find out who I am, would I? Wouldn't want anyone to know that my mother was a dockside whore."

"It doesn't matter, Hunter."

He rounded on her and her charitable absolutions. "Well, it does to me, madam. My mother brought men to her bed to put food on our table."

He had hoped to mortify her, to send her running into the house. But her face softened and a light wind caught up her hair, drifting it across her chest.

"Then she must have loved you very much, Hunter."

"Loved me? That's difficult to say. I don't even recall what she looks like."

His wife said nothing, only stood there beside her fire, watching and listening. He scrubbed his hand across his face and turned away, started gathering wood into his arms again.

"I was a mudlark, madam. I made my living plucking flotsam from the Thames. Glass, metal, coal, the occasional corpse—"

"Hunter, you needn't tell me this—"

"Oh, but isn't that why you ask all your questions? Not a stone unturned? Well, you'll listen now. Sit!"

He pointed to the tree stump he'd been using as a chopping block. When she hesitated, he took a step toward her and she sat down. She would hear it all tonight.

"I gave up mudlarking for stealing coal right off the barge: I hired myself out as a laborer and then 'accidently' shoveled my portion over the side. And I was making good money—bought myself shoes and ate a meal every day, till I was caught by the collier and sent to a workhouse. And there, my dear, I learned the craft of making shoes for ladies."

"Dear God . . ." Her shocked little gasp gave him mild satisfaction. "I didn't know."

"And for that reason I made quite a fool of myself in Blenwick, didn't I?"

"No, Hunter. You were very brave."

"Ballocks!" Hunter went back to stacking wood, leaving her to hang her head in some kind of compassion-born guilt. The memories pushed at him, loosed by his wife's hell-bent curiosity. He would sate her tonight and then he would be done with her, done with everything. It was just a matter of time.

"I escaped the workhouse when I was nine, and went to sea. I invested my salary in the ship's cargo and made three guineas at the close of the voyage. A sizeable sum to a boy of nine. Damn, I liked the weight of three guineas in my hand."

Hunter could feel the money even now; shook his fist next to his ear, and heard the echo of his jangling fortune. These were raw memories, tainted by anger but sweetened by time.

"I learned the pickpocket trade next, and added to my treasure whenever our ship was in port, investing all my ill-gotten funds in the cargo's profits. After two years I had earned myself the tidy sum of five hundred pounds—which was exactly the amount snatched from me by a man who said he had shares to sell in a canalway. Showed me an official looking piece of paper, and promised me I'd be rich in a matter of weeks. My God, I was gullible."

Hunter remembered the blinding anger and the

shame he'd felt at the time, but now found himself oddly amused at his own folly. He turned and caught Felicity's worried frown.

"Oh, but remember, madam, I was resourceful. And that's when I knew I had to learn to read, and joined myself to that venerable institution, the Beggar's Academy. You know the place."

Her frown had deepened, and now her eyes flashed with the anger of the righteous. He moved away, added another piece of wood to her ritual fire.

"Then I bought myself a new suit of clothes and started haunting the coffeehouses, studying the shipping news. I took deep profits on insurance paper, invested in the cargoes themselves, just like the brokers at Lloyd's. By the time I was fifteen, I began financing my own cargoes. I was too young to be taken seriously, so I invented a holding company, and I was just the clerk—'placin' orders for th' boss,' I used to tell them. I hid my profits in the Bank of England. And then, one bright day ten years ago, I arrived in London, on a ship from New York, speaking the Queen's English, dressed like a young lord, with my pockets lined with banknotes. And the rest, madam, you can read about in the back issues of the *Times*."

She had said so little that he didn't know what she was thinking. Appalled, probably. He was.

"I love you, Hunter."

His throat closed off entirely on a breath that had threatened to become a sob. He hadn't expected those words from her, though he should have known they were in her somewhere. She seemed to love so easily. Puppies and stray children, household staff, even Tilson. He didn't want to be one of those.

"I thought you should know that, Hunter. And that I could never do anything to hurt you. But I had been wondering—"

"Christ, woman! Another question? There is nothing left to tell! Nothing that I haven't fed to the *Times* for my own purposes. You were wondering *what?*"

She stood up.

"I was wondering . . ." Now she was biting at her lower lip, looking skyward and then down at her fidgeting fingers. "I had begun to hope that . . . Well, that . . ."

He set his teeth together. "You had hoped that what?"

"I had begun to hope, Hunter, that maybe we could . . . that maybe you would agree to . . ."

Hunter stalked to where she stood beside the tree stump, thinking he'd have to wring this last question from her.

"Agree to what, damn it?"

"Agree to . . . extend our marriage . . . like a monthly lease—"

"A what?" He hadn't heard right. "A lease?"

"After the year is out, Hunter, and you finally have my railway shares, I was thinking that we might stay married until you . . . well, until you didn't want . . . you know . . . And then you could give me a month's notice, and then I would—"

"Damn it, Felicity!" Hunter tore the book out of her hand. It hit the fire with the ungainliness of a slain robin, sending up a explosion of sparks. He gave it no more than a glance. His wife had felled him already.

"Hunter—"

"Extend our marriage like a lease on a piece of property?"

"I know you'll never forgive me, Hunter. I should have burned the book myself. And if I could take back today, I would."

Hunter suddenly didn't give a damn about the day, or the night, or what the morning would bring. To have confessed his greatest weakness to her, handing her the power to destroy him, and believing that she wouldn't—She was surety, and trust, and he wanted her; wanted to lose himself inside her and in this circle of light.

Hunter gave a curse and dragged her into his arms as

if he were hauling her up from the edge of a cliff, chiding himself for listening to her nonsense even as he raked his fingers through her hair and held her against him, afraid she would fly away from him, afraid she would stay.

"I won't take a lease on our marriage, Felicity." He caught her face between his hands. He couldn't get enough of her, speaking every word against her mouth and her eyelids and into her hair. Her eyes sparkled and her face was wet with her delicious tears. He took in a breath and lifted her in his arms, then stood her on the tree stump so he could look up into her star-born eyes. "No lease. It's a marriage, or nothing."

"What do you mean, Hunter? What about the settlement? Article One and all the others?"

He saw joy poised on her face, as if she awaited word of a great happiness. He lifted her hand and put his lips against her wedding band.

"We'll have a regular marriage, Felicity: unending, irrevocable." He waited, too, for this woman to accept him as he was, common and deeply flawed.

Her smile trembled before it broke. "An irrevocable marriage, to the man I love? Oh, yes, Hunter. Please."

He caught her tear-salted words with his kisses, held them as tightly as he held her. "Promise me, Felicity. Promise me—"

"Oh, Hunter!" Felicity put her fingers to his lips— she didn't want him to beg, or to have to ask again. "I'll not forsake your name, Mr. Claybourne. Not ever. Nor will I ever forsake you."

Her husband was smiling, at long last. A singularly magnificent smile that lodged itself inside her heart.

"Then come to me, love." He slipped his feverish hands beneath her skirts and slid them slowly up her cool, bare legs.

"Married!" Her sweet husband had found the slit between her pantalets and was playing his thumbs and his fingers along the opening, teasing as if he couldn't find his way.

"You, my wife, nearly drove me through the roof of my brougham with these drawers of yours."

Felicity felt lighter than air standing there on the tree stump, able to fly but unwilling to leave his hands. "Maybe then we wouldn't have gone to Lord Meath's party, and you wouldn't have found the book."

He paused in his magnificent wandering and brought her face down closer to his. "Which book is that, my dear?"

Felicity followed his glance toward the fire, and saw nothing of the book—only a hot, cleansing flame that sharpened the majestic angles of Hunter's finely chiseled face. Perhaps the blood of a prince or a duke coursed through his veins—it didn't matter, only that she pitied a father who would never know such a remarkable son.

"Oh, nothing, Hunter, I was just— Oh, my!"

Hunter wanted to kiss her there, where warm fleece and ardent flesh met pristine linen. Then, as if her thoughts were his, the bulk of her skirt dropped onto his arms, and with it, the single petticoat. He let the tangle of fabric fall around her ankles and cover the tree stump at her feet.

"You amaze me, wife."

He pulled aside a pantalet leg and spread his hand inside across her belly. She was woodsmoke and breezes, the damp fragrance of the earth. And she was quaking, digging her fingers into his shoulders and calling his name. He parted her gently with his fingertips, playing softly there to hear her sighs, until she was open to him like a flower. Then he slid his tongue along the sleek ridges and lush folds.

"Oh, Hunter!" She gave a sighing sob, and her knees buckled. He cradled her backside and took her weight in his hands as she pressed her magnificence against his mouth. He made love to her fire, and she lifted her voice to the night wind.

His whispers caught and danced in her moist curls; his fingers moved inside her, feeding the deepest part of her hunger. She felt as wild as the night, afraid she would begin to bay at the clouds that crossed the moon.

"Come to me, Hunter. Please!"

But Hunter wanted to kiss her more deeply, and urged her legs apart; then kissed these lips as he would those which put a melody to his name.

"Please, Hunter," she repeated, a whimper now, a plea.

Hunter slid his mouth upward, his fingers working at the annoyingly tiny buttons on her bodice. It was a workingwoman's shirt, built like a man's but tailored to her shape, and uncorseted. He met her hands halfway up the panel of buttons and the shirt fell open, and her firm, tawny nipples dragged across his lips and tongue, giving him solace and driving his need for her. He cupped her breast and played at its velvet peak, and his hand found its way back to the seductive split in her drawers, to waiting flesh and her gasping sighs.

"I need you, Hunter!"

Yet he wondered if she needed him as deeply, or as profoundly, as he needed her. He had almost walked out of her life; he'd offered her freedom, and she hadn't taken it.

"Wrap your arms around my neck, sweet."

She did as he bid, leaving a moan and then a flickering tongue against his ear. He lifted her backside and fit her dampness against his belly as he sat down with her on his lap. The dying fire gilded her brow, smoothing her skin to golden velvet. Then she was working at the buttons of his trousers, and then his drawers.

"Aren't you cold without a shirt?" she asked.

His "no" was more of a groan as she slipped her cool hands into his trousers and cradled him. Ice and heat, and he was blinded by ecstasy.

"Do you think, Hunter, that Lord and Lady Meath have ever done this sort of thing?"

"What kind of question is that? Ah, woman!" Her

hands seemed to be everywhere at once, an erotic bliss pinning stars to the backs of his eyes.

"I mean"—she whispered as she nibbled the ridge of his shoulder and fondled him—"have they ever found pleasure in their glasshouse among the ferns and the orange trees?"

"God, Felicity, how should I know?" Hunter dropped his forehead onto her shoulder. He blocked the urge to sheath himself deeply; such an out-of-control moment would send him over the edge, and he wasn't yet ready to leave the circle of her arms, nor hide himself from her fiery fingers. "That isn't the— Ahh . . . ! Not the sort of thing we discuss at the Claybourne Exchange."

Felicity rocked forward and fit him against her. "I was just wondering if this was . . . well, ordinary."

"Dear wife," Hunter said, gazing through a soft haze at the dying fire and the ring of trees and the wild halo of gold that the lamp made of her hair. "I haven't done anything ordinary since I met you. And I doubt I ever will again."

Her shirt hung open, exposing a perfect breast made milky in the moonlight. He lifted his hips as she enveloped him, and the pleasure was so great he went still. She sucked in her breath and held him, as motionless as he, her arms as sure as her faith in him.

"Oh, how I love you, Hunter." Her laughter caressed his cheek and then his shaft, and his restraint finally fragmented.

"Wife!" He thrust himself to the hilt, a peaceful and tormenting place to be held. The love in her eyes kept him as tightly bound as her sheath, and Hunter wondered how his dread had turned to such unfamiliar delight. Half an hour ago he had wished her out of his life, and now he couldn't imagine living without her.

"Come with me, Hunter. Stay with me forever." Felicity felt the solid shaft of him quake and shudder inside her, felt the hot spill of his seed, and followed him into an ecstasy that rolled on and on, until she was spent and drifting. And he was calling her name, calling her *wife*.

Felicity began to giggle, try as she might not to.

"I'll thank you not to laugh, woman." He was still gasping for air and looked overly outraged.

"I'm sorry, Hunter, but I suddenly had a very clear image of Lord Meath chasing after you and his wallet down Threadneedle Street—"

"I made a point of not looking into faces."

She settled her cheek against his shoulder. "Well, if you ever did steal Meath's wallet, you've repaid him a thousandfold. You have everything to be proud of, Hunter—"

"It's not a matter of pride, Felicity." He was still full and warm inside her, but he stood up with her in his arms, and left her aching when he slipped out of her and set her on her feet. He turned his back while he repaired the front of his trousers.

"I am proud of my accomplishments. But you must understand that I can't risk my reputation—I'd be crucified if they ever found out. Trust is the principal commodity of the Claybourne Exchange. My clients want secure and sizeable profits, and that's what I give them. My honest pledge, my good name—I am made of nothing else. I'm worth nothing if I lose that to a tarnished reputation. I'm a breath away from gaining a position with the Board of Trade, and I won't risk that for anything in this world. Not anything."

He seemed to have placed deliberate emphasis on the word "anything," as if to remind her of her rank in his life.

"I see," she said, cursing the sting of tears for her lack of faith.

"Felicity . . ." He turned back to her, looking as embarrassed as he should for making such a statement. "You see, I . . . it can't be any other way for me."

She wanted to give him a good kick in the shins. "And you still consider me a risk?"

"The very biggest in my life. Ever." He seemed roundly serious and Felicity found a superior kind of contentment in the idea. If he thought her such a risk, then she must mean at least as much to him as his name, perhaps more. The poor man just didn't realize it yet.

"You're a very great fool, Hunter." She plucked idly at the scattering of dark hair on his chest. "When I was a little girl, my father had a saying for those times when I held back in fear of some new adventure."

Hunter looked as if he didn't want to hear it. "Go on."

"Father would say, 'Felicity, although a train is safe in a station, that's not what a train is for.'"

Hunter snorted. "No wonder the man left you penniless."

"Oh, but, he didn't, Mr. Claybourne. He left me the richest man in England."

Chapter 21

"Well done, Felicity!" Mr. Dolan rocked back in his chair and tugged at his mustache, then read on. " 'Among the insupportable evils of the cheap-shoe trade is the employment of apprentice schools' students, wherein innocent and abandoned orphans are subjected to working conditions barely tolerable to the most hardened of adults.' Fine copy!"

"It's the truth, Mr. Dolan. I saw it with my own eyes."

But as usual, Dolan was lost in his reading, and paying little attention to her.

"Oh, and this is good, too: 'No wages are paid to these wretched children, who are fed floured water and must work eighteen-hour days or be strapped for their slothfulness.' Wonderful, Felicity!"

"There is nothing wonderful about it, Mr. Dolan. These apprentice schools are merely pretenses for enslaving helpless children for the purposes of making cheap shoes for the large emporiums and shops. My shoes are now made by hand in Hampstead, by a man whose overindulgent wife feeds him too much roast beef. My aim is to close down all of the apprentice schools."

"Yes, yes," Dolan said, waving away her enthusiasm

as he scanned the pages. "You've got store names, too. Good. Good."

"And proprietors, wherever I could find the names. And holding companies. You remember Adam Skinner, the reporter who left you for the *Times?* He helped me."

"Well, my girl, you've done a right good job of raking up a dust cloud here."

"So, you'll print the article in the *Hearth and Heath?*"

Dolan leaned forward in his oversprung chair and rubbed his palms together. "Oh, I'll make sure it's printed, Felicity. And widely circulated."

"Oh, thank you, Mr. Dolan! Thank you. It will mean so much to the children."

"So much to us all—Mrs. Claybourne." He smiled significantly, and Felicity wished he weren't quite so eager about her name.

"Perhaps I should use a pen name, Mr. Dolan. Or my maiden name."

He lifted himself from his chair and guided her toward the door. "Oh, no, no. You must use your married name, Felicity. Think of the influence you will have over the opinions of the public, with a name like Claybourne. Who would listen to an unknown Felicity Mayfield crying out against the abuse of children? Boohoo!"

"Well—"

"There, you see! No one would give your opinions the time of day. But Mrs. Hunter Claybourne—now, there is a name to take note of. If Claybourne's wife says that these vile, apprentice-school prisons need to be closed down and their proprietors sent to jail, then people in authority are bound to listen."

Felicity was quite sure that Hunter hadn't invested his money in any company that used these apprentice schools, nor did he employ children. And she saw no possible way his name could be sullied by his association with such a worthy cause. Lady Meath herself had

praised him for allowing his wife to do charity work in
the slums. He would be admired, not vilified. And no
one would have any reason to question his past as a
result of her story.

"All right, Mr. Dolan. We'll use my married name."
Miss Felicity Mayfield might not be able to save all the
children single-handedly, but Mrs. Hunter Claybourne
was going to set the public's collective ears on fire.

Felicity left Dolan's office and met Branson on the
stoop.

"A good meeting, Mrs. Claybourne?" he asked,
helping her into the carriage.

"A fine meeting, Branson." The man seemed to have
endless patience with her errands, and she blessed
Hunter for letting her use Branson's services whenever
she needed him.

She sat down and found Giles sitting across from her
in the carriage, looking more apple-cheeked than ever.

Branson stuck his head in the doorway. "The boy
said he had a delivery for you."

Giles patted a huge, paper-wrapped bundle on his
lap. "Donations," he said, his grin too sly.

"Donations of what?"

"Shirts."

"Where did you get them?" Felicity picked up the
bundle and unwrapped it.

"In Leicester Street."

"And someone gave these shirts to you as a dona-
tion?"

Giles laughed hard. "Give 'em to me? Oh, no, Mrs.
Claybourne, I 'propriated 'em from a cart out back o'
the linen shop."

"Oh, Giles." Felicity groaned. "You stole them?"

He threw up his hands. "Well, they ain't going to
just give 'em to me."

Felicity glanced at Branson. He'd been waiting for
directions to the next errand. He raised an eyebrow.
"To Leicester Street, ma'am?"

Felicity nodded. "Thank you, Branson."

Giles threw himself back into the seat and pouted. "They have a million shirts in that shop. They're not going to miss a few."

"That's not the point, Giles. Stealing is wrong. And besides, if you're caught, you'll find yourself stitching shoe tops again. And then I'll have to rescue you again, and Mr. Claybourne will be very angry, and I know you don't want to go through that again, anymore than I do."

"If I get caught."

"*When.* Don't forget, Giles, in just a few years you'll be a young man, and too old for the mercy of the court. You'll spend your life locked up in Newgate. No more stealing, Giles. We'll simply ask for donations."

"Good luck, Mrs. Claybourne. I wouldn't give up nothin' of mine."

"Oh, but you already do give up something very valuable of yours, every day, Giles."

He snorted and locked his arms against chest. "I don't give nothin' to nobody."

"You are very generous with your time. You help me and Gran, and you help the children who can't read as well as you."

"Ballocks!" He blew air out from between his lips. "That's nothing."

"Exactly as it appears to you. And so we must teach our donors that the act of giving won't cost them any more than a moment of their time. We'll just go back into that shop and—"

Giles made a grab for the door, but Felicity hung on to his collar band.

"I'm not going in that linen shop with you!"

"Oh, yes you are. We're going to be honest and . . . we're going to walk out of that store with two bundles of shirts, instead of one! And they will be given to us with sincere blessings by the owner himself."

"A chocolate says we don't."

"It's a deal, Mr. Pepperpot."

*   *   *

The owner of the linen company looked warily between Felicity and Giles as they stood together in his upstairs office.

"So this boy stole these shirts from me, and now you want me to just give them to you for your school? That's quite a dodge you have going there, Mrs. Claybourne." He scowled and pointed a finger at her. "I think I'll have you both brought up on charges."

Felicity shook her head sagely. "Oh, but my husband wouldn't like that, Mr. Malstowe. Hunter Claybourne is a man who values charitable work. And I'm certain that he wouldn't want anyone falsely accusing his wife of stealing—"

"Hunter Claybourne? You mean of the exchange—"

"Yes, Mr. Malstowe. That's exactly the Claybourne I am Mrs. to. Not that his name should influence your charity in any way. I only wish to enlighten you to the progress we are making at the Beggar's Academy, where Mr. Giles Pepperpot"—Felicity put her hand on Giles's shoulder—"lately a thief and pickpocket, is now learning to mend his ways, just as he learns to read and write."

Giles toed his shoe into the floor. "I'm sorry, Mr. Malstowe, sir. I thought I was bein' ever so 'elpful to the children."

Felicity hoped that at least a speck of Giles's apology was from the heart. "There, you see. Where the boy would have once sold the shirts for his own gain, he just now brought them directly to me, Mr. Malstowe, thinking to aid the poor children of the school, who wear rags instead of clothing. You can see that his heart was filled with compassion, and that he is learning the difference between right and wrong."

Malstowe looked anything but convinced. "But, I say—"

"We will gladly take your damaged goods, sir, and anything else that needs mending. We have developed a program that teaches young women the art of dressmaking, and we could also use—"

"Oh, all right. Here! Take the shirts." Mr. Malstowe shoved the bundle into Felicity's arms. "Come with me." He took off down the hallway.

Felicity smiled at Giles and lifted her eyebrows as Hunter would have done, then followed after Malstowe.

They left the linen shop with four bundles, which included not only shirts but also drawers, kerchiefs, and socks. Giles was silent and surly as Branson stowed the donations in the carriage boot.

"Now, about that chocolate, Giles?" Felicity asked.

"I don't have any money," he snarled, and kicked the wheel.

"Oh, but I do, young man. And since I won, I have to buy you a chocolate."

Giles had the most genuinely bright smile when he was caught off guard, and when his teeth were clean. "You do?"

"Of course. Will you join us, Branson? There's a tea shop in Threadneedle."

"I'd be pleased to, Mrs. Claybourne." He smiled across the top of Giles's head and led her to the carriage door.

Giles brushed Branson out of the way and took Felicity's hand. "After you, miss."

Felicity wanted to kiss the little scamp, but he would probably have thrown himself under the next wagon in embarrassment. So she exchanged a nod with Branson and stepped into the carriage.

Giles was learning.

Hunter stopped his horse at the top of the rise, and gazed down on Clabourne Manor. The sight pleased him to the deepest part of his soul. If he'd been gone these past few months of marriage to Felicity, and only now returned, he'd have thought himself arrived at the wrong house. But the transformation had happened before his very eyes, and the drive up to the house would soon resemble Versailles, with its tidy boxwood hedges and immense stone lions, the banks of roses and chrysanthemums.

Felicity.

His heart nearly bursting with the need to see her, Hunter quickly stabled his horse. As he entered the foyer, he heard the ripple of female laughter from the back parlor and wondered what enterprise Felicity was governing today.

Where he had once been greeted by cold, gray stone and the empty echoes of his own footsteps, now he was met with tapestries and portraits, carpets and settees, and total strangers wandering the halls. And in the midst of all the commotion, he would always find his wife.

He ached to see her. She had hung her nightgown in his closet the morning after their encounter in the woods, and in the following few days the rest of her wardrobe had managed to make its way across the hall to his chamber. To *their* chamber.

In the last month, it had become that much and more: a place where he could relax, where his wife could dance around in her nightgown until his blood was boiling, where he awakened each morning to her arms and legs draped over his chest, or his fingers tangled in her hair. And she was always ready with her kiss, and more than ready for his.

Making love in the morning had done wonders for his general mood, and roused him for the day's work. He had recently found himself whistling his way up the stairs to his office at the Claybourne Exchange, and had only that morning given Tilson a raise when the man's wife had appeared to deliver his daily lunch. The look of astonishment on Mrs. Tilson's face had seemed out of all proportion, but he accepted her thanks and had felt exceptionally good the rest of the afternoon.

Yet his days at the office had become grueling and

overlong as he juggled his normal routine with negotiations about the fate of Hudson's investments. And his impending Board committee nomination was due to be announced any day.

He now strolled down the gallery toward the noise at the end of the corridor, wondering what manner of activity he would encounter. Last week it had been Lady Meath, Lady Oswin, and three wives of parliament members sitting in the dining room. They had been assembling kits of needle and thread, going on about gardens and traveling, and had giggled like schoolgirls when he had greeted them.

Not wanting to suffer the same fate today, he peered quietly into the south parlor and discovered a sewing works installed in his home. There were three odd-looking machines, each sitting on its own table, and women bent over them in concentration. One of the women was his wife.

She raised her head and looked directly at him.

"Hunter! You're home early!" She looked startled and a little distressed. Her dark-blue dress was strung with bits of thread, and her hair was stuck through with at least four pencils and some kind of dangerous-looking hook.

"Good afternoon, ladies," he said mildly.

The other five women cowered from him, tucked themselves behind their sewing contraptions and piles of woolens. The taint of Bethnal Green was obvious only to him, but he tried, for Felicity's sake, to ignore the thickening in his throat. He was getting better at it.

He'd begun to look forward to reports of her new ventures. Felicity Claybourne was no dewlapped, moist-eyed, philanthropic matron. She was knee-deep in goodness, a patch of warm sunlight that grew ever brighter. And sometimes he was made breathless and blinded by his consuming need for her to hold him. His passion for her was always near the surface: scratch at his thoughts and it would be there, banked and ready to flare.

"Hunter?" Felicity was staring at him.

"Ah, yes, love. Just came to say hello."

"We're making winter clothes for the schoolchildren. And the ladies are learning the sewing machine."

Hunter looked charmingly confused.

"Come see." Felicity slipped her hand into his and took him to the machine she had been working on. She sat down, steadied the wool beneath the needle, and then started up the treadle with her foot. The needle rose and fell and set its astounding stitches in a line along the fabric.

"Isn't it wonderful, Hunter?" She slowed the treadle and the needle stopped.

He peered closely at the head of the machine. "Where did you get this thing?"

"They were in the cellar."

"I bought them?"

"You must have. And I have put them to good use. We're all learning together." Felicity stood up and put her arm around Mrs. Lytle. "In truth, Marguerite seems to have a natural way with the beasts."

Mrs. Lytle shied, and turned her face away.

Hunter bowed slightly. "My compliments to you, Mrs. Lytle, for your genius. I'm afraid I would stitch my own fingers together."

"Dear me, thank you, sir!" Mrs. Lytle put her hand to her lips and exchanged a nervous giggle with her compatriots.

Felicity's heart was racing as she beamed at Hunter. He was too much of a distraction, and she led him toward the door. "Out of here, Mr. Claybourne. Or else we will put you to work."

"Heaven help me."

Hunter pulled her around the corner into the gallery and swept her into his arms. She loved his eager mouth and his quick arousal. She slipped her hands around his waist, and he backed her against the wall.

"Oh, I missed you, Hunter."

"I miss you perpetually."

"Do you?" Felicity gave a tug on his neckcloth, and his heady moans turned to deep-chested growling.

"Tonight, love," he whispered, at the lobe of her ear. "We have a private box at the Royal Opera House in Covent Garden."

"Do you mean to make love to me at the theater, Hunter?" She felt his arousal flare against her thigh.

"That wouldn't be wise. Though now that you've loosed the idea in my head, I hope I can keep my hands to myself."

Felicity ducked out of his embrace. She turned back to him at the door to the sewing room. "I hope you can't."

She saw him roll his eyes, and watched in deep appreciation as he straightened his coat and strode purposefully down the gallery toward the library.

What a fine and gentle man he was! Misguided sometimes, but willing to listen. He'd looked like a terrified wolf just now when he had stood among the sewing machines and the disarray of fabric, pretending interest and trying not to cast his judgment on the women she had brought to his home.

He was doing his best, and she loved him madly for it.

Loved him even more, because she was almost certain she was carrying his child.

Felicity tried to pay close attention to the stage and to the young tenor, who was struggling valiantly to propose marriage to his aging soprano. But Hunter was sitting decorously beside her, splendidly handsome in his cutaway and crisp linen, calmly unbuttoning the underside of her black, elbow-long glove.

"Dear husband," she whispered a bit breathlessly. "You ought to be watching the stage!"

He brushed his warm fingertips deliciously along her forearm, and she sighed.

"Watch the stage, my dear, when I have you here

beside me? I think not." Hunter looked far too roguish
in the shadowy, gas-dimmed light. He held her hand
in his bare palm as if it were porcelain, tugging on one
tiny button and then the next, unusually patient in his
efforts, his smile brazenly crafty.

"Aren't you at all interested in that woeful young
man and his sweetheart?"

She'd never seen his brow so devilishly slanted.

"My interest lies with you, madam." His fingers
were like fire, his eyes as dark as a moonless ridge of
shale.

"Hunter Claybourne, what are you planning?" Their
private box was visible from the galleries above them;
anyone could look in.

"I'm planning to kiss my wife." His whisper was a
phantom caress, slipping itself around her heart, making her smile.

"Here in the theater?"

"Here," he said, kissing her bared wrist. "In the
theater." His words twined themselves around each
other like a sultry vapor.

"Oh, Hunter," she murmured.

He kissed her lingeringly, again, on the soft place
just above her wrist. Felicity caught herself in a delighted moan.

"Silently, love," he warned. He stroked his naked
fingers deliciously between her palm and her glove as
if they were his mouth and tongue, tugged and per-
suaded until he had freed each of her fingers. "Your
other hand, my sweet."

Felicity giggled even as she tried to frown at him. "I
hope you plan to stop with my gloves."

His laughter was low and gentle. "For now."

Felicity gave him her other hand. Though he never
touched more than her hand, he never took his eyes off
her, and she felt quite thoroughly kissed when he
finished. She flushed to her hairline as he tucked her
gloves into his breast pocket like a shared secret.

"I love you, Hunter."

His face was shadowed, lending an enigmatic glint to his eyes. "And that, my dear, makes you the most remarkable woman I have ever met."

"For loving you?"

Felicity was altogether certain that he loved her, even if he couldn't tell her so. It just wasn't his way. But he'd begun to court her as if she were the most important thing in his life. He'd made a desk for her in his library; left her sweet notes, and blush-making ones. She found fresh flowers in her shoes, and a ready partner to walk the grounds in the evening and listen to her plans for the knot garden and the herbarium.

"I am not loveable, Felicity. Ask anyone in London." He nodded in the direction of the three thousand other people packed into the theater, as if they knew him and would agree.

"Ha! Let them ask *me*. I'm the expert."

He raised an eyebrow. "Are you, now?"

Two months ago, Hunter would have been terrified by the thought; now it pleased him to his soul. She knew him intimately, as no one ever had, and yet she loved him. He wanted to confess his heart to her, would do it now, but he didn't really know how to form such an elemental thing into words. She was the electrifying tumult that banged around in his chest; she had become his pulse and the substance of his days. But he grew hopelessly tongue-tied whenever he set out to explain himself to her. Yet she seemed to know already, seemed to find some amusement in his hesitation, as if it added to her estimation of him. Another secret she held against him.

He prayed for her patience, and would have swept her into his arms just then, but the first act of the opera seemed to be over and the gaslights had begun their annoying hissing toward brilliance.

"Well, I'm disappointed, Hunter! The woman turned the tenor down and sent him on his way. He must feel awful."

"He's an incompetent fool."

"Hunter! How can you say that about a man in the throes of love?" She was frowning deeply, nearly pouting.

Hunter had little patience for men, fictional or otherwise, who didn't know their own minds. He lifted his wife's fingers to his lips. "If the blighter really loved the woman, he'd have simply offered her the choice between marriage and jail."

"But . . ." She looked startled for an instant, then her entire face softened in a smile that spoke of miracles.

He had tipped his heart toward her in the space of a second, and it seemed to fill up and spill over again immediately. "In fact, my love," he said as she cupped his cheek and whispered his name against his mouth, "I recommend it highly."

"Oh, Hunter, I love you."

His heart hammered, and his breath was caught up in his throat. He kissed her softly, though he yearned to wrap her in his arms and sing his love into her hair. But they weren't alone; the galleries above and the boxes on either side were thick with people tonight. "We should take a tour of the lobby, love. Before I make a fool of myself here in the box."

She laughed quietly, and touched his mouth with her fingers, hiding a secret from him, he was sure.

"Yes, we'll wait till we get home, Hunter. Some things are best said in private."

Inflamed but in control of his passions, Hunter led her from the box into the crowded lobby, exhilarated from his near-confession. Another few moments alone with her and he might have been on his knees, babbling love words like a poet gone lunatic. Even now she was close enough to whisper to, her lovely ear framed in wispy curls and inviting his mouth. And he wanted her to know how much he cared, how much he loved her. "Felicity—"

"Hunter, there's Lady Oswin. She's calling me over. Would you mind if I spoke with her?"

Hunter took her hand and kissed her wedding band. "The woman makes my ears ache."

"It's probably about the academy. She's very enthusiastic. And she's thinking of giving us a new coal heater."

"If I promise you two heaters, will you stay here with me?"

"Hunter, you're incorrigible." Yet there she was, with her fingers tucked into his waistcoat again, tugging at him.

He didn't give a fig for Lady Oswin; he wanted to corner his wife and fill her with words of love. He could see down the front of her bodice, where the sleek, black satin draped precariously across the rise of her breasts, tempting him to explore. And her eyes, flirting and ever faithful, tempting him to love her all the more. But there would be time enough later, in the private box and in the brougham, all the way home and for the rest of his life.

"Certainly, my love." He caressed the small of her back and snuggled a kiss against her ear. "I'll bring you a champagne."

She touched a blissful kiss to his cheek, and he watched her glide through the crowd toward Lady Oswin.

Temptation. Yes, she was that. A temptation to believe that nothing else mattered but her love for him, and the home she'd made of her heart. Dear God, it was comfortable there, and sheltered. He could look out onto her goodness and feel that some of it was his. Her benevolence had become his conscience, his penance, and it had begun to fit him very well.

A temptation to believe in redemption.

"Damn you to hell, Claybourne!"

Hunter turned from his reverie and found Lord Meath at his elbow. The man looked apoplectic: red-jowled and irrational. Hunter had calmed Meath more than once when one of the man's unadvised investments had gone awry. What the devil could be wrong now?

"Lord Meath. What is it?"

Meath only got redder. "Don't act the damned fool, Claybourne. It doesn't become you."

Hunter resented the implication, yet he felt suddenly, inexplicably, shoved to the edge of a towering cliff, and he was terrified. Meath's goodwill meant everything to him: legitimacy and the assurance that his fortunes would thrive.

"Sir, you have me at a disadvantage—"

"I'll bury you, Claybourne!" Sputtering in his rage, Meath yanked a folded magazine from his breast pocket. "What about this travesty? And don't tell me you know nothing about it."

Mercantile Weekly. Hunter calmly took the magazine, trying to keep his hands from shaking as he leafed through it, page by page. "And what am I to look for, Lord Meath?"

"Your wife's handiwork," Meath spat, slapping the next page.

"My wife—"

Hunter saw her name then—his own name, the one he'd given to her. His hands went cold. He tried to keep a steady focus, but the letters only blurred in his efforts, and he discovered himself a child again unable to make sense of the scratchings. "I hesitate to say, Lord Meath, that I don't know what is contained in here."

" 'The Tragedy of Workhouse Children?' Can't you guess?" Meath hushed his voice and threw a brief glance around them at the crowded lobby. "Half my fortune, Claybourne, and my business, my very *legal* business—denounced as evil, and slandered by your wife in a trade magazine! There for all the world to see!"

Felicity's words focused and then blazed past Hunter's eyes as he read snatches of the piece. The foulness, the wretched wraiths, the cruel masters. She had spared no detail, and Hunter's stomach reached up into his throat. And there in the list of the buyers and sellers of these slop-trade goods was the Harling Street Emporium—Lord Meath's own company.

Damn it, Felicity! What is this?

"Seven irreplaceable orders canceled today, Claybourne. Seven! Thousands and thousands of pounds gone elsewhere!"

"My humblest apologies, sir." Hunter knew before he'd said them that such words meant nothing to a man like Meath. How could they? Where was the profit in apologies? Hunter would have felt the same if his own name had been dragged through this particular muck.

"Damn your worthless apologies, Claybourne! My name has been irrevocably linked to workhouses and to labor scandals! And all because of you! That's the end of it! I was about to grant my support to your nomination as secretary to the Railway Trade Committee. Well, sir, if you can't control your wife, I doubt you're capable of maintaining control over a Board committee."

"Sir." Everything inside him hardened, even as the noise rose around him and inside him. A roaring rushed into his ears, built up against his temples and began to pound. His focus had gone toward the horizon, toward his wife and her flawless profile. A salted mine, an encumbered railway—she'd been nothing but trouble to him. And he'd walked right into it, blinded by her sunlight and by her reckless promises. He gathered his focus and his resolve and fixed them both on Meath.

"Sir—"

"Do you hear me, Claybourne?" The man was still squawking, an insignificant parasite, preying on anything that got in his way. Wives and children and reputations. And now he was holding the name Hunter Claybourne in his fat, unscarred hand.

"I hear you, sir." He could hear little else.

"Good. Because you'll get no nomination from me, Claybourne, nor from anyone else on the Board. And you can expect a great migration from the Claybourne Exchange. As you can see from your wife's libelous misrepresentations, there are others involved here, others affected—"

"Lord Meath—" But Hunter stopped himself. He wouldn't beg, though his guts had twisted up on themselves and sweat ran down his back. He hadn't begged since he was a boy, and he wasn't about to start again now. He would fix this with Meath, and with the others. But it wouldn't come from begging. It would start elsewhere. She had become a liability.

"There's your wife now, Claybourne. If you know what's good for you, you will keep her locked up. You'll be hearing from my solicitors." Meath disappeared into the crowd.

Locked up, locked away? Yes, that would have been the right choice after all. It was what he had always done with thieves and liars. She had deserved nothing less.

Trust me, she had said. *Whisper your secrets to me, Hunter. I love you.* And so he had trusted her, unconditionally, with everything that had ever been dear to him.

And then she had betrayed him.

"Hunter?"

He turned sharply away from the hotly familiar hand on his arm. He didn't want to look at her, not yet. He needed strength to stand against her and her all-deceiving righteousness.

"Hunter, you look pale. What's wrong?"

Felicity had missed him even in the short minutes they'd been apart. She sought her husband's eyes when he finally turned; but they had never seemed so shadowed and inaccessible, nor so stingingly fixed on hers. A chill poured off him, coating her in icy fear and making her hug her wrap around her shoulders.

"What's happened, Hunter? Have you and Meath quarrelled?"

He seemed to lose focus for a moment, lifted his hand and stumbled a step toward her, as if he had wrestled a terrifying violence and had caught himself. She watched words form on his lips and then disappear in disgust, as if they tasted vile on his tongue.

"Hunter—"

"Come!" His deep voice shook with bottled rage. He stalked away, toward the Bow Street entrance.

Her heart lodged itself in her throat, not letting her breathe. A sinking dread crept over her, a torn seam left unmended and now splitting wide. What was it?

She hurried after him across the emptying lobby. Hunter was already through the iron gate and down the four steps of the deserted portico when she reached the exit door. He was barking for his carriage when she reached his side.

"Tell me what's happened, Hunter. You're frightening me. Is there trouble at home? At the exchange?"

His face was granite and his eyes as brittle as spun glass when he looked down at her. "Don't you think it's a bit too late for you to worry about that, Miss Mayfield?"

"What are you talking about, Hunter?" She touched his elbow and he shook it off with a wild gesture.

"Don't!" He climbed back up the stairs to stand beside one of the thick stone pillars, watching the street, his arms gone rigid at his side.

Frightened to death by his cold anger, Felicity followed him up the steps. "What happened in there?"

"It happened in *here*, Miss Mayfield." He brandished a tightly rolled magazine, then threw it backhanded to the ground. It skidded across the portico and stuck beneath the bars of the iron gate.

Suddenly fuming at his unwarranted hostility, Felicity retrieved the magazine.

"You have no right to treat me this way, Hunter, no matter what had happened between you and Meath."

She unrolled the magazine as he stood his watch over the street. "The *Mercantile Weekly*? What is it? I've never heard of it."

"Liar."

Furious and frightened, she took a step toward him. "Hunter, I've never seen this magazine before."

"Then who the hell is the Mrs. Claybourne on page seven?"

Her hands began to shake as she opened to it. "The Tragedy of Workhouse Children," by Mrs. Hunter Claybourne. This was Dolan's doing, another of his weeklies.

"It's my workhouse article, Hunter," she said softly.

His eyes were obsidian when he turned to her. "And *my* insurmountable obstacle to the Board of Trade."

"What . . . ?" She still couldn't understand his cold rage.

"That was Lord Meath's business you reviled. And I'm the one who must pay for your folly." He stuck his fists into his pockets and paced to the edge of the portico, dismissing her as he looked out onto the noisy traffic.

The Board of Trade. The endorsement of all his achievements. Dear God, what she had done to him! "Hunter, I didn't know about Meath. He wasn't on the list. I wouldn't have . . . I'm sorry—"

He barked a laugh, but didn't spare a look at her. "Feeble words, those. 'I'm sorry.' I tried them myself— Lord Meath wouldn't have them. He doesn't trust me any longer. Finds my name and my reputation objectionable. He's taking his business elsewhere and slapping me with a liable suit. Well, I can't afford that, Miss Mayfield."

"Hunter, no!"

He turned to her then, his face wintery and the light gone from his eyes. "And I can no longer afford *you*."

"No longer . . ." Her heart paused in its racing. "What do you mean?"

"Branson will be here momentarily. You will pack

your things and be gone from Claybourne Manor in the morning."

"Gone, Hunter?" Her throat thickened and failed in a sob. "And that's it? Our irrevocable marriage? Gone?"

"I gave you every warning—"

"You're a coward, Hunter!" He had just discharged her, simply and cleanly. Now he was looking through her, all his connections with her efficiently severed. Shaking with anger and nearly hobbled by the pain in her chest, Felicity held out the magazine.

"You, above anyone, can do something to stop this barbarous practice, Hunter. You should condemn it! Lord Meath's part in this foul business is indefensible."

He glanced away from her and went back to his traffic-watching. They might have been strangers waiting for separate hackneys.

"You'll be amply provided for, Miss Mayfield. Separation papers will be delivered to you as soon as you forward your new address to my solicitor."

"Separation." Felicity put her hand to her stomach, a shield for the child that might be growing there. "And love counts for nothing, Hunter?"

He only nodded toward his carriage as it came around the corner on Bow Street. "Branson's here. You've become a liability to me, Miss Mayfield," he said flatly. "A risk I can no longer sustain."

He turned without a glance, and walked back into the theater.

Her desolation pushed her backward against the pillar and pinned her there, trembling. The pain in her chest was so hot it burned away the tears before they got to her eyes.

"You're wrong, Hunter." She had struck him a terrible blow, but he was wrong. Her disappointment in him blazed as fiercely as her loss.

If Hunter couldn't stand up to Lord Meath, a man who built his trade on the backs of helpless children like Arleigh and Giles and Betts, then Felicity could have nothing more to do with him anyway, no matter how much she loved him. She would continue her fight for as long as she could draw breath.

Branson hadn't seen her yet, and he was climbing the steps on the far side of the portico to take her back home to Claybourne Manor.

Home?

Felicity slipped into the shadows and left the Royal Opera House. She had a new home now—with Gran McGilly and the children at the Beggar's Academy.

Chapter 22

Hunter had stormed back into the theater intend-ing to find Lord Meath and make a start at repairing the damage. But his focus was blurred, and dangerous. The image behind his eyes wasn't Meath's seething anger; it was his wife's look of absolute despair, her sea-misted eyes, her lower lip caught fearlessly in her teeth: a too-recent ghost that would not be shaken.

And now he sat starkly alone in his private box, neither listening to the music nor plotting his next meeting with Lord Meath. He was trying to control his quaking. How the devil could he talk coherently and convincingly with Meath when his hands were quaver-ing, and his throat was closed off to all but the shallowest breath?

She had betrayed him. He'd begun to believe in her lies, in her gallant beliefs. *Save the child and you will save the man.* Well, he didn't need saving. He'd been perfectly fine all these years. He would be so again. He would bleed, but he would heal.

And now he'd had no choice but to rid himself of her. He couldn't risk the next headline, his low-born past thrown up at him: pickpocket, thief, scoundrel. Old habits die hard, they would say.

Already he would be years repairing his name and his reputation. Protecting his clients had been his doctrine, the bedrock of the Claybourne Exchange. He had survived personal terrors and financial setbacks of all kinds, yet he'd always come back stronger and wiser than ever.

He couldn't let one impulsive young woman tear it all down. Not even if he loved her more than he loved himself. Not even then. The fact had no bearing on the matter of his fortune and his future.

He was in no mood to think, or to plot, least of all to see Lord Meath. So he sat in the hissing darkness of the theater, dismissing the scent of vanilla, with the aching pressure of her gloves still lodged against his heart. He rose before the end of the final scene, unable to recall the name of the opera or even a single melody, and made his way onto Bow Street to hire a cab.

Branson met him at the portico.

"I waited two hours, Mr. Claybourne, sir, and your missus didn't show up."

Hunter glanced around, half-expecting to see her. "You didn't take her home?"

"Never saw her, sir. I thought she'd decided to stay."

"That decision wasn't hers to make." Hunter fought a groundless panic. It didn't matter. She was gone from his life; he would teach himself not to care. "She must have found her own way home."

"Yes sir." But Branson was frowning.

Hunter rode all the way to Claybourne Manor, having convinced himself that she had taken her own cab home just to spite him. He expected to find her stalking the foyer with a well-rehearsed diatribe against him and his breed. Heartless magnate, purveyor of poverty, thief.

Let her come with her accusations. He was ready. He would not bend. She was a pariah to him, and nothing she could say would soften the truth. It couldn't possibly. This time the truth was undeniable.

But she wasn't in the foyer or in his chamber, or in
hers. She hadn't used her room in weeks, except to
dress in when she needed more light and a longer
mirror. And now her chamber looked as it had when
they'd left it for the theater, the bed in disarray from
their lovemaking. He smoothed his hand across the
rumpled sheets. He'd caught her here in her dressing
gown and had stripped her of it. As ever, she was eager
and inventive, and had wrapped him in her selfless
splendor. And afterward they had talked of children—

Children.

"She's not in the house, sir." Branson stood at the
door alongside Mrs. Sweeney, both of them looking
confused and lost.

Mrs. Sweeney cuffed Branson. "You louts have misplaced our girl!"

Branson started away. "I'll go back for her, sir. We
can't leave her to—"

"No, Branson." The sooner the break was made, the
sooner his life and the house would return to normal.
"Have this room cleaned and closed up tomorrow," he
said abruptly. "Mrs. Claybourne won't be back."

"Won't—"

But Hunter dismissed them with a fierce scowl and
brushed past them into his own chamber.

The windows were open and the breeze tucked itself
in and out among the folds of the drapes. Felicity
likened fresh air to sleeping in the wild, and had
promised to show him the delights of the Lakes. That
was impossible now, and seemed a bleak and desolate
notion. He closed the window and drew the drapes.

He'd find no sleep in this room tonight.

He made his way to his library and sat at his desk,
pen in hand, ready to devise a scheme that would
bring Lord Meath around. The man would need something of great worth to make up for the loss of
business. High profits and little risk. He'd also have to
pay for the loss of integrity that Meath and the others

were sure to suffer at the hands of the press, when Felicity's story made the *Times*.

He hadn't known of Meath's investments in the apprentice schools, but it didn't matter now. As it wouldn't have mattered then. It was simple commerce; he couldn't let it matter.

But he could wonder if Felicity was sleeping tonight on a bench in Waterloo Station—if he would see her again.

He had given her the power to ruin him and she had wielded it with precision, even when she had promised she wouldn't. He had no choice but to take that power back from her.

He set aside Lord Meath's scheme and forced his pen to write the words that would begin his separation from his wife. The phrases swam in front of him. He blinked them clear, and blotted the page where the ink now ran salty. He would *not* weep for the woman. Her sweetness had been most seductive; he had slipped his hand into hers, had rested his heart inside hers, had raised his hopes and renewed his dreams . . .

But he was nothing without his name and his fortune.

And so he would learn to live without her.

Felicity spent the night on a narrow bench in the schoolroom, and awoke from a dream where Hunter loved her and she was wildly contented, where a child slept in her arms and it was his, and he was smiling down on them both with a love that would endure any hardship.

And her arms still ached from wanting him.

The impossible sweetness followed her through the morning. The children had hugged her and begged for her stories, and she had worn herself weary with their energy. She had changed from her gown into a clean but tattered brown skirt and a high-collared bodice, whose blue had long ago faded to gray. She needed to return the expensive gown to Hunter before the lush black satin was ruined by little handprints or stolen by hungry fingers. And since the sewing parlor at Claybourne Manor was filled with goods that actually belonged to the Beggar's Academy, she would need to make arrangements for their return.

And she was still wearing the pearl necklace he had given her. Worth ten times the price of the Beggar's Academy, it was too precious to keep on the premises, and it would only serve to remind her of him.

It seemed she had business at the Claybourne Exchange, and the sooner done, the better. Felicity left the school at noon with the gown and the pearls, and by the time she reached Cornhill Street, her temper was heated to the boiling point. She'd married an arrogant, hard-hearted man. Then she'd gone and fallen in love with him. And now, she probably had his child tucked beneath her heart.

The doorman smiled when he recognized her, but raised his eyebrows at the reduced state of her clothing. "Good afternoon, Mrs. Claybourne."

"Miss Mayfield," she corrected as she passed him.

Felicity kept up a strong head of steam as she climbed the pristine staircase, for fear of losing the momentum she would need when she met Hunter face-to-face.

She plowed through the outer office. "Good afternoon, Tilson." And threw open the doors of Hunter's office.

He was alone. Peering out the drape-darkened window, his finger caught in the velvet folds.

"Hunter." His name came too softly to her lips, tasted bittersweet.

He turned his head: a glacial precipice in motion, yet firmly rooted in the earth. She wanted to run to him, but he looked monumentally unapproachable.

"Yes?" he said, no more interested than if she were a client about to inquire into the state of her business affairs.

God forgive the man his coldness. Felicity closed the door behind her and stepped resolutely into the room.

"I've come to return the gown I wore last night," she said, draping the dress over a chairback.

"It's yours, Miss Mayfield. Keep it." His voice was so relentlessly solid, it settled like a lead weight in her chest.

"Then I leave you to burn it, Hunter." She bit back her tears as she withdrew the string of pearls from her pocket, and let the strand clatter into a loose pile onto the table. "These are yours, too."

He turned away then, back to the window. "Keep them. Sell them, if you wish. They mean nothing to me."

"They've meant a lot to me, Hunter, because they were a gift from you, my husband. But I have no use for the money or the pearls now. However, there are clothes and unfinished projects in the sewing parlor at Claybourne Manor, given to the academy—"

"Take the lot of it, Miss Mayfield." He left the window and went to his desk. "Strip the house bare, if it pleases you."

"I'll have to arrange—"

"Speak with Branson about it." He unlocked the top drawer and drew out a sheaf of papers. "Anything else, Miss Mayfield?"

Felicity absorbed the smell of leather, paper, and ink, the arid aroma of commerce, and she felt stronger for it, able to see past some of her grief and into the business at hand.

The breaking of her heart away from his.

"I'm returning your name to you, Mr. Claybourne." She saw him pause in his paper-shuffling.

"Fine." He continued adding documents to the sheaf, and she wanted to weep.

"You've never given me the chance to be anything more than Miss Mayfield to you, a very temporary wife. I never knew from one day to the next which name you felt me worthy enough to wear. So I'm taking back my old name and returning yours, worse for the wear it seems, but obviously the best course for the both of us."

His movements were aggravatingly mechanical.

"Very well, Miss Mayf—"

"Hunter, you have to believe that I am sorry—"

"Enough, Miss Mayfield."

"No. You'll hear me out. I'm sorry about your position with the Board of Trade. I know what it meant to you, and I wouldn't have taken that from you for the world."

"But the truth is that you *have* taken it." He leafed through his papers, looking bored. "You and your squandered benevolence."

"Hunter Claybourne!" Felicity went to the front of his desk, shamed to her soul at the change in him. "I'm not going to apologize for the article. It was long past due. I plan to investigate other apprentice schools, and to write many more articles. I will be ruthless in my criticism of men like Lord Meath. I have to be a champion—for Giles and for Arleigh and Betts. And for you, Hunter—"

"I don't need your pity, Miss Mayfield."

"I've never once offered it to you, Hunter."

His face was masked and deeply planed, the shadowy man she had met at the Cobson's sponging house. A stranger who wanted for nothing, and needed no one, who could calmly sort through a stack of documents while her stomach roiled and her shoulders shook.

"You simply don't understand the nature of business, Miss Mayfield."

"Then I don't want to know."

"In business there are carefully calibrated balances—"

"Balances? The life of an innocent child balanced against what? A penny? A pound? A railway? What possible transaction can you justify for stealing Arleigh's childhood from him? For leaving wounds that never heal. You know yourself how they fester—"

"Enough! You will listen for once, and then you will leave me!" He tossed the documents into his attaché. "Cheap labor is the foundation of manufacturing, do you understand me? And manufacturing is the foundation of this country—of this century, and the one to come. Every extra ha'penny that is paid out between the hide and the shoe seller raises the price of the shoe by a factor of four and reduces the profit—"

"Profit? That's your justification—"

"Yes, profit. It is no crime. No shame." He came around the desk as if he thought to intimidate her into agreeing with him. "Cheap shoes make for affordable shoes, Miss Mayfield. It's the law of profits. Neither evil nor good, it's just a matter of profit—"

"Oh, curse you, Hunter, and all your kind."

He grabbed her hand and turned her palm toward him. "Ah, but you can't see the blood on your own pristine hands, can you, Miss Mayfield?"

His hands were icy and huge. He touched her ring, lingered there, and she prayed he wouldn't take it. Not her ring. Not yet. "Blood on *my* hands? There is none!"

"Are you so certain?" He paused, then dropped her hand abruptly. His eyes were colder than ever. "You pride yourself on making winter coats for your miserable wretches. Well, where the hell do you think the woolens come from?"

"A mill, of course." Felicity backed away from him toward the cold, tile-fronted heater. He was a storm about to lay waste to a field of ripe clover.

"And have you ever seen the inside of a woolen mill, Miss Mayfield?"

"No." He'd backed her against the enamel tiles, and now she was forced to crane her neck to see into his face.

"No?" He raised an arrogant brow, and she knew that he found great triumph in his truth. He growled and pushed himself away, then went back to the window, lifting back the heavy drape with his hand. "Well, I suggest you visit one next time you're in the country. You'll find it most illuminating, but then you'll have to swear off woolens and start weaving your own cloth. Visit a coal mine next, Miss Mayfield, and you'll freeze the next winter in your protest against those shocking conditions. And the same holds true of the factories that make your lovely ribbons and the pencils that you write with—"

"Stop it, Hunter! It won't work. You can't hobble me with my own guilt. Not like you've done to yourself." He had never seemed so much a stranger, so much the coolly calculating industrialist as he watched out the window, aloof from everything and everybody. "I know that my garden is small, that its soil is exhausted, and that I'm as insignificant as a drop of rain in the ocean—but I will see that these few children grow and prosper. And they will know compassion, Hunter, will reach out gladly to those whose fortunes aren't as bright as their own—"

"Good day, Miss Mayfield." Hunter dropped the drape against the window and went back to his desk, presenting his broad back to her.

Felicity ached for him, wanted to hold him one last time. She had hurt him immeasurably. But he had put himself past caring. She envied that in him, but refused to shrink from her own grieving. To do that would be to deny that she loved him.

"You're a good man, Hunter—far better than you know. And I would state that fact, unreservedly, even if I didn't love you."

She had never gotten the chance to tell him about the baby; she still wasn't certain herself. He had promised his support when the time came, and that's when she would ask for it. Not now, when her emotions were raw and she might do or say something foolish in front of him. If it were true, she would tell him months from now, when it might be easier to meet his eyes again.

Felicity gathered her courage and went to the door. She paused with her hand on the latch.

Hunter turned, knew that if he could watch her leave, he could let her go. *Just let her go.*

"Good-bye, Hunter."

Then she was gone. Gone in her sagging-brimmed bonnet and her ragged brown skirt, leaving her soft fragrance to accuse him. Gone, at last.

He wanted to follow after her, but he was cemented in place by his fears, and by his relief that she had survived the long night, that she'd been standing here in his office adorned in her rags and stinking of her orphans. He knew she had spent the night at the school. He'd heard Branson wheel the carriage into the darkness, and had been waiting for him when he returned with the news. But he couldn't tell her that.

His throat ached. He felt obscene and soiled again. He closed his eyes but he could still see the hollow-eyed children, could smell the stink of the workhouse on his skin.

She had made him see too clearly, had absolved him with her charity, and then she'd convicted him for it.

I don't need you, Felicity. He needed the Claybourne Exchange, and nothing else.

Already bluntly worded notes had begun to arrive from other men of Lord Meath's rank and influence, asking pointed questions about exposure and trust. How could they trust a man who couldn't control his own wife? How could he allow her to traipse the countryside? How could he not condemn her?

How could she be so beautiful?

And now he'd been summoned to a swiftly called meeting, deep in the bowels of the Bank of England. That meeting was to be about him.

A question of his integrity. His honor. Hunter Claybourne's name held up to its finest scrutiny.

Whatever the cost, he was prepared to pay.

Hunter descended the steps of the exchange and crossed Cornhill Street on foot, and then Threadneedle—shouldering his way past memories, feeling himself shed of his years, his reputation, and his tattered coat, too large and stolen from a shopkeeper's rack. His pulse quickened with a familiar exhilaration and the scent of success tainted by fear. He had been the very best of pickpockets, distracting his quarry with a nudge, then a feint; risking little to chance because he'd known even then what was at stake.

Now he stood on Threadneedle Street staring up at the Bank, feeling exposed and raw.

"Come to face the music, Claybourne?"

Hunter swung around, half-expecting to find a damp-faced magistrate bearing down on him. The urge to bolt into the afternoon throng dissipated slowly, and left a searing hole in his chest.

It was Meath, alighting from his carriage, and an impulse came over Hunter to lift the man's wallet. His fingertips itched with a long-dormant memory of a proud young man and his determination to prosper, but he turned his back on Threadneedle and started up the lofty steps of the Bank.

"Come, Meath. You wouldn't want to miss the bloody spectacle."

"This is a catastrophe, Claybourne! When a man of Lord Meath's stature is jeopardized by such scandal, so is each one of us in this chamber. Mark me, you will pay for this!" Lanford sat at the distant end of the polished table, presiding over the council like a king over his court. Meath sat beside him, bending the man's ear in a hissing whisper.

Hunter steadied his anger and looked around at the sea of granite faces glaring back at him from their overstuffed, high-backed chairs. He was disgusted with himself and with this unholy commerce. But he stood steadfastly, refusing to buckle under their pressure. He had made the fortunes of half the men in this chamber, and could unmake them with a flick of his pen. But such a reprisal wouldn't serve his own fortune—and that was the purpose of his life.

"Well, say something, Claybourne!" Meath bellowed as he leaned forward on his elbows. "You saw the *Times* this morning."

The headline had been impossible to miss. " 'Slopshop Scandal.' Yes, I saw it, Meath."

"And, sir?" Lanford sat forward, too, his thick fingers wrapped around the handle of his gavel.

"And, as usual, the press have got hold of a stinking bone and they will shake it until another comes along to distract them."

Meath jumped to his feet and pointed at Hunter. "It is *my* ankle they have hold of, Claybourne. Not yours. And all because of your wife's outrageous slander."

His wife. *Felicity.* His ruthless champion. Hunter could feel her hand in his, her lips upon his brow. His heart began to pound, and he unclenched his fist to rid himself of her memory.

"Slander, my lord Meath, implies the spreading of falsehoods. I'll grant the woman's impulses were foolish, and she has paid dearly for them, but she reported the facts as they stand."

The chamber roared to life then; the truth set free of its hive to sting wherever it found a home. Nearly every man here was guilty of the same kind of legal immorality as Meath, yet each now denied it with a righteous fury. Lanford banged his gavel repeatedly on the table.

And Meath was shouting over it all, "Facts without proof, Claybourne!"

"Without proof?" Hunter stalked toward Meath, stood over the man and his sweat-smeared spectacles as the chamber grew still. Bile rose into his throat. "Perhaps we should adjourn from these chambers to meet in your apprentice school, Meath; to see the crooked-limbed children for ourselves. Would their sunken cheeks and broken fingers serve as proof enough?"

"Enough, Claybourne!" Lanford said.

"And you, Lanford, ought to look to your own woollen mills. What sort of foulness would the *Times* discover at the Broadworks, I wonder?"

"Are you threatening me, Claybourne?" Lanford's veined jowls shook.

"I'm trying to save our collective hides." Hunter stilled the quaking in his hands and opened his attaché. "And if you cannot recognize that, if you persist in trying to destroy me, then you can take your business elsewhere. As it is, I see two dozen stubborn men whose grand plan is to crawl into a stinking hole, and pull the dirt down on top of them. Is that what all of you want? Do you want your critics to win?"

Hunter scanned the faces at the table; each had gone damply crimson, or had paled to chalk. Lords and Commons, members of the Privy Council, and the Board of Trade—each and every man squirming in their seats. Cowards.

Sir John Eagan rose on his gouty legs, and every eye turned to the man. "What do you suggest we do, Mr. Claybourne?"

Hunter tasted the first stirrings of triumph, and a dizzying brush with his past: Sir John sat on the Queen's Bench—a strict magistrate, and a name Hunter remembered from his youth. If the man knew whose help he was requesting—

Hunter scrubbed that terror from his thoughts. He would walk from this chamber the same man who entered; no one would know of the street urchin that still lived inside him. "First of all, Sir John, we must all agree that there is great profit to be had in cheap labor."

They grumbled their ascent as a body, Meath among them, hunkered over a glass of brandy.

"And," Hunter continued, knowing his next statement would rankle, "that we are a contemptible breed."

The grumbling rose and then fell back on itself as Sir John sat down quietly. "Go on, Mr. Claybourne."

Hunter knew he was dancing dangerously on the edge of a very sharp blade. He turned and felt every eye on his back as he went to the window that looked down onto Threadneedle Street.

"We are the power in England. Financiers, industrialists, demigods. We lay the railways, and erect the factories; we tear down unprofitable rookeries to rebuild and collect higher rents; and we do it all on the backs of people who live and who work under the most appalling conditions—"

"Damnation, Claybourne!" Meath was on his feet behind Hunter. "It isn't our business who these people are—"

"They are children, Meath, and mothers, and hardworking fathers." And Felicity was their champion, *his* champion.

"I can't help that they breed like rabbits, Claybourne. I didn't bring them into this world. To hell with you and your opinions! You have been censured here, sir. And I, for one, will enjoy seeing the Claybourne Exchange slide into the muck of the Thames."

Hunter held his breath and fixed his focus on the watery windowpane. "That will never happen, Meath. Not while I'm alive. I have given each of you my word to protect your interests, and I am here to deliver on that promise."

"Ballocks!" Meath was at Hunter's back. "You're a traitor, Claybourne. A bloody traitor to your class."

Traitor. Hunter swallowed back the knot in his throat and stared out onto Threadneedle Street. It looked as it always had, absorbed in itself and prosperous, tolerating thieves and tycoons in equal numbers. He had been both in his time, and now he was neither. A stranger even to himself.

Damn you, Felicity.

He would play their game because he must, and because he'd forgotten how to play any other. He'd tried to explain to her the practical balance of business, but she wouldn't listen.

Then her hand was in his again, as tangible and warm as if she stood beside him. *They will know compassion, Hunter, and will reach out gladly—* Irrational little fool. She'd deluded herself into thinking that he was respectable man, a good man.

"Gentlemen," Hunter said, his voice remarkably steady as he turned from the window and the woman he loved, to face his accusers. "I am prepared to offer you absolution."

"How?" Lanford stood beside his chair, his face a mask of indignity. "How do we repair this kind of damage?"

"By confessing your part in it."

"What!" Meath staggered backward a step, his balance stolen by too many brandies.

"By confessing your horror and revulsion at finding such loathsome, disgusting activity going on at your own apprentice schools and at your factories."

"Have you gone mad?" Now Sir John was on his feet again.

"No, my lord. You will deny prior knowledge of any such villainy. You will set up a charitable foundation to remedy the situation immediately. Publicly voice your concerns for the wretched poor, for the crippled children." If Hunter had ever had a soul, it was lost to him now. He was nearly sick to his stomach. "Gentlemen, you'll emerge from this filthy pit as patrons of the poor, not rogue capitalists. I will begin by pledging thirty thousand pounds of my own."

The noise in the chamber rose swiftly as one man turned to the next with sudden smiles, the peace of divine clemency in their eyes.

Lanford was at Hunter's side, pumping his arm and calling him brilliant. Meath even offered him a grudging nod.

And Hunter's head reeled. He closed his eyes and she was there inside him, whispering her own kind of absolution, complete and absolutely calamitous.

You're a good man, Hunter—far better than you know.

Damn the woman!

She'd given him back his name, and he'd worn it into battle as his shield, only to find that it no longer fit, that it pinched and offended him.

Damn you, Felicity!

Chapter 23

✦✦✦

"And so the good Robin Hood let fly his arrow and split the sheriff's bolt in twain.'" Felicity looked up from the storybook, across the eager faces and shiny cheeks. Gran was sitting in the upholstered armchair beside her, her lap overflowing with snuggling children. She dearly loved the old woman.

Lady Meath was at the back of the room, contentedly combing Betts's hair. Felicity admired the woman for her courage; she had ignored Lord Meath's prohibition against returning to the school. Lady Oswin was washing up one of the endless piles of dishes, something she knew the woman had never done at home. These ladies of delicate sensibilities seemed as ruggedly committed to the Beggar's Academy as she was.

Indeed, there were miracles left in the world.

"Please, read it again, miss." Arleigh pried the book open to the page she had just turned. "Here! Where Robin Hood beats the sheriff."

Now the other children were calling out for the same, and Felicity resigned herself to a third go-round for the archery tournament.

She was grateful for the distraction. Anything to keep her thoughts off Hunter. He'd been so cold that afternoon, so unlike the man she'd come to love and respect. She cleared her throat of her tears and began to read again.

" 'There came the day when the bandits of Sherwood Forest . . .' "

Hunter had Branson drive him directly from the Claybourne Exchange to Shoreditch Road. He stepped down from the carriage into a caustic evening fog. He clutched his breast pocket and found the document in place, the ink barely dried, and his heart raging inside his chest.

He was doing the best thing he knew how. His business with his wife would be quick. A simple signature, and he would be done with it, made whole again.

Shoreditch was clogged with rattling carts and gravel-voiced costermongers, people shoving and pressing their way home. The alleyways feeding onto it sluiced their foulness into the brew.

"I'll wait here, Mr. Claybourne."

Hunter raised an unsteady hand to Branson and took a last unadulterated breath before he started through the stream of foot traffic.

He hesitated at the mouth of the alleyway, holding back taking his first breath, fearing the black, blinding headache that would surely swamp him. He dizzied for lack of air, caught hold of the green-slick wall, then hung his head and let his lungs fill to bursting.

He gagged as the decay and the hot memories washed over him. The pounding came to his head in a surging rush, drawing bile high into his throat, spilling its scalding bitterness into his mouth, and sending him whirling back to his boyhood.

She had done this to him. Forced him to remember it all: the scurrying between piles of refuse; the bitterness of a withered turnip, sauced in whatever muck he'd found it in. She'd brought him here to face his torment, to name it, to grind it back into his skin, into his nostrils.

He spat the bile from his mouth and stumbled forward into the dimness, cursing the dry heaves that racked him and his water-shot eyes that blurred and disoriented him. He crashed into a stack of crates and a man cursed him.

Hunter dodged the flying cudgel that would have felled him, disgusted with the strength of the native-born instinct that pulled him deeper into the alley, following a foul, ghastly memory so deep-rooted he could track the twisting course without sight.

All this because of her, his wife. *Felicity.* She was his beacon, and his abyss. His past and his future. And he wanted to be done with all the misery.

Hunter broke out of the stifling alley onto a tightly spoked intersection of five streets, ill-lit and hostile.

But he knew the place. It was seventeen years gone from his life, and yet nothing had changed. Not the smell or the taste, or the empty faces.

Two more lanes and he was standing in front of the Beggar's Academy, a boy again, frightened and sweating, knowing there were better dreams for him somewhere else.

Knowing that he had to go inside to find them.

Something prickled Felicity's spine and made her raise her eyes to the door.

It was Hunter. Her pulse took off and left her breathless.

He was huge, and filled the small, sagging portal like a mountain, his fingers white-knuckled and seized-up around the doorframe. His eyes were damp and darkly shadowed, unreadable in the wobbling light of the candles. His coat hung askew, and he was breathing as if he'd run all the way from Cornhill Street.

But he said nothing, so Felicity went back to her reading, stumbling over familiar words and smearing the tears with her fist as they fell upon the page. When he finally moved from the doorway, she watched him from under her lashes, followed the sound of his

uncertain footfalls as he skirted the room and came to
stand behind her.

"May I see you?" he asked, his voice craggy and
deep and tugging at her.

She stood up and turned to him, aware of her every
nerve and of every breath between them. And deeply
aware of the effortless love she bore him. She steeled
herself against her tears.

"What is it you want, Mr. Claybourne?"

"Your signature," he said in that flat, fiscal tone of
his. He was stern-faced and still winded as he lifted a
document from an inside pocket and handed it to her.

The bound paper was folded thickly and tied off in
red ribbon. It looked coldly official. Separation papers,
no doubt. She had expected his solicitor, not him. How
could he do this to her, in person, and here at the
school?

"What is this, Mr. Claybourne?" Angry that he
would take precious time from the children to serve
these on her, Felicity finally looked up at him, ready to
chasten him.

But his eyes were soft and red-rimmed. His lower lip
was damp and chaffed. "It's a transfer of title, Mrs.
Claybourne."

Felicity thought that a strange name for separation
papers. But leave it to Hunter to equate the end of a
marriage with the transfer of property. If he had come
to punish her, he'd found his way.

"I'll only be a moment, children," she said, trying to
keep her voice steady. They wouldn't understand at all
if she broke down and wept. Their dark eyes were
fastened on the stranger beside her, their mouths
agape, and Robin Hood forgotten.

For all but Giles. He had fit his fingers through hers,
and he was watching her face with a stern countenance. "You don't have to go, miss. I'm here, y' know."

"I know that, lad." Felicity squeezed his hand. "I'll
be all right. Will you keep reading for me, Giles?
Come, Mr. Claybourne. I will sign your document."

Choosing not to look up at Hunter, Felicity touched Gran's shoulder to gain a measure of comfort, then stepped away to find a more private corner. Giles brusquely took up the story of Robin Hood.

Felicity reached the table and turned, only to find Hunter still standing where she'd left him, looking almost forlorn. He was scanning the room, his eyes never resting on anything for more than a moment.

The Beggar's Academy—

She'd forgotten entirely that this had been his school, the place he had reviled and then forsaken. His gaze was unyielding as he studied the room, frowning as if he remembered each plank and every post and was paralyzed by the memory. She could almost see the boy again, a tender spirit, so easily and so often wounded.

Tears welled in her eyes for the scarred man he'd become, and she wanted him gone from here.

"Please, Mr. Claybourne," she said, in her most efficient voice. "You can see that I'm busy."

But then she saw his gaze meet with Lady Meath's. He reared back in surprise, shaken from his reverie. He looked ready to bolt, but then offered both women a half-smile.

"Good evening, Lady Meath, Lady Oswin." His voice sounded raw, but steady.

"It's very good to see you here, Mr. Claybourne. You ought to come more often." Lady Meath nodded and then whispered something to Lady Oswin that drew girlish giggles from them both.

The pallor was gone from Hunter's face, and his color had risen dark against his crisply stiff collar. But he was breathing like a charging horse.

And Giles was still attempting to read, although his audience's attention had wandered back to Hunter.

"Who's that man standing behind you, Giles?" Jonathan was on his knees pointing at Hunter.

Giles stopped his reading and scowled deeply at Jonathan. "He's—"

"I'm Mr. Claybourne," Hunter said, swallowing hard to keep the unrelenting sob from escaping his throat.

The room and all its vile memories had nearly swamped him at the door. He'd nearly run away. But she'd been sitting there among the children, his remarkable wife, blessing them with her love, healing them of their cares, and so he had stayed. He cleared his throat, then raised his voice and spoke to the children sitting on the floor beneath him.

"I am Mrs. Claybourne's husband."

Felicity's suspicious, sea-green eyes were on him as he stood rooted to this very painful and electrifying brink. She was frowning, and must have thought him a lunatic. He doubted his own sanity as he teetered here between his past and his future. One more step, and he would be free.

Did these children know how fortunate they were to have her looking after them? Fresh paint, sunlight, windows, her soft hands feeling a fevered brow. She had gifted him unselfishly, and yet he had scorned her.

Oh, patient love. He'd returned to this foul place looking to buy back his honor, to win back a wife, and instead he'd found his heart, right here where he'd left it.

"I . . . was a student here." Hunter's words hung in the damp air like a benediction.

"Dear God, Hunter." Felicity's whisper brushed at him from across the room. He heard admiration and dread. A prayer and a song.

"It was . . . a very long time ago." He had to struggle to put order to his thoughts; there were too many that wanted the light of day.

"Hunter, do you know what you're doing?"

"Yes. Finally." He heard a sob catch in her throat, or had it come from his own? "You, see . . . children. I learned to read here . . . at the Beggar's Academy."

"Mr. Claybourne?" Lady Meath had come to the edge of his vision, her grim frown a dark reminder of his folly. Ruination would come swiftly now. But he ignored her for the wonder in the children's faces.

"And I studied my sums . . . because I knew—" His voice broke into jagged pieces, but he cleared his throat and a rebellious kind of bliss tumbled over him. "Because it was . . . and it still *is* . . . the only way out, my young friends. The *only* way."

The book dropped from Giles's hand. "You, sir?"

"Yes, me. I was a pickpocket, Giles. A thief and a stray." Hunter knelt down to the boy, felt the childhood elation of comradeship, of belonging. "But I didn't let them beat me down, lad. Do you know who I mean?"

Giles's mouth hung open and he nodded. "Yes sir."

"Good. I fought them, and I won. And now I build grand fortunes for them, lad, and even grander fortunes for myself."

The room had gone completely silent.

Hunter stood up and glanced at Felicity, his champion. He loved her eyes: a meadowland, and the sea. Her hair had come free of its moorings, her breathing reduced to quaking. She was beautiful in her tatters and in her frowning distress.

"Hunter, you told—"

He laughed and knew he must sound completely mad. "Well, Mrs. Claybourne, haven't you read that thing yet?"

"No." Felicity felt as if he'd just struck her. Her extraordinary husband had just confessed his closely hoarded past to the world via Lady Meath and Lady Oswin and all the children, and now he was impatient with her? The man was as imperious and coldly unpredictable as ever! He was standing behind Gran— an odd-looking pair, Hunter in his fine, starkly black coat, and Gran's worn-through linsey nearly obscured by all the children in her arms.

"Read it, madam," he said again, cocking his head. "Or didn't you learn how? What sort of school did you go to?"

The children giggled, and Gran smiled. And Hunter seemed to like that immensely, gaining some kind of power from it. In fact, he seemed a bit unbalanced. Now he was taking his time coming toward her, sauntering almost, his gaze heating her as it fixed on her mouth and then her eyes.

"Hurry, please, Mrs. Claybourne." He was standing in front of her, his voice gathered low in the space between them. He was close enough to kiss her, poised and looking down at her as if he would. Yet he only lifted his hand; brushed his fingers against her cheek.

Unable to escape him, Felicity fixed her concentration on the separation papers, the breaking of her heart.

Transfer of Title, just as he had said. But there wasn't a single word about a separation. Only—

"My railway shares . . . ?" He'd come here about her miserable railway shares? "I told you that I wouldn't fight you, Hunter. Just as it says here, the Drayhill-Starlington will officially become yours a year from the date of our marriage, at which time—" But then the words took off on some jumbled track, and her heart went with them.

"At which time, my love, my wife," Hunter whispered, as he tucked a strand of her hair behind her ear, sending her pulse singing, "I will take on as equal partner, in said railway, the institution known as the Beggar's Academy. You'll have your funding, madam, and then some."

This still made no sense, nor did his delicious mouth against hers. Her head was reeling and she shoved him away.

"But, Hunter, you told them about yourself. What will they say? Lady Meath and Lady Oswin . . . didn't you see them?"

"Good God, woman, do you think it matters anymore?"

"Hunter, what happened? What did Meath do to you?"

He only held her and brushed his lips against her ear. "I'm afraid I took the easy way, love. I let all the rats scurry out of their holes and into the sunlight. But please don't despise me for it. I shall hold them to their word."

"To their word, Hunter?" Felicity had no idea what he was talking about, only that he seemed inordinately pleased with himself. "What have you done?"

"I'm thinking of running for the Commons. Do you suppose anyone would elect a true man of the streets?"

Lady Oswin appeared at Hunter's elbow. "Oh, if I could vote, Hunter Claybourne, I would cast my ballot for you!"

Lady Meath was behind her, her eyes damp and her hair sprung from its golden pins. "We won't tell what we've heard here, Mr. Claybourne. Not a word."

Hunter only grinned. "But you must. I will."

"Hunter, are you sure?"

He gazed down on her, held her face between his huge hands. "I love you, Felicity. I have been censured, and my name reduced to nothing. I've lost an irreplaceable post on the Board of Trade—one I thought meant more to me than anything else I could have imagined. But then . . . never in all my life could I have imagined such a priceless treasure as *you*. I am nothing without you and your goodness."

"Oh, Hunter!" He cradled her head against his chest. Felicity soaked up his scent and the magnificent feel of his arms, and then his salty-sweet mouth seeking hers.

Then he was kissing every inch of her mouth. "I will promise to amass great fortunes, my love, if you'll promise to spend them for me. I'm no good at that, and you seem to know where it will do the most good. But just now, I want to take you back to our home—"

"Home? And what if I'm not sure I want to go there?" Her eyes blazed as she pulled herself away to look hard at him.

Hunter panicked. "Not go home?" He never considered—

"You dismissed me, Hunter! You got angry and then dismissed me, as if I were a housemaid caught stealing the silver. I will *never* be dismissed by you again."

"Oh, my love, you never were." His heart was pounding a terrified dirge. "Turning from you was the most difficult thing I have ever done in my life. And I could never do it again. I *never* will."

"Then from now on, when you get angry with me, Hunter, you will take your miserable hide out to the clearing and chop yourself a cord of wood. Then you'll come back inside, and we will discuss the matter rationally. And we will love each other through it all. Is that clear?"

"As crystal, madam." He cradled the back of her head. His eyes went wonderfully soft, and the light of his heart blazed there. "I will be your husband irrevocably and forever more, my love. If you'll have me."

Felicity was about to answer when she felt a tug at her skirt, and looked down at Betts. "Yes, love?"

"Is the big man happy again, miss? Is he?" She looked so full of hope.

Gran was grinning, and nodding her gray head in twinkle-eyed mischief. Lady Meath and Lady Oswin were gripping each other's hands, and the children were all waiting.

Felicity smiled up at Hunter; touched his mouth with her fingers just to assure herself that he was real.

"Oh, I think Mr. Claybourne is going to find himself irrevocably happy."

Then he kissed her madly, while the whole of the Beggar's Academy looked on and applauded.

Epilogue

"Did you ask after the ship's load line, Giles?"
Hunter crossed his arms behind his head
and lay back against the soft grass. The March sun was
marvelously warm on his face, and the sweet, rich
aroma of Felicity's herb garden made him grin with
lusty memories.

They'd had to modify their lovemaking in the last
month, when her child-ripe belly had become unwieldy. In the process, Hunter had discovered that his
wife was as inventive as she was passionate. She'd
wanted him to meet her here, and so he would wait,
most happily.

"And what would a load line be, Mr. Claybourne?"

Hunter watched out of the corner of his eye as Giles
stretched out noisily on the grass, matching Hunter's
own pose, even to the bent knees and the fingers laced
across his chest. It seemed he'd grown a full six inches
since Felicity had brought him to live with them.

The first few months had been rocky, with Giles
following him around, baiting him like a belligerent
shadow and then darting away. But the boy had
excelled with the tutor, showed a remarkable skill with
numbers, and he'd recently taken up reading the *Times*
and asking perceptive questions about shipping news.

"If you're going to invest your shillings in a cargo, son, you'd best see how the ship lies in the water when its full."

"Ah, I see." Giles rolled up onto his elbow and nodded sagely at Hunter. "Can't have the ship lying too low in the water. Too risky."

"Exactly. But don't count on the shipping company to protect your investment, Giles. You've got to learn to protect it yourself."

Giles's brow darkened and he plucked at the grass. "But it isn't my money. Not really. You gave it to me. I didn't work for it, didn't earn it."

Hunter sat upright, wondering where the sudden brooding had come from. "Ah, but you have earned it, son. You've made my wife very happy. And that makes you worth more to me than I could ever pay you."

Hunter watched helplessly as huge tears gathered in Giles's eyes. The road had been a rough one, but Hunter had begun to enjoy this fatherly role. Yet he hadn't the slightest idea how to tell that to the boy. He thought back on what he would have liked to have heard as a child. Then he realized—

"You've made *me* very happy too, Giles. And damned proud."

"Have I?" Giles blinked and hiccuped, and a pair of huge tears splashed into the grass. "Thank you, sir. I . . ." He gave a cry and launched himself into Hunter's arms, all gangly limbed and too big to be weeping.

Hunter's own throat constricted as he patted the boy's back and held him. Home. Yes, that was the thing, that was the need.

"This is your home now, Giles. It's a bit on the grandish side for a pair like you and me, but it's home. And it's all right to love till it hurts."

Giles continued to weep, and Hunter couldn't blame him. He'd been overcome himself more than a few times in the last few months; it happened nearly every time he laid eyes on his wife. His happiness made his heart ache.

"Hey, now," Hunter said, lifting the boy off his shoulder. "What say you and I pay a visit tomorrow afternoon to the West India Docks, and I'll show you what I mean about load line?"

"Really?" Giles sat up on his knees and scrubbed his face with the sleeve of his once-starched white shirt. "You and me, sir?"

"I'll introduce you to a few of the captains, a few of the owners, perhaps—"

"Yes sir! I'd like that!" Then Giles was looking over Hunter's shoulder, and frowning.

"Hello, Giles." Betts plopped herself down possessively in Hunter's lap, her short legs dangling across his folded ones, and handed him a pink ribbon. "Could you please tie my hair, Papa? You're ever so good at it."

Hunter had to swallow hard nearly every time Betts called him Papa. He'd get use to it some day—the sourceless guilt, as well as the overwhelming sense of belonging that fatherhood had brought to him. Three children, and another to come only weeks from now. Who could have imagined?

"Where is your mama?" Hunter asked, as he gathered Betts's hair into a short, curly rope at her nape. Her hair had grown to her shoulders in bright springy curls, and she was forever bringing him ribbons to tie it all up.

"Mama's in the kitchen with Arleigh and Mrs. Sweeney. Do you like lollipops, Papa? Giles does, don't you Giles?"

"No." Giles was still frowning, obviously irked that their father-to-son conversation had been interrupted by Betts and her silly ribbons. "We're going to the West India Dock tomorrow. Mr. Claybourne and I."

"I'm going with you!"

"No, you're not."

"Yes, I am. Aren't I, Papa?"

"She can't go!" Giles's face had gone red, and he was up on his knees again. "Tell her she's too young, Mr. Claybourne, and besides, she's a girl!"

"Course I'm a girl." Betts leaned forward just as Hunter had gotten the bow tied, and her silky hair slipped out of the ribbon and fell back on her shoulders. "You and I couldn't ever get married, if I weren't."

"Get married!" Giles looked stunned, and Hunter held back his laughter. "You're a lunatic! I'm not going to marry you! Tell her, Mr. Claybourne!"

"Papa, why does Giles call you Mr. Claybourne and not Papa?" Betts was a master at piercing Giles with her words. She knew just what to say and when to say it.

Hunter had never insisted, but he could guess Giles's reasons. "Giles is my son now, as Arleigh is, and that's all that matters. He can call me anything he likes: Mr. Claybourne, Hunter, Father, Papa—"

"Pinchfist!" Betts said, with a boisterous giggle.

"Pinchfist?" Hunter growled and pretended outrage. He tickled Betts's ribs and raspberried the back of her neck.

"Not fair!" She shrieked with laughter and launched herself toward Giles, her ribbon sailing like a streamer into a bush.

"Don't—!" But Giles caught Betts square in the chest, and went sailing backward with her into the grass.

"I got you, Giles!" Now Betts was tormenting the boy with her quick little fingers, and he was laughing too hard to stop.

Hunter was about to rise and rescue Giles, when a pair of short, chubby arms came around his head from behind. He saw the red lollipop only an instant before it affixed itself to his forehead.

"It's for you, Papa!" Arleigh shrieked, and hugged Hunter tightly.

"Your papa loves sweets, Arleigh."

Felicity's voice swept around him like a vapor, drew him to his feet with Arleigh clinging to his back.

"You look wonderful, Mrs. Claybourne." Hunter knew he was smiling like a fool, but it felt good to stand there and just stare at his wife.

"I feel like a steamship," she said, frowning as she pressed her hand against her lower back.

"Giles and I had just been discussing load lines."

"Yours is pretty low, Mama." Giles laughed as he pulled Betts to her feet. "I do believe you'd sink." He turned to Hunter. "What do you think . . . Papa?"

Papa. Hunter's throat seized up for a moment, but he managed to nod, and held out his arm to collect his son against him.

"But she's a good risk, Giles. I'd put my trust in her every time."

Felicity felt her eyes well up with tears, but brushed them away so that she could take a good look at her family. Giles was standing close enough to Hunter to be his shadow, and holding Betts's hand as she beamed up at him. Arleigh was clinging to Hunter's neck, his head resting on Hunter's shoulder.

Hunter stood as steadfast as a spreading oak, grinning at her, a red lollipop still stuck to his forehead. What a dear man she had married. Her champion, her love.

She would have gone to him, but another pain had begun to plague her, a great squeezing pressure low in her back that made it difficult to breathe.

Hunter yanked the lollipop from his forehead and frowned at her. "Felicity?"

She managed to smile, even managed to speak. "Giles, would you take Arleigh and Betts into the house? It's nearly dinnertime, and I need to speak with your father."

"I'll get 'em washed up." Giles gave Felicity a watery grin as he collected Arleigh off Hunter's back. "Come along, Betts. I think Mama and Papa want to be alone." Giles threw the boy over his shoulder, then took Betts's hand again, and started toward the house.

"I only have a moment, Hunter—"

Before she could say another thing, Hunter had swept her into his arms and was kissing her.

"I have a great need for you, wife. It seems I can never get enough of you." His breath was fresh with rosemary. "I think of it all day at the exchange, through those foundation meetings that have become so popular—"

"Hunter, tomorrow is our anniversary."

"One year; I haven't forgotten. Couldn't ever."

"Do you mind if your gift comes today?"

He looked charmingly confused, and his forehead tasted of cherries when she kissed him there.

"I don't need a gift, Felicity. I have you."

"Well, this one is coming today, Hunter, and you do need it. And I know you will love it. As you love all our children."

"Children?" She saw the light dawn in his dark eyes. He stood away from her and formed his hands across her belly as he had so often. "The baby?"

She nodded. "I love you, Hunter."

"And you, love, are the stars and the moon to me, and all the goodness in my life." His eyes were soft and damp now as he enfolded her in his arms, touched his salty mouth to hers.

Felicity kept the rising pain to herself, needing this last, quiet moment with her magnificent husband, the most grand-hearted man she had ever known.

"Oh, Hunter, what lucky children we have."

"Not half so lucky as their foolish father has been— to have found you—"

"And a railway in the bargain." She grinned.

Hunter's laughter echoed across the gardens. And as he lifted his exquisite wife into his arms and carried her and her kisses toward the house, he offered up a prayer for Uncle Foley's safe return from the gold fields.

He owed the man a miracle.

Avon Romances—
the best in exceptional authors and unforgettable novels!

THE PERFECT GENTLEMAN   by Danice Allen
78151-4/ $5.50 US/ $7.50 Can

WINTER HEARTS   by Maureen McKade
78871-3/ $5.50 US/ $7.50 Can

A LOVE TO CHERISH   by Connie Mason
77999-4/ $5.99 US/ $7.99 Can

FOR MY LADY'S KISS   by Linda Needham
78755-5/ $5.99 US/ $7.99 Can

THE LOVER   by Nicole Jordan
78560-9/ $5.99 US/ $7.99 Can

LADY ROGUE   by Suzanne Enoch
78812-8/ $5.99 US/ $7.99 Can

A WOMAN'S HEART   by Rosalyn West
78512-9/ $5.99 US/ $7.99 Can

HIGHLAND WOLF   by Lois Greiman
78191-3/ $5.99 US/ $7.99 Can

SCARLET LADY   by Marlene Suson
78912-4/ $5.99 US/ $7.99 Can

TOUGH TALK AND   by Deborah Camp
TENDER KISSES
78250-2/ $5.99 US/ $7.99 Can

If you enjoyed this book, take advantage of this special offer. Subscribe now and get a

FREE
Historical Romance

No Obligation (a $4.50 value)

Each month the editors of True Value select the four *very best* novels from America's leading publishers of romantic fiction. Preview them in your home *Free* for 10 days. With the first four books you receive, we'll send you a FREE book as our introductory gift. No Obligation!

If for any reason you decide not to keep them, just return them and owe nothing. If you like them as much as we think you will, you'll pay just $4.00 each and save at *least* $.50 each off the cover price. (Your savings are *guaranteed* to be at least $2.00 each month.) There is NO postage and handling – or other hidden charges. There are no minimum number of books to buy and you may cancel at any time.

Send in the Coupon Below

To get your FREE historical romance fill out the coupon below and mail it today. As soon as we receive it we'll send you your FREE Book along with your first month's selections.
